TOO LATE

a novel

C. HOOVER

Too Late

Edited by: Murphy Rae, www.murphyrae.net

Cover designer: Murphy Rae, www.murphyrae.net

Interior Formatting by Elaine York,
Allusion Graphics, LLC/Publishing & Book Formatting
www.allusiongraphics.com

Dear readers,

This book started out as a project I would work on during writing blocks. I never intended to release it, because it's nothing like the other books I write. It's morbid, it's twisted and it was a fun escape when I'd find myself stuck on another book or plot twist. I released the first few chapters on a free website two years ago because I had mentioned writing it and a few readers requested to read what I had written. I then would occasionally add chapters to it on the free website.

What had started out as something I never intended for anyone to read, quickly grew into something I couldn't wait to finish. I would write and update the chapters almost daily, so the story was written in real time, unlike the rest of my novels. The immediate release and feedback of each chapter became an addiction for myself and the readers who were fans of the story. So much so that even when I finished it and wrote "The End," I just couldn't stop writing. I wrote several epilogues and even broke rules and placed a prologue in the back end of the book. These chapters were written and posted just as they are placed in this book. I also decided to leave the chapter headings in the paperback as I had originally titled them. I'm doing this because I want readers who are experiencing this book for the first time to read it exactly how it was written and in the order it was written.

Because this book and the experience writing it are so different from my other works, I wanted a way to keep them separate for readers. I am releasing this book using my initials rather than my full first name so the readers who love my published works can easily differentiate between the books I create and deliver through my publisher and the books I create on the side for fun.

I originally wrote and released this book for free. I stated that it would only be on the free website and would not be available in print. However, I have had many requests for those who wish they could read the book on their Kindle or have the book in hand. The book has been available for almost a year now for free online, but not through the platform readers have most requested it to be on. Therefore, I have decided to make this book free through Kindle Unlimited, as well as in paperback, for a limited time only. Thank you all so much for your support while working on this. Please do know that this book is not in any way appropriate for children and young teens. This book deals with much darker subjects than my others and includes extreme adult content. Proceed with caution.

Sincerely,
Colleen Hoover

This book is dedicated to all the members
of the Too Late Facebook group.

Thank you for making this one of my most
favorite writing experiences.

Especially you, Ella Brusa.

ONE

Sloan

Warm fingers entwine with mine, pressing my hands deeper into the mattress. My eyelids are too heavy to open from the lack of sleep I've had this week. The lack of sleep I've had all month, really.

Hell, this whole damn *year*.

I moan and attempt to squeeze my legs together, but I can't. There's pressure everywhere. On my chest, against my cheek, between my legs. It takes me a few seconds to pull my mind out of its sleepy haze, but I'm awake enough to know what he's doing.

"Asa," I mumble, irritated. "Get off me."

He thrusts his weight against me repetitively, groaning against my ear, his morning stubble cutting into my cheek. "I'm almost done, babe," he breathes against my neck.

I attempt to pull my hands out from beneath his, but he squeezes them tighter, reminding me that I'm nothing more than a prisoner in my own bed, and he's the warden of the bedroom. Asa has always had a way of making me feel like my body was at his disposal. He's never mean or forceful about it; he's just needy—and I find it really inconvenient.

Like right now.

At six o'clock in the damn morning.

I can guess the time by the sunlight peeking through the crack under the door, and the fact that Asa is just now coming to bed after last night's party. I, however, have to be in class in less than two hours. This isn't how I would have chosen to be torn from sleep after only three hours of it.

I wrap my legs around his waist and hope he thinks I'm into this. When I act half interested, he gets it over with more quickly.

He palms my right breast and I let out the expected moan, just as he begins to shudder. "*Fuck*," he groans, burying his face in my hair, slowly rocking against me. After several seconds, he collapses on top of me and sighs heavily, then kisses my cheek and rolls onto his side of the bed. He stands up and removes the condom and tosses it into the trashcan, then grabs a bottle of water off the bedside table. He brings the bottle to his lips, raking his eyes over my exposed flesh. His lips pull into a lazy grin. "I love that I'm the only one who's ever been inside that."

He stands confidently naked by the bed, gulping the last of the water. It's hard to accept compliments when they come from someone who refers to your body as "that."

Despite his good looks, he has his faults. In fact, his looks may be the only thing about him I *don't* find fault in. He's cocky, quick-tempered, hard to handle sometimes. But he loves me. He loves the hell out of me. And I'd be lying if I said I didn't love him in return. There are so many things I would change about him if I could, but right now he's all I have, so I deal with it. He brought me in when I had nowhere else to go. No one else to turn to. For that reason alone, I put up with him. I have no other choice.

He brings his hand up and wipes his mouth, then tosses the empty bottle into the trashcan. He runs his hand through his thick brown hair and winks at me, then drops back onto the bed and leans in, kissing me softly on the lips. "Goodnight, babe," he says as he rolls onto his back.

"You mean good morning," I say as I reluctantly pull myself out of bed. My t-shirt is bunched around my waist, so I pull it down and grab some pants and a different shirt. I walk across the hallway to the shower, relieved that one of our countless roommates isn't occupying the only upstairs bathroom.

I check the time on my phone and cringe when I realize I won't even have enough time to stop for coffee. It's the first class of the semester and I already plan to use it to catch up on sleep. This isn't looking good.

There's no way I can keep this up. Asa never goes to class on a regular basis, yet he always passes with near-perfect grades. I'm struggling to keep my head above water, and I didn't miss a single day last semester. Well, in physical form. Unfortunately, we live with so many other people, there's never a quiet moment in the house. I catch myself falling asleep in class more often than not; it's the only time I get peace and quiet. The parties seem to go on all hours of the day and night, regardless of who has class the next day. Weekends have no separation from weekdays in our house, and rent has no bearing over who lives here.

I don't even *know* who lives here half the time. Asa owns the house, but he loves being around people, so he likes the revolving-door free-for-all. If I had the means, I'd have my own place in a heartbeat. But I don't. That just means one more year of pure hell before I graduate.

One more year before I'm free.

I pull my shirt over my head and drop it to the floor, then pull the shower curtain back. As soon as I reach down for the nozzle, I scream at the top of my lungs. Passed out in the tub, fully clothed, is our newest full-time roommate, Dalton.

He jerks awake and smashes his forehead into the faucet above it, letting out a yell. I reach down and grab my shirt just as the door bursts open and Asa rushes in.

"Sloan, are you okay?" he says frantically, spinning me around to check me for injuries. I nod feverishly and point to Dalton in the tub.

3

Dalton groans. "I'm not okay." He palms his freshly injured forehead and attempts to crawl out of the tub.

Asa looks at me, down at my naked body being covered by the shirt in my hands, then looks back at Dalton. I'm afraid he's about to get the wrong idea, so I start to explain, but he cuts me off with a loud, unexpected burst of laughter.

"Did you do that to him?" He's pointing at Dalton's head.

I shake my head. "He hit his head on the faucet when I screamed."

Asa laughs even harder and reaches a hand down to Dalton, then pulls him the rest of the way out of the tub. "Come on, man, you need a beer. Cure for hangovers." He pushes Dalton out of the bathroom and follows behind him, closing the door when he leaves.

I stand frozen, still clutching my shirt to my chest. The sad part is, this is the third time this has happened. A different idiot every time, passed out in the tub. I make a mental note to check the tub from now on before undressing.

TWO

Carter

I pull the schedule out of my pocket and unfold it to look for the room number. "This is such crap," I say into the phone. "I graduated college three years ago. I didn't sign up for this shit so I could do homework."

Dalton laughs loudly, forcing me to pull the phone several inches away from my ear. "Boo fucking hoo," he says. "I had to sleep in a damn bathtub last night. Suck it up, man. Acting the part is part of the job."

"Easy for you to say. You were signed up for one class a week. I have three. Why'd Young only give you one?"

"Maybe I give better head," Dalton says.

I look down at my schedule and up at the number on the door in front of me, finding a match.

"I gotta go. *La clase de Español.*"

"Carter, wait." His tone is more serious. Dalton clears his throat and prepares for his "partner pep talk." I've been suffering through them on a daily basis since we started working together. "Try to make it fun, man. We're so close to getting everything we need...

You'll be here two months, tops. Find a hot piece of ass to sit by; it'll make the days go by faster."

I look through the window of the classroom door. It's practically at full capacity with only three empty seats. My gaze immediately falls on a girl in the back of the room next to one of the empty chairs. Her dark hair is spilled over her face while she rests her head on her arms. She's asleep. I can sit by the sleepers; it's the incessant talkers I can't tolerate. "Look at that. Already found me a hot piece of ass to sit by. I'll check in with you after lunch." I end the call and swing open the classroom door as I turn off the volume on my phone. I hoist the strap of my backpack onto my shoulder as I make my way up the steps to the back of the room. I squeeze past her to the empty seat, tossing my backpack on the floor and my phone onto the table. The sound my phone makes when it meets the solid wood jolts the girl from her sleep. She immediately sits up, wide-eyed. She looks around the room, frantic and confused, then down at the notebook on her desk. I pull the chair out and sit down next to her. She glares at my phone lying on the table in front of us, and then looks at me.

Her hair is a wild mess and there's a shiny trail of drool running from the corner of her lip, down her chin. She's glaring at me like I've interrupted the only minute of sleep she's ever had.

"Late night?" I ask. I bend over and open my backpack, pulling out the Spanish textbook I could more than likely recite from memory.

"Is class over?" she asks, her eyes narrowed at the book I'm placing on the desk in front of me.

"Depends."

"On what?"

"On how long you've been passed out," I say. "I'm not sure which class you're here for, but this is the ten o'clock Spanish class."

She throws her elbows onto the desk in front of her and groans, running her hands over her face. "I've been asleep for five minutes? That's it?" She leans back into her seat and slouches down, resting her head on the back of her chair. "Wake me up when it's over, okay?"

She's looking at me, waiting on me to agree. I tap my finger to my chin. "You've got a little something right here."

She wipes at her mouth and pulls her hand back to inspect it. I expect her to be embarrassed by the fact that she's got drool running down her face, but instead, she rolls her eyes and tucks the sleeve of her shirt under her thumb. She wipes the puddle of drool off the table with her sleeve, and then slouches back down in her seat, closing her eyes.

I've been through college before. I know how it is with the late nights, the partying, the studying, and never having time for it all. But this girl seems stressed to the max. I'm curious if it's due to maybe having a night shift or way too much partying.

I reach down into my backpack and pull the energy drink out that I picked up on the way here this morning. I'm thinking she needs it more than I do.

"Here." I set it on the desk in front of her. "Drink this."

She slowly pries her eyes open as if her eyelids weigh a thousand pounds each. She looks down at the drink, then quickly grabs it and pops the top. She gulps the contents frantically, like it's the first thing she's had to drink in days.

"You're welcome." I laugh.

She finishes the drink and sets it back on the table, wiping her mouth with the same sleeve she wiped away the drool with earlier. I'm not gonna lie; her unkempt, sloppily sexy demeanor is a major turn-on, in a weird way.

"Thanks," she says, wiping the hair out of her eyes. She looks at me and smiles, then stretches her arms out behind her and yawns. The door to the classroom opens and everyone shifts in their seats, indicating the entrance of the instructor—but I can't take my eyes off of her long enough to even validate his presence.

She combs through the strands of her hair with her fingers. It's still slightly damp and I can smell the floral scent of her shampoo when she flips her hair back over her shoulders. It's long and dark and thick, just like the lashes that line her eyes. She glances toward the front of the room and opens her notebook, so I mirror her movements and do the same.

The professor greets us in Spanish, and we return his salutations in collective, broken responses. He begins giving instructions on an assignment when my phone lights up on the table between us. I look down at the incoming text message from Dalton.

Does this hot piece of ass you're sitting next to have a name?

I immediately flip the phone over, hoping she didn't read it. She brings her hand to her mouth to cover her laugh.

Crap. She read it.

"Hot piece of ass, huh?" she says.

"I'm sorry. My friend... He thinks he's funny. Also likes to make my life hell."

She arches an eyebrow and turns toward me. "So you *don't* think I'm a hot piece of ass?"

With her facing me head-on, it's the first chance I've actually had to get a good look at her. Let's just say I'm officially in love with this class now. I shrug my shoulders. "With all due respect, you've been sitting down since I met you. I haven't even seen your ass."

She laughs again. "Sloan," she says, extending her hand. I take her hand in mine. There's a small crescent-shaped scar on her thumb. I run my thumb across it and twist her hand back and forth, inspecting the scar.

"Sloan," I repeat, letting her name roll off the tip of my tongue.

"This is usually the point during introductions that one would reply with their *own* name," she says.

I glance back up at her and she pulls her hand away, looking at me inquisitively.

"Carter," I reply, keeping in character with who I'm supposed to be. It's been hard enough referring to Ryan as Dalton for the past six weeks, but I've gotten used to it. Calling myself Carter is another story. I've more than once slipped up and almost used my real name.

"*Mucho gusto*," she says in an almost perfect accent, turning her attention toward the front of the room.

No, the pleasure is *mine*. Believe me.

The professor instructs the class to turn to the closest partner and state three facts about the other person in Spanish. This is my fourth year of Spanish, so I decide to let Sloan go first so I don't intimidate her. We turn toward each other and I nod my head at her. "*Las señoras primera*," I say.

"No, we'll take turns," she says. "You first. Go ahead, tell me a fact about myself."

"Okay," I say, laughing at how she just took control. "*Usted es mandona.*"

"That's an opinion, not a fact," she states. "But I'll give it to you."

I tilt my head in her direction. "You understood what I just said?"

She nods her head. "If you intended to call me bossy, then yes." She narrows her eyes, but a tiny smile forces its way through. "My turn," she says. "*Su compañera de clase es bella.*"

I laugh. She just complimented herself by telling me that my class partner is beautiful? I nod in unabashed agreement. "*Mi compañera de clase esta correcta.*"

I can see the blush rise to her cheeks, despite her tanned skin. "How old are you?" she asks.

"That's a question, not a fact. And in English, no less."

"I need to ask a question to get to the fact. You look a little older than most sophomore Spanish students."

"How old do you think I am?"

"Twenty-three? Twenty-four?" she says.

She's not too far off. I'm twenty-five, but she doesn't need to know that. "Twenty-two," I say.

"*Tiene veintidos años*," she says, stating her second fact about me.

"You cheat," I reply.

"You have to say that in Spanish if that's one of your facts about me."

"Usted engaña."

I can tell by the arch in her eyebrow that she wasn't expecting me to know that one in Spanish.

"That's three for you," she says.

"You still have one more."

"Usted es un perro."

I laugh. "You just accidentally called me a dog."

She shakes her head. "It wasn't an accident."

Her phone vibrates, so she pulls it out of her pocket and gives it her full attention. I lean back in my chair and grab my own phone, pretending to do the same. We sit silently while the rest of the class finishes the assignment. I watch out of the corner of my eye as she texts, her thumbs flying quickly over the screen of her phone. She's cute. I like that I'm looking forward to this class now. Three days a week doesn't seem like enough all of a sudden.

There's roughly fifteen minutes left of class and I'm doing my damnedest to keep myself from staring at her. She hasn't said anything else since she referred to me as a dog. I watch as she doodles into her notebook, not paying attention to a single word the instructor has said. She's either bored out of her mind, or she's somewhere else entirely. I lean forward, attempting to get a better look at what she's writing. I feel nosey, but then again, she did read my text earlier, so I feel justified.

Her pen is frantically moving over the paper, possibly a result of the energy drink she downed. I read the sentences as she jots them down. They don't make a lick of sense, no matter how many times I read them.

Trains and buses stole my shoes and now I have to eat raw squid.

I laugh at the randomness of all the sentences sprawled across her page, and she glances up at me. I meet her gaze and she grins mischievously.

She looks down at her notebook and taps her pen against it. "I get bored," she whispers. "I don't have a very good attention span."

I normally have a great attention span, but apparently not while I'm sitting next to her.

"Sometimes I don't either," I say. I reach across the desk and point at her words. "What is that? A secret code?"

She shrugs her shoulders and drops her pen, then slides the notebook closer to me. "It's just something stupid I do when I'm bored. I like to see how many random things I can think up without actually *thinking*. The more they don't make sense, the more I win."

"The more you win?" I ask, hoping for clarification. This girl is an enigma. "How could you lose if you're the only one playing your game?"

Her smile disappears and she glances away, staring down at the notebook in front of her. She delicately traces her finger over the letters in one of the words. I wonder what the hell I just said to change her demeanor so drastically and so fast. She picks her pen up and hands it to me, shaking away whatever thoughts just darkened her mind.

"Try it," she says. "It's highly addictive."

I take the pen from her hand and find an open spot on her page. "So I just write anything? Whatever comes to mind?"

"No," she says. "The exact opposite. Try not to think about it. Try not to let *anything* come to mind. Just write."

I press the pen to the paper and do exactly what she says. I just write.

I dropped a can of corn down the laundry shoot, now my mother cries rainbows.

I lay the pen down, feeling slightly stupid. She covers her mouth to stifle a laugh after she reads it. She turns to a fresh page and writes, *You're a natural*, then hands me the pen again.

Thank you. Unicorn juice helps me breathe when I listen to disco.

She laughs again and takes the pen from my hand just as the professor dismisses class. Everyone throws their books in their bags and slides out of their seats in a hurry.

Everyone but us. We're both staring down at the page, smiling, not moving.

She puts her hand on the notebook and slowly shuts it, then slides it down the table and into her backpack. She looks back at me. "Don't get up yet," she says as she stands up.

"Why not?"

"Because. You need to sit there while I walk away so you can determine whether or not I really am a fine piece of ass." She winks at me and spins around.

Oh my god. I bite my knuckles and do exactly what she says, planting my eyes directly on her ass. And just my luck, it's perfect. Every bit of her body is perfect. I sit completely still as I watch her descend the stairs.

Where the hell did this girl come from? And where the hell has she been all my life? I curse the fact that whatever just happened between us is all that could ever happen. Relationships never begin well with lies. Especially lies like mine.

She glances over her shoulder before she walks out the door, and I bring my gaze back up to her eyes. I give her a thumbs up. She laughs and disappears out the classroom door.

I gather my things and attempt to get her out of my head. I need to be on point tonight. There's too much riding on this to be distracted by such a beautiful, perfect ass.

THREE

Sloan

I finish the day's homework at the library, knowing I won't be able to concentrate once I step foot back in the house. When I first moved in with Asa, I was one night away from being evicted from the couch I was crashing on...not to mention all the other financial issues I dealt with. We had only been dating two months, but I had nowhere else to go.

That was over two years ago.

I knew based on the cars he drove and the size of his house that he had money. What I wasn't sure of was whether or not it was old money or if he was involved in something he shouldn't have been involved in. I was hoping it would be the former, but me and hope have never had good results. He hid it pretty well for the first couple of months, excusing his spending habits on the illusion that he had a big inheritance. I believed him for a while. I had no choice but to believe him.

When people I didn't know began showing up at odd hours of the night, and Asa only spoke to them behind closed doors, it became more and more obvious. He tried to explain his reasoning and swore he only sold "harmless" drugs to people who were going to find it somewhere else anyway. I didn't want any part of it, so when he refused to stop, I left.

The only problem was, I had nowhere to go. I crashed on a few friends' couches, but none of them had room or money to keep supporting me. I would have resorted to a homeless shelter before going back to Asa, but it wasn't my life I was worried about; it was my little brother's.

Stephen has never had it easy. He was born with a lot of issues, both mentally and physically. He was receiving state funding for his care and had finally been put in a good home I could trust with him, but when that was cut off, I couldn't risk him being sent back home to my mother. I didn't want him back in that life, and I'd do anything to make sure he wasn't a part of it ever again.

I was gone all of two weeks when I had no one else to turn to other than Asa. Walking back through his doors and asking for his help was the hardest thing I've ever had to do. It was as if running back into his arms was the equivalent of relinquishing my self-respect. He let me move back in, but not without consequences. Now that he knew exactly how much I had to depend on him, he stopped hiding his lifestyle. More and more people came over, and transactions were out in the open rather than behind closed doors.

Now, there are constantly so many people in and out of the house that it's difficult to differentiate between the people who live here, the people who crash here, and complete strangers. Every night is a party, and every party is my nightmare.

Every week that passes, the atmosphere becomes more and more dangerous, and I want out more than ever. I've been working part-time on campus in the library, but they don't have a student worker position for me this semester. I'm on a waiting list, and I've been applying for other jobs, trying desperately to add to my escape cash. It wouldn't be so hard if it were just myself I had to care for, but with Stephen in the picture, it'll take money that I don't have. Money that I won't have for a while.

In the meantime, I have to keep up appearances by acting like I still owe my life to Asa, when in reality, I feel like he's ruining it. Don't get me wrong, I do love him. I love who he used to be and who I still see small glimpses of when we're in private. I love who I know he could be again someday, but I'm also not naïve. As many promises as he's made me that he's scaling down the business in preparation to get out, I know he won't. I've tried to talk some sense into him, but when you've got the power in your hands and the money in your pocket, it's hard to walk away. He'll never walk away. He'll either do this until he's in prison...or until he's dead. And I don't want to be around for either.

I don't even try to identify the vehicles in the driveway anymore. Every day there's a new one. I park Asa's car and grab my things, then head inside for another night of hell.

When I walk inside, the house is eerily quiet. I shut the door behind me and smile, relishing in the fact that everyone's out back at the pool. I never get a chance for solitude, so I take advantage and put in my headphones and begin cleaning. I know it doesn't sound like fun, but for me it's my only chance to escape.

Not to mention, the house is a constant pigsty.

I start in the living room and throw away enough beer bottles to fill a thirty-gallon trash bag. When I reach the kitchen and witness the mountain of dishes piled in the sink, I actually smile. This should waste at least an hour. I organize the dirty dishes to the left of the sink and begin filling the basin with water. I begin to sway to the music spilling into my ears from the headphones. I haven't felt so at peace in this house since the first two months I lived here. Back when the *good* Asa was around.

As soon as memories of the Asa I fell in love with flood my mind, I feel his arms wrap around me from behind and he begins swaying to the music with me. I smile and keep my eyes closed and wrap my hands in his, then lean back against his chest. He kisses my ear, then laces his fingers with mine and spins me around to face him. When I open my eyes, he's smiling down at me with a genuinely sweet expression. I haven't seen this look in his eyes in so long, it actually makes my heart ache, knowing how much I've missed it.

Maybe he really is trying. Maybe he's tired of this life, too.

He takes my face in his hands and kisses me—a long, passionate kiss that I forgot he was even capable of. Lately, the only time I get kissed is when he's on top of me in our bed. I wrap my arms around his neck and kiss him back. I kiss him desperately. I kiss the old Asa, not knowing how long I'll have him here with me like this.

He pulls back and takes the headphones out of my ears.

"Somebody wants a continuation of this morning, huh?"

I kiss him again and smile, nodding my head. I do. If this is the Asa I'll get in my bed, I actually do.

He puts his hands on my shoulders and laughs. "Not in front of the company, Sloan."

Company?

I squeeze my eyes shut, scared to turn around, unaware that we were being observed.

"There's someone I want you to meet," he says. He spins me around and I open one eye, then the other, hoping the shock I feel in my stomach isn't clearly sprawled across my face. Leaning up against the doorframe with his arms folded across his chest and a hard look in his eyes, is all six feet of Carter.

I gasp, mostly because he's the last person I expected to see here. Standing in front of him now is suddenly more intimidating than sitting next to him in class was this morning. He's a lot taller than I thought—taller than Asa, even. He's not as defined as Asa, but then again, Asa works out every day and, based on the size of his biceps, probably dabbles in steroids. Carter is more naturally built, with a darker complexion and darker hair—and at the moment, very dark, angry eyes.

"Hey," Carter says, easing his expression with a smile, extending his hand to me without a trace of recognition on his face. I realize he's pretending not to know me for my own benefit—or perhaps for *his* own benefit, so I return his handshake, introducing myself to him for the second time today.

"I'm Sloan," I say shakily, hoping he can't feel my racing pulse through the palm of my hand. I cut the handshake short and pull back. "So how do you and Asa know each other?" I'm not sure I want to know the answer, but the question spills out of my mouth anyway.

Asa puts his arm around my waist and spins me in the other direction, away from Carter. "He's my new business partner, and right now we've got business to conduct. Go clean somewhere else." He pats me on the ass, attempting to shoo me away like a dog. I spin around and scowl at him, but it's not nearly as intense as the hatred spilling out of Carter's eyes as he watches Asa.

I normally don't push things with Asa, especially in front of other people, but I can't help my temper right now. I'm furious at his cavalier attitude about bringing in someone else, despite the fact that he promised me he was getting out. I also can't deny the fact that I'm pissed that it's Carter. I'm angry at myself for developing a false first impression of him in class today. I thought I was better at reading people, but the fact that he's involved with Asa shows me that I don't know a damn thing about reading people. He's just like the rest of them, but I should expect it by now. As hard as I try—as hard as it was leaving my childhood home in order to get away from this same type of lifestyle, only to end up right back in it—it makes me feel ignorant. How can I crave and work toward a normal life so incredibly bad, yet I keep falling right back in the middle of this shit? It's a damn curse.

"Asa, you promised." I toss my hand in Carter's direction. "Hiring new people isn't getting out...it's getting in deeper."

I feel hypocritical asking him to stop doing what he does. Every month I let him send a check for Stephen's care with the same dirty money I wish he wasn't making. But it's easier for me to allow that, since it's not for me. I'd take the dirtiest money there is if it meant my little brother would be taken care of.

Asa's eyes grow dark and he takes a step toward me. He gently places his hands on my arms and rubs them up and down. He leans his mouth in toward my ear and increases his grip on my arms, squeezing with all his force until I wince from the pain.

"Don't embarrass me," he whispers quietly enough that only I can hear him. He eases his grip and runs his hands down to my elbows, then kisses me lovingly on the cheek for show. "Go put on that sexy red dress. We're having a party tonight to celebrate."

He steps back and releases me from his grip completely. I glance at Carter, who's still standing in the doorway, eyeing Asa like he could rip his head off at any second. He cuts his eyes to mine and for a second they grow softer, but I don't hang around long enough to be positive. I turn and run up the stairs to the bedroom. I slam the door and fall onto the bed. The muscles in my arms are throbbing from the pain, so I try to rub it away. It's the first time he's ever physically hurt me in front of someone, but the injury to my pride hurts so much worse. I never should have questioned him in front of someone. I know better.

But I also know that I don't deserve what he just did to me. No one does. I want to grab my bags and pack everything I own. I want to leave and never come back. I want out. I want out, I want out, I want out.

But I can't leave. It's not just me who would be affected.

FOUR

Carter

"Sorry about her," Asa says, turning back to me.

I unclench my fists and attempt to hide my disdain. I've known him all of three hours, and I've never despised someone more in my entire life.

"It's all good," I reply. I walk over to the bar and casually ease myself into one of the seats at the table, despite the fact that I want to run upstairs and make sure Sloan's okay. My mind is still reeling from the fact that Sloan is involved in this. She was the last person I expected to run into coming here. Watching Asa kiss her like he did, and watching her respond like she did, made me officially regret taking on this assignment. This just became a hell of a lot more complicated.

"She live with you?" I ask.

Asa hands me a beer out of the fridge and I untwist the top, then bring it to my mouth. "Yep," he says. "And I'll cut off your dick if you so much as look at her the wrong way."

I eye him, but he doesn't skip a beat. He shuts the door to the refrigerator and saunters to his seat on the other side of the bar as though the sentence never even left his mouth. That he can physically hurt her like he just did, then act like he gives a shit about her, has me floored. I want to bust the fucking beer bottle against his head, but instead I grip it harder, keeping my temper in check.

He opens his beer and raises the bottle. "To money," he says, clinking the bottle against mine.

"To money." *And watching assholes get what they deserve.*

Dalton walks in, interrupting with perfect timing. He looks at me and nods, then turns his attention to Asa. "Hey, man. Jon wants to know what to do about the alcohol situation. Is it BYOB tonight, or are we providing, because we don't have shit."

Asa slams his beer down on the bar and shoves his chair back, standing up. "I told that asshole to stock up yesterday." Asa storms out of the kitchen.

Dalton nudges his head toward the front door and I get up and follow him outside. Once we're alone in the middle of the front yard, he turns toward me and takes a swig of his beer, mostly for show. Dalton hates beer.

"How'd it go? You think you're in?" he asks.

I shrug. "I guess. He's desperate for someone who can speak Spanish. I told him I was good, but not fluent."

Dalton gapes at me. "Just like that? No questions asked?" He shakes his head in disbelief. "God, he's such a dumbass. Why do the new ones think they're so untouchable? Fucking pretentious prick."

"Yep," I say in whole-hearted agreement.

"I warned you about this job, Luke. It'll fuck with your head having to live like this. You sure you want in on this one?"

There's no way I can back out now, knowing how close Dalton and the others are to nailing him. "You just called me Luke."

"Shit." Dalton kicks at the ground with his shoe and looks back up at me. "Sorry, man. We still on to meet tomorrow? Young wants a full report now that you're in."

"Some of us have class tomorrow," I say, rubbing it in yet again that I got the shitty end of the assignment. "I'll be out by noon, though."

Dalton nods and turns back toward the house. "You invite that hot piece of ass from your Spanish class to the party?"

"Nope. This isn't her style." *Not to mention the fact that she doesn't need an invite. She's smack dab in the middle of this shit.*

He nods, knowing inviting someone into this lifestyle is something I would never do. Dalton can take on and absorb his role like nothing I've ever seen. He's had long-term relationships while undercover, even went so far as to propose once, just to keep up appearances. Of course, once the job's over, he has no problem disappearing. There's still a huge part of me that knows every person I meet while I'm Carter, is still that...a *person*. I don't want to mislead anyone unnecessarily, so I make it a point to be on guard and never let these things go too deep.

He closes the door behind him and I stand alone in the front yard, staring at the house that has just become my assignment for at least the next two months. Undercover work wasn't really what I joined the force for, but it's what I'm good at. Unfortunately, I've got a really bad feeling about this one...and I've only been here a day.

I spend the next couple of hours being escorted in and out of rooms by Asa, shaking hands with more people than I can count. At first I try to keep mental notes of everyone I meet and the way they interact with Asa, but by the fourth beer that is shoved into my hands, I stop trying. There'll be plenty of time to get to know everyone; I don't need to be too focused right now. I'm still so new to this crowd, I don't want to give anyone reason for suspicion.

I finally break away long enough to go look for a bathroom. When I find one, the guy I now know as Jon, and two girls who can't be older than nineteen, occupy it. I close the door faster than I opened it, then head upstairs hoping to find one that isn't being used as a brothel.

I remain in the bathroom for a good ten minutes longer than I need to. I pour my beer into the sink and fill the bottle with tap water, having gone well past my personal quota for the night. I need to spend the next few weeks completely sober.

I stare at myself in the mirror, hoping I can pull this off. I'm not from this area, so I'm not worried about being recognized. What I'm worried about is the fact that I'm not like Dalton. I can't just turn it on and off like he does. The things I see here are the things I see when I close my eyes at night. And based on what I saw between Sloan and Asa today, I won't be getting much sleep.

I run a washcloth under the water and wet my face, willing myself to sober up before I exit the bathroom. I toss the washcloth into the hamper of clothes. I stare at the hamper, full to the brim of dirty laundry, and wonder if Sloan is the only girl who lives here. I'm assuming she's probably the one who gets stuck with all the laundry. Not to mention the rest of the house.

When Asa and I walked in on her cleaning the kitchen this afternoon, he stopped in the doorway and watched her clean for a moment. I stood over his shoulder, taken aback by the fact that it was the same girl from class this morning...but more so by just how beautiful she was, swaying to the music. The lyrics to the iconic Rick Springfield song, *"Jessie's Girl,"* were running through my mind as I stood behind Asa, watching him watch her. I wanted to be the one watching her like that.

Like she was mine.

I inhale deeply and open the bathroom door. My eyes are pulled to the vision standing in the doorway across the hall. She spins around when she hears the bathroom door open, and her slinky dress spins with her. When she comes to a standstill, I can't pull my eyes away from the dress. It hugs her in all the right places, the spaghetti straps holding up a barely-there top that squeezes her breasts together, leaving no room for any type of bra. It pisses me off that I'm mentally thanking Asa for telling her to put on this dress.

Breathe, Luke. Breathe.

I finally bring my eyes to meet hers, and the look on her face doesn't match the sexy, confidant attire she's sporting. It looks like she's been crying.

"You okay?" I ask, taking a step toward her. She glances at the stairwell with a look of fear in her eyes, then back up at me. She nods and starts to head toward the stairs, so I reach out and grab her hand, pulling her back. "Sloan, wait."

She faces me. The girl I'm looking at right now is not the girl I met in class today. This girl is fragile. Scared. Broken.

She takes a step toward me, folding her arms across her chest. She stares down at the floor between us, tugging on her lip with her teeth. "Why are you here, Carter?"

I don't know how to answer her. I don't want to lie, but I also can't tell her the truth. I'm pretty sure it would be frowned upon if I told the girlfriend of the guy I'm trying to bust the real reason why I'm here.

"I was invited," I say.

She darts her head up. "You know what I mean. Why are you even involved in all of this?"

"You're dating the very reason why I'm here," I say, referring to our mutual involvement with Asa. "It's just a job."

She rolls her eyes as though she's heard that excuse before. Probably from Asa. But the difference between my excuse and Asa's, is that mine is the truth. She just doesn't know exactly how much of a job it really is.

I sigh and try to ease some of the tension between us. "Sloan, I think it's safe to say we both left a few important facts out of our class assignment today."

She releases a pained laugh. "Yeah. He should have assigned us more than three. I think five would have covered it."

"Yep," I say. "Five facts probably would have been enough to clue me in to the fact that you have a boyfriend."

She glances up at me, her chin tucked in. "I'm sorry," she says quietly.

"For what?"

She drops her shoulders and lowers her voice even more. "For the way I acted in class today. For flirting with you. I shouldn't have said some of the things I said. I swear I'm not that kind of girl. I would have never..."

"Sloan," I interrupt, hooking my finger under her chin. I stare down at her, knowing full well I need to drop my hand and back the fuck away from her. "I don't think that about you at all. It was harmless fun, that's it."

The word *harmless* looms in the air like a dark, ominous cloud. We both know that Asa is anything but harmless. Talking to her in class, standing with her in this hallway...it's the harmless moments like these that, if they occur enough, will end up being a hell of a lot more than just harmless. Asa's threat from earlier repeats in my mind. Everything about this girl is off limits. Asa has made that clear...my *career* makes that clear. Why can't I see it that clearly?

I begin to drop my hand when a voice from behind us causes us both to jump.

"You're missing the party, man."

I spin around and Dalton is at the top of the stairwell, eyeing me like he's about to beat my ass. He has every right to, considering the mess I almost just got myself in.

"Yeah." I take a deep breath and turn back around to face her. "We'll talk in class," I whisper. She nods and lets out a breath, relieved that the voice at the top of the stairs belonged to Dalton and not Asa. She's not the only one relieved by that.

She turns around and heads back into her room, rather than downstairs. I can see now, based on her environment, why she doesn't get any sleep.

As soon as the door closes behind her, I spin around and come face-to-face with Dalton. His nostrils are flaring, a dead giveaway that he's about to hit me. He shoves me against the wall and wedges his arm between my chest and throat.

"Don't fuck this up," he seethes. He slaps his palm against the side of my head. "Play smart."

FIVE

Asa

I fold my arms behind my head and lean back on the pillow. "Take off your panties."

She grins and bends forward, hooking her thumbs in her panties as she slowly slides them down over her hips. Her breasts are pushed together nicely in a transparent black bra. I think I'll let her leave that one on.

"Come here."

She bends down on the bed and crawls toward me, her long blonde hair tracing up my legs as she slowly glides up my body. She positions herself above me, straddling me. This chick knows what she's doing. That can be both good and bad. I like a girl who knows how to fuck, but it also makes me wonder how many guys she's had to fuck in order to get so good. I reach over to the nightstand and grab a condom, handing it to her.

"Put it on," I command. She keeps her eyes trained on mine as she opens it, then brings her hands to my dick. I grab her wrists and shake my head. "With your mouth."

She grins and begins to lower her head when I hear the footsteps. Then the bedroom doorknob makes an unsuccessful turn. *Fuck.*

"Asa, open the door!" Sloan yells from outside the room.

"Fuck!" I shove the girl onto her back. I stand up and grab my pants, pulling them on as the girl on the bed looks back and forth between the door and me. I pick her clothes up off the floor and throw them toward the closet, pointing for her to go hide.

She stands up and scoffs at my demand, shaking her head.

If this bitch really thinks she's about to walk out of this room with Sloan on the other side of the door, she's delusional. I grab her by the shoulders and shove her toward the closet.

"Just for a few minutes," I whisper. She starts to object, so I cover her mouth with mine. Whatever it takes to shut her up. I drop my hand between her legs, feeling her rely on me for support as her knees begin to buckle beneath her. Needless to say, her anger dissolves with each stroke. She moans into my mouth and I push her farther into my closet, just as Sloan beats on the door for a second time.

"Two minutes," I whisper. "I'll get rid of her."

I kiss her again, then shut the closet door. I grab a towel and wipe my hands, then walk to the bedroom door and open it.

"It's four o'clock in the afternoon, why are you asleep?" Sloan says, shoving past me.

She's heading toward the closet, so I grab her by the waist and pull her down onto the bed. "I had class all day. I'm tired," I say, knowing the lie will ease her resolve.

It does.

She relaxes and curls into my chest. "You actually went to class today?"

I nod and bring my hands to her face, wiping a stray strand of hair out of her eyes, then tucking it behind her ear. I roll her onto her back and hover over her. The distinct bruises on her arms catch my eye, and it reminds me that I never did apologize for that incident in the kitchen.

"I did go to class," I lie, running my fingers down her arm, over the marks I left on her. "I'm taking it seriously, Sloan. Everything I've promised you. I want to make it better." I bend down and kiss the fingertip bruises. "I love you, babe," I say softly. "I didn't mean to hurt you. Sometimes I forget how fragile your skin is."

She presses her lips into a thin line and swallows. I can tell she's trying not to cry. This is going to take a little more work than I thought. "God, Sloan. I don't deserve you. I swear to you, I'll make it better. I'll make it better for both of us, okay?" I take both of her cheeks between the palms of my hands and I kiss her deeply. I know a girl likes it when a guy holds her face while he kisses her; like kissing is his only intention.

It's bullshit. If guys had their way, their hands would never venture above the tits.

"I love you," I say again as I glide my hand down to her waist. My dick swells in my pants, getting a hell of a lot harder than the whore in the closet could get it.

As many girls as I've been with, I can honestly say Sloan turns me on more than any of them. I don't know what it is about her that I find so much more attractive than the rest of them. Her tits aren't that big and she's not even that curvy.

I think it's her innocence. I like knowing I'm the first and only guy who's ever fucked her. I like knowing I'll be the only guy who'll *ever* fuck her.

I slide my hand underneath her shirt and pull the lace of her bra down. "Let me make it up to you," I whisper. I press my mouth to the thin layer of shirt covering her nipple, and I take it between my teeth. She moans and arches her back, but pushes against my chest.

"Asa, I just left the gym. I'm all sweaty. Let me take a shower first."

I release her nipple from my mouth and attempt to change her mind by running my hand between her legs, rubbing at the denim of her jeans. "You're perfect," I say, licking at the sweet, sweaty skin of her neck. She stiffens, so I increase the pressure of my hand. "Relax," I whisper. She fights it, but I can feel her slowly melting against my hand. I let the subtle movement of her hips guide my hand to the right spot. I work her up, harder and harder, until she's on the verge of falling apart beneath my fingertips.

She gives in to my coercion and relaxes her arms above her head. I sit up on my knees and unbutton her pants, easing them down her hips far enough to give me access. I slip my fingers underneath the edge of her panties and ease two of them inside of her. She moans and grasps at the sheets, balling them up in knots between her white-knuckled fists. I slowly ease my fingers in and out of her, teasing her clit with the pad of my thumb. I rake my eyes over her body as I build up speed with my hand. As soon as I feel the shudders rising up from her, I cover her mouth with mine and kiss her hard. She lets out a scream that's completely muffled by my mouth. God, I love it when she screams into my mouth. Her breath slides down my throat in labored waves, mixing with mine. I continue rubbing her until she stiffens beneath me and tries to pull my hand away. I slip my hand out of her panties, pulling them back into position.

"You can go shower now." I kiss her again and she grabs my face, then pushes me onto my back and rolls on top of me.

"What about you?" she asks, reaching down to unzip my pants.

I grab her hand and pull it away. "I owed you one," I say. "Now go shower. We're going out tonight."

She smiles. "Like on a date?"

"Not *like* a date. It *is* a date."

She grins and hops off of me, heading toward the door.

"Lock it on your way out," I say.

She pauses and turns around. "Why?"

I grab the bulge in my pants. "I need to finish what you started."

She crinkles up her nose and rolls her eyes, but she locks the door behind her. I jump up and check the lock, then turn around, just as whatever-her-name-is comes barging out of the closet. She points her finger at me and practically spits venom when she speaks. "You sick fuck!"

I grab the hand that's pointing in my face and spin it around, wrapping her arm behind her back. I lean into her ear and press my hard-on against her stomach. "Hey, hey," I say quietly, attempting to calm her down. I run my fingers down her cheek and lightly kiss her lips. "I saved the best part for you." I press her down onto the bed, ass first. I drop my pants and kick them off, then reach for the condom and slide it on. The girl lies back on the bed and spreads her legs open.

Fucking whore.

I kneel down on the bed and position myself between her legs. I slide my hands underneath her back and bring them up from behind, gripping her shoulders with a firm hold. I wait silently and listen for the water to start running across the hall. When the shower starts up, I grip her tighter and slam into her so hard, she screams. I immediately put my hand over her mouth and continue slamming against her. I can't tell if she's screaming into my hand because she likes it, or because I'm fucking her so hard it hurts. The fact that I can't tell the difference turns me on even more.

It doesn't take me long at all. Knowing I just made Sloan scream in this same spot less than two minutes ago is enough to make me finish without even having my dick balls-deep in some whore. I squeeze my eyes shut and slam into her one last time, holding my position for several seconds while her moans are still being suppressed by my hand. I drop onto my elbows and take one of her nipples in my mouth, sucking and pulling on it until every last bit of me is released.

I relax against the girl's chest and pull out. She whimpers, squeezing her thighs against my hips, wanting more. The thought of making two girls climax beneath my fingertips just minutes apart is more than even *I have* ever accomplished. I toss the condom into the trash, then lie down beside her. I push her thighs apart, then shove two fingers deep inside her, watching as her eyes roll back in her head.

I press my cheek against hers and ease my fingers in and out. "You like this?" I whisper in her ear. She moans and breathes a *yes,* so I force a third finger inside her, feeling her stretch around my hand. She breathes a much louder *yes* this time.

I shove the fourth finger inside her, watching as she grimaces in pain. I rub my thumb over her clit and cup my fingers upward, finding the exact spot that sends her into a tailspin.

"You like it when I fuck you with my hand?"

She becomes louder, moaning and grunting and yelling my name. I have to cover her goddamn mouth again with my free hand.

I pull back and look her in the eyes. "Did you watch me fuck my girlfriend with this hand? Did that turn you on?"

Her eyes grow wide and she doesn't respond, so I ask her again.

"*Did* it?" I say, pausing the movement of my hand, causing her to whimper. I know how close she is to releasing, so I use her desperation to my advantage.

"Tell me you liked it."

She moans, pressing herself against my hand, silently begging me to keep going. I pull my fingers out of her and bring them up to her mouth.

"Taste her," I say, tracing my wet fingers along her bottom lip.

She turns her face to the side, not wanting to take my fingers in her mouth. My dick is hard again, so I position myself on top of her. The need growing between her legs makes her desperate. She tilts her face back toward me, just like I knew she would, and reluctantly opens her mouth. I grab her jaw with my other hand and force her mouth open wider, shoving two of my fingers inside.

"Suck," I demand. She closes her lips over my fingers and sucks them.

"Does she taste good?" I ask, rubbing myself against her faster and harder, bringing her right to the edge with me.

She moans and nods her head, grabbing my wrist with her hand, taking turns sucking each of my fingers down to the knuckles. The feel of her tongue sliding up and down my fingers nearly makes me bust it all over her. "Fuuuck," I groan. I pull my hand out of her mouth.

"Let me taste," I say. I kiss her, licking the sweet aftertaste of both of them off of her tongue. She arches her back and it doesn't take her long before she's writhing beneath me. I pull back from her mouth and continue to rub against her. When she finally starts to reach her peak, I can feel the scream wanting to escape her lips, so I do to her what I just did to Sloan. I cover her mouth with mine and let her scream her little heart out, while she shudders and shakes beneath me. I close my eyes and groan as I lift up slightly and press my dick against the girl's stomach, releasing myself all over her.

When she's finally calm beneath me, I roll off of her and hand her a shirt from the floor to clean up with.

"Get dressed," I say. "I have a date tonight."

SIX

Sloan

slip into the bathroom before class for a quick hair and makeup check. I've never cared before if I looked like I just rolled out of bed, but knowing Carter will be sitting inches away from me for the next hour has me more concerned than usual.

The fluorescent lights are unforgiving. The bags under my eyes tell their own truth about last night. Just looking at my reflection, all I see is a girl who stayed up way too late worrying about the guy who promised her a date but never showed.

Asa left with his friend Jon while I was in the shower yesterday, getting ready for him to take me out for the first time in over five months. Despite the fact that neither of them was home, the house was still full of people. I stayed up worried about him until I couldn't keep my eyes open anymore. When he finally crawled in bed, then proceeded to crawl on top of me, I was so pissed I just started crying.

He didn't even notice. Or he didn't *care*.

I cried the entire time he was on top of me, fucking me like he didn't give a shit *who* was under him, as long as *someone* was under him. When he finished, he rolled over and fell asleep without a single word. Not an apology. Not a thank-you. Not an *I love you.* He just rolled over and fell right to sleep without a single thing on his conscience. I rolled over and continued to cry.

I cried for the fact that I allow him to do what he does to me. I cried for the fact that I feel like I have no other choice. I cried for the fact that I'm still with him, despite the person he's become. I cried for the fact that I have no way out, no matter how much I want to leave. I cried for the fact that despite everything horrible about Asa, I was still worried sick when he didn't come home. I cried because I realized that no matter who he's become, a part of me is still in love with him...because I don't know how *not* to be.

I turn away from my reflection and head to class, because I don't want to look at myself anymore. I'm ashamed of who I've become.

Carter is already seated at our table when I walk into Spanish class. I can see him watching me out of the corner of my eye, but I refuse to look at him.

After spending an hour with him in class the other day, I think it's safe to say I developed a slight crush. The thought of getting to spend time with him three days a week had me giddy; a feeling that had become all too foreign to me. But seeing him in my house, with Asa of all people, crushed any fantasies I may have had. I never intended for anything to happen with Carter. How could it have? There's no way I can get out of the situation I'm in with Asa, and I'm not a cheater. I was simply looking forward to having a crush. Looking forward to flirting a little bit. Looking forward to feeling desirable.

Knowing now that Carter is more like Asa than I could have imagined, I don't want any part of it. Any part of him. The fact that he's now another constant fixture at our house makes him even more off limits. If Asa even had a suspicion that another guy was speaking to me, that guy would be dead. I'd like to say that isn't a literal statement, but it is. Seeing as how he doesn't seem to have a conscience, I one hundred percent believe that Asa is capable of murder.

Which is exactly the reason I'm not putting Carter in that situation. I keep telling myself that Carter is just another Asa, in different clothing. Not worth the risk. I treat this situation with Carter exactly as it is: another roadblock to my eventual escape.

I glance around the room for a vacant seat that isn't next to his. I must have spent too much time in the restroom, because the class is almost full. There are two seats on the second-to-top row that are empty, but they're directly in front of the seat Carter is occupying. I avoid his gaze and walk to the empty seats with my head tucked down. I don't know if I can pull off pretending I didn't notice him, but I'm sure as hell going to try.

I take one of the seats and sit down, then pull my books out and place them on the table in front of me. I hear a sudden commotion coming from the top row and can't help but turn around. Carter is scooting across the table behind me with his backpack in hand. He hops off the table and pulls the empty chair out next to me, then plops down into it.

"What's this all about?" he asks, twisting in his chair to face me.

"What's *what* all about?" I ask, opening the text to where we left off on Monday.

I can feel him staring at me, but he doesn't say anything. I continue to pretend-read, and he continues to silently stare at me until I can't take it anymore. I turn to face him.

"*What?*" I ask, irritated. "What do you want?"

He still doesn't say anything. I slam my book shut and turn my body toward his. The fact that our knees are pressed together doesn't go unnoticed. He glances down at our legs and I can see a hint of a grin playing at the corners of his mouth.

"Well," he says. "I sort of liked sitting by you the other day, so I thought I'd do it again. I take it that's not what you want, so..."

He begins to gather his books and a huge part of me wants to rip them from his hands and make him stay here, right where he is. But an even bigger part of me is relieved that he's taking the hint.

He shoves his notebook in his backpack and I keep quiet. If I say anything, I know it'll be nothing but a pathetic plea for him to stay put.

"You're in my seat," a flat, monotone voice says.

Carter and I both look up to see a guy standing in front of us, staring down at Carter with an indifferent expression.

"I was just moving, man," Carter says, pulling his backpack onto the table.

"You should have never sat there in the first place," the guy says. "*I* sit there." The guy turns to me and extends his arm straight out, pointing at me. "And you don't sit right there. A different girl sat there on Monday, so you can't sit there."

The guy's expression is troubled. He's terribly disturbed that we're in different seats today. I feel sorry for him, recognizing features of one of my own brothers when I look at him. I start to tell him we'll move—that he can have his seat—but Carter's anger intercepts my response. He stands up.

"Get your finger out of her face," he says to the guy.

"Get out of my seat," the guy replies, turning his attention back to Carter.

Carter laughs and drops his backpack on the floor. "Dude," he says. "What is this? Kindergarten? Go find your own fucking seat."

The guy drops his arm and looks at Carter in shock. He starts to reply, but snaps his mouth shut and walks toward the back row, defeated. "But that's my seat," he mumbles, walking away.

Carter pulls his notebook back out of his backpack and sets it on the table in front of him. "I guess you're stuck with me," he says. "No way I'm moving seats now."

I shake my head and lean in toward him. "Carter," I whisper. "Give him a break. I think he has Asperger's, he can't help it."

Carter snaps his head in my direction. "No shit? Are you serious?"

I nod. "My brother had Asperger's. I know the signs."

He runs his hands over his face. "Shit," he groans. He quickly stands up, reaching for my hand when he does. I stand up with him.

"Get your stuff," he says, pointing to my backpack and notebook. He turns around and throws his stuff on the table behind him, then reaches for my backpack and does the same. He looks up at the guy and points down to the seats we were just occupying. "Sorry, man. I didn't realize they were your seats. We'll move."

The guy quickly walks back to the row we're in and claims his seat before Carter changes his mind. Realizing most of the class is probably watching the commotion between the three of us, I still can't help but smile. I love that he just did that.

We both walk back to the seats we occupied on Monday, then unpack our stuff onto the table.

Again.

"Thank you for doing that," I say to him.

He doesn't respond. He gives me a half-smile, then looks down at his phone until class starts.

Things are a little awkward once the lecture begins. Not wanting to sit by Carter has left him questioning me. I can tell, because it's written clearly in front of me in black ink as I stare down at the paper he just scooted toward me.

Why didn't you want to sit by me?

I chuckle at the simplicity in his question. I pick up my pen and write a response.

Dude. What is this? Kindergarten?

He reads my response and I swear I can see him frown. I was trying to be funny, but he missed the humor, apparently. He writes something down, something long, and slides the note back to me.

I'm serious, Sloan. Did I cross some sort of line the other night? I'm sorry if I did. I know you're with Asa and I respect that. I honestly just think you're fun and want to sit by you. Spanish bores the hell out of me and sitting next to you makes the urge I have to gouge my own eyes out a little less imminent.

I stare at his note for a lot longer than it actually takes me to read it. He's got incredibly impressive handwriting for a guy, and an even more impressive way of making my heart race.

He thinks I'm fun.

It's a simple compliment, but one that affects me way more than I wish it did. I have no idea what to say in response, so I press my pen to the paper and don't even think when I write.

People in Wyoming don't really exist, and I can never find the right outfit to wear when I shop for penguins.

I slide the paper back to him and when he laughs out loud, I put my hand over my mouth, covering my smile. I love that he gets my sense of humor, but hate it at the same time. Every second I spend with him just makes two *more* seconds I want to spend with him.

He slides the paper back to me.

Mosquitos whisper sweet nothings into my barrel of monkeys that took too long to bring me the pizza I ordered.

I laugh, then clench my stomach. Seeing the word *pizza* reminds me of just how hungry I am. I was too upset to eat dinner last night, so it's been over twenty-four hours since I've eaten anything.

Pizza sounds good.

I lay my pen down but don't slide the note to him. I'm not sure why I wrote something down that I was actually thinking this time.

"It does," he says aloud.

I glance up at him and he's looking at me with a smile that actually hurts. He's everything I want, and everything I don't need, and it literally, *physically* hurts.

"After class," he whispers. "I'm taking you for pizza."

It comes out of his mouth so fast, it seems like he knows he shouldn't be saying it, much less *doing* it.

But I nod.
Dammit, I nod.

SEVEN

Carter

After class is over, she walks next to me as I lead her toward the parking lot. I can tell by the grip she has on her backpack and the way she keeps looking behind her that she's about to back out. When she pauses, turning toward me on the pavement, I don't even give her the chance to speak.

"It's lunchtime, Sloan. You need to eat. I'm taking you for pizza. Quit trying to make it more than it is, okay?"

Her eyes widen in shock that I knew exactly what she was thinking. She presses her lips together and nods.

"It's lunch," she says with a shrug, casually trying to convince herself that this is perfectly okay. "*I* eat lunch. *You* eat lunch. What's the big deal if we eat lunch at the same time? At the same restaurant?"

"Exactly," I say.

There are smiles on both of our faces, but the fear in our eyes speaks volumes.

We're crossing a line, and we both know it.

When we reach my car, I naturally start toward her door to open it for her, but change my mind and go straight to the driver's side instead. The less I treat her like my date, the less it'll *feel* like a date. I don't want to make her more nervous about our "casual lunch" than she already is. The truth is, I'm nervous enough for the both of us. I don't know what the hell I think I'm doing, but whenever I'm around her, all I can think about is how much more I want to be around her.

We both shut our doors and I crank the car, then pull out of the parking lot. Pulling away from the college with her alone in my car feels almost like playing a game of Russian roulette. My pulse is racing and my mouth runs dry, knowing my being with her is potential career suicide. Not to mention what would happen if Asa found out.

I wipe him from my mind and look over at her, deciding that if this may very well be my last day on Earth, I'm going to focus on her and enjoy the hell out of it.

"I have a confession," she says, looking at me, embarrassed.

"What is it?"

She clicks her seatbelt into place and folds her hands in her lap. "I don't have any money."

I want to laugh at her confession, but in all honesty, it makes me sad for her. "My treat," I say, because it would have been, regardless. "But if I hadn't taken you to lunch today, how would you have eaten?"

She shrugs. "I usually don't eat lunch. Lunch costs money, and money is something I don't have in abundance right now. I'm saving up for something more important."

She glances out the window, a clear sign that she doesn't have intentions of elaborating on what it is she's saving up for. I don't push it. But I *do* push for an answer as to why she doesn't have money to eat on.

"Why don't you just ask Asa for money? He's got it. I bet if he knew you weren't eating lunch, he'd make sure you had some."

She shakes her head. "I don't want his dirty money," she spits out. "I'd rather starve."

I don't respond. I don't want to remind her of the fact that she's under the impression that I'm working for Asa, so I'll be paying for our lunch with that same dirty money. Instead, I change the conversation to a lighter subject.

"Tell me about your brother," I say as I steer the car in the direction of the freeway.

"My brother?" she asks, questioning me. "Which one?"

"The one with Asperger's? I don't know a lot about it. I had a neighbor kid back in Sacramento who had it. I didn't know it was something you could overcome, but you said your brother *had* it... like as in past tense."

Her eyes drop to her lap and she laces her fingers together. "It's *not* something you can overcome," she says quietly.

But she referred to it in the past tense. Or...I guess she referred to *him* in the past tense. *I'm an insensitive dumbass. Why the hell did I bring it up?*

"I'm sorry." I reach over and give her hand a quick squeeze. "I'm really sorry," I repeat.

She pulls her hand back to her lap and clears her throat. "It's fine," she says, forcing a smile. "It was a long time ago. Asperger's wasn't the only thing he dealt with, unfortunately."

And on that note, we reach the restaurant. I pull into a parking spot and turn off the car. Neither of us moves. I think she's waiting on me to get out of the car, but I feel like I just ruined her good mood.

"I officially sucked the fun out of that drive," I say. "Got any remedies?"

She laughs lightheartedly and grins. "We could take the writing game to another level," she says. "Try to lighten the mood a little bit. Instead of writing random things without thinking, we could just spend lunch *saying* random things without thinking."

I nod and gesture toward the restaurant in front of us. "After you," I say. "Walrus tusks cloud my vision like chocolate pudding."

She laughs and opens her door. "One-legged tiger sharks are better for you than vegetables."

EIGHT

Asa

"**J**on!"

I'm gripping my phone so tight, I wouldn't be surprised if it crumpled in my hand. I breathe in through my nose and out through my mouth, calming myself, attempting to give her the benefit of the doubt before I completely flip out.

"Jon!"

I finally hear his footsteps bounding up the stairs. My door swings open and he walks into the room. "What the hell is it? I was taking a shit."

I look down at the GPS report on my phone. "What's at 1262 Ricker Road?"

He looks up at the ceiling, drumming his fingers against the doorframe. "Ricker Road," he repeats to himself. "Mostly just restaurants, I think." He looks down at his phone and types in the address. "Why? We got a delivery?"

I shake my head. "Nope. Sloan's on Ricker Road."

Jon cocks his head. "Did your car break down? She need a ride somewhere?"

42

I roll my eyes. "She doesn't need a fucking ride, dumbass. She's on Ricker Road when she should be on campus. I want to know what the fuck she's doing there and who the fuck she's with."

Realization finally dawns on his face. "Oh, shit. You want to go check it out?" He scrolls through his phone some more. "Looks like Italian. Something called Mi Amore."

I toss my phone across the mattress and stand up, pacing the room. "No," I say. "It's half an hour away. Forty-five minutes with traffic. She'll be gone before we even get there." I take a deep breath and grip the bridge of my nose between my fingertips, willing myself to remain calm.

If she's fucking around, I'll find out. And if I find out, she's fucking dead. The bastard she's fucking around with won't be as lucky.

"I'll figure it out," I say to Jon. "Tonight."

NINE

Sloan

Carter holds the door open for me. It's the first time I've been inside a restaurant in months; I forgot how good they smell.

Thoughts of Asa finding out I'm here keep flashing through my mind, despite doing my best to focus on the fact that I'm just eating lunch. As innocent as I can pretend this is, if Asa found out...

I don't even want to think about what Asa would do.

The hostess smiles at us, grabbing two menus. "Table for two?"

"Yes, please," Carter says. "Bananas like boiled water in Reno," he adds with a straight face.

I bust out laughing. The hostess shoots us both a confused look, then shakes her head. "Follow me."

Carter reaches down and grabs my hand, pulling me forward. He doesn't just grab my hand to lead me to our seat; he intertwines his fingers with mine and smiles at me, causing my heart to pound like a kick drum.

Oh, God, this is wrong, wrong, wrong.

When we reach our table and he pulls his hand from mine to take his seat, it literally makes my heart ache, having to let go of his hand. We both scoot into the booth and rest our elbows on the table between us. I look down at his hands...at the one that just held mine. There's nothing particularly special about his hand. It's odd how the slightest touch from that simple hand can cause such a disturbance inside of me. It's just a hand. *What the hell is so special about his hand?*

"What?" he says. The sound of his voice pulls me out of my trance and I look up at him. His head is tilted to the side and his eyes are focused on mine. Hard. Like he's attempting to read my mind.

"What?" I ask him in return, feigning ignorance.

He leans back into the booth and folds his arms across his chest. "I was just wondering what you were thinking. You were looking at my hands like you wanted to cut them off."

I didn't realize my expression was a dead giveaway. I can feel the heat rise to my cheeks, but I refuse to look embarrassed. I lean back in my booth and scoot toward the wall, so that I'm not sitting directly in front of him. I prop my feet in the seat next to him and cross my ankles, getting comfortable.

"I was just thinking," I reply.

He props his feet up next to me, crossing them at the ankles as well. I can't tell if he's just getting comfortable, or if he's mimicking me.

"I know you were just thinking. I want to know *what* you were thinking."

"Are you always this nosey?"

He smiles. "When it comes to the safety of my limbs...yes."

"Well, I wasn't thinking I wanted to cut off your hands, if that makes you feel better."

He keeps his eyes locked on mine, his head resting casually against the booth. "Tell me," he says again.

"You're pushy," I say, picking up the menu. I hold it up in front of me, blocking the sight of him. His piercing dark eyes are hard to say no to, so I just choose not to look at him at all.

His fingers slide over the top of the menu and he pulls it down, eyeing me, still waiting for an answer. I drop the menu and sigh.

"Internal thoughts are internal for a reason, Carter."

He narrows his eyes and leans forward in the booth. "Should I not have held your hand? Did that piss you off?"

The sensually smooth sound of his voice alone tickles the inside of my stomach like a feather, but I try to convince myself that I'm just hungry.

"It didn't piss me off," I say, still skirting around his demand for answers. The problem I had with him holding my hand was that I liked it. A lot. But I'm not telling him that.

I pull my gaze from his and pick the menu up again. I don't want to see his reaction. I read the selections on the menu for a while, very aware of the silence poised between us. The fact that he isn't saying anything is driving me crazy. I can feel him staring, silently challenging me to look at him.

"Can I get a pizza?" I ask, breaking the silence and changing the subject.

"Get whatever you want," he says, finally picking up his own menu.

"Pepperoni and onions." I drop my menu back on the table. "And water's fine. I'm going to the restroom."

I move to slide out, but his feet are still propped up in the booth next to me, blocking my exit. I'm forced to look up at him, but he's still staring down at his menu. He slowly pulls one foot off the booth, then the other, a small smile playing on his lips the whole time. I scoot out of the booth and head to the bathroom, locking the door behind me. I press my back to the door and close my eyes, letting out a deep, pent-up sigh.

Damn him.

Damn him for sitting by me in class.

Damn him for showing up at my house.

Damn him for being involved with Asa.

Damn him for bringing me here.

Damn him for holding my hand.

Damn him for being so nice.

Damn him for being everything I wish Asa was, and everything I wish I could have.

I wash my hands no less than ten times, but I can still feel him. I can still feel his fingers laced with mine...the rough skin of his palm pressed against my hand...the way he pulled me behind him, guiding me through the restaurant...the tingle on my palm that won't go away, no matter how hard I scrub.

I squirt more soap into my hands and wash them for the eleventh time, then work up the nerve to finally exit the bathroom and take a seat back in the booth.

"I figured you'd want some caffeine," Carter says, pointing to the soda in front of me. He figured right.

Damn him.

I slide the drink closer to me and place the straw between my lips.

"Thanks."

He props his feet up on my side of the booth, blocking me in again. "You're welcome," he says, shooting me a smile that's on the verge of seductive, and even a little bit cocky. I catch myself staring at his lips for a beat too long, and his smile widens.

"Don't smile at me like that," I snap, annoyed that he's making this harder on both of us with his subtle flirtations. I force my back against the booth and kick my legs back up into the seat next to him.

The smile disappears from his face and he drops his gaze down to my arms. Anger returns to his eyes when he notices the fading bruises plastered on me like I've been branded.

That's how they make me feel, anyway.

I run my hands up my arms and cover them, suddenly feeling exposed.

"You don't want me to smile at you?" he asks, a confused expression strewn across his face.

"No," I say sharply. "I don't. I don't want you to smile at me like you like me. I don't want you to sit next to me in class. I don't want

47

you to hold my hand. I don't want you to flirt with me. I don't even want you to buy me lunch, but I'm too hungry to really care about that one right now." I bring my drink to my mouth to shut myself up.

He looks down at his glass and runs his hands up it, wiping off the condensation. He slowly inhales, staring down at his glass the entire time, then expels a long, deep breath.

"So, you want me to be mean to you, then?" He looks at me with an expression so cold, I don't even recognize him. "You want me to treat you like shit? The way Asa treats you?" He leans back in the booth, folding his arms over his broad chest. "Funny. I didn't peg you as a doormat."

I return his heated stare with just as much fury. "Funny. I didn't peg you for a dealer."

We hold each other's gazes, refusing to be the one who cracks first.

"I guess I do have that going for me," he says with a smug grin. "Dealer? Check. Asshole? Check. What else would it take, Sloan? What else do I need to do to get you to fuck me? You want me to slap you around a little bit? Seems to work wonders for Asa."

His cruel words are like a direct punch to my gut, knocking the breath out of me.

"Fuck you," I say through clenched teeth.

"No thanks. Apparently I'd have to hit you first, and that's not my style."

I bite my lip and hold my breath, fighting back tears. I've spent the last year and a half teaching myself how not to cry in front of assholes. I've got this.

"Take me back to my car," I say.

He closes his eyes and rubs his hands over his face. He groans out of frustration, then clasps his hands together behind his neck. "I'll take you after you eat something."

I scoot over in the booth until my thigh meets his feet. "I'm not hungry. Let me out."

He doesn't move his feet, so instead I pull my legs up and stand up in the booth, then jump over him. I head for the door, never having wanted to get away from someone so quickly in my entire life.

"Sloan," he calls after me. "Sloan!"

I swing the door open and walk outside—a rush of wind colliding with my face as I gasp for air. I bend over and put my hands on my knees, inhaling through my nose and out my mouth, over and over. When the threat of tears subsides, I straighten up and walk toward his car. The alarm beeps twice and the doors unlock. I turn around, but he isn't following me—he's still inside the restaurant.

Damn him. He just unlocked the car for me.

I slam the door as hard as I can after I climb inside. I wait for him to walk outside, but he doesn't. Several moments pass, and I realize he has no intention of following me. He's actually going to eat first. He's an even bigger jerk than I thought.

I grab the baseball cap off the console and put it on my head, pulling it down over my eyes to block the sun. If I have to wait for him to eat lunch before he takes me back to Asa's car, I might as well get a nap out of it.

TEN

Carter

"**C**an we get these to go?" I ask, handing our drinks to the waitress. "And the pizza?"

"I'll have it right out," she says. She walks away and I lean forward, dropping my head in my hands.

I have no idea what just got into me. I've never let a girl get to me like this. Much less a girl I'm not even dating.

But damn her! She's so frustrating. I don't understand how she can be so headstrong and confident when she's around me, but at her own home she acts like Asa's fucking doormat.

Then, out of the blue, she accosts me for being *nice* to her? What the *hell*? I realize some women are drawn to men like Asa. I've been in this career long enough to see that. But Sloan is different. She's smarter than that. Which is why it's so damn painful having to sit back and watch it, because I don't know what's keeping her there. Even if it's not my place, I can't be alone with her like this and not use it as an opportunity to convince her she's better than this. Although, I'm pretty sure calling her a doormat and saying the shit I said isn't how to convince her of that.

I'm a fucking idiot.

"Your order is at the counter," the waitress says, handing me the bill.

I grab it from her and pay it, then head outside with Sloan's food.

When I approach the car, I pause before opening the door. She's sitting in the passenger seat with her feet propped up on the dash. She's got my ball cap on, tugged down over her eyes. Her dark hair is swept over her right shoulder, spilling down over her arms that are folded across her chest.

Seeing her in her red dress the other night messed with my mind so bad, I didn't sleep all night. But seeing her here...asleep in my car...wearing my ball cap?

I don't think I'll ever be able to sleep again.

I open the door and she pulls her feet off the dash, but doesn't pull the ball cap from over her eyes. She shifts her body more toward the passenger door, a move that causes me to wince.

I hurt her. She's so damaged, and I hurt her even more.

"Here," I say, holding the to-go cup out to her. She lifts the brim of the cap and looks up at me. I'm surprised to see that her eyes aren't red. I assumed the hat was to cover up the fact that she was crying, but she hasn't shed a single tear.

She takes the drink from my hands, so I hold the pizza box out to her. She takes it, and I slide into the driver's seat. She immediately opens the lid to the pizza and grabs a slice, shoving it into her mouth. She turns the box so that the pizza is facing me, then lifts it to offer me a slice. I take one and start to smile at her, but remember she ordered me not to. Instead, I take a bite of the pizza and start the car.

We don't speak on the way back to campus. She's finishing up her third slice when we pull into the parking spot next to her car. She takes a big swig of her soda, then closes the lid to the pizza and places the box in the back seat.

"Take the pizza with you," I say, my words ripping a hole through the silence and tension built up between us.

She places her drink in the cup holder and pulls off my baseball cap, smoothing back her hair. "I can't," she says quietly. "He'll wonder where I got it."

She shifts her body toward me and reaches between us into the back seat to grab her backpack. She faces forward again and tucks her backpack underneath her arms.

"I would thank you for lunch," she says, "but it pretty much ruined my day." She opens the car door and rushes out before I can process her words. When her door slams behind her, I kill the engine and get out of the car.

"Sloan," I say, walking around my car until I reach her. She throws her backpack inside and shuts her back door. She opens the driver-side door and uses it as a barrier between us.

"Don't, Carter," she says, refusing to look up at me. "Don't apologize. You made your point, but I'm too pissed to listen to apologies right now. So just don't."

She can tell me not to apologize all she wants, but there's no way in hell I'm letting her get in that car before I say my peace.

"I'm sorry," I say anyway. "I shouldn't have said those things. You didn't deserve that, but dammit, Sloan! You're better than this. Give yourself some credit."

She refuses to look at me when I speak, so I run my hand under her chin and tilt her face up to mine. She darts her eyes to the right, still stubbornly refusing to make eye contact. I squeeze between her door and my car and make my way around until she's directly in front of me. I take her face in both hands, desperate for her to look at me. I need her to listen to what I have to say.

"Look at me," I plead, keeping a firm hold on her face. "I'm sorry. I was out of line."

She continues to keep her eyes locked on mine while a lone, thick tear trickles down her cheek. She wipes it away with the back of her hand before I have a chance to.

"You have no idea how many times I've heard that same, uniform apology."

My hands are still on her face and she's looking at my chest, avoiding my eyes. I try to lift her face to mine, but she refuses to budge.

"It's *not* the same, Sloan. You can't compare me to him."

She tilts her eyes up to the sky and laughs, trying to hold back more tears. "You're no better than he is. The only difference between the two of you is that nothing Asa has ever said to me has hurt as much as what you said today." She pulls my hands away from her face and climbs into her car. She reaches for the door handle and looks back up at me. "You're no different, Carter, so don't you *dare* judge me. Go save someone else." She pulls the door shut and I'm forced to take a step back. I watch as she completely breaks down inside the car. She doesn't look at me again, but I can see the tears spilling down her cheeks as she pulls away.

"I'm sorry," I say again as I watch her drive away.

ELEVEN

Asa

After everything I've done for her—after everything I'm *doing* for her—she better have one hell of a good excuse for putting me through this.

She'd be nothing if it weren't for me. I took her in when she had nowhere else to go. If it weren't for me, she would have had to crawl back to her crack-whore mother. Just based on the things she's told me about her childhood, she's way better off with me and she knows it. A mother who brings home a new sleazy husband every other month? I'd like to see her go back to that shit.

But if she's fucking around, that's the first place I'll drop her off. I'll be the first one to shove her right through her crack-whore mother's front door—back into a trailer full of rotating step-fathers who get off on hiding in her closet while she changes clothes.

"Do you want me to try something else?" Jess says, pulling my focus back into the moment. She's on her knees at the edge of the bed. "It's not getting hard."

I lift up on my elbows and look down at her. "If you knew how to fucking do it right," I say. I stand up and scoot her a few inches across the floor and brace my hands against the wall. I close my eyes and imagine she's Sloan kneeling in front of me instead. Except I imagine she's crying, begging me to keep her. Pleading for me to save her again, just like I had to do the last time she did something this stupid.

The thought of Sloan is all it takes. I grab Jess by the hair and shove my dick in her mouth. I keep one hand braced against the wall and the other hand tangled in her hair while she does her job.

Who in their right mind would take Sloan to a restaurant, knowing she belongs to me? To Asa Jackson? Whoever he is, if he knew the things I could do to him—he never would have done it. No one has that kind of death wish.

"Fuck," I say, irritated at the way the rubber gets in the way of feeling her tongue. I pull out of her mouth and rip the condom off.

"Oh, God," I groan when her tongue greets me skin to skin. "That's more like it."

I pump into her mouth a few times while she twists her hand around my dick. She's good, but I know she can do better.

"Take it all," I say, moving her hand away. I wrap my hands in the back of her hair and press myself into her mouth until I can feel the back of her throat. The gagging sound she makes every time I push a little farther into her makes me explode within seconds. I grip the back of her head with both hands while she struggles to pull away, but I hold her head firmly in place until I'm finished. She's clawing at my thighs, trying to pull away so she can breathe. I finally release her head and watch as she falls to her hands on the floor, coughing and gasping for breath.

I pull my pants up and button them. "Tell Jon thanks for sharing," I say to her. "Your boyfriend is a hell of a lot more generous than I am."

She wipes her mouth and stands up.

"Fucking bastard," she says. She slams the door on her way out.

"Fucking whore," I mutter.

When I go downstairs, Jon is seated at the bar with Dalton and Carter. I grab a beer out of the fridge and take a seat with them.

"You didn't tell me she could deep throat," I say to Jon, twisting the top off the beer. "Lucky bastard."

Jon glares at me, leaning back in his chair. "I didn't know she could."

I laugh. "Well, I don't think she knew she could either until about five minutes ago."

Jon sighs and shakes his head. "God dammit, Asa. I told you to go easy on her."

I laugh and take a sip, then set the beer back on the table. "The only girl I go easy on is Sloan."

Carter lifts his beer to his lips, eyeing me while he tilts his head back and gulps. This kid has a major staring problem.

"Speaking of Sloan," Jon says, pulling my attention back to his. "When will you return the favor?" He laughs and takes a swig of beer.

The jackass is laughing? He thinks he made a fucking joke? I pull my leg back and kick his chair as hard as I can, sending him and his beer backwards onto the ceramic tile. I stand up and look down at him, my hands clenched in fists.

"*Sloan's* not a fucking *whore!*" I yell.

Jon pulls himself up off the floor, then proceeds to bow up to me like the idiot that he is. "She's not? Guess you found out why she was on Ricker today. She wasn't off fucking some guy like you thought?"

I lunge forward and punch him in his goddamned filthy mouth. He falls to the floor and I kick him in the ribs. I drop to my knees and try to punch him again, but Dalton and Carter are pulling me off of him before I have the chance. He scoots away from me and wipes at his bloody mouth. He looks down at his hand and back up at me.

"Fucking bastard," he says.

"Funny. That's the same thing your girlfriend called me when I pulled my dick out of her throat."

Jon scrambles to his feet and lunges forward again, so I step into his swing, allowing him to square me in the jaw. Carter steps between us, pushing him back against the fridge while Dalton tightens his grip on my arms.

"Go upstairs!" Carter says to him. "Go check on Jess and calm the fuck down."

Jon nods and Carter releases him. Dalton doesn't let go of me until Jon clears the stairs.

I push my hand against my jaw and pop my neck. "I'll be out back. Let me know as soon as Sloan gets here."

TWELVE

Carter

Asa walks out the back door and I grip the back of my neck and squeeze.

"Shit!"

"I know," Dalton says, not having any clue as to what's actually going through my mind at the moment.

"I need to make a phone call," I tell him. "Wait in here and make sure they don't get into it again." I walk out the front door and head straight to my car. I pull my phone from my pocket and scroll through the numbers, checking for Sloan's. Dalton said he entered everyone's number who lives here into my phone once I was assigned this job. I scroll through the S's but don't see her name. Just as I'm about to throw my phone out of frustration, the contact *Asa's girl* catches my eye. I press it. I press it over and over, willing it to dial faster.

I hold the phone to my ear and listen as it rings. On the fourth ring, she finally picks up.

"Hello?"

"Sloan!" I say her name desperately.

"Who is this?"

"It's Lu...Carter. It's Carter."

She sighs heavily into the phone.

"No, don't hang up," I say, hoping she holds on long enough to hear I'm not just calling her to apologize again. "He knows. He knows you went to lunch today on Ricker Road."

She doesn't say anything for several quiet seconds.

"You told him?" she asks, her voice full of hurt.

"No. No, I would never...I heard Jon say something about finding out who you were with at lunch. He doesn't know it was me."

I glance behind me, making sure I'm still in the clear. Dalton is standing at the window watching me.

"But...how could he know?" she asks, fear in her voice.

"Maybe he tracks your phone," I say. "Where are you?"

"I just left the gym. I'm five minutes away. Carter, what do I do? He'll kill me."

The fear in her voice makes me regret every second of today. I should have never put her in this situation.

"Listen to me. The box of pizza is still in my back seat. I'll keep him occupied out back. When you get here, grab the pizza and bring it to the backyard. Act like you have nothing to hide. Tell him you were hungry so you went out to a restaurant for lunch and bought a pizza and then offer us some. If you bring it up first, you should be fine."

"Okay," she says, breathing heavily. "Okay."

"Okay," I say back.

Several silent seconds pass and my pulse slowly begins to regulate.

"Sloan?"

"Yeah?" she whispers.

"I won't let him hurt you."

She's quiet for a moment. I hear her sigh, then the call is dropped. I look down at my phone and take a deep breath, then head inside.

"Who was that?" Dalton asks, eyeing me curiously when I walk back through the door. "Hottie from Spanish?"

I nod. "Yep. I'm going out back. You want to help me calm Asa down?"

Dalton falls into step behind me. "Looks like *you're* the one who needs calming down," he says.

I swing open the door and Asa is seated on a lounge chair by the pool, drumming his fingers on his knees. I take a seat next to him and kick my feet back, attempting to appear as relaxed as my nerves will allow me. I don't care if he finds out it was me who was with her at lunch. I don't care if he follows through with his threat. All I care about is that he doesn't lay another finger on Sloan.

Dalton and I keep Asa occupied with talk about an upcoming deal he wants to make. A while later, we hear Sloan pull into the driveway. I can see Asa tense up and he clamps his mouth shut mid-sentence. He starts to pull himself up, I assume to go meet her in the front yard. I do whatever it takes to distract him.

"So, this Jess chick?" I say.

He turns toward me. "What about her?"

"Just curious. Can she really deep throat?" Even just having to pretend I'm interested makes me feel like an asshole.

Asa smiles and opens his mouth to respond when the back door swings open. Sloan walks outside with a pizza box in her hand. I can feel the anger seeping off of Asa as his hands ball into fists.

"Hey, guys," she says, sauntering toward us. "Anyone hungry? I have leftovers." She holds out the pizza box and keeps the smile plastered on her face.

Dalton jumps up and meets her, grabbing the box out of her hands. "Hell yeah," he says, taking a slice. He hands the box to me, so I grab one, too. I hand the box to Asa just as Sloan takes a seat on the lawn chair with him. She leans in to kiss him, but he pulls back.

"Where'd you get this?" he asks, closing the lid to read the top of it. She shrugs, careful not to look at me at all. "Some Italian place. One of my classes was cancelled today and I was hungry, so I grabbed lunch."

"Alone?" he asks, setting the box on the concrete next to him.

She smiles. "Yeah. I'm so tired of campus food." She reaches down to the box and grabs a slice. "Taste it," she says, handing it to him. "It's really good. I brought it home so you could try it."

Asa grabs the slice of pizza out of her hands and drops it back onto the box. He leans forward and grabs Sloan by the hand, pulling her to him.

"Come here," he says, pulling her onto his lap and grabbing the back of her head to kiss her.

I look away. I have to.

Asa stands up with Sloan still wrapped around him. I can see him out of the corner of my eye as he hoists her up by the ass, kissing her neck. He walks toward the house and I look up, just as she glances at me from over his shoulder. She watches me wide-eyed until he carries her through the back door and into the house; more than likely all the way up to his bed.

I lean back in my chair and let out a huge-ass sigh, running my hands through my hair. How am I expected to just sit here, knowing what's going on in that house?

"I wish we could bust his ass today," I say to Dalton.

"I don't like the way she looks at you," Dalton says with a mouthful of pizza. I glance over at him and he's still staring at the back door. "She's trouble."

I pick up the box of pizza and grab another slice. "Jealous?" I laugh, trying to appear nonchalant about his comment. "You can always have Jess. I hear Jon's a lot more generous than Asa."

Dalton laughs and shakes his head. "These people are so fucked up."

Not all of them.

"I think we could use her," Dalton adds. I look over at him and can see his wheels turning.

"Use her how?"

"She's into you," he says, sitting straight up in his seat. "You have to use that to your advantage. Get close to her. She probably knows more about the people Asa works with than we'll ever be able to find out from our positions."

Shit. The last thing I want to do is get her involved. "I don't think that's a good idea."

Dalton stands up and says, "Bullshit. This is perfect. That girl is the break we've been waiting for in this case." He starts dialing a number on his phone, walking toward the back door.

Using women to get closer to cracking a case is nothing to him. He's done it in almost every job we've worked together.

It's just not something I'm willing to do.

But it may not be a choice that's left up to me...

THIRTEEN

Sloan

"**Y**our heart is beating so fast," Asa says, dropping me onto the mattress.

Of course it is. This was probably the scariest five minutes of my life, not knowing if I could pull off the lie. Thanks to Carter, it worked.

"You kissed me the entire way through the house," I say. "Of course it's beating fast."

Asa slides on top of me and presses his lips to mine, kissing me gently. He runs his hand through my hair, kissing down my chin and neck, until he gets to the base of my throat. He pauses and looks me straight in the eye.

"Do you love me, Sloan?" he says, his question coming straight out of left field.

I swallow and then nod.

He pushes up onto the palms of his hands. "Well then, say it."

I force a smile as I look up at him. "I love you, Asa."

He stares at me a moment as if he has an internal lie detector and he's waiting to see if I passed. He slowly lowers himself on top of me and buries his head in my neck. "I love you, too," he says. He rolls onto his side and pulls me to him. He holds me, rubbing his hand in soft circles over my back. I don't remember the last time he touched me in this bed without it being directly related to sex. He kisses the side of my head and sighs.

"Don't leave me, Sloan," he says firmly. "Don't you ever fucking leave me."

The fierce yet desperate look in his eyes paralyzes me. I shake my head. "I won't, Asa."

His eyes scroll over every inch of my face. Lying here wrapped in his arms, watching him watch me with such intensity—I don't know if I should feel loved or terrified. It's a little of both.

He presses his mouth to mine and kisses me hard. He shoves his tongue deep into my throat like he's trying to claim every inch of me from the inside out. There's nothing tender about it, and when he tears his mouth from mine, he's gasping for breath. He lifts up onto his knees and pulls his shirt over his head. "Tell me again," he says, reaching to me and pulling both my shirt and bra over my head. "Tell me you love me, Sloan. That you'll never leave me."

"I love you. I'll never leave you," I whisper, praying the latter will soon be a lie.

He brings his mouth back to mine and runs his hands down my stomach until he reaches my pants. He's kissing me with such intensity, it's hard to catch my breath. He tries to pull my pants down, but he can't seem to break away from my mouth long enough to do it. I lift my hips and remove my clothes, just like the whore I've become for him.

Because is this not the definition of a whore? Someone who compromises his or her self-respect for personal gain? Even if my personal gain is something selfless and has nothing to do with me and everything to do with my brother, it doesn't change the fact that I'm having sex with him in exchange for something. Which... by definition...makes me a whore.

His whore.

And from the possessive look in his eyes, that's all he'll ever allow me to be.

FOURTEEN

Carter

There are few things worse than my sense of timing. As soon as I open the back door to walk inside the house, my ears are met with the final sound of Asa's grunts coming from upstairs. I pause in the kitchen, not even sure why I'm listening to what he's doing to her. Just the thought of it makes my stomach turn, especially after knowing what he just did to Jess a matter of two hours ago.

When I hear footsteps upstairs and the bathroom door shut, I snap out of my trance and walk to the refrigerator. There's a magnetic dry-erase board, covered in phone numbers, stuck to the front of the fridge. I grab one of the markers and press it to the board and write. Footsteps descend the stairs and I snap the marker back into place, then turn around just in time to see Asa round the corner.

"Hey," he says. He's barefoot and the only thing he's wearing is his unbuttoned blue jeans. His hair is in disarray and he has a smug grin on his face.

"What's up?" I lean against the counter and watch him as he walks to the cabinet and grabs a bag of potato chips. He opens it and leans against the counter across from me.

"How'd it go last night?" he asks. "I haven't even had a chance to ask you."

"Good," I say. "But I was curious. What if we could get to his supplier directly? There really isn't a need for a middleman anymore, if the only reason you were going through him was for translation."

Asa pops another chip into his mouth and licks his fingers. "Why do you think I brought you in?" He sets the bag of chips down and turns to the sink, running his hands under the water. "My hands fucking taste like pussy," he says, scrubbing them with soap.

This is one of the few moments in my career when I wish I had chosen something a little lamer. Something a little less emotionally draining. I should have been a poetry teacher.

"How long have you been dating that girl?" I ask. Part of what I'm here for is to pry, but the only questions I seem to want to know the answers to are questions related to Sloan.

He dries his hands on a towel and grabs the bag of chips, then takes a seat at the bar. I stay where I am.

"A while. Two years maybe?" He shoves a handful of chips into his mouth and wipes his palm down the leg of his jeans.

"Doesn't seem like she approves of what you do," I say, treading lightly. "You think she'd ever out you?"

"Hell no," he quickly replies. "I'm all she has. She's got no choice but to accept it."

I nod and grip the edge of the counter behind me. I don't trust a word that comes out of his mouth, so I'm really hoping the fact that he's all she has is just another one of his lies.

"Just making sure," I say. "It's hard for me to trust people, if you know what I mean."

Asa narrows his eyes and leans forward. "Don't ever trust *anyone*, Carter. *Especially* the whores."

"I thought you said Sloan wasn't a whore," I challenge.

He keeps his eyes locked with mine—unmoving and angry. For a moment, I'm worried he might do to me what he did to Jon earlier. Instead, he brings his hand to his jaw and pops his neck, then leans back in his seat again. The flash of anger in his eyes dissipates with the sound of Sloan's footsteps descending the stairs. She walks into the kitchen and comes to a pause when she sees both of us.

Asa takes his eyes off me and looks at Sloan. He laughs and stands up, scooping her against him. "People have to earn my trust," he says, looking over her shoulder at me. "Sloan earned hers."

She puts her hands against his chest and pushes against him, but he doesn't release her. He sits back down and pulls her against him so that she's standing between his legs with her back to his chest, facing me. He wraps his arms around her stomach and rests his chin on her shoulder, making eye contact with me again.

"I like you, Carter," Asa says. "You're all business."

I force a half-smile, gripping the counter with all my strength as I try not to look in her eyes. I can't handle the fear I see in them every time he has his hands on her.

"Speaking of business," I say, "I'll be back in a couple of hours. I've got a few things I need to do." I straighten up and walk past Sloan and Asa toward the front door. When I do, she looks up at me with appreciation in her eyes.

Asa bends down and kisses her neck, then lifts a hand to her breast. She squeezes her eyes shut and grimaces, then turns away from me.

I keep walking and head for the front door, feeling completely helpless. I have to remind myself that I'm here for one reason and one reason only—and she isn't it.

I text Dalton before I pull out of the driveway and tell him I'm going to the station to do a few write-ups. Instead, I just start driving, not having a clue as to where I'm going. I turn on the radio and try to rid the murderous thoughts I'm having of Asa, but all my other thoughts are of Sloan...and every thought I have of Sloan leads back to murderous thoughts of Asa.

I realize I have a duty. My duty is to complete the job I'm being paid to do...which is to bust the largest campus drug ring in collegiate history. The drug problem at the local university has multiplied tenfold in the past three years alone. Rumor has it that Asa is the sole reason for that. Asa and all the people in his circle, which is why Dalton and I are here—to identify the key players. Dalton and I are only a small part of this sting, but it's the small parts that make up a huge whole, and every one of our roles is vital.

Asa is ruining countless lives and Sloan's is just one of them. I can either focus on what I'm here to do and help take down everyone involved in his entire operation, which will in turn save lives...or I can save one girl from her abusive boyfriend.

Having to separate what I'm here to do and what I *want* to do makes this situation feel like General Patton's theory, how sometimes it's necessary to sacrifice the lives of the few for the good of the many.

It feels like I'm sacrificing Sloan's life for the sake of all the others that Asa is ruining. And the thought of that kills me.

I find myself second-guessing whether or not I'm cut out for this profession for at least the third time in the last week.

After an hour of driving around, I decide to head back to Asa's. Dalton stays there most of the time, but he told Asa I live on campus during a conversation they had a couple of months ago. Therefore, I had to actually get an apartment on campus in case Asa ever decides to run a check on me. I'm at Asa's more often than not, though, because that's where I'll ultimately get most of the info. Well...from being around his "crew" and...possibly Sloan.

I know Dalton is right. I know I need to utilize Sloan for the advantage of the investigation, but that would mean she would have to remain in the situation she's in. I'd much rather sneak her some cash and force her to run as far away from Asa as she can get.

When I close in on Asa's street, I notice Sloan sitting at a park bench two blocks from their house. She's seated alone with books laid out in front of her on a picnic table. I slow down the car and pull over to the side of the road. I scope out the area, ensuring she's alone.

I sit in my car and watch her awhile, contemplating what I should do. If I were smarter, I would keep driving and refocus my attention where it needs to be. If I were smarter, I wouldn't be shutting my car door, preparing myself to cross the street.

If I were smarter...

FIFTEEN

Sloan

've never seen Asa study a day in his life. I study every day, regardless of how crazy things get around me. Like right now, having to leave the house and walk to the park just for peace and quiet.

How in the hell does he have a 3.5 average GPA? I wouldn't put it past him if he were paying off his professors.

"Hey."

I grip my keys, complete with pepper spray, and slowly turn around. Carter is walking up behind me with his hands tucked inside the pockets of his jeans. His dark hair is unkempt and hangs down his forehead, swooping into his eyes.

He pauses a few feet from me, waiting for me to give him permission to approach. He isn't smiling at me this time. *At least he minds well.*

"Hey," I say flatly. I drop my keys back on the table. "Did Asa send you to summon me?"

He walks to the picnic table and swings his leg over the bench and straddles it. He's facing me with his hands still in his pockets.

I stare down at my textbooks and refuse to look at him. The mild crush I developed on him in class turned into what could have been a very serious shit storm after having lunch with him. I need to keep my distance, and looking at him makes me *not* want to keep my distance.

"I was just driving by. Saw you sitting here, thought I'd check on you."

"I'm fine," I say, returning my attention to the homework in front of me. I feel like maybe I should thank him for the heads up today. If he hadn't called, there's no telling how that situation would have turned out. But then again, he could have just been warning me to save his own ass.

But I know he wasn't. I could hear the concern in his voice before I hung up the phone. He was scared for me. He was scared for me, just like I was scared for him.

"Are you?" he asks skeptically. "Are you really fine?"

I glance up at him. He can't just leave things alone, can he?

I drop my pencil on the table and turn to face him. He's always pushing for more truth. Always wanting to know what the hell I'm thinking. If this is what he wants, we might as well get it over with. I take a deep breath and prepare to answer all the questions he's ever asked, and even ones he hasn't gotten around to asking yet.

"Yes, I'm fine. I'm not great. I'm not terrible. I'm just *fine*. I'm fine because I have a roof over my head and a boyfriend who loves me, despite the fact that he makes bad choices. Do I wish he were a better person? Yes. If I had the means, would I leave him? Yes. Absolutely. Do I wish there wasn't so much constantly going on at my house that I could actually find a quiet place to do homework, or heaven forbid, get some sleep? Hell yes. Do I wish I could graduate sooner and get out of this mess? Yes. Am I embarrassed by the way Asa treats me? Yes. Do I wish you weren't a part of this? Yes. Do I wish you could be the guy I thought you were the first time I met you in class? Yes. Do I wish you could save me?"

I let out a short, defeated sigh and look down at my hands. "So much, Carter," I whisper. "I wish you could save me from all this shit so, so much. But you can't. I'm not in this life for myself. If I were, I would have left a long time ago."

How could he save me from this life? He's a *part* of this life. If I ran from Asa and into Carter's arms, it would be the exact same lifestyle...just a different pair of arms. And Carter has no idea that the only reason I'm still in this situation isn't even about me or what I used to feel for Asa.

I shake my head at this entire unfortunate situation we're in and try to blink back tears. "I left him once," I say to Carter. "In the beginning, when I found out how he was making his money. I didn't have anywhere to go, but I left him because I knew I deserved better." I pause, searching for the right words. When I look up at Carter the first thing I notice is the genuine concern in his eyes. It's a strange feeling to trust someone you barely know more than the person you share your own bed with.

"I had two younger brothers growing up. They were born when I was only two. Twins. My mother was an addict, so they were both born with complications. Drew died when he was ten. The other—Stephen—needs a lot of care. Care I can't provide on my own if I want to build a good life for us. When he turned sixteen, he was finally approved for a group facility where he'd be able to live and have twenty-four-hour care. And I could go to college and make a better life for us. Things were great until a few weeks after I decided to break up with Asa. Stephen's funding was pulled by the state and I had no place for us to live—no place to care for him. My only other option was paying the fee out of pocket, which is thousands of dollars a month. I couldn't afford it, but the last thing I wanted was for him to be forced to move back in with my mother. It's not safe for him there. When I realized the situation I had put us both in, I didn't know where else to turn. And when Asa showed up, begging to take me back with promises of paying for Stephen's care, I couldn't say no. I moved back in with him. Now I'm forced to pretend that he's enough for me. I pretend to turn a blind eye to the awful things he does. And in turn, he sends a check every month to pay for Stephen's expenses. And that's why I'm still there, Carter. Because I have no other choice."

Carter stares at me, completely silent. For a moment I almost regret being so open with him. I've never told anyone that. As much as Asa doesn't deserve me, I'm still ashamed that I'm only with him because he helps me. It's embarrassing to admit the truth to someone.

Lunch with him today seems like it was a world away from right now. So much has happened between this morning and this moment. He looks different now. Not the playful Carter he was in class this morning. Not the apologetic Carter he was after our lunch today.

Right now he just looks...I don't know...like a different person altogether. Almost as if he's been pretending to be someone he's not and this is the first time he's looking at me with truth behind his eyes.

He glances away for a second and I see the slow roll of his throat as he swallows and then speaks. "I respect what you're doing for your brother, Sloan," he says. "But what good are you going to be to him if you end up dead? That house isn't safe for you. Asa isn't safe for you."

I sigh and wipe away a rogue tear. "I do what I'm able to do, Carter. I can't afford to worry about the *what ifs*."

His eyes follow the tear down my cheek and then he lifts a hand to my face and wipes it away.

Of all the tears I've cried to Asa, he's never once attempted to wipe them away.

"Come here," Carter says, taking hold of my hand. He pulls me toward him as he scoots closer to me. I look down at his hand, holding on to mine, and I attempt to pull it back. He squeezes it and grabs my elbow with his other hand. "Come here," he whispers soothingly, pulling me closer. He wraps his arms around me and guides my head to his shoulder. He squeezes me tightly, cradling my head with one of his hands. He presses his warm cheek against the top of my head and he holds me.

That's all he does.

He doesn't make excuses. He doesn't lie and tell me everything will be okay, because we both know it won't. He doesn't make promises he won't be able to keep like Asa does. He just holds me out of nothing more than a simple desire to bring me comfort—and it's the first time I've ever felt this.

I scoot closer and relax against him, listening to the sound of his heart beating rapidly inside his chest. I close my eyes and try to imagine a time in my crazy, fucked up life that I've ever felt cared about, but I come up empty. I've been living on this earth for twenty years, and this is the first time I feel like someone actually gives a shit.

I clench his shirt in my fists and try again to scoot even closer to him, wanting to curl up inside of him and relish in this feeling forever. He lifts his cheek and lightly presses his lips against the top of my head.

We remain clasped together, holding on to each other as if the fate of the world depends on this embrace.

The thin layer of his shirt is damp from the tears that are pouring down my cheeks. I don't even know why I'm crying. Maybe it's because, until this moment, I had no idea what it felt like to be valued. What it felt like to be respected. Until this moment, I had no idea what it felt like to be cared for.

No one should have to experience a life never feeling truly cared for—not even by the parents who created them. Yet I've lived that for twenty years now.

Until this moment.

SIXTEEN

Carter

I close my eyes and continue to hold her while she quietly cries against my chest. I hold her until dusk turns into dark and what was left of the light is engulfed by a blanket of stars.

I hold her until I hear a car about to turn on the street. I glance up, but they turn and go in the opposite direction. She remains pressed against my shirt, but the thought of Asa or even Dalton seeing me with her right now is at the forefront of my mind.

I shouldn't be here comforting her. It can only cause more problems for her.

Because she's right. I can't save her. As much as I want to, we're both stuck. I can't risk ruining something that is so much bigger than just the two of us. I can't sacrifice what it is I'm here to do for the sake of helping her leave. That's something she'll have to do on her own and when she's financially able.

And every moment I hold her, every time I grab her hand, every time I sit next to her in class, every time I put her in more and more of these harmless situations—I'm pushing her closer and closer to the edge of a cliff. If I don't figure out how to back away from her...I'll end up watching her fall.

I release my hold from around her and pull back, but she remains clutched to my shirt. I grab her hands and pull them away from me. She lifts her head and looks up at me, her eyes as red and swollen as I suddenly wish her lips were.

Stop thinking like this, Luke.

I stand up and she grabs at my shirt to pull me back, confusion rampant in her eyes.

"Let go," I whisper.

Her hands fall to her lap and she breaks our stare. She pulls her feet up onto the bench and hugs her knees, crying into her arms. Walking away from her is about to take all the strength I have.

"You're right, Sloan," I say as I back away from her. "I can't save you."

I turn around and begin walking back to my car, each step harder than the last. I don't turn around when I open the door. I climb inside the car and drive to her house without once looking back.

———

When I walk through the front door, I can tell by the state of the living room and the noise from the backyard that this is going to be a long night.

I make my way through the house and to the backyard. There are several people scattered around. No one even looks up when I walk outside. There are four girls in the pool putting on a spectacle. Two of them have the other two perched up on their shoulders and they're trying to knock each other off into the water. Jon and Dalton are standing beside the pool, beers in hand, cheering for whomever they've bet on.

Asa is sitting at the side of the pool with his feet dangling in the water. He isn't staring at the girls. He's staring straight at me—eyes hard and suspicious. I nod in his direction, acting oblivious to the look in his eye.

Dalton sees me and says, "Carter!" He rushes around the pool, unsteady on his feet. He's laughing the whole time, spilling half his beer. When he reaches me, he wraps his arm around me and leans in.

"Don't worry, I'm not as fucked up as I look," he says. "Did you get anything out of Sloan?"

I pull back and eye him. "How did you know I was with Sloan?"

He chuckles. "I didn't. But good job," he says, squeezing my shoulder. "You work fast. I think she knows more than we think she does."

I shake my head. "I don't think she knows shit," I tell him. "Focusing on her will be a waste of our time."

I glance over Dalton's shoulder and see Asa staring at us. He pulls his feet out of the water and stands up.

"He's coming over here," I say.

Dalton raises an eyebrow and then backs away, raising his beer in the air. He grins and spins around. "A hundred bucks says I can stay under water longer than any of you fucks!"

Jon immediately takes him up on the bet. They throw their beers aside and dive into the pool.

Asa walks toward me and then straight past me as he makes his way into the house, never once making eye contact with me.

I don't know what unnerves me more. The fact that I'm suspicious of every move he makes or the fact that he seems suspicious of *me*.

SEVENTEEN

Sloan

It took me half an hour after Carter walked away to finally regain my composure enough to pack my things and walk back home. It's been ten minutes since I reached the edge of my dark driveway. I've been staring at the pavement, following the winding path with my eyes. It would be so easy to keep walking. There's nothing in that house I want. Nothing I even need. I could keep walking along the pavement until I'm too far to turn back.

I wish it were as easy as it sounds, but once again...it's not just about me. And no one *but* me is going to be able to change any of this.

Carter can't save me. Asa sure as hell isn't going to save me. I just need to continue saving my money until I have enough to make it on my own and bring my brother with me.

I take a step onto the grass, toward the house, but I hesitate. It's the last place I want to be right now. I want to be back at the park, back on the bench, back in Carter's arms. I want that feeling again, but I'm ashamed to admit I want more than that, too. I want to know what it feels like to be kissed by someone who respects me.

Just having that thought makes me feel incredibly guilty. To my knowledge, Asa is faithful to me. He provides for me. He takes care of my brother financially...a responsibility that isn't even his. He does this because he loves me and he knows I want to see my brother happy. I can't discredit that. It's more than anyone has ever done for me in my entire life.

I throw my backpack of completed homework in Asa's car and walk through the front door. I just keep walking until I get to the kitchen. I'll do like I do every night and take something to eat and drink up to my room. I'll stay there alone and try to sleep amidst the sound of music and laughter and sometimes the occasional muffled screams. I'll fall asleep and hope that Asa gives me at least four good hours before he wakes me up again.

I set the timer on the microwave and fill my cup with ice. I shut the freezer and go to open the refrigerator door when the familiar handwriting on the dry-erase board catches my eye. My breath hitches when I read it.

Worries flow from her lips like the random words that flow from her fingertips. I reach out and try to catch them, clenching them in my fists, wanting nothing more than to catch them all.

I look at his words, written clearly out in the open for anyone to see, but I know they're meant only for me. It's obvious he played the game wrong. He actually *thought* about what he was going to say before he wrote it this time. *Cheater.*

I erase the words, but not before imprinting them on my mind. I pick up the marker and press it to the dry-erase board.

EIGHTEEN

My hands are wet from sweat. The air conditioner is broken again and it's too hot to go outside. I run my sweaty palm along the leather arm of the couch, leaving a streak of sweat behind the path of my hand.

I wonder where sweat comes from?

I wonder where leather comes from?

My mother told me it's made from cows, but I know she's a liar, so I don't believe her. How could leather be made out of cows? I've touched a cow before and they're sort of fuzzy. They don't look like leather to me. Leather looks more like it's made from dinosaurs than cows.

I bet leather really is made out of dinosaurs. I don't know why my mother always lies to me. She lies to Daddy, too. I know she lies to him, because she gets in trouble for it a lot.

Daddy always tells me not to trust whores. I don't know what a whore is, but I know it's something my Daddy hates.

Sometimes when he gets mad at my mom, he calls her a whore. Maybe a whore is another word for liar and that's why he hates them so much.

I wish my mother wasn't a whore. I wish she would stop lying, so she wouldn't get in trouble so much. I don't like watching her get in trouble.

Daddy says it's good for me, though. He says if I want to grow up and be a man, I need to see what a woman looks like when she cries. Daddy says a woman's tears make men weak, and the more I see their tears when I'm younger, the less I'll believe their lies when I'm older. Sometimes when he punishes my mother for being a whore, he makes me watch her cry so that I'll grow up knowing that all the whores cry and it shouldn't bother me.

"Don't trust anyone, Asa," he always tells me. "Especially the whores."

I grasp the leather strap tethered around my arm and pull it tighter, then slap at my skin. I realize now that leather isn't made from dinosaurs.

My mother wasn't lying about *that*, at least.

I don't remember a lot about the fight in their bedroom that night. The yelling had become a daily occurrence, so it wasn't new to me. What was so different about that night was the silence. The house had never been so quiet. I remember lying in bed, listening to myself breathe because it was the only noise in the entire house. I hated the quiet. I *hate* the quiet.

No one found out what he did to her for a few days. They found her body wrapped in a bloody sheet, shoved under the house and half-covered in dirt. I know this, because I snuck outside and watched them pull her out from under the house.

After the cops arrested my father, I was shipped to my aunt's house where I lived until I ran away at fourteen.

I know he's in prison somewhere, but I've never looked for him. I haven't seen or heard from him since that night.

I guess you shouldn't trust the *men* who marry the whores, either.

I press the tip of the needle into my arm and apply a little pressure. Once it pierces my skin, I draw the process out as long as possible. The initial insertion and sting is the best part for me.

I push my thumb down, feeling the warm burn move from the point of insertion, down to my wrist and straight up through to my shoulder.

I slide the needle out and drop it to the floor, then untie the strap of leather, letting it fall as well. I curl my arm up to my chest and hold it with my other hand while I lean my head back against the wall. I close my eyes and smile to myself, relieved I didn't end up with a whore like my mother.

Thinking Sloan was with another guy today made it crystal clear why my father hated whores. I don't think I truly understood him until that moment—when I felt the hatred for Sloan that he felt for my mother.

I'm so relieved Sloan isn't a whore.

I let my arm fall limp to the mattress.

Fuck, this feels so good.

I hear Sloan's footsteps ascending the stairs.

She'll be pissed that I'm doing this in our bedroom. She thinks I simply sell the shit—that I don't actually sample it.

After what she put me through today already, she better not say a damn word about this when she walks into this bedroom.

Fuck...so good.

NINETEEN

Carter

She returned home about ten minutes ago. I saw the lights turn on in the kitchen.

I'm sitting by the pool with Jon, Dalton, and some guy named Kevin. They're engrossed in a live poker tournament, watching it on a laptop that Kevin has propped up on the table. Apparently they've somehow got stake in it.

I'm aware that Dalton is mentally taking notes, following the conversations like it's a ping pong match. I let him. My mind is too exhausted from this day to keep up, and I can't stop worrying about where Asa disappeared to, and what Sloan is doing right now.

My gaze is fixated on the house. I watch the windows as she moves around the kitchen, making herself something to eat. Once it looks like she disappears upstairs, I use the opportunity to take a breather. I need to regroup—place my focus back on the conversation around me. I just need a few minutes alone in order to do that. Some people recharge by having the energy of other people around them.

I am not one of those people.

I read once that the difference between an extrovert and an introvert isn't how you act in a group setting. It's whether or not those group settings give you fuel or drain you. An introvert can outwardly appear to others to be an extrovert, and vice versa. But it all comes down to how those interactions influence you internally.

I am definitely an introvert, because people drain me. And now I need silence to refuel.

"You want a beer?" I ask Dalton. He shakes his head, so I stand up and head inside to the kitchen. I don't even want a beer. I just want silence. How Sloan lives with this on a day-to-day basis and still functions is unbelievable.

I walk through the back door and the first thing I notice when I get to the kitchen is the new sentence scripted across the dry-erase board. I take a step closer and read it.

He unclenched his fists and dropped her worries, unable to catch them for her. But she picked them back up and dusted them off. She wants to be able to hold them herself now.

I read it over and over, until the bedroom door upstairs slams and breaks me out of my trance. I take a step away from the fridge, just as Sloan rounds the corner into the kitchen. She stops suddenly when she sees me. She pulls her hands quickly up to her face and wipes at the tears. I see her glance at her words on the refrigerator, then back at me.

We both stand silently, just two feet apart, staring at each other. Her eyes are wide and I watch as her chest heaves up and down with each breath she takes.

Three seconds.

Five seconds.

Ten seconds.

I lose count of how much time passes while we both just watch each other, neither of us knowing what to do about the invisible rope between us, tugging and pulling us together with strength so much stronger than our willpower.

She sniffles and then rests her hands on her hips as her eyes fall to the floor.

"I hate him, Carter," she whispers.

I can tell by the hurt in her voice that something happened when she went upstairs. I look up at the ceiling toward their bedroom, wondering what it could have been. When I look back at her, she's staring at me.

"He's passed out," she says. "He's using again."

I shouldn't feel relieved that he's passed out, but I am. "Again?"

She takes a couple of steps toward me and then rests her back against the countertop, folding her arms together. She wipes at another tear. "He gets..." She inhales a breath and I can tell it's hard for her to talk about. I walk over to her and stand next to her.

"He gets paranoid," she says. "He starts to think he's about to get caught and the pressure gets to be too much for him. He thinks I don't notice these things, but I do. And then he starts using and when that happens, things...things turn bad for all of us."

I'm warring with myself right now. Part of me wants to comfort her—part of me wants to selfishly push her for more information. "All of us?"

She nods. "Me. Jon. The guys who work for him." She nudges her head in my direction. "*You.*"

She says that last word with a dose of bitterness. Her top teeth press into her bottom lip and she looks in the other direction. I continue to stare at her. Her hands are twisting into the sleeves of her shirt as she hugs herself tighter and tighter.

She isn't crying anymore. She's angry now and I'm not sure if she's angry at me or Asa.

I look back at the words on the board.

He unclenched his fists and dropped her worries, unable to catch them for her. But she picked them back up and dusted them off. She wants to be able to hold them herself now.

Rereading those words and watching her right now gives me clarity. All this time I've been worried for her. Concerned that she was being brainwashed and had no idea what kind of person Asa is.

"I was wrong about you," I tell her.

She looks at me again; this time her lips are pressed together, her eyebrows drawn together in curiosity.

"I thought you needed protection," I clarify. "I thought maybe you were naïve when it came to Asa. But you aren't. You know him better than anyone. I thought he was using you...but you're the one using *him*."

Her jaw tightens with those words and she grits her teeth. "I'm *using* him?"

I nod.

Her curiosity turns into anger as she narrows her eyes. "I was wrong about you, too," she says. "I thought you were different. But you're a bastard, just like the rest of them."

She turns to walk away, but I grab her elbow and pull her back. She gasps when I spin her around and grip her forearms. "I'm not finished," I tell her.

Her eyes are full of shock now. I loosen my grip on her arms, rubbing my thumbs back and forth to hopefully put her anger a little more at ease.

"Do you love him?" I ask her.

She inhales slowly, but doesn't respond.

"No," I say, answering for her. "You don't. You probably used to, but the only thing love relies on for survival is respect. And you don't get that from him."

She remains silent as she waits for me to get my point across.

"You don't love him. You're still here—not because you're too weak to leave—but because you're too *strong* to leave. You put up with this shit because you know it's not about you. It's not about your own safety. You do it for your brother. Everything you do, you do for other people. Not many people have that kind of courage and strength, Sloan. It's fucking inspiring."

Her lips part and she sucks in a soft rush of air. Based on her reaction, I'd say she's not used to being complimented. And that's sad.

"I'm sorry I said those things to you at the restaurant," I tell her. "You aren't weak. You aren't Asa's *doormat*. You're..."

A tear trickles out of her left eye and trails down her cheek. I lift my hand and press it to her cheek, letting the tear fall against my thumb. I don't wipe it away. If anything, I want to bottle it up and save it. This is probably the first tear she's ever cried as the result of a compliment, rather than an insult.

"I'm what?" she asks, her voice soft and hopeful. She's looking up at me, wanting—*needing* me to finish my sentence.

My eyes drop to her mouth and my chest constricts at the thought of what her lips would feel like sliding against mine. I swallow hard and finish saying the words I know she needs to hear.

"You're one of the strongest people I've ever met," I whisper. "You are everything Asa doesn't deserve. And..." I take a step closer and she tilts her head up as I lean in toward her and whisper, "And everything I want."

She sighs softly and we're so close I can feel her breath on my lips—so close I can already taste her. I run my hand through her hair to pull her toward me, but the second our lips almost meet, the back door to the kitchen begins to open. We both separate, facing opposite directions. I open the refrigerator just as Jon walks into the kitchen. I look away from him, but not before seeing the knowing look he shoots me. The suspicion.

Shit.

I hear Sloan open a cabinet behind me. I reach inside the refrigerator. "Want a beer?" I ask Jon, holding it out toward him.

He takes two deliberately slow steps toward me, eyeing me hard, and takes the beer from my hand. He glances behind me at Sloan as he twists off the cap. "What did I just interrupt?"

I wait to see if Sloan wants to answer, but she doesn't. There's just a long stretch of silence. I grab another beer out of the fridge and then close the door, glancing in Sloan's direction. Her back is to both of us as she pours herself a glass of water from the sink.

I could act like Jon is overreacting. I could feign innocence. But Jon would know better. I know what it looked like when he walked in here—both of us turning in opposite directions, separating, looking guilty.

Jon doesn't know me. For all he knows, I'm just like him. Making him think I'm not worried about repercussions would probably gain me more respect from him than not. Making him believe I think Sloan is just another "whore" (as Asa would say) would be better in his eyes than if I actually thought she was anything different.

I look back at Jon and smirk as I take a step toward him. "Wouldn't you like to know." Just as I pass him, I wink, allowing him to think whatever the hell he wants.

I walk confidently outside and as soon as the door shuts behind me, I press my hand into the wall and let out a huge rush of air.

I can feel the pull in every part of me—the blood rushing to my head as my lungs drag in all the breaths Sloan took from me in that kitchen. Or took from Luke, rather. Because that was all me just now, pulling her to me, wanting to put my mouth on hers. That had nothing to do with why I'm here.

And I got exactly what I deserved for allowing it to happen. Jon knows he walked in on something and now I have to figure out how to fix that before Asa finds out.

Shit just got real.

TWENTY

Sloan

My hands are shaking as I take a sip of water. I know Jon is still in the kitchen, standing somewhere behind me, but I don't want to turn around. He disgusts me almost as much as Asa, and knowing he thinks he saw something between me and Carter gives him a leg up. I know how he works. I'm not stupid.

I set the glass down and glance behind me. Jon is standing against the fridge, staring at the words I wrote. He lifts his hand and traces his index finger around the words on the dry-erase board, then he runs his finger through them, erasing them. "What the fuck does this even mean?" he says, glancing back at me.

I face him full-on, folding my arms over my chest. I hate how his eyes scroll down my body. I hate how he looks at me—like I'm the one thing he can't have. Only now that he thinks Carter almost had me, I somehow seem more attainable to him.

My heart feels like it slips up my throat. I can feel my pulse beating in my neck as Jon begins to take a few steps toward me. "Where's Asa?" he asks, his eyes roaming over my breasts rather than my face.

"In our bedroom," I say, wanting him to know that Asa is right here in the house. I don't mention that he's passed out and probably won't wake up for several hours.

It's funny how things work sometimes. I fear Asa more than anyone—but Asa is also my only protection against people in this house.

Jon glances up at the ceiling. "He asleep?"

I shake my head. "No," I say. "I came down to make him something to drink."

I can see in his eyes that he knows I'm lying. He knows I'm only trying to protect myself. He takes another step forward until he reaches me. Something changes in his expression. I see the sinister look in his eyes—the hatred—and I open my mouth to scream. I want to yell for Carter to come back inside. I want to yell for Asa to come downstairs. But I can't, because Jon's hand clamps around my throat, stifling my voice.

"You want to know what I'm sick of?" he asks, glaring at me as he squeezes his hand tighter. My eyes are wide, but I'm unable to nod or shake my head. I'm gripping at his hand around my throat as I try to pull it away from me.

"I'm sick of Asa getting everything he wants," he says. "And not letting me have shit."

I squeeze my eyes shut. Someone will walk in soon. Carter, Dalton—someone will stop this.

Just as that thought passes through my mind, the back door opens and relief washes over me. I open my eyes and Jon spins around, still gripping my throat.

My wide eyes meet Kevin's. He pauses in the doorway, staring at us. I barely know him because he's not here at the house much, but I don't care. He's here and Jon just got busted. He'll be forced to release me.

"Get the fuck out of here," Jon growls at Kevin.

Kevin takes in the scene: Jon pressed against me, one of his hands gripping my hips, the other around my throat, the fear in my expression. I try to shake my head to silently beg Kevin not to walk away, but he misreads the situation, because he laughs. Or...maybe he doesn't misread it. Maybe he doesn't care. Maybe he's just as sick as Jon. Kevin holds up his hands and says, "My bad, man," and steps back outside.

What the fuck?

Jon spins me around and pushes me toward the living room, out of the kitchen. I try to scream, but nothing comes out. His hand is still clamped around my throat.

The living room is dark and empty and I try to fight my way out of his grip, but I'm getting weaker by the second with every drop of air he's refusing to let me inhale. I can feel the panic set in, but I force it back down. I can't lose control of myself right now.

He pushes me onto the couch and as soon as he releases his grip around my throat, I drag in gasp after gasp of air, coughing and sputtering until I have enough air in my lungs to scream. But before I'm able to do that, something cold is placed against my throat. Something sharp.

Oh, God.

I squeeze my eyes shut as soon as Jon's other hand begins to push my knees apart. I have never felt terror like I feel right now. I've been in dangerous situations before—usually at the hands of Asa. But I've never feared for my life at the hands of Asa.

Jon is different. Jon would hurt me just to punish Asa.

His hand runs up my thigh and settles between my legs. I can feel my legs shaking from the fear that's overtaking my entire body.

"Asa thinks everyone else's girls are fair game, but he's the only one who gets a piece of this?" He lowers his mouth to my ear. "He owes me a few favors, Sloan. And I need you to repay one right now."

"Jon," I choke out. "Please stop. Please."

He brings his mouth to mine. "Say please again," he whispers.

"Please," I plead one more time.

"I like it when you beg." His mouth crashes against mine and I immediately taste bile as it makes its way up my throat. There's nothing gentle about his mouth as his tongue forces its way past my lips. The more I try to fight to free myself, the harder he presses the blade against my throat.

Through all the fear and all the struggling, I'm somehow still able to hear the quiet click of a gun.

Jon freezes on top of me and when I open my eyes, I see the metal tip of a gun pressed against his temple.

"Get the fuck away from her," Carter says.

Oh, God. Thank you, Carter. Thank you, thank you, thank you.

Jon's hand slowly leaves my throat. He presses it against the back of the couch. "You're gonna regret this," he says to Carter.

I look up at Carter, seeing something in his eyes I've never seen before as he stares down at Jon.

"You're wrong," he says, his voice steady. "The only thing I'll regret is not shooting you three seconds ago."

Jon swallows and slowly begins to back away from me. Carter never pulls the gun from his head as Jon pulls himself to a seated position. Carter moves the gun to Jon's forehead and stares down at him.

"Apologize to her."

Jon doesn't waste a breath. "I'm sorry," he says, his voice shaking.

I pull my legs away from him and scramble off the couch. I back away from the couch, behind Carter. I bring my hand to my throat and rub at it, trying to massage away the pain from Jon's grip.

Carter takes a step away from Jon, but keeps the gun pointed at him.

"I think we both have secrets we'd like to keep from Asa. You didn't see me in the kitchen with Sloan and I didn't see you forcing yourself on top of her. You agree?" Carter says to him.

I don't know how I feel about that—being their bartering tool. But I know if Jon goes to Asa with his suspicions of what he saw between me and Carter in the kitchen, Asa will hurt Carter. And that's the last thing I want.

Jon nods. "I never saw a thing."

Carter says, "Good. We're on the same page then." He presses the tip of the gun back to Jon's forehead, shoving Jon's head against the back of the couch. "But if you touch Sloan again, I won't even worry about having to inform Asa because I'll fucking kill you myself." Carter uses all his force to smash the gun against the side of Jon's head. Jon doesn't even have the chance to react. He falls against the arm of the couch—his whole body limp. Out cold from one blow to his head.

I'm staring in shock at Jon when I feel Carter grip my face. I glance up at him and he's giving me the once-over, checking for injuries. "Are you okay?" he asks.

I nod. As soon as I start nodding, the tears start coming. Carter pulls me to him and my whole body starts to shake with sobs.

He runs his hand down the back of my head and presses his lips against my ear. "Sloan, I hate to ask you this because the last place I want you to be is with Asa right now. But you're safer up there. Go to your room and don't come out for the rest of the night, okay?"

I nod, because I know he's right. Asa is the devil himself sometimes, but at least he would never allow anyone in the house to hurt me. Besides, he's out cold. Just like Jon.

Carter walks me to the base of the stairs. "Do you have your cell phone on you?"

"Yes."

"Call me if you need me tonight. Otherwise, I'll see you in the morning," he says, running a soothing hand over my cheek.

I completely forgot about tomorrow. I have school tomorrow. Class with Carter. The thought of being with him at school—away from all this shit—is the only thing I have to look forward to right now.

"Okay," I say, my voice still shaking from the result of the last half-hour.

He leans in and kisses me on the forehead, then releases me. Jon starts to stir on the couch, so Carter nods up the stairs, wanting me out of the room before Jon wakes up. I turn to walk up the stairs, in shock over how different life inside this house is compared to what it's like outside this house.

Normally, when someone gets attacked, it's reported to the police. But inside this house, it's handled internally. It's used as a bargaining tool. And instead of going to the police, I go upstairs to a guy who is ten times more dangerous than the person who almost raped me.

This house doesn't follow the same rules as the outside world. This house is a prison with its own set of rules.

And Asa is the warden. Always has been.

I just don't think Asa realizes that now that Carter is here, he could easily be overthrown.

I hope he never *does* realize it. Because that wouldn't be good for any of us.

TWENTY-ONE

Asa

My mouth is fucking dry. It tastes like I've been sucking on a goddamn towel all night.

I roll over to reach for one of the bottles of water Sloan always keeps by our bed. I can't open my eyes because my whole head feels like it's about to explode, so I feel around the nightstand until I find one. My hands are shaking. I already want another hit. This time I'll be smart about it. I won't do it when I'm so torn up on whiskey, I pass out and waste my fucking high like I did last night.

I bring the bottle of water to my mouth and down the entire contents in two huge gulps. I toss the empty bottle across the room and fall back onto my pillow.

I'm still thirsty.

I stretch out my arms and accidentally hit Sloan in the shoulder. I glance over at her, but my head is too groggy to focus. She rustles a little, but she doesn't wake up. I look at the alarm clock and squint. It's 4:30 a.m. She still has two hours before she has to get up and get ready for school.

I give myself a minute to adjust to the darkness until I can see her really well. Then I roll onto my side and watch her sleep.

She sleeps on her back now. Never on her side, never on her stomach. When I was a kid, my dad always slept on his back, even when he'd pass out on the couch from whatever substance he was abusing that day. I asked him why he slept like that once and he said, "When you're on your back, you're prepared for anything. It's easier to wake up and protect yourself. If you get too comfortable, you're left off guard."

It makes me wonder if Sloan sleeps on her back as a protective method. Then it makes me wonder if she sleeps on her back to protect herself from *me*.

No. She doesn't fear me like that. She fucking worships me.

She used to sleep on her stomach, though. Maybe I just need to buy a new mattress. Maybe she just doesn't like this bed.

She also used to sleep naked, but she hasn't done that in over a year. She claims it's because there are too many people in this house and she doesn't feel comfortable. It used to bother me when I'd crawl on top of her at night, only to find she was wearing fucking pajamas and I couldn't slide inside of her until after I got them off of her.

After complaining enough, she finally compromised and only sleeps in a T-shirt now. Easier access, but I'd still rather her be naked.

I pull the covers down, careful not to wake her. Sometimes I just like to look at her while she sleeps. I like to think she's dreaming about me. Sometimes I touch her, just soft enough not to wake her, but enough to make her moan in her sleep.

Her T-shirt is bunched up around her waist. I lift it, slowly, inch by inch until her breasts are exposed. And then I lean back, reaching under the covers and into my boxers. I grip myself and begin stroking as I watch her sleep—watch her soft breasts move up and down with each slow breath she inhales.

She's so fucking beautiful. All that long, dark hair. Those lashes. That mouth. I've honestly never seen another girl as beautiful as her in real life. I knew she'd be mine the first time I laid eyes on her. I couldn't allow something this perfect to be with anyone else.

But I wouldn't allow myself to pursue her right away, because I liked the way she looked at me. I could see the innocence in her eyes as she would stare at me in class. I made her curious. And even though I pretended not to notice her, she made *me* curious. I could tell she was different from any girl I'd ever been with.

Nothing scares me—not since I was a kid. But the way I obsessed over the thought of her came pretty damn close to scary. The thought of being able to corrupt something that sweet made me think about her more than anything else in my life.

Before Sloan, I wasn't the type of guy who loved girls. Not in the traditional sense, anyway. I used them for what the majority of them are good for. A quick late-night fuck, sometimes a pre-breakfast fuck, but never anything after 8:00 a.m. or before 8:00 p.m. Guys who allow girls in their life between the hours of 8:00 a.m. and 8:00 p.m. have shit for brains.

That's a direct quote from my father.

I used to remind myself of this every time I'd look at Sloan, before she was mine. Every time I'd catch her staring at me in class. Every time my dick would jerk in my pants when I thought about her.

Shit for brains.

The more I observed her, the more I started to question my father and whether or not he even knew what the hell he was talking about when I was younger. He probably never experienced a girl like Sloan. A girl who had yet to be corrupted by another man. A girl who was too timid to know how to flirt with a guy. A girl who hadn't had the chance to become a whore yet.

I told myself I'd test her out. See if she was the exception to the rule. I caught up with her after class one day and asked her if she wanted to go to lunch. It was the first time I'd ever asked a girl on a date, come to think of it. I expected her to smile and shyly agree, but instead she looked me over, turned away, and kept walking.

That's when I realized I was wrong about her. She wasn't shy. She wasn't unfamiliar with how cruel people could be. She knew *exactly* how cruel the world was and that's why she kept her distance from everyone.

Little did she know, her fake disinterest made me want her even more. It made me want to pursue her until she wanted every part of me...even the cruelty. It made me want her to *beg* for it.

It wasn't as hard as I thought it would be. It's amazing how far good looks and humor can get you.

And...manners. *Who knew?*

You hold a fucking door open for a girl, she automatically thinks you're a gentleman. She thinks you're the type of guy who would treat his mother like a queen. Girls see guys with manners and think there's no way they could be dangerous.

I held every fucking door open for Sloan that I could find.

I even held an umbrella for her once.

That was a long time ago, though. That was back when she used to sleep on her stomach. *Naked.*

Sometimes I wonder if she's not as happy as she used to be. She left me once and I fucking hated it. Every second she was gone, I felt like I had turned into every single thing my father feared I'd grow up to be. *A lovesick fool. Shit for brains.*

But I do love her. Fuck him and his idiotic bullshit philosophies on love. She's the best thing that's ever happened to me, and when she left me, I knew that.

I knew if she left for good, she'd eventually find someone else. I couldn't bear the thought of another man's mouth on hers. His hands on her. His fucking disgusting dick inside of her, when she'd only ever had me there. She was mine.

And I did what I needed to do to get her back—even if she doesn't realize it had anything to do with me. I did it for her benefit—because I love her. And I know she loves me. When she came back to me and asked for my help, it was the proudest I've ever been of myself. Because I knew at that point it was a done deal. She was mine forever.

But there's still that one tiny flaw in our relationship that makes me question the permanence of it. She refuses to accept my lifestyle—always makes me promise her I'll get out someday. We both know that'll never happen, though. I'm good at what I do. But I guess maybe I need to prove to her that I can do both. Be what she needs without it compromising my lifestyle.

I need to ensure she never goes anywhere. I need to make her part of my life permanently.

I could marry her. I could buy her a house—one where just the two of us lived. Of course I'd be in *this* house between the hours of 8:00 a.m. and 8:00 p.m., since I seem to be the only one who knows how to properly operate things around here.

But Sloan could be at the home we would share together, growing babies. When I came home at night, she could feed me, we'd make love, I'd sleep with her by my side. And she'd sleep on her stomach.

I've never thought about marriage before. I wonder why this brilliant idea is just now coming to me.

She's never brought up marriage, though. I'm not even sure she'd agree to it. But if she got pregnant, she wouldn't have a choice. Unfortunately, she uses birth control with more routine than I get my dick sucked. Not that her birth control isn't something I couldn't tamper with. But on top of that, she also forces me to use a goddamn condom every time I have sex with her.

But...condoms are something else I could tamper with.

I wonder what it would feel like to be inside her without a condom. She's let me inside of her for a few seconds before—just to prep her before putting on the condom. But I've never finished inside of her.

Her warm pussy squeezing tight around my dick while I release into her, feeling every single sensation without a barrier.

I groan at the thought of it and start pumping my fist faster. Fuck, this feels good. Watching her, thinking about being inside of her. I need to touch her. I lean forward, bringing my mouth to her exposed breast. I normally try not to wake her, but it won't be the first time she wakes up to me jacking off on her.

I slide my tongue against her nipple and tease her, circling it slowly. She stretches her arm out against the pillow and moans. I like that she's still asleep. I like to see how close I can get her to an orgasm before waking her up.

I wrap my lips around her nipple and suck gently. It instantly hardens inside my mouth.

"Mmm," she moans again, her sleepy voice breathless. "Carter."

My jaw clenches with her fucking nipple still in my mouth.

What the fucking fuck did she just say?

I immediately pull away, letting her nipple pop out of my mouth. I look down at her fucking face and release my grip on my dick. It just went limp at the sound of that name passing her lips.

What the fuck?

What.

The.

Fuck?

My chest hurts. It feels like someone just crushed it. Dropped a brick on it. Dropped a whole fucking *building* on it.

Somewhere between moaning his name and regaining consciousness, Sloan pulled her shirt down over her tits.

Somewhere between moaning his name and regaining consciousness, I wrapped my hand around her throat.

She's staring at me. Her eyes are wide with fear. I'm sure it's a scary thing to wake up to your boyfriend's hand around your throat, but she should be lucky she's not feeling what *I'm* feeling right now.

"Are you fucking him?"

It takes all the effort I have not to scream those words at her. Instead, my voice is calm and collected, unlike every other part of me. I'm not squeezing her throat with any significant force.

Yet.

I simply have my hand around it, so she *should* be answering me right now. She's able to speak, but she's not. The fucking whore is just staring at me like she just got caught.

"Sloan? Are you fucking Carter? Has he been inside you?"

Sloan immediately begins to shake her head. She presses her palms into the mattress and pushes herself up against the headboard. My hand doesn't leave her throat.

"What are you talking about?" she says. "No. Of course not. *God*, no."

She's looking at me like I'm crazy. She's very convincing.

My mother was convincing, too. Look where that landed her.

I tighten my grip, watching her face as it slowly turns a shade pinker. She winces and fists the sheet at her sides. Her eyes begin to fill with tears.

Good thing my father taught me not to let a woman's tears fool me.

I lean in toward her until I'm a mere two inches from her. I scroll over her eyes, her mouth, every fucking lying part of her goddamn face. "You just said his *name*, Sloan. I had your fucking nipple in my mouth, trying to *please* you. But then you whispered his fucking name. You said *Carter*."

Sloan shakes her head. She's so adamant about it, shaking it with such intensity, I ease my grip around her throat so she can speak. After inhaling a gasp of air, she blurts out, "I didn't say *Carter*, you fucking dipshit. I said *harder*. I was awake and could feel you kissing me. I wanted you to do it *harder*."

I stare at her.

I let her words sink in.

I let her explanation massage the ache in my chest until I can breathe again.

I slowly slide my hand away from her throat, down her neck.

Fuck.

I'm being paranoid.

Why would I ever think she'd dream about another guy when she sleeps next to *me*? She wouldn't cheat on me. She *can't*. She has no one else. It would be the worst mistake she ever made and she knows it.

I need to get her out of this house. Away from all these people. I'm more certain now than I was ten minutes ago that I need to make her a mother. Make her a wife. Give her a place of our own where other men are never around to make me this fucking paranoid.

Sloan leans forward and reaches to the hem of her shirt, pulling it over her head. She tosses it on the floor and then pushes me back against the headboard, sliding onto my lap.

And just like that, I'm hard again.

She presses her breast against my mouth and offers herself to me. I take her nipple in my mouth again and I give her what she wants. I suck her *harder*. So hard it hurts her. I want her to feel the ache my mouth left on her for the rest of the fucking day.

She wraps her hands in my hair, pulling me against her as she moans and says my name. She says, *"Asa."*

She says it *three times*.

My name.

I grab her hips and lift her slightly until she's positioned right over my dick. I bring her back down until I'm buried inside her, almost certain I've never been this deep. God, she feels good. It feels so good when I don't hate her.

I didn't like how it felt to hate her.

"You're mine, Sloan," I say, dragging my lips up her neck and to her mouth.

She whispers, "Yours, Asa."

I slide my tongue in her mouth until she moans, and then I pull away from her. I grip her throat again with my right hand and guide her hips up and down with my left. She winces a little when I squeeze her throat, and it makes me wonder if I hurt her neck earlier. I move my hand and can already see a handprint. There's even a little bruising.

Fuck. I did. I hurt her a lot more than I intended to.

I lean in and kiss her softly on the neck, giving her a silent apology. Then I look into her eyes as she rides me. "I want to marry you, Sloan. I want to make you mine forever."

She doesn't say anything right away. Her whole body stiffens and she stops moving against me. "What did you say?" she asks, her voice shaky.

I grin and rub my hands down her back, gripping her ass. "I said marry me, baby. Be my wife."

I lift her off of me and push her onto her back. I slide back inside of her, relishing the fact that I don't have on a condom. I move in and out, savoring every sensation while she stares up at me, speechless.

"I'll buy you a ring while you're at school today. The biggest one I can find. I just need you to say yes first."

A tear falls out of her eye and that's when I know for sure that she loves me. The thought of spending forever with me just made her cry.

I somehow find a way to push into her even harder this time and she winces. I want to be as deep inside of her as I can reach. I want her to feel every piece of me. I want her to feel how much I love her. Her fingers dig into the flesh of my arms as she pushes against me, her body's natural reaction to the pressure between her legs. I don't care how many times we've done this, I know it still hurts her sometimes. She's so tight and I barely fit inside her, having to force myself against her so hard it makes her wince and push against me.

Just like she's doing now. I probably shouldn't like it when she's in pain, but I do. I fucking love it when my dick hurts her. I like knowing that even when the sex is over, she'll feel me inside of her for hours with every movement she makes.

God, I love this girl.

I speak between thrusts, staring straight down at her tear-filled eyes. "I love you, Sloan. So fucking much. I need to hear you say yes."

I groan, feeling how close I am to finishing. Finishing *inside* her. Experiencing something with her that we've never experienced together before. I kiss the side of her head and then lower my mouth to her ear. "I need to hear you say yes, baby."

She finally releases a quiet, "Yes."

That word makes me so goddamn happy, it only takes one more thrust for me to come. And I release inside her. *Deep* inside her. Inside my *fiancée.*

My legs shake and my whole body jerks against her like nothing I've ever experienced. I'm shaking—practically trembling when I'm finished, but she's still in shock. She remains completely still, unable to move or speak beneath me. I know that felt as good to her as it did to me. She's just still in shock because she wasn't expecting a proposal. Especially in the middle of the fucking night. Or morning. However you look at it.

I pull out of her and roll onto my side. I immediately bring my hand between her legs, wanting to feel what I left inside her. Warmth trickles out of her and I spread it around with my hand, touching her, circling my fingers against her wetness.

I already want to fuck her again. But that can wait. Right now I just want to make her come and then fall asleep next to her. Next to my fiancée. My naked fiancée who's going to start sleeping on her fucking stomach.

She closes her eyes while I touch her. *Squeezes* them shut, actually. I watch her face while I continue to stroke her. I wait for the moans to pass the lips that just spoke the word *yes* to me when I asked her to marry me.

I didn't even have to convince her. This is already so much easier than I thought it would be.

Asa and Sloan, happily ever fucking after.

Fuck my father and his bullshit philosophies on love.

TWENTY-TWO

Carter/Luke

'm not telling you again. I don't want her involved."

Dalton—*Ryan*—clenches his fists and leans back in the chair, frustrated with me. "She's already involved, Luke. You're not putting her in danger—she lived there before we ever got involved." He leans forward again. "This wasn't an issue in the last job. Remember Carrie?"

I remember Carrie. "Carrie was *your* project. Not mine. I've never gotten involved with a girl for the sake of an assignment, Ryan."

He cocks an eyebrow. "But you'll get involved with one while you're *on* a job, just not *for* the job? You'll allow your feelings for her to put us both in danger?"

I push my chair back and stand up. "I'm not putting us in danger. Nothing is going on. I don't know how many times I have to repeat that."

I hate that he's right, but I'll never admit that to him. I face the one-way mirror of the interrogation room and stare at myself. I look tired. I run a hand through my hair and close my eyes.

"Do you really believe that whatever is going on with her is innocent? That it isn't putting us at risk in some way?" Ryan says. "Did you not attack Jon—Asa's *best friend*—because he was kissing Sloan last night?"

I find his reflection in the mirror and I eye him hard. "*Kissing* her?" I spin around and face him. "He was about to *rape* her, Ryan! What'd you want me to do, walk back outside and double down on the fucking poker game?"

I face the mirror again and watch him. He knows he would have done the same thing if he had walked in on that.

It's fitting that we're doing this inside an interrogation room at a nearby precinct, because this case review is starting to feel just like an interrogation.

We're both quiet for a while. I run my hands down my face and sigh.

"How is leading this girl to believe I have feelings for her going to help this case?"

Ryan shrugs. "I don't know. It might not help. But it's worth a shot. Especially since you already seem to have some sort of friendship with her that she values. Her guard would be down around you. She might tell you things in confidence that we don't already know."

He stands up and walks around the table, then leans against it.

Technically, he's my superior. I have to remind myself of that sometimes with the way we have to interact and with as many undercover jobs as we've done together. He's been doing this about five years longer than I have and I know he knows what he's talking about. As much as I don't want to admit it.

"I'm not asking you to fall in love with the chick. I'm not even asking you to *pretend* you love her. All I'm asking is that you take advantage of her feelings for you. For the sake of this investigation."

"And how do I do that?" I ask. "Asa is always around. It would be more dangerous for us to get her involved."

"There are ways," Ryan says. "You have class with her today. Start there. I know she goes to visit her brother on Sundays. Go with her this Sunday."

I laugh. "Yeah, I'm sure Asa would be absolutely fine with that."

"He won't know. He mentioned something to Jon about us all going to the casino Sunday. We'll be gone all day. Just pretend you have something else to do and offer to go with Sloan instead. You'll get a full day with her, uninterrupted and unmonitored by anyone who knows him."

I know I should tell him no. But the truth of the matter is, I'd offer to go with Sloan whether it helped the case or hurt it. That's how pathetic I've become at my job lately. Nothing should come before the job. Especially someone on the other *side* of the job.

"Fine," I say. I grab my jacket and pull it on. Before I open the door to exit, I pause. I slowly turn and face him. "How did you know I have class with her?"

Ryan grins. "She's the hottie from Spanish, Luke. I'm not an idiot." He grabs his own jacket and pulls it on. "Why the fuck do you think you were signed up for that class?"

TWENTY-THREE

Sloan

I'm still shaking when I walk into the building. It's been hours since the incident with Asa, but I'm still sick over it. I've never been that scared. Not even last night when Jon was on top of me with a knife to my throat.

I can't believe I said Carter's name out loud while I slept. Not only could I have gotten myself in a serious situation with Asa—I could have been responsible for whatever Asa would have done to Carter.

I don't know how I recovered from that one as well as I did. And thank fuck Carter's name rhymes with harder.

But one thing I'm not relieved about is what happened afterward. The things Asa said to me. Him bringing marriage into it.

Him not using a condom.

I don't know what Asa does when I'm not around. I've never been told he cheats on me other than what Jon said last night, but I don't even know what he meant by that. I've also never caught him cheating, but I don't trust him enough to put my health and my life at risk.

But that happened this morning and it's at the forefront of my mind. The second it turned 8:00 a.m., I called my doctor and made an appointment for next week to be tested. I'm on the pill and I take it religiously, so I'm not at all worried about him getting me pregnant. But I am worried about everything else he could give me.

I'll try not to think about it until next week. And I'll do whatever I can to make sure that doesn't happen again. I was just honestly too scared for my life to say anything this morning. I've never seen him look at me with so much hatred as he did when he thought he heard me moan Carter's name.

When he did hear me moan Carter's name.

Before I walk to class to face Carter, I stop by the bathroom and try to calm myself down. Now that I'm not in the same house with Asa, I can breathe easier. But I have no idea how to ensure I don't talk in my sleep again. If it means just never sleeping in the presence of Asa again, I'll figure out a way to do that.

When I'm finished in the bathroom and walk out into the hallway, the first thing I see is Carter, propped up near the door of our classroom.

He's waiting for me.

When he sees me, he stands up straight and waits for me to reach him.

"You okay?" he says, his eyes immediately falling to my neck. There are bruises there from what Jon did to me last night, but it'll probably look even worse by the end of today, thanks to what Asa did this morning.

God, what kind of fucking life am I living right now that I'm choked by two different men in the span of twelve hours?

"I'm fine," I say unconvincingly.

Carter lifts his hand and touches a finger to my throat. "It's bruised," he says. "Did Asa notice?"

He runs the back of one of his fingers across my neck. I know it's out of concern, but whenever he makes any sort of contact with me at all—no matter the reason—I seem to forget just how capable

I am of actually feeling things. I've learned to numb myself over the past couple of years with Asa, and Carter negates all that effort.

"He noticed, but he wasn't suspicious. He thought he did it himself."

My words cause Carter to flinch. His eyes flick back to mine. "Sloan," he whispers, shaking his head. He pulls his hand away from my neck and runs it through his hair. I can see the roll of his throat as he swallows back what looks like pure hatred at the thought of Asa's hands on me. He's obviously worried about me, which I completely understand. But he also knows why I stay, and he doesn't seem to judge me for it. He actually understands my situation and sympathizes with it. I like that about him—his empathy.

Something Asa has probably never felt for anyone his whole life.

Carter lays a gentle hand on my elbow. "Come on. Let's get our seats." He makes an attempt to direct me toward the door, but I pull back.

"Carter, wait."

He turns around to face me again, stepping aside to let two students enter. I glance down the hallway to the left and then to the right. "I have to tell you something."

Concern overtakes whatever residual anger he felt. He nods and leads me down the hallway, away from the door, looking for somewhere more private. We pass another door and he checks the window, then the doorknob. It turns, so he pulls open the door and leads me inside.

It's an empty music room, flanked with various instruments against one wall and several desks arranged in a circle in the middle of the room. When the door closes behind us and we finally have privacy, I expect Carter to ask me what I need to tell him. Instead, as soon as I turn around, he pulls me to him, wrapping his arms tightly around me, cradling my head against his shoulder.

He hugs me.

That's all he does. He hugs me tightly without a word, yet I can feel everything he's saying. And I realize that since last night—since everything that happened with Jon—he's probably been worried sick about me. He probably wanted to hug me and reassure me last night. As soon as he saw me this morning. But simple hugs aren't so simple in my life.

I wrap my arms around him and bury my face in his shirt, inhaling the subtle hint of his cologne. He smells like the beach. I close my eyes and wish we were there. Away from all this bullshit.

We stand in silence for several minutes, neither of us moving. After a while, I can't tell who is hugging whom—who is holding whom. It's like we're both barely suspended, clinging to each other, afraid we might fall down if either of us lets go.

"I said your name in my sleep," I whisper, slicing through the silence.

Carter immediately pulls back and looks at me. "Did he hear you?"

I nod. "Yes. But I think I covered it pretty well. I told him he misheard me—that I said something else. But he was really angry right after it happened, Carter. Angrier than I've ever seen him. And I just...I thought you should know. I think we need to be more careful. I mean, I know there's nothing really going on between us, but—"

Carter interrupts and says, "Isn't there, though? I know we technically haven't acted on it, but this isn't innocent, Sloan. If Asa even knew I had class with you..."

"Exactly," I say.

Carter nods, knowing what this means. He can't talk to me at the house. Hell, he shouldn't even look my direction anymore. After what happened early this morning, Asa will be suspicious, even though he believed me. The last thing I want to do is cause trouble for Carter, but it seems I've already done that.

"I'm sorry," I say to him.

"Why are you apologizing? Because you had a dream about me?"

I nod.

Carter lifts a hand to my cheek and the corner of his mouth lifts into a grin. "If we're apologizing for that, then I owe you about a dozen apologies already."

I bite my cheek to hide my smile. He drops his hand and presses it against the small of my back. "We'll be late if we don't hurry."

I laugh a little at the thought of being tardy. What weight does being late for class hold against all the other shit that's going on in our lives? Very, very little. But he's right.

I follow him out the door and back down the hallway toward the classroom. Before we walk inside, he leans down and whispers, "For what it's worth, you look really beautiful today. I kind of can't catch my breath."

He keeps walking, despite the fact that his words have frozen my feet to the floor.

That's all those were. *Words.* A few simple words strung together, but they held just enough power to physically stop me in my tracks.

My hand goes up to my mouth as I quietly inhale. I force away the smile that wants to break out and I somehow force my feet to walk into the classroom. I glance up and see Carter pulling two chairs out on the top row, so I make my way up to him.

My knees feel like they're about to fail me. *This is how it should be. This is how guys should make girls feel.*

Why the hell did I ever give Asa the time of day?

When I reach my seat, he's still standing, waiting for me to sit down first. I give him a quick smile as a thank-you and take my seat. I take my books out of my bag and he does the same. The professor walks in just as we're settled. He turns and begins writing on the board.

Screamed a little too much at the football game last night. Lost my voice. Go through chapters 8-10 and we'll catch up on lecture next week.

Half of the class laughs at the note. The other half groans. Carter opens his book to the right page. I lean forward and open mine and begin reading. I don't get far before Carter grabs a pen and begins writing a note. I'm giddy with anticipation, hoping it's for me and he's not actually taking notes for class.

I don't even feel guilty. I should feel guilty about this. Especially since Asa sort of proposed to me this morning, and out of fear for my own life, I was forced to say yes.

This is so fucked up. I'm going to hell.

Actually...I might already *be* in hell. Most of the time this life feels more like a punishment for something horrible I must have done in a previous life. Until Carter came along, at least. I don't remember much that has ever made me excited about life before he recently entered it.

Carter slides the note to me. It's folded in half, so I lift the paper and read what he wrote. I expect something random, like the game we've played in class before. Instead, it's just a simple request.

Put your hand under the table.

I read it twice before looking at my hands. The note is a little random, but not like the game I showed him. It's only random because I'm confused by it. I slip the note under my book and then lower my hand under the table and wait for him to hand me whatever it is he has.

To my surprise—he doesn't give me anything. His warm palm slides against mine and he threads our fingers together, resting our hands on my thigh.

And then he returns his focus to his textbook, resuming his reading like he didn't just attempt to set me on fire.

That's exactly what it feels like—my hand wrapped in his—him touching my leg. I feel like someone needs to douse me with water. My heart begins to race and I feel like my whole body is tingling.

He's holding my hand.

Jesus fucking Christ.

I didn't know holding hands could feel better than a kiss. Better than sex. Sex with Asa, at least.

I close my eyes and focus on the weight of his hand against mine. The width of his fingers between mine. The way his thumb occasionally runs back and forth.

After probably fifteen minutes of pretending to read the textbook in front of me, he pulls his hand from mine. He doesn't release me, though. He just begins to make circles with his fingertips against my palm. He traces every part of my hand, my palm, my fingers, *between* my fingers. With every minute that passes, my mind begins to wonder what those fingers would feel like against my leg. My neck. My stomach.

My breathing grows heavier. I begin to take in shorter breaths with each minute closer we get to the end of class.

I don't want class to end. I never want it to end.

When he's explored every part of my hand twice over, his fingers slide to my leg. He begins to stroke my knee, about three inches up the inside of my leg, and back down to my knee. My eyes are closed and I'm gripping the book in my hands. He does this for several more minutes, driving me completely insane, almost to the point that I might have to get up and go to the bathroom to splash cold water on my face.

But I don't, because somehow the fifty minutes of class are up and everyone is packing up to leave.

I find the strength to open my eyes and glance up at him. He's staring at me, his gaze narrowed, eyes heated, wet lips that I can't seem to look away from. He grabs my hand again and squeezes. "I know I shouldn't..."

I shake my head. "You shouldn't."

I'm not even sure what he was about to say, but I have an idea of where his mind is at right now, because mine is right there with his.

"I know," he says. "I just...I can't be this close to you and not touch you."

"And I can't not let you."

He inhales a deep breath, then releases it at the same time he releases my hand. He gathers his book and shoves it inside his backpack. He stands up and throws the backpack over his shoulder. I look up at him and he's staring down at me. I wait for him to say goodbye or walk away, but he doesn't.

We stare at each other for a few more seconds before he drops his backpack and falls back down in his seat. He wraps his hand in my hair and presses his forehead against the side of my head. I have no idea what he's doing, but the desperation in the way he's pressed against me makes me wince.

"Sloan," he whispers, his mouth directly over my ear. "I want everything about you. So goddamn much. To the point that it's blinding me."

I gasp at his words.

"Please be careful," he says. "Until I can help you get out of there. I don't know when that'll be, but please. Be very, very careful."

I squeeze my eyes shut when he presses a kiss to the side of my head. What I wouldn't give for those lips to be pressing against my mouth right now.

How can I have this many feelings for someone I just met? For someone I haven't even kissed yet? For someone who is mostly everything I want, but also involved with everything I despise?

"If I come to your house tonight, I'm not even going to look in your direction," he says. "But know that you're all I see. You're all I fucking see, Sloan."

He releases me as quickly as he grabbed hold of me. He picks up his backpack again and stands up. I hear him walk away and I'm still sitting completely immobile, my eyes closed, my heart thrashing around inside my chest.

I want more of whatever it is he makes me feel. But I want it away from here. Away from this town. Away from Asa. I know Carter wants me to leave and I want to. I want to so bad, but I have to be more prepared for that to be able to happen. And if I leave— Carter has to leave, too. Not only does he need to sever ties with Asa, but I need him to sever ties with this corrupt lifestyle Asa has created.

We both need to leave.

Before it's too late...

TWENTY-FOUR

Asa

've never been the kind of guy who deals with excess bullshit. Another piece of wisdom my father taught me.

"If it doesn't benefit you, it shouldn't fucking matter to you."

That's probably the best piece of advice he ever gave me. I apply that wisdom to every aspect of my life. My friendships. My business partners. My education. My empire.

Yes, I said empire. I'm not quite there yet, but props to positive thinking and all that bullshit, right?

When I first started dealing, I was small-time. Dealt what I could, when I could, to whomever I could. Mostly ecstasy to college kids, weed to college dropouts. Once I realized that wasn't where the money or the power was, I started studying.

There was a full year right around the time I started college that I studied every minute of every day. And I'm not talking the bullshit textbook studying that lands you a full-time desk job making enough salary a year to buy one house, one car, and one wife. I'm talking *real* studying. Meeting people. Becoming the person people want to meet. Sampling the good shit, the heroin, the coke, just to get a feel of what kind of drug fits better with which demographic. Knowing how to not get addicted to the shit. Getting to know your dealer so well that you become best friends with your dealer's dealer. Building trust in whoever has more power than you, but lying low enough that they don't see it coming when you've suddenly got more power than them.

I learned a lot and I learned it the hard way. The *right* way. From the bottom to the top.

I don't deal the petty shit now: X, weed, pills. I especially don't fuck with weed. It's an excess. You want weed? Move to fucking Colorado and buy yourself a gift card to the sweet shop. Don't waste my fucking time.

But if you want the good stuff...the shit that makes you feel like you're kissing the face of the goddamn Creator himself? That's when you come to me. I won't sell you the Ford, but I'll sell you the rarest fucking Bugatti you'll ever come across.

I'm still building. I'll always be building. The second someone in my position feels like they have nothing else to learn is the same second they'll be surpassed by the next guy. As far as I'm concerned, there are no more available spots above Asa Jackson in this city. I have a good team beneath me. Guys who know their places. Guys who know I'll be fair to them if they're fair to me.

I'm still getting to know my newest guy, Carter. Most people are transparent, but he's like a muddy fucking river. Most people, especially the ones who work for me, kiss my ass because they know what a fucking good thing it is to be able to fit inside my back pocket.

Carter is different. He doesn't seem to care one way or another. It's his indifference that unnerves me. He reminds me of myself a little, and I'm not so sure that's a good thing. There's only room for one me.

My oldest guy, Jon, is really beginning to get sloppy. He was once my right-hand man, but lately he's become my fucking Achilles' heel.

Which brings me back to my initial point.

If it doesn't benefit you, it shouldn't fucking matter to you.

I'm struggling to see how Jon benefits me anymore. He seems to just stir up bullshit wherever he goes. Last week he lost one of my biggest clients because he couldn't keep his dick in his pants when it came to the guy's wife. Even *I* know how to draw the line between my dick and my wallet.

Unlike Jon, Carter is a benefit. He's a good translator, he's quiet, he shows up where he needs to be and does what I need him to do. Which is the only reason I haven't gotten rid of him yet, despite my suspicions about him. He's not *excess* yet.

Jon, though. Jon is becoming dead weight.

But Jon also knows too much, which poses an even bigger problem.

For Jon. Not for me.

Aside from the business, I've cut all the other excess out of my life. Other than Sloan. She's far from excess, though. If I had to compare her to a drug, Sloan would be heroin. Heroin is nice. Heroin makes you mellow. As long as you have it in good supply, heroin would be something you could happily inject every day for the rest of your life.

Maybe it's weird to compare people to drugs, but when drugs are all you know, it's normal.

Jon would be meth. He's way too cocky, talks too much, painful at times. Real fucking painful.

Dalton would be coke. Sociable, friendly, makes you want to do more coke. I like coke.

Carter would be...

What would Carter be?

I don't think I know Carter well enough to know which drug he resembles. But for about two minutes last night when I thought Sloan said his goddamn name, Carter was the motherfucking overdose.

But she didn't say his name. She's never even spoken to the guy as far as I know. And if he's smart, that means he's never spoken to her beyond their introduction in the kitchen.

But soon, I won't have to worry about the guys around here because she won't live in this house anymore. She'll be in *our* house.

Shit.

Fuck!

I was supposed to buy the fucking ring today. I knew I was forgetting something.

I go to my closet to get dressed. I debate pulling out the Armani. You know—special day and shit. Instead I grab a dark blue button-up shirt I know Sloan likes and pair it with slacks. It really doesn't matter what I pick out of the closet, it's all fucking spectacular. I've always dressed for the level of respect I want to receive.

And no, my fucking father didn't teach me that one. He'd have probably made it a lot longer in the outside world had he not dressed like the fucking bum that he was.

When I reach the bottom of the stairs and glance in the kitchen, I see Jon standing at the sink with his back to me, holding a bag of ice to the side of his head.

"What happened to you?"

He turns around, and the whole fucking right side of his face is black and blue. "Christ, man. Who the hell did you fuck over?"

Jon drops the bag of ice in the sink. "No one important."

I walk into the kitchen. His face is even worse up close. And if he thinks he's not about to tell me who fucked him up, he's wrong. If he lost us another job, the left side of his face will look a whole lot worse than his right. I grab my keys off the counter and ask him again. "Who the fuck did that to you, Jon?"

He pops his jaw and looks away from me. "Some asshole caught me with his girl last night. Took me off guard. It looks worse than it was."

Fucking idiot. I laugh. "No, I'm sure it looks just as bad as it was." I walk to the pantry and check the alcohol stock. It's empty, as usual. I slam the pantry door. "We're celebrating tonight. Need you to stock up today. I have to run an errand."

Jon nods. "Special occasion?"

"Yep. Got engaged. Make it classy. None of the cheap shit."
I head toward the front door and I hear Jon laugh. When I turn
around, the fucker is still smiling. "Something funny?" I ask,
walking back into the kitchen.

He shakes his head. "Is there anything *not* funny about you
getting married, Asa?"

I laugh. And then I fuck up the left side of his face.

Fucking excess.

TWENTY-FIVE

Carter

I make it to my car in the parking lot. Somehow. I grip the steering wheel and lean my head back.

I have no idea where the line is drawn now, it's so fucking blurred. I'm trying to do the job I'm here to do, but at the same time Sloan is making me question whether this is really the life I want at all. I have no idea if I was Carter just now or if that was all Luke. Luke is becoming Carter.

I'm pulling too much of myself into this job, but I have no idea how to not be myself when I'm with her. All the things I want to say to her. The things I wish I could do to her. The truth I wish I could tell her.

If I told her the truth about who I am and what I'm here to do, though, I'd be risking everything. My life. Ryan's life. Possibly *her* life. The less she knows, the better.

I press my forehead against the steering wheel and try to foresee the inevitable shitstorm that's coming our way.

I want to be with her. I want to be with her as Luke. But that can't happen until we have enough on Asa to put him away for good. And we won't be able to put him away for good until he slips up. He's careful right now. He's smarter than I initially thought.

But the more time it takes to get where we need to be in this investigation, the more danger Sloan is in. And knowing what I know now about Asa, leaving him is the worst thing she could do. There's no way he'd let her leave peacefully. He'd hurt her. And I wouldn't put it past him to hurt her brother, too.

She's stuck until he's gone, and that could be months.

I lean back in my seat again and pick up my phone. As if I'm being punked, I have two texts from Asa.

Asa: Where are you?
Asa: Meet me for lunch at noon. Peralta's. I'm fucking hungry.

I stare at the texts for several seconds. This is out of character for him. He doesn't text on his regular phone when it has to do with a job, so...he literally just wants *lunch?*

Me: Be there in ten.

Twelve minutes later I'm weaving my way through the restaurant to where Asa is seated. He's staring down at his phone when I take my seat.

"Hey," he says, not even glancing up. He finishes the text and then sets his phone aside. "You busy tonight?" he asks.

I shake my head and pick up the menu. "Nope. Why?"

I look over the menu, but I don't have to make eye contact to see that he's smiling. He reaches behind him and then sets something on the table. I lower the menu and my eyes land on a box.

A jewelry box.

What the fuck?

He opens it and holds it out for me to take. I stare down at the ring, the dread making my skin itch. *He's proposing?*

I try not to laugh. He's fucking delusional if he thinks she's going to agree to this. He also doesn't know Sloan as well as he thinks he does, because this ring is nothing like Sloan. This ring is gaudy and showy. She'll fucking hate it.

"You're proposing?" I hand him back the box and pick up my menu again like I'm not really interested.

"No, I did that already. Tonight's the celebration."

My eyes flick away from the menu and straight to his. "She said yes?" I had no idea nods could be cocky until just now. I force myself to smile. "Congrats, man. She seems like a keeper."

Why did she not mention this to me this morning? Why would she agree to marry him? I guess she feels trapped. She can't very well say no to Asa with the position she's in. Agreeing to it was the safe thing to do, even though it makes me sick for her.

I just don't know why she didn't warn me.

He puts the box back in his coat pocket. "She is a keeper. She's heroin."

I lift an eyebrow. "Heroin?"

He shakes off my question and calls over the waiter. "I want a beer. Whatever you have on tap. And a cheeseburger, all the way."

The waiter looks at me. "Same," I say.

We hand over the menus and I feel my phone buzz in my pocket. It's probably Dalton. I texted him on the way here to let him know I was having lunch with Asa. I have no idea what this lunch is about, but I want to make sure the team knows where I am. Especially after Sloan said my name in her sleep. I half expected my agreeing to this lunch was a suicide mission.

I take a sip of the water already sitting on the table. "So when's the big day?"

Asa shrugs. "No idea. Soon. I want to get her out of that fucking house before she gets hurt. I don't trust a single goddamn person around her."

How thoughtful of him. He's about a day late, though, but I'm sure Jon failed to tell him that.

"I figured she liked it there," I lie. "Don't you guys have some kind of open relationship? How does that work?"

Asa's eyes narrow. "No, we don't have a fucking open relationship. Why the fuck would you think that?"

I laugh and casually bring up all the reasons why someone in my position *should* think that, even though I know better. "Jess? The chick you fucked in your bedroom last week? The girl in the pool two nights ago?"

Asa laughs. "You have a lot to learn about relationships, Carter."

I lean back in my seat. I try to keep this conversation going without seeming too interested, but I want to know every detail about why he's wasting Sloan's time.

"Maybe so. I assumed most relationships were between two people, but I guess I'm wrong. Relationships confuse me. As does yours."

"*As does yours*?" he repeats. "Who the fuck talks like that?"

We're interrupted by the waiter delivering our beers. We both take drinks and then he pushes his beer aside and leans forward, tapping his index finger against the table. "Let me teach you about relationships, Carter. In case you ever find yourself in one."

This should be interesting.

"Is your father alive?" Asa asks.

"Nope. Died when I was two." *That's a lie. He died three years ago.*

"Well that's your first problem. You were raised by a woman."

"That's a problem?"

He nods. "You learned about life from a woman. Lots of men do, it's fine. But that's what's wrong with most men. Men need to learn from men. We work differently than society leads women to believe."

I don't respond. I wait for him to continue this rare display of charitable *genius*.

"Men weren't designed by nature to be monogamous. It's engrained in us to spread our seed. To keep the population going. We're breeders by default, and no matter what society tries to force upon us, we'll be breeders until we kill ourselves off. That's why we're so fucking horny all the time."

I glance to my left, at two older women whose mouths are hung open, eavesdropping on Asa's definition of the male species.

"Women are the ones who give birth," I point out. "Are they not also considered breeders? Would it not also be in their chemical makeup to populate the world?"

He shakes his head. "They're nurturers. It's their duty to keep the species alive. Not to create it. Besides, women aren't into sex like men are."

I wish I were recording this. "They aren't?"

"Fuck no. They crave the expression of thoughts...emotions... feelings. They want to form a bond...a lifelong connection. That's why they push for marriage, because it's in their biological makeup to crave a protector. A provider. They need stability, a home, a place to raise their children. Women don't have physical cravings like we do. So it's only fair that we create the families for the women, but we also need an outlet to partake in our natural urges. When men fuck around, it's different than when the women fuck around."

I nod my head like I'm understanding his philosophy, but it's making me ill for Sloan. "So in your opinion, women don't have a biological excuse to sleep with more than one man. But men do?"

He nods. "Exactly. When a man cheats, it's purely physical. We're attracted to a woman's hips, to her legs, to her ass, to her tits. It's all about the sexual act. Dick in, dick out. When a *woman* cheats, it's purely mental. They're turned on by emotions. By their feelings. If a woman fucks a man, it's not because she's horny. It's because she wants him to love her. That's why I fuck around on Sloan. And that's why Sloan is not allowed to fuck around on me. Cheating for a man is different than cheating for a woman, and that's a fact, proven by mother nature herself."

Holy fuck. People like this actually exist. God help us.

"And Sloan is okay with this?"

Asa laughs. "That's the thing, Carter. Women don't understand because they aren't made like us. That's why men were also given the distinct ability to lie so well."

I smile, when all I'd really like to do is reach across the table and put an end to his ability to breed—an end to his ability to create life that might turn out like him.

"So what role do the mistresses play in all this?" I ask.

He smiles sickeningly. "That's why God made the whores, Carter."

I force a smile. He's right about one thing—I can definitely lie well. "So the whores are for nature and the wives are for nurture," I say.

Asa smiles proudly, like he actually taught me something. He lifts his beer. "Cheers to that," he says. We clink our beers together and he takes a sip. "My father used to say something similar to that."

"Is he still alive?"

Asa nods, but I notice the sudden tightness in his jaw. "Yeah. Somewhere."

Our food arrives, but I'm not sure I feel like eating after that twisted lecture on Darwinism.

I definitely don't feel like eating now that I know I'll be seeing Sloan tonight. *At her fucking engagement party.*

"You should give a toast tonight."

I pause, mid chew. "Excuse me?"

Asa takes a sip of his beer. "Tonight," he says, setting it back down on the table. "At the party. You should give a toast after I announce the engagement. You can string a sentence together better than any other fucker that'll be there. Make me look good. Sloan will eat that shit up."

I force the food down my throat. "I'd be honored."

Motherfucker.

TWENTY-SIX

Sloan

I waste as much time as I can before coming home every day. The less I'm here, the better. After classes were finished up today, I went to the gym, then the library. It was after seven when I finally walked through my front door. Jon was sitting on the couch, glaring at me.

I rushed to the stairs and up to my room as fast as I could, but not before noticing his face. I don't know what happened after I walked away from him and Carter last night, but it's apparent Carter wasn't finished with him, because both sides of his face are black and blue now.

I make sure to lock my bedroom door. I don't know if Asa is here or not, but I'm never chancing being alone with Jon again.

Once I'm safe in the room, I toss my backpack on the floor. My eyes instantly fall on the dresser. Specifically on the *jewelry box* sitting on the dresser.

He bought me a ring. He makes promises almost daily and never keeps them. The one time I want him to forget is the one time he actually remembers.

Just my luck.

I walk over to the dresser and open the box. I don't even pick it up; I just push it open with my fingers, not really wanting to see it.

I immediately wince. Of course he would buy me this one; it was probably the biggest one in the jewelry store. Three huge diamonds make up the majority of the platinum ring, each diamond encased by smaller ones.

It's seriously ugly as shit. Am I actually going to have to wear this thing?

There's no hiding this. I knew I should have told Carter earlier today. I just didn't know how to tell the guy I'm developing feelings for that I just got engaged to someone else. To someone he loathes. Even if that engagement means very little to me.

I hear laughter outside, so I make my way to the bedroom window. There are coolers set up everywhere and Dalton is standing at the grill, flipping burgers. Several people are lounging and standing around. Maybe twenty. Asa must have heated the pool. It's like 65 degrees out and the water would be too cold to swim, but there are a few people in the pool already.

Asa only heats the pool for big parties.

Shit.

I spin around at the knock on the bedroom door. "Sloan!"

I rush to the door and unlock it, letting Asa inside. He's smiling before he even makes eye contact with me. "Hey, future wife."

Funny how what he deems a term of endearment can feel like an insult to me.

"Hey...future husband."

He wraps his arm around me and kisses my neck. "I hope you got a lot of sleep last night, cuz you aren't getting any tonight." His lips drag up my neck and stop at the corner of my mouth. "Do you want your ring now or later?"

I fail to tell him I already looked at it, and that the ring just serves as further proof that he doesn't know me at all. I tell him I want it now, because if I say later, that means he'll make a big production out of it. That's the last thing I want.

He reaches over to the dresser and grabs the box. He hands it to me, but then he pulls it back. "Wait. Gotta do this right."

He lowers himself to one knee and lifts the box up, presenting the ring to me. "Will you do me the honor of becoming Mrs. Asa Jackson?"

Seriously? This has to be the worst proposal in history. If you don't count the one he gave this morning right after he had his hand around my throat.

"I already said yes, silly," I say to him.

He grins and slips the ring on my finger. I look at it, holding it up to the light. *I didn't know Hell had so much sparkle.*

Asa stands up and walks over to the closet. He pulls off the blue shirt he's wearing and begins to choose a different one. "We should match tonight," he says. "Black shirt, black dress." He pulls out a shirt and then throws a dress in my direction. I catch it. "I'll be so relieved when we have our own place soon. Separate closets."

My hands make fists around the dress. "Our own place?"

He laughs. "You don't think I'm going to marry you and keep you in this house, do you?"

"*Keep* me?"

He pulls the black shirt over his head. He starts laughing to himself as he's buttoning it up. "I had lunch with Carter today," he says casually, sitting on the bed.

Lunch? What? Our class together ended at lunchtime. Carter left class after making me feel the things I felt, and then went directly to lunch with *Asa?*

Why?

I sit on the opposite end of the bed and attempt to sound disinterested. "Oh yeah?"

Asa begins pulling on a pair of socks. "He's not so bad. I kind of like him. Might even ask him to be a groomsman in our wedding."

He's already planning the wedding?

Asa slips on his shoes and stands up, turning toward the mirror. He runs both hands through his hair. "Have you thought about who you'll ask to be your bridesmaids? You don't really have any friends, do you?"

You make it kind of difficult for me to have friends, Asa.

"We just got engaged this morning," I say to him. "Then I had class all day. I haven't really had time to think about the details of a wedding."

"You could ask Jess to be a bridesmaid," he says.

I nod, but internally I'm laughing. Jess hates me. I don't know why, but the girl hasn't looked my direction in six months, no matter how much I try to reach out. "Yeah," I say. "I could ask Jess."

Asa opens the bedroom door and motions toward the dress still fisted tightly in my hands. "Take a shower and get ready. I want you dolled up tonight for the big announcement."

The door closes behind him. I look down at the dress. I look down at my ring.

This hole I'm digging for myself is getting deeper and deeper. If I don't figure out how to climb out of it, Asa's going to fill it with cement.

Asa likes my hair best when it's straight. I know this, because there have been a couple of times I've put some curl in it and he's asked me to redo it. The first time was right after we started dating, when he was introducing me to Jon and Jess for the first time. And once on our first anniversary when we went to dinner at a restaurant I reserved myself. The anniversary dinner I had to remind him about three times.

He said his mother had curly hair and he prefers for me to wear mine straight.

I know nothing about his family, other than he doesn't have one. And that one sentence about his mother's hair is the only time he's ever mentioned her in the years that I've known him.

Yet...here I am, standing in front of the mirror with the curling iron, adding curls to my hair. Simply because I know Carter likes them. I catch him staring at my hair sometimes when I put curl in it. Like he wishes he could touch it—slide his whole hand through my hair and pull my face to his. And even though he'll be on the opposite end of the room from me, not even looking in my direction tonight, I curl my hair. For him.

Not for my *fiancé*.

The music is loud, the house is full of people, and I've been in my bathroom for an hour and a half getting ready. Of course an hour of that was probably spent staring at myself in the mirror, wondering how in the hell I got myself to this point in life. But I have to stop dwelling on all the bad decisions I've made and figure out how to make better ones.

I go see my brother on Sunday. Now that his care is private pay, I no longer meet with the social worker to sign his annual forms. But I think I'll schedule an appointment with her while I'm there Sunday. I want to figure out what I can do to get his benefits back in place without Asa finding out.

Someone beats on the bathroom door, so I put down the curling iron and switch it off. I open it to find Asa gripping the doorframe. His eyes run down the length of me and then back up again. "Holy fuck," he says, stepping inside the bathroom. He wraps his arm around my waist and his other hand drops to my thigh, crawling my dress up with his fingers. "I was planning on waiting until I got you in bed tonight, but I'm not sure if I can."

His breath reeks of whiskey. I doubt it's even nine o'clock yet and he's halfway to being comatose already.

I push against his chest. "Well, you *have* to wait. I just finished getting ready. I'd like to be able to torture you with this outfit for a *few* hours, at least."

He groans and pushes me onto the counter, pressing himself between my legs. "Sloan, how can one guy be so fucking lucky?"

I close my eyes while he kisses down my shoulder. How can one girl be so *un*lucky?

He grips my waist and pulls me off the counter. He doesn't set me on my feet, though. He scoops me up in his arms and I'm forced to grab him around the neck to steady myself. He carries me out of the bathroom and down the stairs. Before we reach the bottom, he stops and sets me on my feet. "Wait here," he says, disappearing down the rest of the steps and into the kitchen.

I look around the living room at all the people. So many fucking people. My eyes catch Jess's stare and I smile at her. She looks away, but I'm almost certain she cringes before doing so.

I have no idea what I've done to her or why she hates me so much. But honestly, I'm used to people treating me like she treats me. I stopped worrying myself sick about it before I even reached high school.

I bring the fingers of my right hand over to my left and I twist the ring around nervously. I guess the one positive aspect of this ring being so big is that I could probably use it in self-defense. Might come in handy if I find myself alone with Jon again.

I can feel the anxiousness crawl into my stomach before I even notice him staring. Carter is on the other side of the living room. He's leaning against the wall, next to Dalton. His arms are folded together and—true to his word—he's not looking directly at me. Technically. He's looking down at my hand.

I stop twisting the ring, and when I do, his eyes flick up to mine. They're narrowed, his jaw set tight. Dalton is standing next to him, laughing and talking like Carter is completely engaged in whatever he's saying. But just like Carter said earlier, he can't see anything else—he only sees me. His expression doesn't waver. Even when Asa returns with two glasses of champagne and forces one of them into my hands, Carter still doesn't look away. It's almost as if he's torturing himself on purpose.

I try to save him a little bit of pain and look away first. It probably doesn't help that I look up at Asa. I can still feel Carter's eyes on me as Asa raises his glass.

"Fuckers!" he yells. "Turn off the music!"

A few seconds later, the music cuts off. Everyone in the room turns toward us and I suddenly want to run back up the stairs and hide. I force myself not to look at Carter.

Once Asa has everyone's attention, he says, "Most of you already know, because I haven't kept my fucking mouth shut since she said yes." He holds up my hand. "But she said yes!"

Collective cheers and congratulations come from the room, but they quickly dwindle as it becomes apparent that Asa isn't finished speaking.

"I've loved this girl for a long time now," he says. "She's my fucking world. So it's about damn time we make it official." He smiles at me and I'd be lying if I said there wasn't something inside me that feels a little something for him—even if it is only sympathy at this point. Somewhere deep inside, I know he is the way he is because of the hand he was dealt as a child. A part of me can't fault him for that. But just because a lot of his behavior can probably be excused by whatever awful people were around him as a child, doesn't mean I'm required to subject myself to a life of unhappiness simply because he loves me.

Because he does love me. He may love me with his own twisted take on love, but he *does* love me. That much is obvious.

Asa points across the room. "Carter! My man! Help us celebrate this monumental occasion with a toast!"

I close my eyes. Why is he pulling Carter into this? I can't look. I can't.

"Someone get that fucker a glass of champagne!" Asa yells.

I open my eyes and slowly drag them across the room toward Carter, who still has the same expression on his face. Only this time, he's being handed a glass of champagne.

And a chair to stand on.

Fuck my life.

Asa pulls me against him and kisses the side of my head as we both watch Carter step onto the chair. The room is incredibly quiet. He's commanded the room in a way that Asa didn't even command it, and Carter hasn't even spoken a word yet. It feels like they all care more about what Carter has to say than what Asa had to say. Something I hope Asa doesn't notice.

Carter doesn't look at me. He winks at Asa and brings his glass of champagne to his mouth. He downs the entire glass in one gulp before he even makes the toast. When his glass is empty, he holds it out to Dalton, who is holding the bottle of champagne. He refills Carter's glass, and then Carter pulls it to his chest and looks straight at Asa. I can see him blow out a quick, pent up breath right before he begins speaking.

"It's hard to believe we've reached the age of engagements. Marriages. Creating families. But it's even harder to believe that Asa Jackson is the one beating us all to it."

A few laughs break out around the room.

"I've never really seen myself as the type of guy who would settle down. But after spending time with Asa and getting to know him better—witnessing firsthand how much he *values* his relationship with Sloan, he may have just changed my mind. Because if he can end up with a girl as beautiful as her, then maybe it's not too late for the rest of us."

People begin to raise their glasses, but Carter waves a hand in the air to hush them. I can feel Asa tense at my side, but I've been tense since Carter started speaking.

"I'm not finished," Carter says, his eyes roaming over the crowd. "Asa Jackson deserves a longer toast than this, you impatient fuckers."

More laughs.

Carter downs his second glass of champagne and then waits for Dalton to refill it for a third time. My pulse is racing so hard, I'm praying Asa doesn't grab my wrist and feel it.

"While Sloan is very, *very* beautiful," Carter says, making sure not to look at me. "Looks have shit-all to do with love. Love isn't found in the attraction you have to someone. Love isn't found in the laughter you share. Love isn't even found in all the things you have in common. Love is not, in any way, shape, or form, defined by nor found in the abundance of bliss it brings two people." He downs his third glass of champagne and with the same routine, Dalton fills

Carter's glass for a fourth time. I take a sip of my own glass now that my mouth and throat have completely run dry.

"Love," Carter says, his voice a little more slurred and a little bit louder. "Love is not *found*. Love *finds*."

Carter's eyes move across the room until they land on mine. "Love finds you in the forgiveness at the tail end of a fight. Love finds you in the empathy you feel for someone else. Love finds you in the embrace that follows a tragedy. Love finds you in the celebration after the conquering of an illness. Love finds you in the devastation after the *surrender* to an illness."

Carter raises his glass. "To Asa and Sloan. May love find you in every tragedy you face."

The room erupts in cheers.

My heart erupts in my chest.

Asa's mouth finds mine and he kisses me, then he's gone. Disappeared into the crowd of people clamoring to pat him on the back, congratulate him, and inflate his ego.

I'm left standing on the stairs, staring at the guy who is still standing on his chair, staring back at me.

He stares for several seconds and I can't look away. Then he downs his fourth glass of champagne, wipes his mouth, and steps off the chair, disappearing into the crowd.

I put my hand on my stomach and release all the breath I've been holding since he began his speech.

Love finds you in the tragedies.

That's certainly where Carter found me. In the midst of a series of tragedies...

My eyes scan the crowd until I spot Asa on the other side of the room, staring straight at me. Suspicion has replaced the smile that's been affixed to his face all afternoon. His eyes are focused on mine with the same intensity mine were just focused on Carter's.

I can't even find the strength to fake a smile.

Asa downs a shot and slams it on the table next to him. Kevin refills it and he downs that one. Then another. His gaze never once wavers from mine.

TWENTY-SEVEN

Asa

"**A**nother."

"That's five already, Asa," Kevin says. "It's barely after nine. You'll be out by ten if you keep this up."

I tear my eyes from Sloan and glare at Kevin. He concedes, pouring the sixth shot, and I down it. When I look back at the stairs, she's gone.

I glance around the room, but I don't see her. I immediately part through the crowd and make my way up the stairs, toward our bedroom.

When I open the door, I find her sitting on the bed, staring down at her hand. She glances up at me and smiles, but it looks forced. *It looks forced a lot here lately.*

"Why are you up here?" I ask her.

She shrugs. "You know I don't like parties."

She used to. Just like she used to sleep naked. On her stomach.

I take two steps until I'm standing in front of her, looking down on her. "What'd you think of Carter's toast?"

She wets her lips and shrugs again. "It was a little hard to follow. Kind of confusing, actually."

I nod, watching her reaction carefully. "Was it? Is that why you were staring at him after I walked away?"

She tilts her head a little, a move people make when they're confused. Or maybe it's a move people make when they're only *pretending* to be confused.

The one thing about Sloan that I *don't* like is that she's smart. Smarter than most girls. Even smarter than a lot of men I know. She might even be a good liar, because I've yet to catch her in one. I lower my hand to the side of her face and tilt her gaze up to mine. "I've already asked you this once. This is the last time, Sloan."

If I didn't know better, I'd say she was trembling. Could be the six shots rushing through my bloodstream, though. I trail my fingers across her cheekbone. I pause at her lips and then slowly trace them. "Do you want to fuck him?"

Her neck stiffens and she pulls away. "Asa, don't be ridiculous," she says, dismissing my question.

I shake my head. "I'm not stupid, Sloan, so don't treat me like I am. I saw the way you looked at him downstairs. And I'm still not sure I'm convinced it wasn't his name you were moaning in your sleep last night. So tell me...do you want to fuck him? Do you think about his mouth on you?"

She shakes her head. "Don't do this again, Asa. You're drunk. It makes you paranoid." She stands up to come face-to-face with me, and my hand slides down to her waist. She looks me dead in the eyes. "I don't give a fuck about Carter. I don't even know him. I have no idea why you keep bringing him up, but if he bothers you so much, *fire* him. Don't allow him in our house again. I couldn't care less, Asa, and if you're this threatened by him, do something about it. If I wanted anyone else, I wouldn't be wearing this ring."

She holds up her left hand and smiles. "It's beautiful, by the way," she says, admiring the ring. "I was a little speechless earlier, so I forgot to tell you how perfect it is."

I'm either a delusional fuck or she's the best goddamn liar I've ever met. If I'm forced to choose between the two, I choose the former.

I wrap my arms around her waist. "Come downstairs," I tell her. "I want my eyes on you all night."

She gives me a peck on the cheek. "I will in half an hour. I want to stare at my ring for a little bit before all the girls downstairs start demanding to try it on." She twists the ring on her finger, admiring it again.

Girls. They're so easy to please. I should start buying her more fucking jewelry.

I release her and head to the door. "Don't wait too long, you have a lot of shots to catch up on." I open the door to walk out, but pause when she calls my name. I turn around and she's sitting back down on the bed.

"I love you," she says, her sweet lips curling around those words. It makes me fucking ache to be inside her.

I will be. Later.

"I know you do, baby. You'd be stupid not to."

I close the door and walk back downstairs. I probably shouldn't have said that to her, but I'm still a little bitter with the way she made me feel when I caught her staring at Carter. When I cross the room, Kevin is still standing at the table with all the liquor. I grab a shot out of his hand. "One more," I say, pointing at the bottle and downing the one in my hand. I'll need about double what I've already had to get over the way my blood was boiling at the thought of Carter and Sloan.

Speaking of Carter...

I catch him out of the corner of my eye just as he leans in and whispers in some petite brunette's ear. She laughs and slaps him in the chest. My eyes follow his hands and they're gripping her waist, pressing her into the wall behind her.

Sloan is right. I'm being paranoid. If anything were going on between Carter and Sloan, he'd be staring me down or looking around for Sloan. Not sliding his tongue up some girl's neck like he's doing right now.

Good for him. Pretty sure that's the first time I've really seen him let loose. Must have been the half-bottle of champagne he downed during his toast.

I take another shot and walk past them on my way toward the back door. I pat Carter on the back, but I don't think he notices. The chick's legs are wrapped around his waist now. She has some nice fucking legs.

Lucky bastard.

I lightly trail my fingers across one of her legs as I pass them. Carter still has his mouth buried against her neck, but the girl makes eye contact with me when she feels me touch her. I wink at her and then walk toward the back door.

I give her five minutes before she comes up with an excuse to follow me outside.

I should feel bad about this—about stealing Carter's girl right out from under him. But the fucker has gotten inside my head more than enough in the last twenty-four hours when it comes to Sloan. If anything, he deserves this.

TWENTY-EIGHT

"Is he gone?" I whisper in her ear.

Tillie nods and unwraps her legs from around my waist. "Yep," she says, wiping at her neck. "I get that you had to make it convincing, but please don't ever put your tongue on me again. Gross."

I laugh. She straightens her hair by running her fingers through it. "Now disappear. I have work to do. This might even be easier than I thought." She slaps her hand against my chest and pushes me aside, heading out the back door in search of her new project. *Asa*.

Tille has helped out with a couple of jobs I've worked on before, but she's usually Dalton's sidekick. I figured having her here tonight would not only come in handy for my own sake, but for the investigation as well. If anyone could take Asa's eyes off Sloan for any amount of time, it would be Tillie. Not only because of the way she looks, but she's like a chameleon. She can become whoever she needs to be in order to worm her way into a guy's psyche, and Asa Jackson is next up on her list.

When she disappears outside, I glance around the room to make sure no one is paying any attention to me. When I'm in the clear, I head straight for the stairs.

Granted, my sneaking up to Sloan's room is not why Tillie is here. In fact, Dalton ordered me to stay away from Sloan tonight and wait until Sunday to give her any attention—when Asa is far away from both of us.

Luckily, Dalton is outside. So is Asa.

And now, so is Tillie. I've got at least a ten-minute window to check on Sloan.

She's probably confused by the toast I gave downstairs. Hell, I'm still confused as to why Asa asked me to do it in the first place. Either he's beginning to trust me, or it's a *keep your enemies closer* kind of situation.

I don't waste time knocking when I get to her bedroom. I open the door and shut it just as fast. Then I lock it for good measure. She's sitting on the bed and as soon as she glances up and realizes it's me, she stands up. "Carter," she says, wiping at a tear. "You shouldn't be in here."

God, she looks beautiful. I was so sick to my stomach when I saw Asa carrying her down the stairs earlier, I refused to allow myself to take it all in. The way her dark curls are cascading around her bare shoulders, the way her dress hugs at her just like I wish I was doing right now. *Fuck.* I know I had to down half a bottle of champagne in order to get through the toast earlier, but it's really starting to hit me now.

I walk past her without touching her somehow, to the window. I stand to the side of it and look out over the backyard. Asa is on a lounge chair by the pool—Tillie is sitting on the chair next to his. She's leaning forward, engrossing him in conversation. His hands are relaxed behind his head, and even from here I can tell he's staring at her breasts.

Dalton is talking to Jon on the other side of the pool.

I glance back at Sloan and she's standing behind me, shaking her head. "Why are you in here? He's already suspicious, Carter. Are you *crazy?*"

I nod. "Apparently."

She's hugging herself nervously, staring up at me. My heart feels like it's about to tear through my chest. It does that sometimes when I do stupid shit like this. "Do you want me to leave?" I ask her.

She pulls her bottom lip in and chews on it for a second. "Not yet," she whispers.

I reach to her and pull her left arm away from her chest. I slide my fingers around her ring. "I can't do this while you're wearing this ring." I slip the ring off her hand and toss it on the bed.

"Do what?" she whispers, looking up at me with a considerable amount of anticipation.

I close the gap between us. "Kiss you." I lift my hands to her face, slowly sliding them through her hair to the nape of her neck. "I'm going to kiss you until I sober up or get caught. Whichever comes first."

Her chest rises with her gasp. "Hurry," she says, breathless.

Hurry is the *last* thing I'm gonna do when it comes to her.

I tilt my head, feeling her fists clench the front of my shirt. I barely touch my lips to her lips, feathering my mouth against hers. We both release shaky breaths the second we make contact—breaths we've been holding since that first day we saw each other in class.

She's on her tiptoes now, needing me to kiss her fully, to finally give her what we both want. Instead, I pull back and look down at her. When she realizes I'm doing the exact opposite of what she wants, she opens her eyes.

I stare down at her mouth, wanting to savor it for one more second before devouring it. I move my right hand back to her cheek, slowly rubbing the pad of my thumb over her bottom lip.

"What's taking you so long?"

I stare at her mouth as I trace my thumb over her top lip. "I'm worried that once we start, we won't be able to stop."

She slides her hands up my neck, sending chills down my back. "I think you should have thought that through before you walked into my bedroom. It's a little late to change your mind now."

I nod, pulling her to me. I wrap one hand around her back and keep the other wrapped in her hair. "Yep. Definitely too late." I press my lips to hers and my pulse begins to rage beneath my skin. Her lips part to make room for my tongue, and I when I finally taste her, she's so goddamn sweet I groan. Her mouth is warm, her lips are cold, and the way she kisses me back makes the room feel hotter than hell. I try to pull her closer, to kiss her deeper, but it isn't enough. We're grasping at each other, attempting to get more from this kiss than we know we're allowed. But her lips, her gasps, her moans...I can't stop.

I can't stop.

We end up with her back flat against a wall and my hands beside her head. Our kiss slows down, speeds up, slows down again.

Stops.

We're practically panting as I stare down at her. She's looking up at me with the most tragic expression. I kiss her softly on the lips, then on her cheek. I pull back and press my forehead to hers as we catch our breath.

"I should go home," I whisper. "I need to go before my stupidity gets you killed."

She nods and then desperately grips my arms. "Take me with you."

I don't move.

"Please," she says, her eyes filling with tears. "Let's go. Now, before I change my mind. I want out of here and I never want to come back."

Fuck.

Is she really saying this?

"*Please*, Carter." Her words are desparate. "We can discharge my brother so Asa doesn't use him against me. And wherever we end up, I'll find a way to get him back in the care he needs. Let's just go."

My heart is deflating, just like her hope is about to. If she only knew how much I wish I could do that. I start to shake my head and she moves her hands from my arms to my cheeks. A huge tear spills out of her eye. "Carter, *please*. You don't owe him anything. You can get out. We both can. Right now."

I squeeze my eyes shut and roll my forehead to the side of her head. My lips are directly over her ear when I whisper, "It's not that easy, Sloan."

If it were all up to Luke, and Carter didn't have to exist, we'd be halfway across the state already. But if I took her tonight...if we just ran away and I abandoned Ryan in the middle of all this...it would compromise the entire investigation. It would make Asa even more dangerous. And I'd be letting down a whole fucking lot of people, not to mention giving up my entire career. I wouldn't even have a way to support her.

"I want to get you out of here, Sloan," I whisper. "I just can't leave yet. I can't explain why and I don't know when I can, but I will. I promise. I swear."

I press my lips to the side of her head, just as she starts to cry. And as much as I'd give to hold her in my arms until her devastation passes, I can't. Every second I'm in this room with her is another second I'm risking her life.

I press my mouth to hers once more and then pull away from her. She lets her head fall back against the wall and she's so much sadder in this moment than when I even walked inside the room to begin with.

She's still gripping my wrist as I try to walk away. When she refuses to let go, I lift her fingers from around my wrist, releasing her. I watch as her arm falls limp to her side. Having to walk away from her like this is nothing short of devastating.

It's tragic.

And that's where love finds you...in the tragedies.

TWENTY-NINE

Sloan

'**ve** never missed a single Sunday visiting my brother. And even though I've been in bed since Carter walked away Friday night, pretending to be sick, I somehow pulled myself out of my slump today.

Asa and all his friends went to the casino. It's about a three-hour drive north, and my brother is an hour drive south. It's sad, but I feel like the more distance I put between Asa and myself today, the better I'll feel. The more I'll be able to breathe.

Right before I walk out of my bedroom, I pause in the doorway. I reach to my left hand and slip off the ring, setting it on the dresser. I'll be home way before Asa gets back, so he won't notice I didn't wear it today.

But my hand will feel a million pounds lighter.

I stop in the kitchen to make myself a drink for the road. When I reach for the freezer to grab ice, my hand tightens around the door handle. My eyes fall to the new words written on the dry-erase board.

Pickles don't feel guilty when people yodel, so why aren't the sheets ever folded on Tuesday?

145

I have no idea when Carter wrote this, but I know he wrote it to try to make me feel better about the way he had to leave Friday night. He wrote it to try to make me laugh.

It works, because I'm smiling for the first time in two days when I open the freezer.

I fill my cup with ice and soda, then grab an extra soda for Stephen. They don't let him keep sodas in his room due to his health restrictions, so I always sneak him an extra one on Sundays as a treat. With his doctor's permission, of course. I just don't tell Stephen that.

I grab my purse, my keys, and the drinks and start to head for the door when I receive an incoming text. I wait until I'm at my car to pull my phone out of my purse and read it.

Carter: Pick me up on the corner of Standard and Wyatt. I want to go with you.

My cheeks heat up at the unexpected text. I thought he was with Asa and the guys today. I start to text him back, but another text comes through.

Carter: Also, never respond to my texts. And delete both of these.

I do what he requests and then I back out of my driveway and head to the corner of Standard and Wyatt. It's only a few streets down, and I know he wants me to pick him up there because it's safer than leaving his car in the driveway. But I'm still confused as to how he knew I was even going anywhere.

I'm filled with anticipation as I search for him. When I round the corner of Standard, he's right where he said he'd be, standing alone on the curb, hands shoved in the back pockets of his jeans. He smiles when he sees me and it hurts. And feels incredible. When I come to a stop, he opens the door and climbs inside the car.

"What are you doing?" I ask.

"Going with you to visit your brother."

"But...how? How did you get out of gambling? And how did you even know when I was leaving?"

He smiles at me and then leans across the seat and wraps his hand in my hair. He rests his lips against mine and says, "I have my ways." He kisses me and then moves back to his side of the seat. He pulls on his seatbelt. "If you think it's too risky for me to go inside the building with you, I don't mind waiting in the car. I just really needed some time alone with you."

I try to smile, but having him this close reminds me of Friday night, and how pathetic I sounded when I tried to beg him to run away with me.

I wasn't thinking things through. I can't just up and leave, I'm in the middle of getting my college degree. I can't pull Stephen out of his facility and drag him on a cross-country road trip. He's happy there and I'd be doing him a disservice.

I just want out so bad, and after feeling what I felt when Carter kissed me, I got emotional. And it made me wish he was wrong—that he really could save me.

Carter reaches across the seat for my hand. "Sloan. Can you make me a promise today?"

I glance over at him. "Depends on what it is."

"I can see in your expression that you're thinking about Friday night. Let's not talk about Asa today. Or what we both know needs to happen. I don't even want to discuss the possibility of getting caught, or how stupid I am for coming with you. Let's just be Sloan and Luke today, okay?"

I raise an eyebrow. "*Luke?* Who is Luke? Are we role playing?"

His jaw twitches and he says, "I mean Carter. I used to go by my middle name when I was younger. Hard habit to break."

I shake my head and laugh. "Do I make you that flustered that you can't even remember which name you go by?"

He grips my hand tighter and smiles. "Stop making fun of me. And don't ever call me Luke. Only my grandfather called me Luke and it's weird."

"Okay, but I'm not gonna lie. I kind of like Luke. Luke."

He reaches over and squeezes my knee. "Sloan and *Carter*. Let's be Sloan and Carter today," he corrects again.

"Which one am I?" I tease. "Sloan or Carter?"

He laughs, then unbuckles his seatbelt and leans across the seat. He presses his mouth to my ear and slides the palm of his hand over my thigh. I hold my breath and grip the steering wheel when he whispers, "You be Sloan. I'll be Carter. And on our way home this afternoon, we'll pull over somewhere quiet and you can be Sloan in the back seat *with* Carter. Sound good?"

I exhale with my nod. "Uh-huh."

THIRTY

Carter

"When is the last time Asa visited?" I ask her.

She turns off the car and begins gathering her things. "Two years ago. He's only been here once. He said it made him uncomfortable."

Of course he'd say that.

"So no one would think it's odd that I'm walking in with you?"

Sloan shakes her head. "I think the employees are so used to seeing me alone, they'd only be curious that I finally showed up with someone. But they wouldn't be suspicious or tell Asa, because they don't even know Asa." She drops her keys and her phone in her purse and then grips the steering wheel. She stares out over the parking lot in front of us. "That's really sad, isn't it? That I have no one? *Literally* no one. It's always just been me and Stephen against the whole goddamn world."

I reach over and tuck a strand of hair behind her ear. I want to comfort her—to tell her she has me. But she's being so honest right now, I don't want to feed her another lie. She doesn't even know my real name, and the more lies I tell her in moments like these, the harder it'll be for her to forgive me when she finds out the truth.

Which she almost *did* earlier. I swear to God, sometimes I wonder how I ever got this position to begin with. I am the worst undercover detective that ever existed. Seriously, they should call me The Pink Panther.

Sometimes I think maybe she could handle it if I told her the truth. That maybe she would be able to help out in some way. But that would only put her in more danger and I already do that enough.

Maybe in time, if I can get her to earn Ryan's trust, he'll see the benefit of filling her in. But for now, it's better she doesn't know.

She's still staring blankly out the window, so I pull her to me and hug her. She wraps her arms around me and sighs against my neck, and I wish Asa would fucking die on the way back from the casino.

Shit. That was really harsh.

But can he not see how much better the lives of those around him would be if he didn't exist?

Of course he can't. You see nothing outside the realm of yourself when you're a sadistic narcissist.

"You give really nice hugs," Sloan says.

I hug her tighter. "I think you just haven't been given enough hugs in your lifetime."

"That too," she says with a sigh.

I keep my grip on her for a moment longer, until she whispers against my neck. "Fifty-six king crabs ate shoelaces for Easter dinner and then they coughed up Rainbow Brite through their nostrils."

I laugh and kiss her on top of her head. "You can't buy illegal butter with a bike wheel or silly string."

I can feel her smile when she finds my mouth and kisses me.

That's all I wanted before we got out of this car—for her smile to return.

"You said he didn't like Asa," I say on our way down the hall toward Stephen's room. "So if he doesn't communicate, how do you know if he likes or dislikes someone?"

She's been filling me in on her brother's condition during the walk to his room. She listed off about five things he's been diagnosed with, but I can't even remember the names of them, so the least I can do is try to understand them.

"We have our own way of communicating," she says. "I've practically raised him since he was an infant." She rounds the corner and points down a hallway. "He's down here at the end."

I still have questions, so I pull on her hand until we come to a stop. "But you're only a few years older than him. How did you raise him?"

She looks up at me and shrugs. "I did what I had to, Carter. No one else was around to do it."

I don't know that I've ever met anyone like her. I kiss her, partly because I want to get as many kisses in as we can today, and partly because she deserves a little more affection in her life. *Selfless* affection. I don't mean for the kiss to be anything more than a second or two, but we haven't been able to kiss like this since our first kiss. I'm instantly pulled into it and everything else fades away.

Until someone clears their throat behind us. We pull apart to see a nurse attempting to exit the doorway we're blocking. Sloan apologizes and then starts laughing as we rush down the hallway to Stephen's room.

She knocks on the door and then pushes it open. I follow her inside, immediately impressed with the facility. I expected more of a nursing home or hospital room setup, but these are more like miniature apartments. There's a small living area attached to a sleeping area and a kitchenette. I notice there's no stove or microwave though, which probably means he has to have all his meals prepared for him.

Sloan walks into the living area to greet her brother, but I wait in the entryway, not wanting to interrupt them.

Stephen is sitting on the couch, watching the television. He glances up at Sloan and I can immediately see the resemblance. They have the same hair color, same hair texture, same eyes.

But his face is expressionless. He turns back to the TV and my heart instantly aches for Sloan. The one person in this world she loves doesn't have the capacity to express his love in return. No wonder she seems so lonely. She's probably the loneliest person I've ever met.

"Stephen, there's someone I'd like you to meet," she says, pointing in my direction. "That's my friend Carter. We go to school together."

Stephen looks at me, but then looks back at the TV just as quick.

Sloan pats the couch next to her, requesting me to come sit by her. I walk over and sit down, watching her interact with him. She begins pulling things out of her purse. Nail clippers, paper, a pen, a soda. She talks to him the whole time, telling him about the drive over and giving him her thoughts on the new resident she noticed next door.

"You want ice?" she asks.

I glance at Stephen, but he gives no indication that he wants ice. Sloan points in the kitchen area. "Carter, will you make a glass of ice for him? And get the blue straw out of the top left-hand drawer?"

I nod and go to the kitchen to make his cup of ice. I notice she grabs a pen and starts writing something down. She slides the paper over to Stephen and he instantly looks at it, grabs the pen, and leans forward to write something in return.

He can read and write? She didn't mention that.

When I'm finished with the cup of ice, I walk back to the living room and hand it to her. She finishes writing something else and hands the paper back to Stephen, then pours his soda into the glass. As soon as she sticks the straw in it, Stephen grabs it out of her hand and begins drinking it. He hands her back the paper and she hands it to me. I read what she wrote first.

Books made out of jellybeans get really sticky when you wear furry gloves.

I read what Stephen wrote next. His writing isn't as legible as hers, but I can make out what it says.

Baskets of lizards on my head break the cotton in half for you.

I glance at Sloan and she shoots me a small smile. I recall our first day in class together when I saw her doing this for the first time. She said it was just a game she plays sometimes. I guess this is what she meant. She plays it on Sundays with Stephen.

"Can he read almost anything?" I ask her.

She shakes her head. "He doesn't really comprehend. I taught him how to read and write when we were younger, but stringing full thoughts together has never been something I've seen him do on paper. It's his favorite game to play."

I look over at Stephen. "Can I write something, Stephen?" I reach out for the pen and he hands it to me, but he still doesn't look at me. I press it to the paper.

Your sister is amazing and you're very lucky to have her.

I hand Sloan the paper and she reads it before handing it to Stephen. She blushes and nudges me in the shoulder, then passes the pen and paper off to him.

And that's what we do for the next ten pages. Stephen and Sloan write random words back and forth, and I just write down a bunch of compliments about Sloan.

*Your sister has great hair. I especially love it
when she curls it.
Did you know your sister cleans up after several men
who don't know how to lift a damn finger? And no
one has probably ever told her thank you. Thank you,
Sloan.
Your sister's ring finger looks beautiful and bare today.
I like your sister. A lot.*

After about an hour, a nurse comes in and interrupts the game
to take Stephen to physical therapy.

"Is the social worker in today?" Sloan asks.

The nurse shakes her head. "Not on Sundays. But I'll leave a
note in her box when he's finished with therapy so she'll know to
contact you tomorrow."

Sloan tells her that would be great and then she walks over
to give Stephen a hug. When she's finished with her goodbye, I'm
honestly not sure what to do. I don't want to pretend I'm an expert
at interacting with individuals like Stephen, but I also don't want to
do something I shouldn't do.

"Does he shake hands?" I ask Sloan.

She shakes her head. "He doesn't really let anyone but me
touch him." She slips her hand through mine.

"It was nice meeting you, Stephen," I say to him. Sloan grabs
her purse and we begin to walk out of the room so the nurse can
do what she needs to do to prepare him for therapy. When we're
almost to the door, I feel a tap on my shoulder. I turn around to find
Stephen standing in front of me, eyes on the floor, rocking back and
forth on his heels. He hands me the pen and a blank sheet of paper.
I take it from him, not really knowing how to tell him we're leaving
and we can't keep playing.

I glance at Sloan to see what she wants me to do, and I'm
confused by her expression. Stephen walks back into the living
room, away from us. I look down at the blank sheet of paper and
pen.

"He wants you to come back," she whispers. When I glance up at her again, she's smiling, shaking her head back and forth. "I've never seen that happen before, Carter." She covers her mouth with her hand and lets out a mixture of what could be both a laugh and a cry. "He likes you."

I look back at Stephen and his back is to us now. When I look back at Sloan, she stands on her tiptoes and kisses me, then leads me out of the room. I fold up the paper and slip it and the pen in my back pocket.

I don't know what I was expecting today, but it certainly wasn't that.

I'm glad I came, but now it's not only because of Sloan.

THIRTY-ONE

Asa

I remember this being a hell of a lot more fun last month.

I double down on the bet and run my hand through my hair, squeezing the back of my neck. I'm hungry. I look over at Kevin and Dalton who are engrossed in conversation with some bartender who looks more like a girl Jon would take behind the building than either of them would entertain.

The only reason why Jon probably *isn't* fucking her behind the building right now is because he left with two lot lizards from the truck stop next door. Probably took them to the men's room. Which surprises me that he was even able to do *that* with the way his face is puffed up like a fucking blueberry.

He should be back by now, though, because I'm pretty sure he can't last more than two minutes with a chick. There were two of them. That's only four minutes, but I haven't seen him in over an hour.

Where the hell is he?

I look around, and when I don't see him in the vicinity, I cash out my chips. I yell across the table—*over the obnoxious fucking slot machine bells*—and tell Dalton and Kevin I'm going to look for Jon. Dalton nods.

I make it to the other side of the casino without finding him. I turn back and walk past a blackjack table when my eyes fall on a guy slurring something to the dealer. "Every time I come to this goddamn casino, I see the same miserable motherfuckers hunched over these tables, handing over their hard-earned wages to you goddamn motherfuckers and you just keep taking. Taking, taking, taking."

The dealer scoops the chips out from in front of the guy. A man across the table says, "And nine times out of ten that miserable motherfucker is you."

I laugh and make eye contact with the man who just spoke.

I stop laughing.

He glances away from me without even a flash of recognition.

The guy doing the complaining pushes his stool away from the table and stands. He points at the guy I'm staring at and says, "You got lucky, Paul. That's all. Won't last."

I'm clenching my fists so hard, I'm drawing blood. I can feel it seeping out of my palm.

I didn't even have to hear his name confirmed to know it was him. A son doesn't forget his father.

No matter how easy it was for that father to forget his son.

I turn my back to him and wipe the blood from my hand onto the leg of my jeans. I pull my phone out and do a quick Google search. After a few minutes of scrolling through the results and glancing back and forth from him to my phone, I finally find what I'm looking for.

The motherfucker was paroled last year.

I slide my phone into my pocket and walk over to the empty seat across from him. I've never been this tense, but it isn't because I'm scared of what he'll do to me anymore. I'm tense because I'm scared of what I want to do to *him*. I lay down my bet and try not to make it obvious that I'm staring, but he isn't paying me any attention. He's focused on the dealer.

His hair is so thin, he might even be considered bald if it weren't for the last few strands he's pathetically holding on to. I run my hand through my hair. It feels as thick as it always has.

Maybe he lost his hair because of stress and it isn't hereditary. God I hope nothing about this man is hereditary; he looks like a fucking waste of space.

I remember my father being much taller. Much broader. Much more intimidating. I'm a little disappointed.

Actually, I'm a lot disappointed. I've always hated the motherfucker, but the memories I have of him made me think he was invincible. Which made me feel like maybe I got a little of that from him. But seeing how he's turned out really puts a fucking wrinkle in my pride.

"Hey, kid," he says, snapping his bony fingers. "You got a smoke?"

My eyes meet his and he's staring at me, trying to bum a cigarette off of his only fucking child, and he doesn't even recognize me. Not even a little bit.

"I don't fucking smoke, asshole."

He chuckles and holds up a hand, palm out. "Whoa, there, buddy. Bad day?"

He thinks that was me having an attitude? I turn a chip over in my fingers and lean forward. "You could say that."

He shakes his head and we're silent for the next round of bets. An older chick with tits more wrinkled than my old man's knuckles sidles up next to him and puts her arm around him. "I'm ready to go," she whines.

He sticks his elbow out to shove her off of him and says, "I'm not. I told you I'd find you when I'm ready."

She whines some more until he pulls a twenty out of his pocket and tells her to go play some penny slots. When she's gone, I nudge my head in her direction. "That your wife?"

He chuckles again. "No. Fuck no."

I flip my first card over. It's a ten of hearts. "You ever been married?" I ask him.

He brings his hand up to his neck and pops it, but doesn't look at me. "Once. Didn't last long."

Yeah, I know. I was there.

"Was she a whore?" I ask him. "Is that why you aren't married to her anymore?"

He laughs and makes eye contact with me again. "Yeah. Yeah, she was."

I blow out a slow breath, then flip over my second card. An ace of clubs.

Blackjack.

"I'm getting married," I say. "But she's not a whore."

I don't think I'm making any sense to him, because he tilts his head and his eyes narrow a little. Then he leans forward and taps the edge of the table. "Let me give you a piece of advice, son."

"Don't call me *son*."

He pauses for a second and I recognize a flash of the condescending look he used to give. Then he says, "They're *all* whores. You're young, don't settle down. Enjoy your life."

"I *do* fucking enjoy my life. I enjoy it a whole fucking bunch."

He shakes his head and then mutters, "You're the angriest son of a bitch I've ever met."

He's right. I am.

I've never been angrier than I am in this moment.

I want to climb across this table and shove my cards down his throat, despite the fact that it's a winning hand.

The dealer pushes my winnings in front of me, but I stand up and walk away before I do something stupid inside a building full of security cameras and security guards.

"Sir!" The dealer calls after me. "You can't walk away from your chips!"

"Keep the fucking chips!"

I walk as fast as I can from one side of the casino to the other. I finally find Jon, flanked by the two lot lizards at a fucking pussy-ass Wheel of Fortune game.

"Go find Dalton and Kevin. We're leaving."

I walk toward the exit and as soon as I shove open the doors, I bend forward, gasping for breath.

I'm not like him.

I'm *nothing* like him.

He's pathetic. He's weak. He's fucking *bald*, for Christ's sake!

My hands are shaking.

"Hey!" I get the attention of a man who just exited. "Can I bum one of those?"

He puts his cigarette in his mouth to reach into his pocket for another one. He hands it to me, then offers me a lighter. I light it and mutter thanks, then inhale a long drag of it. I'm still pacing when the guys finally make it outside.

But not far behind them, I see him, the wrinkled-tit lot lizard flanked to his arm. They're making their way toward the exit.

"Let's go," Jon says, once they're all outside.

I shake my head and don't take my eyes off my father. "We'll leave in a second."

I continue staring at them as they walk toward the exit. Once they push through the doors and are outside, his eyes land on me. He notices the cigarette in my mouth as he passes me.

"I thought you said you didn't smoke."

"I don't," I say, blowing smoke toward him. "This is my first."

Again with the condescending looks. They're the same condescending looks he used to give me when I was a kid, only this time they aren't served up with a beating.

From his end, anyway.

They keep walking, and when they're about five feet away, I say, "You have a lovely afternoon, Paul Jackson."

My father stops walking, waiting a few seconds before turning around. When he finally does, I see it. The recognition. He cocks his head and says, "I never told you my name."

I shrug and then drop my cigarette to the concrete, snuffing it out with the heel of my shoe. "My bad. Guess I should have said *Dad*."

There's no second-guessing whether that's recognition on his face now. "Asa?" He takes a step forward, but that was his second mistake.

His *first* was not remembering me to begin with.

I stride over to him and come down on him with both fists. The pathetic fuck hits the ground before I even follow through with a full swing. I can feel one of the guys trying to pull me off of him. The bitch is screaming in my ear, scratching at my face, trying to get me off of him.

I punch him again. I punch him for every year he left me alone. I punch him for every time he called my mother a whore. I punch him for every piece of fucked up advice he ever gave me. I keep punching him until my fists are covered in blood and I can no longer see my father's face. There's so much blood, I'm pretty sure I even mistake the concrete for his head, because that punch hurts the worst.

When the guys finally pull me off him and start dragging me toward the car, I feel the wet shit on my face. The shit my father told me is what makes the difference between men and pussies.

Yes, I'm talking about tears. I can feel them and I can't fucking stop them and I've never felt so powerful and so weak in my whole fucking life.

I have no idea how I make it to the passenger seat, or who even put me here, but I'm fucking beating the dashboard, punching it so hard it cracks. Kevin is peeling out of the parking lot, I'm sure trying to beat security before they find the bloody mess I left at their front entry.

Jon reaches around my seat and tries to pull my arms behind me, but he's stupider than I thought if he thinks he can hold me back. I tear my arms from his grip and start punching the dash again. I'll punch it until my hands are numb or this shit stops coming out of my fucking eyes.

I'm not turning into him. I'm not fucking turning into that pathetic bastard.

I don't want to feel this anymore.

"Somebody fucking give me something!" I yell.

It feels like my bones are trying to tear through my skin. I pull at my hair, I punch the fucking window. "I can't fucking breathe!"

Kevin rolls down the window, but it doesn't help.

"*Give* me something!" I yell again. I turn around and try to grab Jon, but he leans back and lifts his fucking leg up like that'll protect him from me. "Now!"

"It's in the trunk!" Jon yells. "Christ, Kevin! Pull over so we can calm him the fuck down!"

I turn around and punch at the dash again. Several punches later, Jon returns to the back seat. "Give me two seconds," he says.

He's a fucking liar, because it's more like ten seconds before he hands me the needle. I pull the cap off with my teeth and shove it in my arm.

I lean back in my seat.

"Go," I say to Kevin.

I close my eyes and feel the car begin to move.

I am nothing like him.

And they are not all whores. Sloan is not a whore.

"She's heroin," I whisper. "Heroin is nice."

THIRTY-
TWO

Carter

"What are you hungry for?" I ask her.

She wanted me to drive back, so I've been looking for a restaurant for the last five miles.

"I don't care," she says. "Anything but Greek."

"You don't like Greek food?"

She shrugs. "It's okay. There's just not a Greek restaurant until the next town and I'm hungry. If you wanted Greek, I'd have to wait too long to eat."

I laugh. She's so goddamn adorable. I reach over to take her hand, but receive an incoming text. I normally wouldn't text and drive, especially with Sloan in the car, but Dalton said he'd warn me if they decided to come back early.

And sure enough, the text is from Dalton.

Dalton: Time for you to head back. Asa's not in good shape.

Oh, shit. Did my death wish curse him earlier?

Me: Were you guys in a car wreck?
Dalton: No. He just beat the shit out of his father
and he's having a major fucking breakdown.
Dalton: He keeps rambling about how Sloan better
be there by the time he gets back. Never seen him
like this, man.

I delete the texts and then set my phone back in the cup holder. I grip the steering wheel. "Sorry, but we can't stop and eat. Dalton says Asa had a breakdown and they're on their way back."

"A breakdown?" Sloan says.

"Yeah, something about his father? Apparently he beat him up at the casino."

Sloan looks out the window. "His father is alive?"

I glance over at her. She doesn't know about his father being charged for murder? I guess it makes sense that Asa wouldn't tell her. That's not really something you would want your girlfriend to know.

"He doesn't know you're with me. We don't have to get back before them. I'm hungry," she says.

I hate that I'm forcing her to go back home when she needs to stay the hell away from there. "Dalton says he's adamant that you be there. Apparently he's in pretty bad shape."

She sighs. "That's not my problem. Why does Dalton know you're with me, anyway? I don't trust Dalton. Or Jon. Or Kevin."

"Don't worry. I trust Dalton with my life." I reach over and take her hand, pulling it onto my lap. "I'll park at my car and then come over later tonight. I think there should be some distance between you getting home and me showing up."

She nods, but she doesn't say anything else on the drive home. We're both dreading the inevitable, which is coming face-to-face with an unstable Asa Jackson. He's bad enough when he's in a *good* mood. I don't even want to think of how he's going to treat Sloan tonight.

When we reach my car, I look around to make sure I don't see anyone. I parked a couple miles from her house and then walked the rest of the way this morning.

Before I get out of the car, I pull her to me and kiss her. She kisses me back with a sigh and it's kind of sad. Like she's tired of saying goodbye like this.

"How come it seems every time we take a step forward, we're forced to take ten steps back?" she asks.

I push a strand of hair off her forehead. "We'll just have to start taking bigger steps forward."

She forces a smile and then says, "I hate that I won't get to talk to you when you come over tonight. Or touch you."

I kiss her forehead. "Me, too," I say. "We should have a sign we can use in place of being able to talk tonight. Something subtle that only we'll notice."

"Like what?"

I lift my hand and rub my thumb across my bottom lip. "That's mine," I tell her.

She crinkles up her nose while she tries to think of one.

"You should twirl a strand of hair around your finger," I suggest. "I like it when you do that."

She smiles. "Okay. If you see me doing that it means I wish I could be alone with you." She pulls at a strand of her hair and twirls it around her finger.

I lean forward and kiss her, then force myself out of her car. I wait until she drives away before texting Dalton again.

Me: Don't let him alone with her before I get there. I'm scared of what he might do.

Dalton: Noted. Not sure what's going on with him. He shot up, slept for ten minutes, now he's talking incessantly. He keeps saying he wants spaghetti and that his hair is really thick. He's not making any sense. He even made Kevin run his hand through his hair.

Fuck. He's already unpredictable. This isn't good.

Me: Let me know as soon as you all get back. I'll wait an hour and then head that way.

Dalton: Good idea. BTW, he just looked at me and said you were LSD. What do you think that means?

Me: No fucking clue.

Dalton: He said, "Carter causes the worst hallucinations and he's hard to fucking locate. He's LSD."

Me: He's out of his fucking mind.

THIRTY-THREE

Sloan

My phone is ringing as soon as I walk through the front door. I glance down at the screen and see that it's Asa. *Great.*

I slide my thumb across the screen to answer it. "Hey."

"Hey, baby," he says. He sounds like he just woke up, but I can tell he's still in a car. "Are you home?"

"Yep. Just walked in the door. Are you still at the casino?"

"Nope," he says. "On our way back."

So I heard.

"We're hungry. We want spaghetti. Can you cook some?"

"I have a lot of homework to do. Wasn't really planning on cooking tonight."

He sighs and says, "Yeah, well, I wasn't really planning on craving spaghetti."

"Sounds like we have a dilemma," I say, uninterested.

"Not to me. Make some fucking spaghetti, Sloan. *Please.* I'm having kind of a bad day, here."

I close my eyes and fall onto the couch. This is going to be a long night. I might as well make it as easy on myself as possible.

"Okay. I'll make you spaghetti. Would you like meatballs with that, dear?"

"I would love meatballs. We want meatballs, right, guys?"

I hear a couple of the guys in the car mutter, "Sure."

I kick my legs up on the arm of the couch and put the phone on speaker, resting it on my chest. "Why are you having a bad day?"

It's quiet for a minute, and then Asa says, "Have I ever told you about my father, Sloan?"

"No."

He sighs. "Exactly. There's nothing to fucking tell."

Jesus. What in the hell did that man do to him? I rub my fingers against my temples. "When will you be back?"

Asa doesn't answer my question. Instead, he says, "Is Carter there?"

I immediately sit up on the couch. Blame the paranoia, but my voice grows a little weaker. I try to hide it when I say, "No, Asa. He's with you."

There's a short pause. "No, Sloan. He *isn't*."

The phone grows even quieter, and when I look down at it, I realize he hung up. I press the phone to my forehead. *What does he know?*

An hour later, they all walk through the front door. I'm not finished with the spaghetti yet because I had to go to the store to get the damn noodles. Asa walks into the kitchen, and I gasp when I look up at him. His shirt is covered in blood and his fist is almost unrecognizable. I immediately rush to the first aid kit in the pantry. "Come here," I tell him, directing him to the sink.

I run water over his hand, trying to find where the blood is coming from, but it seems like it's coming from everywhere. His whole fist looks like raw flesh. My stomach turns, but I force myself to finish cleaning it so I can bandage it up and not have to look at it.

"What in the hell did you *do*, Asa?"

He winces and looks down at his hand. Then he shrugs. "Not enough."

I put ointment all over his hand and then wrap it, but that's hardly going to help. He probably needs stitches. Several stitches.

I feel his hand clamp tightly around mine, and my eyes dart up to his.

"Where's your fucking ring?"

Shit.

"On the dresser. I didn't want to get it dirty while I cooked."

He stands up and yanks my arm, pulling me toward the stairs. I can feel the pull all the way up to my neck. "Asa, stop!"

He doesn't let go of me, and when he drags me behind him, through the living room, Dalton stands up. "Asa," he says.

Asa still doesn't stop. I have to run just to keep up with him as he takes the stairs two at a time, so I don't fall down. He swings the bedroom door open and grabs my ring off the dresser, pulling my left hand up between us. "You keep your fucking ring on your hand. That's why I bought it for you, so people would know they can't mess with you."

He slaps my hand on the dresser and then opens the top drawer, holding my hand down flat with his.

"What are you doing?" I ask, fearing the answer. He opens the second drawer and rifles through it.

"Helping you remember never to take it off," he says, grabbing a tube and slamming the dresser drawer shut. My eyes land on the bottle of super glue in his hand.

The hell he is.

I try to yank my hand back, but he uses even more force to hold down my wrist. He pulls the cap off the super glue and starts squirting it on my finger, spreading it under my ring.

The tears begin stinging at my eyes. I've never seen him like this and I don't want to push things even more. I stop fighting and stand as still as I can, aside from my heart racing in my chest. Carter isn't here, and I'm honestly too scared to fight back right now because I'm not sure that any of those guys downstairs would come to my defense.

Asa tosses the super glue on the dresser and lifts my hand, then blows on it to dry the glue. He stares at me the whole time he's blowing on my finger. His eyes are black. Huge and black and terrifying.

"You finished?" I whisper. "I don't want to overcook your spaghetti."

He blows on my hand for a few more seconds and then leans in and kisses my palm. "All done. Now you won't forget."

He's crazy. He's fucking crazy. I think I've always known he wasn't a great person, but I had no idea how crazy he was until looking at his eyes just now.

Asa follows me out of the bedroom and down the stairs. Dalton is standing at the base of the stairs, and I can see the concern in his eyes.

I still don't trust him.

I walk back into the kitchen and straight to the stove. I pull the noodles off the burner and begin pouring them into the strainer just as a car pulls up in the driveway.

Carter.

I finish straining the noodles, staring down at my ring the whole time.

It's not even straight. It'll be a bitch peeling off the super glue and will probably take me days. The least the asshole could have done was make sure he glued it on straight. It's going to drive me crazy.

I make sure not to look at the front door when it opens. I go back to the stove and stir the spaghetti sauce, then check the meatballs in the oven. Asa is washing blood off his arms at the sink when Carter walks into the kitchen and opens the refrigerator.

"What happened to you?" Carter says.

I can't make out what Asa says, thanks to the pulse still pounding in my ears, but Carter laughs. "You guys win any jackpots?"

I turn around and walk to the sink, catching a glimpse of Carter out of the corner of my eye.

Asa shakes his head and says, "Not a goddamn thing. Not like that jackpot you had wrapped around you Friday night."

It feels like all the blood completely leaves my heart. I can't look at Carter right now. I can't. Either Asa is testing me to see if I react to that statement, or Carter isn't at all who I thought he was.

"She was a mother-fucking firecracker," Asa adds. "Good job, man. I was definitely impressed."

I walk to the oven to check on the meatballs, but only so I can get a glimpse of Carter's face. He takes a sip of his beer, not making eye contact with me. "She's just a friend," he says.

I have to grip the oven door with all my strength, because it feels like I'm about to crash to the floor.

What girl? When? Friday night was when Carter came to my room and kissed me. How in the world did I not know he was here with someone else?

I feel like more of a fool in this moment than I've ever felt dating Asa. At least I've always known Asa is an asshole.

I honestly thought Carter was different.

"A friend my ass," Asa says. "Do you hump Dalton against the living room wall like that? Jon? Where I come from, friends don't do that to friends, my man."

I pull the meatballs out of the oven and am forced to walk the long way around the island back to the stove, just to avoid either of them seeing the tears in my eyes. A few seconds later, I feel Asa's arm slip around my waist. He kisses my neck, and fuck if I don't turn around and plant my mouth on his. As much as I hate him and as much as I want to cut his dick off for what he just did to me upstairs, this kiss isn't at all about him.

I want Carter to feel what I just felt. Like there's a huge gash in my chest.

Fucking bastard. They're all fucking bastards.

I pull away from Asa. "You're making it hard to concentrate. You guys get out of the kitchen so I can finish cooking."

I have no idea how I'm able to speak, because each of my words wants to turn to sobs. I drop all the meatballs into the sauce, and as I'm pouring the noodles in, Dalton walks in the kitchen.

"Christ, Asa. Go take a fucking shower. We'll all lose our appetite if we have to stare at all that blood while we eat."

I use Dalton's distraction to glance over at Carter. He's staring right at me, his eyes full of concern. It's like he's trying to tell me a million things right now. He lifts his hand and runs his thumb over his bottom lip.

I don't twirl my hair around my finger. Instead, I rub my mouth with my middle finger and then turn to face Asa. He pushes my hair over my shoulder. "You should come shower with me. It'll be kind of hard to do it one-handed."

I shake my head. "Later. I have to finish cooking."

Asa runs his fingers down my arm, sliding them over my hand and over my ring. He turns and walks out of the kitchen. Dalton follows him. As soon as I'm alone with Carter, he's rushing across the kitchen toward me. He stops when he reaches me and comes as close as he can without it looking suspicious. I grip the counter in front of me and don't look up at him.

"It wasn't like that, Sloan. I swear. You have to trust me."

His words come out in a rushed, desperate whisper.

I don't look at him when I say, "You were making out with another *girl*?" I slowly turn my head and make eye contact, and I can almost swear he's about to risk getting caught and pull me to him.

He starts shaking his head. "I wouldn't do that to you. It wasn't like that."

His words are slow and precise this time. Everything about him makes me want to trust what he's saying, but everything about every single male from my past tells me never to trust anyone with a dick.

He glances around to make sure no one can see us. All the guys in the living room have their backs to us and they're facing the TV.

Carter leans in and squeezes my wrist. "I would never do anything to hurt you. Ever. I swear on your brother's life, Sloan."

And that's when I *really* get angry. No one swears on my brother's life. It's over before I even realized I did it. I slapped him so hard, all the guys in the living room turned around in their seats.

I can't believe I just slapped him. I can't tell who's more shocked by it. Me, him or all the guys who are now staring at us. I'm more hurt than I've probably ever been in my life, but I'm still smart enough to know I need to cover up the fact that I just slapped him so it doesn't appear personal. "Don't dip your finger in the spaghetti sauce, asshole! That's disgusting!"

Carter immediately realizes what I'm doing. He forces a laugh and rubs his cheek, but I can see the disappointment in his eyes as he turns and walks toward the living room. I don't feel bad for him. My brother and I have had enough bad luck. The last thing we need is for Carter to be telling lies and making empty promises while swearing on Stephen's life.

I spin around and I stir the fucking spaghetti. I pause to wipe tears away with the sleeve of my shirt, and then I start stirring again. A minute later, Dalton appears at my side and reaches across me. He grabs a spoon and dips it in the sauce, then puts the spoon in his mouth to taste it. He nods and then tosses the spoon in the sink, right before leaning into me. "He's telling you the truth, Sloan."

He walks away, and that's when I can't control the tears any longer. I don't know what to believe. Who to trust. Who to be mad at, who to love. I go to the sink and wash spaghetti sauce off my hands.

I need out of this house.

I walk to the back door and yell over my shoulder. "Your fucking spaghetti is ready, you goddamn asshole motherfuckers!"

THIRTY-FOUR

Carter

I rinse out the last of the bowls and place them in the dishwasher.

Asa never made it down to eat. Sloan never came back inside. I texted Dalton a few minutes ago and asked him to go upstairs and check on the status of Asa before I risk going outside and talking to Sloan.

I wipe down the countertop and start the dishwasher. I hear Dalton coming down the stairs at the same time I get a text from him.

> **Dalton: He's passed out naked on his bed. Looks like he'll be that way for a while, but I'll text you if he starts to come downstairs. Make sure your phone is on.**

I double and triple check the sound and vibrate settings on my phone, then slide it in my pocket. I head outside to smooth things over with Sloan.

She's in the middle of the swimming pool, floating on her back, staring up at the stars. She doesn't look at me when she hears the back door shut.

As I'm making my way toward her, I notice her shirt and jeans are thrown over a lounge chair.

Fucking hell.

She's swimming in her underwear.

That may be normal practice for her around here, but it just feels like I'm stepping on a landmine by being out here while she's not technically in a bathing suit.

I reach the edge of the pool and stare down at her, but she still won't look at me. The water is covering most of her face, but with the light from inside the house, I'm able to see the redness in her eyes.

It's kind of fucked up if you think about it. She's upset that I might be messing with other people, but all the while she's sleeping in another man's bed every night.

Hell, she fucking *kissed* him just to spite me earlier.

But I get it. And I don't blame her, because I know how much she was hurting. How much she is hurting.

And that's the hardest part of this. It's not that I'm about to have to convince her that I really do have feelings for her. The hardest part is knowing what she feels right now as she doubts them.

If I could just come out and tell her the whole truth, it would make things so much easier. But that's a violation of my job. It would be disobeying a direct order from Ryan. And as unstable as Asa is right now, the less Sloan knows, the better.

When Asa mentioned Tillie in the kitchen, the color completely drained from Sloan's face. I could have killed him right then and there.

Sloan fans her arms out and kicks her legs, giving herself a push back toward the middle of the pool. "He forgot to turn off the pool heater this weekend," she says quietly. "It feels really good. I think I might just stay here forever."

Her voice is sad. I want to kick off my shoes and dive in the water and stay there *with* her forever. Just not in this pool or at this house.

"What's her name?" she asks, still quiet and staring at the night sky.

I squeeze the back of my neck, wondering how much I should actually reveal. "Tillie."

She laughs, but not because she finds it entertaining. "Is she your girlfriend?"

I sigh. "She's just a friend, Sloan. Sometimes she does favors for me."

Sloan's whole body sinks under the water. She sinks all the way to the bottom. When she emerges, she's shooting daggers at me. It isn't until I see the look on her face that I realize what I just implied.

I bring my hands up behind my head. "Not *those* kinds of favors, Sloan. Jesus."

She pushes her wet hair off her forehead and I try not to look at any other part of her other than her face, but it's really fucking difficult when she's soaking wet.

"What favor was she doing for you Friday night that required you to have your hands all over her?"

I hate how calm she is because I know she's raging on the inside. Which means she's likely to explode any minute now. I feel like the edge of this pool is the edge of a volcano.

"Answer me. What favor was she doing for you Friday night?" she repeats.

I answer honestly. "She was helping me to try and convince Asa that I'm not interested in fucking you."

I don't have to be staring at her chest to notice her gasp. She tries to hide it, though. She stares at me for a moment and then dips under the water again. She swims to the shallow end and then stands up and walks out of the pool. Both her bra and underwear are nude, completely see-through, and making me paranoid as fuck. I'm half-afraid Asa will be able to hear my pulse from his room.

Sloan continues walking around the pool until she's standing right in front of me. Even then, she steps closer. So close, I can feel the wetness from her bra pressing against my chest.

"*Are* you? Interested in fucking me?"

Jesus Christ. What is she doing?

I fight my own hands as they slide to her hips. "Not really," I say, my voice rough. "I'm much more interested in making love to you."

She's breathing heavily now, but nothing compared to me. I want to fucking kiss her so bad, but it would definitely be the kiss of death, because I would never stop.

That, or she'd kill me if I tried. I can't tell if she's still angry with me or not. She acts like she wants me to touch her—to kiss her. But she's looking at me like she wants to throw me in the pool and hold my head underwater.

She slides her hand to her hip, covering my hand with hers. She wraps her fingers around mine and then drags my hand slowly across her stomach and up to her breast.

I swallow hard and glance up at her bedroom window. "What are you doing, Sloan?"

She leans in and stands on her toes until her breasts are pressed against me. I close my eyes and slip one of my hands around to her lower back. My fingertips dip into the back of her underwear and I pull her to me.

Her lips meet my ear, and she whispers, "Do you get a promotion if you make it to third base with your subject's fiancée?"

My eyes pop open.

I carefully thread my fingers through her hair, tugging her head back so I can look down at her. "You aren't making any sense, Sloan."

She smiles, but the betrayal in her eyes is much more evident. "I know what you are," she says. "I know what you're doing here. And now it all makes sense why you're so interested in me."

She pulls away from me, stepping back until my hands are no longer on her. She's shooting daggers at me with her eyes. "Don't fucking speak to me ever again or I'll tell every last one of them you're undercover. Luke."

She tries to walk past me, but I immediately step in front of her and cover her mouth with my hand. She tries to scream and my eyes flick to the back door. No one has seen us yet, but I need to get her somewhere more private before she does something to get us both killed.

She tries to pull my hand away, clawing at it with her fingernails. I wrap my arms around her and force her to walk to the side of the house with me. She gets even angrier when she realizes what I'm doing, so she starts fighting me with all her strength. I hate having to use this much force on her, but it's for her own protection. When I finally get her to the side of the house, behind the protective shield of trees, I push her against the wall and keep my hand over her mouth.

"Stop, it Sloan," I say, looking her dead in the eyes. "*Listen* to me. Be quiet and listen to me. *Please.*"

She's breathing heavily against my hand, gripping my wrist with both of hers. When she finally stops struggling, I press one hand against the house beside her head and I slowly begin to remove the other from her mouth.

She's panting with fear by the time I put my other hand beside her head. I press my forehead to hers. "Everything I've ever said to you. Every look I've given you. Every time I've touched you. It was never for the job, Sloan. Not one fucking time. Do you understand that?"

She doesn't respond.

I wince, because I hate that I've put her in this position. I hate that she even doubts me. I hate that I've given her all the reason in the world to. And I hate that I don't know a single goddamn thing I could say to make her believe what I feel for her.

I lean in and kiss the side of her head, then I lower my arms and wrap them around her.

I don't try to convince her with more words.

I don't feed her apologies that are way too late.

I just hug her, because I can't stand to know she's feeling what she's feeling.

After several moments of being frozen stiff in my arms, she slowly begins to relax. Her hands come up and fist my shirt, and she begins to melt against me. She presses her face against my chest and starts crying, so I cradle her as tight as I can.

I squeeze my eyes shut and whisper in her damp hair. "You're all I see, Sloan. Beyond the job, beyond right and wrong. You're all I see."

I press my lips to the side of her head, and when I feel her mouth press against my neck, I pull her closer. She's still gasping for breath, probably a combination of fear, anger, and our current proximity. We find each other in the dark, and when our lips finally meet, it's as if she's silently begging me to kiss away her doubts.

I do. Our mouths war in desperation. I push her against the wall of the house again. Every second that passes is a second that never should have passed at all, but I can't stop what's happening. All I can think about is how I can get more of her.

When I press into her, she moans against my mouth, and that sound pushes away everything else. The anxiety, the common sense. My need for her completely takes over, and based on the way her hands are sliding inside my shirt, so does hers.

I'm in the fog and I don't see myself finding my way out of it anytime soon.

Fucking hell.

My mouth works its way down her neck. I bring one of my hands up to her breasts and slide it between her skin and her bra. I'm met with skin as smooth as silk. "God, Sloan," I whisper, dragging my mouth up her neck again. When I reach her lips, she dips her tongue in my mouth and her hands fall to the button of my jeans.

I lift one of her legs to my side. Then the other. "My car," I whisper, wrapping her around me.

It's dark enough outside and the property is encased with enough trees that I'm not worried about neighbors seeing us as we climb in my back seat. The only thing I'm worried about is the fact that her fiancé is inside the house and getting caught would mean...

I don't even want to think about that right now. Dalton hasn't texted me yet, so we've got time.

I shut the back door and reach over the front seat, grabbing a condom out of the glove box. When I fall back against the seat, she's sliding on top of me, mouth on mine, hands on my chest.

Down my chest.

I lift her bra over her breasts and work my mouth over her at the same time she frees me from my jeans.

Once I get the condom on, I grab her hips and position her on top of me while she pulls her panties aside. I lean my head back against the seat so I can watch her face as I enter her.

We make eye contact and I begin to lower her on top of me, slowly. Everything grows much quieter in the car as we both hold our breaths. My eyes never leave hers the whole time she's taking me in. When we're finally skin to skin and I'm fully inside her, we simultaneously release a sharp exhale.

"My God," I whisper.

It's the best thing I've ever felt—finally being inside her.

It's the *guiltiest* I've ever felt—knowing how much danger my lack of willpower is putting her in.

She leans forward and wraps her arms around my neck. "Luke," she breathes against my lips.

I fucking die.

She called me Luke.

My mouth finds hers again and I kiss her the way she deserves to be kissed. With conviction. With respect. With feeling.

She begins to move on top of me and she's all I see.

I close my eyes and she's all I fucking see.

THIRTY-FIVE

Sloan

I had no idea it could feel like this.

That sounds so cliché, even as I'm thinking it. But his hands, his mouth, the way he touches me—it's like my response is what he lives for.

And right now, the only thing I'm focused on is the way he's moving his hand against me, touching me in just the right place that I'm afraid I might not only wake Asa up, but the entire neighborhood. As if he can sense this, he covers my mouth with his, stifling my moans as I crush myself against him. My legs begin to shake, my arms, my whole body, as the greatest sensation I've ever felt slams through me.

"Luke," I moan against his lips.

As weak as I am in this moment, I find the strength to continue moving until I'm the one having to stifle *his* sounds. His mouth is incredible. He tastes like fruit. He tastes sweet.

Nothing like the bitterness I swallow when I kiss Asa.

When we're both no longer shaking, and I'm still on top of him, he leans forward and feathers his lips across my shoulder.

I don't know how I went from hating him two hours ago in the kitchen to feeling more for him in this moment than all the days before combined.

Knowing that he's not like Asa...that's he's the complete *opposite* of Asa...it's so...*attractive*.

He's good. He's a *good guy*. They actually exist.

It all came together like an epiphany while I was floating in the pool. Him calling himself by the wrong name. Him taking a Spanish class that is years beneath his ability, only to conveniently be in there with me. The way he continued to reassure me that I needed to trust him, but he would never say *why*. Using another girl as a decoy.

That was the kicker. I figured that one out before he even came clean at the pool.

When Dalton said Carter...or *Luke,* rather...was telling the truth, I knew there was more to it. More to her. More to him blatantly making out with someone else when he's in the same house as me. I told myself that if he came outside and denied ever being with her that I would know then that he's a liar. That he's just like Asa.

But if he came outside and told me the truth—that he was using her to throw Asa off—then I knew I was right. I had him pegged.

I just didn't know which one I preferred to hear. That he was just like Asa...or that he'd been using me this whole time.

As soon as he realized I had figured it out, I was expecting that to be the end of us. I thought he would fear for his job and try to cut some kind of deal with me to keep me quiet. Because guys like him...guys with careers, who are good and successful and kind... they don't fall for girls like me.

Or at least that's what I was raised to believe.

But I was wrong, because he's not worried about his job. When he says all he sees is me, I believe him. Because all I see is him. And right now I want to soak up every second of him.

His arms are wrapped around me and we're both just trying to catch our breath. This was stupid. We both know it, but right now I would say it was completely worth it.

"As much as I wish you could stay right where you are forever, you should go back inside," he says.

I know he's right, but I wish he wasn't. Inside is the last place I want to be after this. I run my fingers through his hair and can smell the fresh scent of shampoo. I bend forward and sniff his hair. "You showered? Before you came back to the house?"

He smiles, I can see it even in the dark.

"So you showered *and* you had condoms in your car? Were you expecting to get laid tonight?"

He drops his head against the headrest and a slow, satisfied grin stretches across his lips. "I showered because I like to look good for you. I have a condom in my car because I like to be prepared. And it's been there for six months, in case you're curious."

I was, but I don't have a right to be. He knows what still happens between Asa and me at night. If I could stop it I would, but it's just not an option right now. Not until I'm no longer in this house.

But we don't talk about that. About the fact that I'm still with Asa, and about how what just happened between Luke and me wasn't right, no matter how right it felt. But I honestly don't care that I just cheated on Asa. I should feel guilty, but I don't.

Karma's a bitch, Asa Jackson.

Luke runs his thumb over my arm and pushes down my bra strap. He dips his thumb under it, rubbing back and forth. "Sloan?"

I'm tracing his jaw. He has a great face. Masculine in all the right places, but a hint of soft femininity to his lips. "Yeah?"

"How did you figure it out?"

I grin. "You're all I see, Luke. And I'm really smart."

He nods. "Yes, you are." He presses his palms against my back and pulls me against him, but before his lips meet mine, my back hits the seat and he's hovering over me, covering my mouth with his hand. "Be still," he whispers, looking out the front window.

My heart feels like it climbs up my throat.

We're dead. We're dead.

We. Are. Dead.

I hear a heavy pounding against the window, but I'm not so sure it isn't just my heart. "Open the fucking door!"

I close my eyes, but feel Luke's mouth press against my ear. "It's just Dalton," he whispers. "Stay down."

I nod and cover myself with my arms as Luke sits up and opens the door. Something comes flying into the back seat, and Luke catches it in his arms. "What the fuck!" Luke says, gathering whatever Dalton just threw at him.

Dalton leans in through the door and looks at me. "Next time you two decide to sneak off and fuck, make sure you take your clothes with you."

Luke hands me my shirt and jeans that Dalton just threw at him. I frantically pull my shirt over my head, embarrassed that we were so careless.

"Is he awake?" Luke asks Dalton.

Dalton eyes him hard, saying so many things with that look that I don't even begin to understand. "No. But you need to leave before you get us both killed." Then Dalton turns and looks at me. "And you need to get back in the house before Carter gets *you* killed."

He stands up, and right before he slams the car door, he says, "We need to talk before you leave, Carter."

I'm struggling into my jeans and Luke reaches over to help me. I really should keep calling him Carter in my head, otherwise I'll likely slip up and call him Luke around Asa.

"Are you in trouble?" I ask him. I button my jeans and then straighten out my shirt. He slides a hand around to the nape of my neck.

"I'm *always* in trouble, Sloan. I wish I could tell you I'm good at my job, but I think this has proven that my priorities are a little out of line."

I laugh. "I personally think your priorities for the past half hour were spot-on."

He kisses me and says, "Go. Be careful."

I kiss him back, hard. And when I walk away from him this time, it doesn't hurt quite as much. Because now I have hope. Hope that he has a plan to get us out of this mess.

I smile the entire time I'm in the shower, because when I opened the back door and walked into a spotless kitchen, I knew without a doubt it had been Carter who cleaned it.

No one—and I mean *no* one—has ever lifted a finger to help me around this house. I'm not sure I've ever heard that cleaning is the way to a girl's heart, but based on my reaction, I'd say it's the way to mine. Because I nearly cried when I heard the dishwasher running.

That's really sad. Loading a dishwasher means more to me than an engagement ring? From the outside looking in, it would seem my priorities are way out of line, too.

But I much prefer them this way.

Asa is passed out on the bed when I walk into our bedroom. He's sprawled across the whole mattress, naked.

Great. I'm going to have to try and wake him up or roll him to his side of the bed, but he's way too heavy for me.

I walk around to his side of the bed and grab his arm and try pulling him across the mattress. He doesn't budge, but he does groan between snores.

Then...he *vomits.*

All over my damn comforter.

I close my eyes and try to remain calm. Of course he would ruin this beautiful night.

He continues vomiting between bouts of groaning, filling the room with an acidic smell. I rush to the desk and retrieve the trashcan, then I lean over him and lift his head so that he's vomiting into the trash can.

He throws up two more times and then finally, after a few minutes of calm, he opens his eyes. When he looks up at me, the terrifying look in his eyes from earlier is gone, replaced with a childlike innocence. "Thank you, baby," he mutters.

I place the trashcan back on the floor and then put my hand on the side of his head. "Asa, I need you to try and stand up. I need to take the comforter off the bed."

He rolls over, away from the vomit, and pulls a pillow to his chest, falling back to sleep almost immediately.

"Asa." I shake him, but he's out again.

I stand up and look around the room, trying to figure out how I'm going to do this without having to go downstairs and ask for help.

There's no way I can do this by myself, and I'm not about to sleep downstairs on the couch. Not with Jon here. I'm praying Dalton or Carter are still here, because letting Jon or Kevin know that Asa is out cold will not be doing me any favors when it comes to my safety.

To my relief, Carter and Dalton are standing at the door preparing to leave when I make it downstairs. Carter stands alert when he sees me.

"I need someone to help me lift Asa so I can change my comforter. He threw up everywhere."

Jon mutters, "Good luck with that," from the couch.

Carter glares in Jon's direction and then immediately starts to head to the stairs. I can see the disapproval in Dalton's eyes, but he begins to follow Carter as well.

When we all make it up to the bedroom, the stench is so bad, I'm forced to cover my nose to keep from gagging.

"Holy shit," Dalton mutters. He walks straight to a window and opens it. We all look down at Asa and I'm a little embarrassed for him that he's naked. But knowing Asa, he wouldn't care. And even if he did, it's no one's fault but his own that he's in this position.

Carter reaches down and tries to shake him awake. "Asa. Wake up."

Asa groans, but still doesn't wake up.

"What the hell did he take?" Carter asks, turning toward Dalton.

Dalton shrugs. "Hell if I know. I saw him chew a few pills on the way to the casino. Heroin on the way home."

Carter doesn't even hesitate when he leans forward and hooks Asa under the arms. He lifts him up and then stands, pulling Asa away from the bed.

I immediately gather the comforter and wad it up. I'm not even going to attempt to wash this one. I set it in the hallway and then change the sheets, just to be safe.

"Which side does he sleep on?" Carter asks, still holding him up beneath his arms. I point to Asa's side of the bed and Carter drags him over there. Dalton helps lift him back onto the bed and I pull another blanket out of the closet and cover him with it.

When I'm tucking it around him, Asa opens his eyes and looks up at me. He runs a hand over his face, wincing. "What's that smell?" he grumbles.

"You threw up on the bed."

He grimaces. "Did you clean it up?"

I nod and whisper, "Yeah. I changed the sheets. Go back to sleep."

He doesn't close his eyes. Instead, he lifts his hand and tugs at a strand of my hair. "You take such good care of me, Sloan."

I stare at him for a second—at this vulnerable version of him. And somehow, even with Carter standing in the room with me, I feel for him.

I can't *not* feel for him.

Asa isn't the way he is because he *chooses* to be. I feel like he is who he is because he was never shown how to be anything different.

For that, he'll always have my sympathy. He'll never have my heart, and he'll likely never even have my forgiveness.

But I can't help but give him my sympathy.

I start to stand up, but he reaches out and grabs my wrist, pulling me back down. I lower myself to my knees beside the bed and Asa wraps his hand over mine. His eyes are closed when he whispers, "One time, when I was five...I threw up on my bed. My father made me sleep in it. Said it'd teach me not to do it again." He releases a small laugh, but then his eyes squeeze together even tighter. "Guess the bastard was wrong about that, too," he mutters.

Oh, God.

My hand goes to my heart as I ache for the little boy in him.

I turn and look at Carter and Dalton, and they're looking at Asa with just as much pity as I am. When I turn back toward Asa, he's rolling onto his stomach, burying his face into his pillow.

He grips the pillow in both fists and presses his face against it so hard, I'm convinced he's trying to smother himself. His shoulders begin to shake as they roll forward into the pillow.

"Asa," I whisper, soothing a hand over his head.

He becomes a wreck of sobs. It's the kind of cry that is so deep and heart wrenching, it's not even accompanied by a sound.

Completely silent.

I've never seen Asa cry. I didn't even know he was capable of real tears.

He won't remember any of this tomorrow. He won't know if I left him here alone or crawled into bed and held him. I continue to sooth Asa's head as I glance up at Carter. Dalton is no longer in the room. It's just the three of us now.

Carter walks over to me and I can see equal amounts of sympathy in his eyes. He lifts his hand and runs it over my cheek, then bends forward and kisses me on the forehead.

He holds his lips there for several seconds before breaking away and walking toward the door. When he reaches the doorway, he turns around and stares at me for a moment. He lifts a hand and slowly runs his thumb over his bottom lip. My heart reaches out for him, but I stay planted on the floor, comforting Asa.

I lift my hand and pull at a strand of my hair, winding it around my finger. Carter's lips stretch into a ghost of a smile as he watches me for a few seconds longer, then closes the door.

I climb onto the bed, under the covers, and I wrap myself around Asa, soothing his tears until I'm convinced he's finally asleep.

But right before I drift off, I hear him whisper, "You better never fucking leave me, Sloan."

THIRTY-SIX

Asa

The first thing I see when I open the refrigerator is a bowl of leftover spaghetti. *Thank God.*

"See, Dad?" I whisper to no one. "She's a fucking godsend."

I put the spaghetti in the microwave and then walk over to the sink to splash water on my face. It feels like I slept with my head in the fucking toilet all night. Hell, based on the stench of the bedroom this morning, I probably did.

I lean over the counter, waiting for the spaghetti to finish heating up. I stare at the bowl as it rotates in circles inside the microwave.

I wonder if I killed him?

I doubt it. It's been almost a day since we left the casino. If he died, the police would have been here by now. And if he lived, I'm almost positive he won't press charges. He knows he deserved what I did to him.

The microwave beeps.

I pull the spaghetti out and grab a fork, then shove a bite into my mouth. I barely get it swallowed before I have to find the trashcan. I throw up twice, rinse out my mouth, and then force another bite of spaghetti into my mouth.

I'll push through this withdrawal like a motherfucker, because I am not turning out like that man.

I eat another bite of spaghetti and swallow it down with my bile.

Push through it, Asa.

The front door swings open and Sloan walks inside. I glance at the clock and notice it's barely after two. She's never home from school this early. Either she doesn't notice me standing in the kitchen or it's that time of the month and she's in a pissy mood, because she rushes straight up the stairs and to the bedroom.

Not a minute later, I hear her making a mess of the bedroom. Stuff falling to the floor. Her feet moving from one side of the room to the other. I stare up at the ceiling, wondering what the fuck she's doing. My head hurts too bad to go up and look for myself. I don't have to, because a few seconds later, she's storming down the stairs.

When she rounds the corner to the kitchen, my dick twitches in my pants. She's angry as hell and it's hot as fuck. I smile at her as she marches toward me.

Before I can even get a word out, she's in my face. She shoves a finger in my chest. "Where is the paperwork, Asa?"

Paperwork?

What the fuck is she talking about?

"What the fuck are you talking about?"

Her chest is heaving, and if she would just step a few inches closer, I would be able to feel it. "My brother's file!" she says. "Where is it, Asa?"

Oh. *That* paperwork.

I carefully place the bowl of spaghetti on the counter and then bring my arms up and fold them over my chest. "I don't know what you're talking about, Sloan."

She inhales a meticulous breath, exhales it with even more precision, and then spins around. She puts her hands on her hips, trying to find the strength to remain calm.

I knew if she ever found out what I did, she'd be pissed. Even so, I've never really given much thought as to how I'd talk my way out of it.

"Two years," she says, gritting her teeth. She spins back around and her eyes are full of tears.

Well, shit. I didn't mean to make her cry.

"For two years I thought you were paying for his care. You showed me the paperwork, Asa. The letters the state sent. The check stubs." She begins pacing back and forth. "The social worker thought I was an idiot today when I asked her if his benefits could ever be renewed. Do you know what she said to me, Asa?" She faces me again.

I shrug.

She takes a step forward, folding her arms over her chest. "She said, '*The benefits were never cancelled, Sloan. Stephen's care has never been private pay.*'"

Tears are streaming down her cheeks now. For the first time since she walked down here, I start to get a little uncomfortable that maybe I took it too far with this lie. She's angrier than I've ever seen her.

She can't leave me.

"Sloan." I take a step forward and put my hands on her shoulders. "Baby, listen. I had to do whatever I could to get you back. You *left* me. I'm sorry you're upset." I move my hands to her cheeks. "You shouldn't be mad about this, though. It took a lot of fucking effort and money on my part. If anything, you should be flattered that you're that important to me."

Her hands come up between mine and she pushes me away from her. "You fucking *asshole!*" she yells. "You forged an entire file to back up your lies, Asa! Monthly letters from the government! Who the fuck *does* that?"

She has no idea how much money I had to pay the fucker who sends those or she'd be thanking me right now.

She points at me from across the kitchen. "You trapped me. This whole time you made me think there was no way out."

I swallow the anger down. I take a step forward. *Did I really just hear her right?*

"I *trapped* you?"

She's so worked up, she's inhaling small gasps of breath. She wipes angrily at her tears and nods, lowering her voice. "Yes, Asa. You trapped me. I've been your fucking prisoner for the last two years, thinking my brother was about to have to go back to my worthless mother. All because you *knew* if you didn't have that to hold over my head, I would have left you."

She doesn't mean what she's saying. She's angry. She would never leave me. Yes, I lied to her. Yes, I paid a shit ton of money to make it look like her brother's benefits were cancelled. But it was a temporary fix. She would have come crawling back to me eventually if it weren't for that. I just made it easier on her.

"Is that what you think? That you've been a prisoner here?" I ask. "Do I not give you a place to sleep? Buy your groceries? Give you nice things? Allow you to go to college? Drive my cars?" I walk across the kitchen and don't slow down when I reach her. I walk her backward until she's pressed against the wall, my hands caging her in. "Don't you dare stand here—in *my* home—and imply that you didn't have every opportunity in the world to walk out that fucking door."

I push off the wall and point toward the living room. "Go. If you don't love me anymore, fucking *leave!*"

She would never leave. I know this, because if she left, that would mean she's been using me for my money these last two years. Using me as a sole means to support her goddamn waste-of-space brother. If that's the case, that would make her a whore by definition.

And I'm not marrying a fucking whore.

Sloan glances at the door and then looks back at me. She shakes her head, and I swear she smiles. "Goodbye, Asa. Enjoy your life."

She begins walking toward the front door. "I do enjoy my life, Sloan. I enjoy it a whole fucking bunch!"

I allow her to reach the front door before I walk after her. She's not even to the grass before I have my arm wrapped around her waist, my hand over her mouth. I turn her around and walk her back into the goddamn house she's so ungrateful for. I carry her straight up to the bedroom and kick open the door. I toss her onto the bed and she tries to scoot off and run around me.

How cute.

I grab her by the hair and swing her back to the bed. She screams, but I put a stop to that with my hand. I climb on top of her, covering her mouth with one hand and holding her wrists down with the other. There's not much I can do about her legs as she does her best to kick her way out from under me, but I have more strength in one finger than she does in her entire body. It feels more like she's tickling me than attempting to hurt me.

"Listen up, babe," I whisper, staring down at her. "If you try to insinuate that you don't love me, I'm going to be really upset. *Really* fucking upset. Because that would mean you've been pretending with me since the day you walked back through my door. That would mean you've been faking every orgasm, every kiss, every word you've ever spoken to me—simply for a monthly check. And if that were true, that would make you a whore, Sloan. Do you know what men like me do to whores?"

Her eyes are wide with fear. Hopefully that means I'm getting through to her. She's no longer attempting to kick her way out from under me, so that's a good sign.

"That was a question, babe. Do you *know* what men like me do to *whores*?"

A tear falls out of her eye as she shakes her head. I can feel the breath from her nostrils slamming against my hand; she's struggling so hard for more air.

I lower my mouth to her ear. "Please don't make me show you."

We lie like this for a few more moments, while I make sure my words are sinking in. I pull back and look down at her. Her expression hasn't changed, but now she's crying so hard against my hand, snot is coming from her nose. It's on my fucking hand now. I pull it away from her mouth and wipe it on the bed. Then I grab the sleeve of my shirt and I wipe her face clean.

Her lips are quivering. I don't know why I've never noticed how fucking attractive that is. I kiss her softly, closing my eyes while her lips tremble against mine. "Do you love me?" I carefully whisper the words against her mouth. "Or are you a whore?"

A shaky breath passes her lips. "I love you," she whispers. "I'm sorry. I was just upset, Asa. I don't like it when you lie to me."

I press my forehead to the side of her head and exhale. In a way, she's right. I probably should have never lied to her about her brother. But if she had been in my shoes, she'd have done the same thing.

"Don't ever get angry like that with me again, Sloan." I pull back and brush her hair out of her face. It's sweaty and sticks to my hand. I run my fingers through it, smoothing it out with the rest of her hair. "I don't like what it does to me," I say quietly. "What it makes me want to have to do to *you*."

She nods. "I don't like it, either," she says.

Her eyes are full of regret, but I don't feel bad. It's her own fault for coming at me like she did. At least that's out of the way, though. It was becoming tedious to keep up with that lie for so long, I was starting to get sloppy with it.

I release her wrists and bring my hand to her face, running the backs of my knuckles across her cheek. "Should we kiss and make up now?"

She nods, and when I press my lips to hers, I exhale with relief. Because for a split second when she was walking toward the front door, I thought maybe she was serious about leaving. I thought maybe I would never get to taste her like this again.

I'm relieved it was an empty threat. I don't know what I'd do if I ever found out she didn't actually love me. She's the only one who does.

She turns her head to the side and gives me access to her neck. As I kiss my way down her body, she begins to relax.

When I finally have all her clothes off, she spreads her legs for me. I press against her. "Do you love me, Sloan?"

She nods, then says, "Yes, Asa. I love you."

My tongue dives into her mouth at the same time my dick dives inside her.

Inside her—where I'm the only man who has ever been. Where I'm the only man who'll ever *be*.

"You're mine, Sloan," I whisper, fucking her just like she likes to be fucked. She grips my arms and squeezes her eyes shut.

She feels it so deeply; she cries the whole time.

THIRTY-SEVEN

Sloan

I close my eyes and allow the spray of water to beat down on my face.

What was I thinking?

Confronting him alone? Not warning Carter what was about to go down? *That was really dumb.*

But in my defense, it's hard to think when you're in a blind rage.

After I left my doctor's appointment this morning, I got the call from the social worker. I had been driving toward campus, and when she revealed that my brother's care wasn't private pay, I lost it. *Completely* lost it. I turned the car around and drove straight to my brother's facility to meet with her. By the time I left, I had never been that angry.

The only thing I could think about was Asa and how I wanted to kill him. Rage really does blind you. When I walked into the kitchen to confront him, I didn't care that he could hurt me. I just wanted to know if it was true—if he'd somehow been sending me forged letters from the government. I didn't want to believe it, because believing it would mean he is certifiably insane. But the only type of person who could invent a lie like that and keep it up for two years *has* to be certifiably insane.

I remember the day he brought over my mail after we broke up the first time. The benefits letter was on top. After I read the letter, I was devastated. The bastard actually comforted me—told me if I ever needed anything, he'd help me in a heartbeat. He said, "That's what you do for the people you love, Sloan. You help them."

That was back when I believed he actually loved me and it was a heartfelt gesture. *Now I think it's more of a psychotic obsession.*

I had nowhere else to go, and thanks to what I thought was about to happen to Stephen, I ended up being forced to ask Asa for help. It was a last resort, for sure. Hell, I even called the number on the form that day to see if I had any other options. Now I realize it was obviously a fake number with one of Asa's friends on the other line, but I didn't realize it at the time.

The hot water mixes with the tears that are now streaking down my cheeks.

How could I have fallen for it for so long? All the pieces are still coming together, right down to why he only lets me use his car on Sundays to go visit Stephen.

The social worker doesn't work on Sundays. There would be no chance I'd ever run into her and strike up a conversation about his benefits.

I still can't wrap my mind around it and it's been hours since I found out. I try to tell myself it took me so long to find out the truth because I had no reason to think he would do something like that. But I had *every* reason.

That's what Asa does.

He's a liar. A cheat. He sabotages people. He sets people up.

I'm so angry with myself right now, I scrub my body even harder, wanting to get his smell off me. I'm scrubbing my neck when the shower curtain flies open. I gasp and move so that my back is against the wall and I can better fight him off if it comes down to that.

Asa is standing in front of me, completely dressed now, in dark blue jeans and a crisp, white t-shirt. It makes the tattoos on his arms look brighter—angrier. But his expression isn't angry right now. He looks confused.

And he's actually staring at my face and not my breasts.

"Do you think it's weird that no one really comes over here anymore?" he asks.

His thoughts are becoming more and more unpredictable. I blow out a breath and turn my back to the water, rinsing the conditioner out of my hair. "I'm not sure what you mean, Asa."

When the conditioner is rinsed from my hair, I glance over at him. He's staring down at the tub, at the water circling the drain. "There used to be so many people here, all day every day, all night. Now it's just like four or five people, unless I have a party."

It's because you're unpredictable and you fucking scare people, Asa.

"Maybe they're all just busy?"

His eyes flick up to mine. They're still full of confusion. A little disappointment. I don't know a lot about drugs, or what it's like coming down from them, but paranoia may be a withdrawal symptom. I hope so, because otherwise, I'm not sure what to make of this version of Asa.

"Yeah," he says. "Maybe they're just busy. Or they aren't and they just want me to *think* they are. Because everyone fucking *pretends* around here."

His words are harsh, but his voice is calm, still with a hint of confusion. I'm praying he's not referring to Carter when he says everyone pretends. Or referring to me.I need to warn Carter. Something just isn't right with him today. I've never been scared for my life like I was when Asa pulled me back inside the house. I'm tempted to not tell Carter about what happened because I know he'll be upset that I confronted him alone.

"We should invite a few people over for dinner tonight. Will you cook?"

I nod. "For how many people?"

He doesn't even hesitate with the answer he spits out. "Me, you, Jon, Dalton, Kevin and Carter. I want the food ready at seven o'clock. I'll text them now."

He closes the shower curtain.

What the hell is wrong with him?

I blow out a steady breath and grab the washcloth. I'm scrubbing the heels of my feet when he opens the shower curtain again. When I look into his eyes, he's still shockingly looking at my face and nothing else. He opens his mouth, closes it, and then pauses for two seconds before, "Are you mad at me, Sloan?"

Is that a trick question?

I fucking loathe you, Asa.

I gauge his expression and then reply with, "I'm not very happy with you."

He sighs, and then nods like he doesn't blame me. Now I really know something is wrong with him. "I shouldn't have lied to you about your brother's benefits. Sometimes I think I could treat you better than I do."

I swallow the lump in my throat. "Then why don't you?"

His eyes narrow with a slight tilt of his head, like he's actually contemplating my question. "I don't know how."

He closes the shower curtain.

The bathroom door slams shut.

My arm clenches my stomach, because I feel like I might puke. Everything he does makes me so nervous to be around him. After that weird conversation, it's increased tenfold.

Thank God he's inviting everyone over tonight, because I really don't want to be alone with him. I need Carter to be here.

I'm about to turn off the water when the bathroom door reopens. Seconds later, the shower curtain opens from the opposite end this time. My hand freezes on the knob when I hear him step inside the shower.

No, no, no. Please don't make me have sex with you again. I breathe in calmly through my nose, hoping he's just waiting for his turn in the shower.

A few seconds pass, but I don't feel him step up behind me. He doesn't say anything. My heart is beating so fast, I get lightheaded.

I straighten up and slowly turn around. His white t-shirt is soaked through and he still has his jeans on. He's leaning against the back wall of the shower, barefoot, staring down at the tub.

I wait a moment to see what he wants. When he fails to move or speak—*he just keeps staring at nothing*—I finally speak up.

The fear cracks the sound of my voice when I say, "What are you doing, Asa?"

My question breaks him out of his trance. His eyes flick up to mine. He stares for approximately five painstakingly long seconds, and then he looks around the shower and back down at his clothes. He runs his hands over them like he has no idea why they're wet. He shakes his head and says, "I don't fucking know."

My knees grow weak at his reaction. I don't even turn off the water. I step out of the shower as fast as I can and grab a towel. I don't even bother getting dressed before swinging open the door to run to the bedroom. I just need to stay as far away from him as I can until Carter gets here and I know I'll be a little safer.

As soon as I step out into the hallway, something to my right catches my eye. I look over and see Jon about to walk into the bedroom at the end of the hall. His hand is on the door and he's staring at me—his eyes scrolling down my towel-covered body.

When I see the disgusting grin stretch across his face, I walk the three feet to my bedroom door. "Don't even think about it you piece of fucking *shit*." I slam the bedroom door and lock myself away from every last one of these crazy assholes. I walk to my phone and I text Carter.

Sloan: He's losing his mind. Please show up early.

I delete the text and wait for the sound of the shower to cut off. It doesn't.

After I'm dressed and about to head to the store, I decide to check on him. I open the bathroom door and he's no longer standing. He's sitting in the tub, still fully clothed, the water beating down on him. His eyes are wide open and the water is running over them.

I grip the doorknob and take a small step back. "I'm going to the grocery store, Asa. What do you want me to cook tonight?"

His head doesn't move, but his eyes scroll across the bathroom and meet mine. "Meatloaf."

I nod. "Okay. You want anything else while I'm there?"

He stares at me for a few seconds and then he smiles. "Get a dessert for the celebration."

Celebration? My throat suddenly becomes itchy and it's hard to swallow. "Okay," I say, my voice weak. "What are we celebrating?"

His eyes leave mine and move straight ahead again. "You'll see."

THIRTY-EIGHT

Carter

I have no idea why Asa invited us over for dinner. We've been at his house almost every night lately; tonight shouldn't be any different. I was hoping Sloan was being paranoid in her text when she said he's losing his mind, but I'm a little worried she's spot-on.

I can smell the food before I even open the front door. When I walk inside and look around, Dalton is the only one not here yet. Jon and Asa are taking up both recliners and Kevin is on the couch.

Asa is leaning forward with his elbows on his knees, remote in hand, flipping through news channels. When he hears the door close behind me, he turns around.

I nod my head in his direction and he turns back to the TV. "Do you watch the news, Carter?"

I glance toward the kitchen to see Sloan standing at the bar, wiping it down with a rag. I can see her from where I'm standing, but Asa can't.

"Sometimes," I say.

Sloan cuts her eyes to mine and lifts a finger to her hair. I run my thumb across my bottom lip. She lifts her other hand to her head and twirls three of her fingers in her hair. Then five. Then all ten. Then she's mock-ripping at her hair with both hands, twirling it in all directions, letting me know she's going crazy.

I want to smile at her, but I force myself to walk into the living room and take a seat next to Kevin. "Why'd you want to know if I watch the news?" I ask Asa.

He flips to another channel. "I haven't heard anything about my father. Just making sure he survived and I'm not about to be arrested for murder."

He says it so nonchalant, like the possibility of being arrested for murder is a daily occurrence. I nod, but fail to tell him that his father survived. He wasn't even hurt that bad, actually. The casino called an ambulance for him, but other than a broken nose and a broken jaw, there isn't any serious damage. The guy didn't even want to press charges. Dalton told me all this after he checked into it today.

He also told me the guy was an addict, he was diagnosed as a paranoid schizophrenic, and he had a shitload of other issues. I hate to say it, I have a little sympathy for Asa somewhere deep down inside. There's no telling what he went through as a child with that man as a father. But sympathy is as far as it goes. You can sympathize with someone and still wish they were dead.

I keep the information about his father's condition to myself. I think it's good that Asa is worried about repercussions. It's not something he probably experiences very often.

Asa sighs after flipping through all the news channels twice and coming up empty. He stands up and throws the remote toward Jon. "You guys make sure and wash your hands. My fiancée worked hard cooking this dinner and I don't want any of you fuckers seated at my table with filthy hands." He heads to the stairs and runs up to his room. His bedroom door closes, and I glance at Kevin, who is staring at the empty stairs.

"He's being really fucking weird," Kevin says.

Jon begins flipping through the channels and says, "What's new?"

Neither one of them bothers going to the kitchen to wash their hands, so I use the opportunity to walk in there. Sloan is pulling the meatloaf out of the oven when I pass her. "Hey, Sloan," I say casually.

She looks at me, but doesn't smile. She shoots me a look that tells me we need to talk. There's just not really a way to do that right now. I turn the water on and she walks the meatloaf to the counter next to me. She sticks a knife between the loaf and the pan and begins working it loose.

"I messed up today," she whispers.

I turn the water to a lower pressure so I can hear her better.

"I found out he's been lying to me about my brother's benefits. I confronted him. Told him I was leaving him. He got really angry."

"Sloan," I say quietly. *Why the hell would she do that?* "Are you okay?"

She shrugs. "I am right now. But something is off with him, Carter. I'm scared. He sat in the shower with his clothes on for half an hour. Then when I got home from the grocery store, I looked out the window and saw him sitting on a lounge chair, staring at the pool. Then he just started slapping his palm against his forehead. He did it thirty-six times. I counted."

Jesus Christ.

She glances up at me and I hate how scared she looks. I should just take her now. Grab her hand, pull her outside while he's upstairs, and get her the fuck out of here.

"Now he keeps saying he has a surprise for me. He's talking like this dinner is some kind of celebration," she whispers. "I'm scared to find out what it is we're celebrating."

Asa's footsteps move overhead, like he's about to head downstairs. Sloan grabs the pan of meatloaf and walks it to the table.

The other two guys must hear Asa heading downstairs as well, because they're at the sink now, preparing to wash their hands like he instructed.

We help Sloan carry the rest of the food to the table, just as Dalton walks through the front door. It's only 6:55, but he sees Asa bounding down the stairs and he apologizes for being late.

"You aren't late," Asa says. "You're right on time."

I take a seat, and it ends up being directly across from Asa. Diagonal from Sloan. It's oddly quiet as everyone passes around the food, divvying it onto their plates. Once all the food has been passed around the table, Asa grabs his fork and says, "Should we say grace?"

No one speaks. We all just stare at him, wondering if he's kidding or if someone needs to start praying before he flips his shit.

He laughs loudly and says, "You stupid fucks." He shoves his fork into his mashed potatoes and swallows a bite.

Jon says, "This is twice in a row we've had dinner here. What gives? Is this what happens when you become domesticated?"

Asa narrows his eyes in Jon's direction, then washes his mashed potatoes down with his beer. "Where's Jess tonight?"

Jon shrugs. "Haven't seen her in a few days. I think we broke up."

Asa chuckles, then he looks at me. "Where's Tillie?"

I run my thumb across my bottom lip. "Working. She might stop by tomorrow night."

Asa licks his lips, taking another sip of his beer. "That would be nice," he says. Then he looks at Dalton. "How come you've never brought a girl over?"

Dalton speaks with a mouthful of meatloaf. "She lives in Nashville."

Asa nods and says, "What's her name?"

"Steph. She's a singer. She's why I was almost late, actually. She signed a recording contract today and she called to tell me about it." He looks proud when he talks about her.

It almost makes me laugh, because there is no Steph. He just made all that shit up on the fly, and Asa swallows it down like a warm glass of milk. "That's cool," Asa says.

Asa likes Dalton. I can tell by the way he looks at him—without any suspicion at all. Not like the way he looks at me.

"Something wrong with your fucking mouth, Carter?"

I glance at him and raise my eyebrow.

"You're rubbing your goddamn lip raw."

I didn't even realize I was still rubbing my lip. I pull my hand from my mouth. "All good," I say, taking a bite of the meatloaf. The last thing I want to do is provoke him. Not with the way he's been acting lately.

Asa takes another bite of his meatloaf, and then he rests his hands beside his plate. "So," he says. "I have a little surprise." He smiles, and then looks over at Sloan. I can see the roll of her throat when she swallows.

"What is it?" she asks cautiously.

Asa opens his mouth to speak, but he's cut off by a loud banging on the front door. I can see the irritation in his eyes as he turns to glance at the living room door. A second loud knock occurs.

He drops his silverware with a loud clank onto the table and looks around at all of us. "Any of you expecting company? In the middle of fucking dinner?"

No one speaks up.

He scoots back from the table and slaps his napkin beside his plate. When he turns to walk into the living room, Sloan glances across the table at me. She looks scared, but also relieved that his big surprise was just interrupted. I turn to Dalton and he raises an eyebrow.

We all look at Asa as he peers through the peephole. He stares for several seconds and then presses his forehead to the door. "*Fuck.*" He turns and rushes to the kitchen, grabbing Sloan by the arm and pulling her up out of her chair. He grips her shoulders and says, "Go up to the room and lock the door. Don't open it whatever you do."

I scoot my chair back and stand up. Dalton does the same. We both look at each other and then back at Asa.

"Who's at the door?" Jon asks, pushing his chair back as well. I don't think any of us have ever seen Asa this worried.

Asa glances up the stairs and around the room like he's trying to find a way to escape. "It's the fucking FBI, Jon. It's the fucking *goddamn* FBI!"

What?

I immediately turn to Dalton, but he shakes his head to let me know he's just as unaware as I am. I also notice his fists clench at his side. "Shit!" he says. To Asa, I'm sure Dalton's reaction is expected. But to me, I know why he's really mad. The FBI are about to walk into this house and ruin the investigation.

More pounding against the door.

Asa pulls his hands through his hair. "Fuck! *Fuck!*"

I see him glance toward the back door. I can already see him trying to plan an escape route. I step forward to get his attention.

"If they're here to arrest anyone, they already have the house surrounded, Asa. They may just be here for questioning about your father. Just open the door and act normal. We'll all stay seated at the table like we have nothing to hide."

Dalton nods. "He's right, Asa. If we all run, they'll have reason to think you're hiding something."

Asa nods, but Jon shakes his head. "Fuck that. We've got shit all over this house. If we open the door, it's over. For all of us."

Asa's eyes are wide as he tries to figure out what to do. We all look at the front door when the banging resumes.

I can see the veins in Dalton's neck, and I know he's fearing that all the work we've put in was basically for nothing. The entire investigation won't mean shit, because it will now be in the hands of someone else.

We've seen this happen a couple of times—an investigation being taken over by a higher-ranking force. But Dalton has put so much into this, it's going to be impossible for him to watch it go up in flames.

"Go to your room, Sloan," Asa orders. "You don't need to be here when I open that door."

Sloan glances at me, concern in her eyes. She wants to know if she should follow Asa's orders—if she should leave the room.

More banging.

I nod softly to let Sloan know she should do what Asa is asking her to do. At least she'll be out of the way of whatever is about to go down.

Asa suddenly strides across the room toward Sloan. He gets in her face. "What the fuck are you looking at *him* for?" he yells, waving his hand in my direction. "What the fuck are you looking at him for?"

Oh, God. I start to walk around the table, but Dalton grabs my arm. Asa wraps his hand around the back of Sloan's neck and shoves her toward the stairs. "Get the fuck up the stairs!"

She doesn't look back as she runs up the stairs.

Asa is looking at me now. Dalton may not be happy that the FBI showed up, but I'm relieved. Chances are, Asa will be arrested for whatever they're here to confront him for. Which means I might survive tonight, because the look he's giving me right now is telling me otherwise.

He knows. He can tell, based on that one look Sloan gave me, that something is going on between us. But between the banging on the front door and the imminent possibility that he's about to be arrested, he thankfully puts it on the back burner.

He points at all four of us. "Sit the fuck down," he says. "Eat. I'm opening the goddamn door." We all take our seats. Asa rushes to the kitchen and opens a cabinet, reaching to the back of it. He pulls out a gun and slides it inside the back of his pants. As he's passing the table, he says, "If I find out any of you fuckers are responsible for this, you're *all* dead." Asa turns toward the door, and right before he opens it, he presses his forehead against it like he's saying a quick prayer. When he pulls it open, he smiles. "How can I help you gentlemen?"

I hear a voice say, "Asa Jackson?"

Asa nods, but then the door swings open and several men swarm him, knocking him to the ground.

When Jon sees what's happening, he scrambles toward the back door, just as it's busted open and three men rush inside. Jon is immediately subdued and thrown to the kitchen floor.

It isn't until this moment that I realize these guys won't have any clue Dalton and I are undercover. I don't even have a badge on me to prove it. They'll just think we're on Asa's side.

The next several seconds are complete chaos.

More men appear through the doorway, guns are pointed at our heads, we're on our stomachs, faces pressed to the floor, hands being cuffed behind our backs.

I'm lying next to Dalton and before they pull him to his feet, he whispers, "Stay calm. Wait until you're alone before saying anything."

I nod, but one of the agents notices us communicating. Dalton is jerked up by his arms.

I can hear Asa being read his Miranda rights as two men jerk me up off the floor by my arms. They're barking orders, separating all of us into different parts of the house. I'm pulled into a spare bedroom off of the kitchen.

All I can think about is Sloan and how freaked out she probably is right now.

The door slams shut behind me and I'm thrown into a desk chair. There are two men in the room with me. One is taller than me with dark blond hair and a beard. The other is shorter, stockier, with red hair and an even redder mustache. The redhead is the one who speaks first. They both pull their badges out of their jacket pockets and flash them at me. "I'm Agent Bowers," he says. "This is Agent Thompson. We're going to ask you a few questions and we'd appreciate your cooperation."

I nod. Agent Bowers walks closer to me and says, "Do you live here?"

I shake my head. "No." I start to tell them what I'm doing here and that they're making a big fucking mistake, but the tall one interrupts me and says, "What's your name?"

"Carter," I say. I don't say *Luke* yet, because I'm still not sure if Asa is even being arrested. The last thing I need is for the fucking FBI to blow my cover.

"Carter?" agent Bowers says. "You just have one name? So you're like Madonna? Cher?" he bends forward, eyeing me. "What's your fucking last name, smartass?"

I twist my hands behind my back, trying to ease the pressure cutting into the circulation in my wrists. My pulse is pounding in my temples, partly because of the entire last few minutes and partly because I'm pissed that they're about to end everything and get all the credit. Sure, they might be here to arrest Asa. And yes, I'm relieved that Sloan is now safe. But knowing the entire last few months were for shit and that I put Sloan in danger more than once *really* hits a nerve.

It grows quiet and I can hear Asa yell, "Fuck you!" from another room.

Agent Thompson kicks my chair, bringing my attention back to him. "What's your last name, son?"

Little does he know I'm aware of how to conduct a proper investigation, and these assholes have already broken at least three rules. But the FBI, and even the police, aren't really known to follow rules to the specifics in situations like these. I know that firsthand.

I open my mouth to respond to them, but I'm cut off by the sound of Sloan's scream coming from upstairs. I immediately jump up, but both of them shove me back down in the chair. "Fucking arrest me, or let me go!" I yell.

I have to get to Sloan. She's probably scared shitless right now, not knowing what the hell is going on. I need to check on her before I fucking lose it, but they won't let me out of the room. "I'm on your side," I say to them, trying to keep my voice calm, when I just feel like screaming at them. "If you take the cuffs off, I'll prove it and then get back to my fucking job!"

Detective Thompson stares at me for a moment and then looks back at agent Bowers and laughs. He points at me. "You hear that?" he says. "He's a cop."

Agent Bowers also laughs, and with a heavy dose of sarcasm, he says, "Our bad. You're free to go," he says, pointing toward the door.

I could do without the sarcasm. I also know I just fucked up by breaking cover, but I'm not sitting in here for another minute with these assholes. I'll worry about dealing with Ryan later. "You'll find my badge taped underneath my passenger seat. It's the black Charger."

Agent Thompson's eyes narrow and he looks at me like he might actually be entertaining the idea that I'm not lying. He looks at agent Bowers and nudges his head toward the door, silently telling him to go verify.

I can still hear Asa in another room, yelling back at whoever is questioning him. He's demanding a lawyer now. I don't think that's going to help him at this point.

Agent Thompson doesn't ask me more questions once we're alone. I take the opportunity to bring up Sloan.

"There's a girl in a bedroom upstairs. Can you make sure she's okay when your partner returns?"

Agent Thompson nods. "Yeah, we can do that. Anyone else in the house we should be aware of?"

I shake my head. I already regret outing myself; the last thing I'm going to do is out Ryan. He can do that on his own time when he sees fit. He'll probably wait until they have Asa in custody.

I hate that it wasn't our investigation that ended things for Asa, but I'm relieved it's finally coming to an end. For Sloan's sake. Ryan, however, is probably fuming right now.

A moment later, the bedroom door opens. I glance up to see if agent Bowers found the envelope that contains my badge. I see the open envelope first, but as soon as I see who's holding it, my relief turns into one big clusterfuck of confusion and dread.

What the fuck is happening?

Asa's eyes meet mine.

What the fuck?

He looks down at the envelope in his hands and slaps it against his palm twice. He glances at agent Thompson and says, "I'd like some privacy with my friend, please."

Agent Thompson nods and walks out of the room. Before he's out the door, Asa points at agent Thompson's blue FBI jacket with the three big yellow letters emblazoned across the back of it. "It looks so *real*, doesn't it?" he says. He glances back at me. "I bought them at the costume store downtown." He laughs and then closes the door. "The shady *actors* were a little more expensive than the jackets."

No.

Fuck.

Fuck.

No.

I fell right into that one.

I can taste the bile in the back of my throat. I can feel the blood trickling out of my wrists as I struggle with everything in me to somehow get out of these handcuffs.

Asa tosses the envelope containing my badge onto the mattress, then he reaches behind his back and pulls his gun out of his pants. He takes a seat on the edge of the bed, his mouth drawn tight in anger.

"How'd you like my surprise? *Luke.*"

I'm looking straight at him...suddenly aware that I've just made the biggest mistake of my career. The biggest mistake of my life.

And all I can think about is Sloan.

I squeeze my eyes shut and all I see is Sloan.

THIRTY-NINE

Asa

"**H**ave you ever seen the movie *Point Break*?" I ask him.

Luke is eyeing me hard—his chest is heaving, nostrils flaring. *I fucking love it.*

He doesn't answer me. It's funny that he's so quick to open his mouth to brag that he's a mother-fucking cop, but when it comes to me, he barely makes an effort to converse.

"I'm not referring to the new piece-of-shit remake, Luke. I'm talking about the original film with Keanu Reeves and Patrick Swayze. Oh, and what's his face from the Red Hot Chili Peppers? The singer?"

I look to Luke to help me out with the guy's name, but he doesn't. He's just staring me down. I don't know why I keep waiting for him to respond. I lean back on the bed and I keep talking. "There's a part in the movie where Keanu Reeves and his team bust a drug house. But what they don't realize is that one of the guys who lives there is an undercover cop. And due to their impatience and lack of planning, they ruin the entire fucking investigation for the poor guy. Months and months of hard work. You remember that part?"

Naturally, he doesn't reply. He just keeps fidgeting with the cuffs behind his back, trying to free himself.

"I was probably only ten when I saw that movie for the first time, but I couldn't stop thinking about that part. I obsessed over it. I always wondered what would have happened had Keanu's team only been *pretending* to be the FBI. I wondered how that scene would have played out had that undercover fucker come clean, only to find out Keanu wasn't with the FBI at all. He was just pretending to be in order to weed him out. Talk about a double plot twist."

Carter's eyes glance to the door like someone is going to walk in and rescue him. I hate to break it to him, but it's not gonna happen.

"Anyway," I say, standing up. "I thought it'd be worth a shot. See if any of you fuckers were really stupid enough to try and betray me, and if you were, maybe you were stupid enough to fall for the double plot twist." I tilt my head and smile at him. "You must be feeling *really* fucking stupid right now."

His jaw twitches. So does mine, because I have no idea how to refer to him now and it's pissing me off. Carter? Luke? *Dead?*

Yes. I'll refer to him as *dead.*

"I mean *really* fucking stupid," I say, laughing. "Why would you be so quick to reveal yourself? I'm no cop, but I'd assume breaking cover is not something you people take lightly."

I pace the room several times, trying to work it over in my own mind. Why would anyone be in such a hurry to get out of a situation that they would compromise their identity? It's like it was life or death for him. If he didn't hurry up and get to someone, it'd be too late.

I slowly sit back down on the bed. "Unless..." I glance over at him. "Unless you broke cover because you're the kind of guy who lets your emotions rule your actions. What do they call those kinds of guys? I'm pretty sure you and I had a conversation about this over lunch recently." I glance up at the ceiling in mock thought. "Oh yeah," I say. "*Pussies.*"

He doesn't laugh at my joke.

That's probably good, because it might have pissed me off had he laughed.

I glance over at the door and can't remember if I locked it or not. I stand up and go check it, then turn around and face Luke again. "But the real question is, *why* would you be so emotional at a time like that? When you should be at the top of your undercover game? What could have been at the forefront of your mind when training and common sense should have won out?"

I take five steps toward him, until there aren't any more steps to take. He maintains eye contact the entire time, lifting his chin to hold his stare. "Oh. That's right. You were too worried about my fucking *fiancée* to do your goddamn job right!" I slam my gun against the side of his face. His head swings to the side. I'm pretty sure that blow was hard enough to knock a tooth or two loose, but he acts like it doesn't faze him. He makes eye contact with me again, looking a little calmer than before I even hit him.

Motherfucker.

I hate that I still like this side of him. The quiet, introspective side of him that doesn't crack from fear. It's impressive.

Too bad the only thing that makes him crack under pressure is Sloan.

I wonder how long he's been brainwashing her? Using her for his investigation? He's probably been slowly turning her against me since the day they met.

I thought the casino incident was bad. I thought unleashing on my father was the angriest I've ever been. But I was wrong. *Boy, was I wrong.*

Seeing Sloan look at him for instruction earlier was by far the angriest I have ever been. *Ever.* I've never wanted to kill someone like I wanted to kill Carter in that moment. But that would have ruined my surprise, so I had to remain patient.

I slowly lift my gun and point it against the side of his head and imagine what it'll be like when I finally pull the trigger. To watch his fucking brains splatter all over the floor. I wonder how much damage it will do to his head. Will he still be recognizable? When I pull Sloan in here to get one last look at him, will she be able to tell it's even him? Or will his whole head explode?

I force myself to pull the gun away from his head because as curious as I am to see what it's going to be like when I kill him, there are a few questions I need answers to before that happens.

I squat down in front of him and rest my arms on my thighs. "Did you fuck her?"

I know in this case, it's a rhetorical question, because he'd be stupid to answer it. But he hasn't proven to be the brightest crayon in the box today. "Where were you when you fucked her the first time? In my house? In my bed? Did she come?"

He folds his lips together, moistening them. But he still doesn't respond. His silence is really starting to get annoying. I stand and walk to the door, double-checking that it's locked. I'm not even sure why I want it locked; the guys have the house under control. One of them was ordered to go straight upstairs and watch Sloan. Four of them are split up between Jon and Kevin, although I'm not worried about either of them. They're too fucking stupid to be cops, but I like the idea of letting them shit their pants for another ten minutes or so.

I'm still not sure about Dalton. But he's in the living room with two guns to his head, so I guess I'll worry about him after I'm finished with Carter.

"You want to know what it was like the first time I fucked her?" I ask.

Since the second I walked in here, he finally responds to one of my questions. He barely shakes his head back and forth, twice. It's so unnoticeable; I don't think he even realizes he did it. He must *really* not want to know what it was like the first time I fucked her.

Well too bad, Carter. I'm gonna tell you all about it anyway.

I sit on the bed again, but this time I sit all the way back until I'm against the headboard. I cross my feet and rest the gun on my thigh. "She was eighteen," I tell him. "Innocent. Untouched. Poor girl had been taking care of her brother for so long she never even had the chance to be a kid. To go out, to have fun, to experience guys. Would you believe it if I told you I'm the first guy she ever kissed?"

He's staring ahead now, refusing to look at me. I can see the veins in his neck bulging. I smile and get even more detailed with my story because I like watching him squirm.

"She wasn't inexperienced because she was shy, let me make that clear up front. She was inexperienced because she didn't trust easily. Grew up with a pathetic mother, didn't even know her father. So when I came into the picture, she didn't know what to think. Didn't have any exes to compare me to, so I didn't have anything to live up to. No one to outdo. I just knew if I was better to her than her own parents had ever been, she'd think she was blessed. And I was, Carter. I was so fucking good to her.

"Thankfully, she wasn't the type of girl who wanted to take things slow. The first time I took her on a date, I kissed her before we even got to the restaurant. Pushed her against a brick wall in some alley and she liked it so much, it was like she wanted to drown on my fucking saliva."

Fucking hell. My dick is hard now just thinking about it.

"I had been to that particular restaurant before, so I knew the perfect time of night to take her so that it wouldn't be crowded. And I knew the perfect table to request so that we'd have privacy. She couldn't keep her hands off me after we sat down. It was like I unleashed this need in her that I didn't even know girls were capable of feeling. And it made me want to bend her over the table, lift her dress up, and fuck her right on top of the appetizers.

"I'll never forget that dress. It was a cute little white dress with tiny straps and yellow flowers all over it. It felt like silk in my hands and I couldn't stop touching it. She wore these white sandals that showed off her pink toes, and she had slipped the shoes off at some point during dinner. I fucking loved it. Are you a foot guy, Luke?"

He's staring at me now. Not sure when that happened, but he doesn't look as calm as he did right after I hit him.

I was right. This is the only subject that breaks him. I smile and keep going.

"The whole time we ate, I charmed her. Told her how beautiful she was, how special she was. How what she was doing for her brother was the most compassionate thing I'd ever witnessed. And the whole time I was feeding her exactly what she needed to hear, my hand was slowly inching up her thigh. By the time they brought the dessert menu, I had already slipped my hand under her panties . The waiter had barely disappeared when my finger went inside of her."

I blow out a breath, trying to control my pulse. I can't even fucking *think* about it without getting worked up. "It'll be difficult describing what happened next, because you just had to fucking be there. But I'm going to try."

I sit up on the bed and run the gun across my cheek. "Her pussy...holy *fuck*. It was the warmest, wettest, tightest thing I'd ever touched. I wanted to crawl under the table and bury my mouth against it. And she was so fucking *responsive*. I guess never having been touched by a guy before, that's natural. But there was something magical...something spiritual that happened inside of me when the tips of my fingers touched her perfectly intact hymen.

"Her very first orgasm hit her in the back of that Indian restaurant with the taste of curry on her tongue, my hand up her dress, my fingers deep inside of her. It was beautiful. Fucking beautiful."

I sigh at the memory, then laugh when I realize I never even got to the good part.

"I had to have her. I needed to fuck through that hymen until she bled all over me, so I drove her straight back to my place. But of course after we made out for half an hour, she asked me to wait. Said we were moving too fast. But I had to have her, Luke. I couldn't fucking *breathe*. So I cuddled with her for two goddamn hours. Waited until the middle of the night, and then I started kissing her. Touching her. Running my tongue up and down her clit, working her up in her sleep so that when she finally did wake up, she'd be begging for it. And that's exactly what happened. She woke up with my head between her legs and within ten seconds, she was begging me for it. The first *night*, Luke. She had just gone on her first official date. Just had her first kiss. Her first orgasm. And then like the miracle that it was, I was easing inside of her, watching her wince, feeling her stretch around me. I put my hand on her stomach because I wanted to feel the pop when I shoved inside of her. She screamed when it happened. It was kind of unexpected for her, the way I just shoved inside of her and took her while she was still half asleep. I don't think she really truly woke up until that moment. And then I started fucking her. Hard. So hard, Luke. I had never felt like I wanted to be a part of someone, inside of someone with more than just my dick. I just kept thrusting, because for some reason, it didn't feel like I'd ever get deep enough. The marks left by my headboard against the wall are still there, actually. I might show them to you before I kill you."

I stand up and rub a hand down my face. "After two years I still think about that night. About what it felt like being the first person inside of her. The first person to make her come. The first person to make her scream out a name. And every time I look at her, I love her a little bit more knowing that what happened between us will always be sacred. That I'll get all those firsts and all those lasts. That she would never allow another man to kiss her. To touch her. To slide his dick inside of her and fucking *ruin* her for me."

I calmly walk over to Luke and squat in front of him again. "If I find out you took all that from me, Luke, she'll be worthless to me. Excuse me while I go upstairs to retrieve her. I think the three of us need to have a serious conversation."

I send two of the fuckers back inside to keep an eye on Luke while I run upstairs to retrieve my Sloan.

FORTY

Sloan

The first thing I did after running upstairs to my bedroom was run to my nightstand for my phone. It wasn't there. I looked on the floor, the bed, *under* the bed.

And then I remember Asa running up here right before dinner. *The bastard hid my phone.*

As soon as I heard the shouting from downstairs, the scuffling, the crashes...I ran to my closet to hide. Less than ten seconds later, someone pounded on the door. When I heard the words, "FBI, open up!" I was filled with relief.

I crawled out of the closet and swung open the door, but I immediately knew something wasn't right. The agent shoved me into the bedroom and slammed the door behind me, pointing a gun at me. He ordered me on the bed and hasn't allowed me to move or speak since he walked in.

It's been a while now. Too long. I can sometimes make out the sounds of Dalton's voice. Sometimes Jon's or Kevin's.

But not Asa's.

And not Luke's.

My stomach coils at the idea that Asa has anything to do with this. But it wouldn't be the first time he's concocted a ridiculously elaborate scheme. It's becoming his forte.

"Am I under arrest?" I ask the agent.

He remains in front of the door, but doesn't answer my question.

"If I'm not under arrest, I'd like to go downstairs."

He shakes his head no.

Fuck this guy.

I stand up and try to walk around him, but he grabs my arm and tosses me back toward the bed. That's when I know for sure something isn't right with this whole situation. I jump back up and attempt it again. "Help!" I scream, hoping to get someone else's attention in the house.

He slaps his hand over my mouth and shoves me against the wall. "I suggest you shut your mouth and sit back down on the bed."

I stomp on his foot, knowing I'm just making things worse for myself. But I'm tired of not fighting back. His hands meet my shoulders and he shoves me against the wall so hard my head slams against it. I wince and try to pull a hand up to my head, but he grabs my wrists and shoves them at my sides.

"You're a feisty little thing," he says, smiling like that's something that's supposed to turn him on.

Where the fuck did this guy come from? The same womb as Jon?

"Help!" I scream again.

This time he shakes his head and says, "Don't know how to keep your mouth shut, do you?" He presses his lips against mine and I fucking *hate* men. I *hate* them. I *hate* them!

My eyes are wide open as I try to keep my lips pressed together against the force of his tongue. I'm looking over the guy's shoulder, struggling to free myself from him, when the bedroom door swings open.

I'm both horrified and relieved to see that it's Asa.

What in the hell is going on?

His eyes scan the room and then land on us—on the guy who's still trying to penetrate my mouth with his tongue. There's a hand now working its way up my shirt. I realize what a fucked up world I live in when I catch myself praying that Asa comes to my rescue, but also fearing for the moment I'm safe with him.

Asa doesn't even take two seconds to process what he's seeing. His eyes turn heated with rage. "I gave you one fucking job, asshole!" he yells, striding toward us. Just when the guy releases me and begins to spin around, Asa lifts his gun and presses it to the top of the guy's head. "*One* fucking job!"

Ringing.

I can't hear anything over the ringing in my ears. The sting of liquid in my eyes—on my face. I cover my ears with my hands and squeeze my eyes shut.

No, that did not just happen.

No, no, no.

I hear the guy fall to the floor and I have to step to the side to get my left foot out from under him. "No, Asa. No, no, no," I repeat, my hands still over my ears, my eyes still shut.

"He probably thought you were a whore, Sloan," he says, grabbing my arm. "Can you blame him?"

Asa yanks me forward and I trip over the guy on the floor. Asa doesn't let go of my arm as he drags me to my feet and yanks me toward the door.

My eyes are still closed. I think I might be screaming, because my throat is stinging, but I can't tell if that's me or the ringing in my ears. I'm suddenly lifted up into the air and thrown over his shoulder.

He carries me down the stairs and the last ten seconds replay over again in my head.

This is not happening.

Seconds later, he lays me down on a bed. I'm still too scared to open my eyes. Several moments pass and I can feel my chest pulling for air. I gasp between tears as Asa's voice comes at me from inches above me.

"Sloan, look at me."

I slowly open my eyes and look up at him. He's kneeling over me on the bed, touching my face, smoothing back my hair. There are specks of blood on his face—across his neck.

I look into his eyes and his pupils have overtaken everything. Two huge black irises stare back down at me, and it sends a shiver over my already trembling body.

"Sloan," he whispers, still smoothing his hand over my hair. I try to look around the room, but he grabs my jaw and forces my eyes back to his. "Baby, I have some really bad news."

I don't think my heart can take whatever it is he's about to say. I'm afraid if I open my mouth to respond to him, I'll puke.

"I know about you and Luke."

My heart crashes to a halt at that name. I fight back the flood of tears attempting to return. *He called him Luke.*

How does he know his name is Luke?

I muster every ounce of strength I can find and I use it to play dumb. "Who is Luke?"

His eyes scroll over my face. His pupils contract and then expand again. A slow smile spreads across his face and then he presses his lips to my forehead. "That's what I thought," he whispers, pulling away from me. "It's not your fault, Sloan. He brainwashed you. Tried to turn you against me. But his name isn't even *Carter*, baby. It's Luke. Ask him yourself." He slips his hand under my back and pushes me up until I'm sitting on the bed.

I'm suddenly face-to-face with my worst nightmare.

Luke is sitting at a desk chair, his hands cuffed behind his back. The agony on his face speaks volumes of what he thinks about our predicament.

No.

Asa is watching me, waiting for my reaction. I try to control it—to hide my fear, my heartache, my own agony. But knowing we're both at the hands of Asa right now leaves little strength for pretending.

Don't react. Don't react. Don't react.

I repeat these words in my head while Luke speaks the same silent words to me with his eyes.

That's what Asa wants. A reaction. I do whatever I can to not give him the one he expects. He's standing now, so I look up at him with the most innocent expression I'm capable of right now. "Asa, what are you talking about? Why is Carter handcuffed?"

He stares down at me like he's disappointed. Like he expected me to come out and say I knew Luke was undercover, or in the least, that I'm sleeping with him. He smirks. "You still think I'm stupid, Sloan?" His eyes slowly slide over to Luke. "So I guess it's okay if I do this then, huh?" He lifts his gun and strides toward him, just like he did in the second before he shot the guy upstairs.

I immediately jump up, grab his arm and scream, "No! Asa, No!"

He doesn't shoot him.

Instead, the hand that's holding his gun swings around and hits me so hard, I fly back onto the bed. *He didn't even need me to admit what was happening between Luke and me. My reaction just gave it away.*

He's on top of me now, gripping my wrists, pressing his forehead to the side of my head. "Sloan, no," he says, his voice instantly strained. "No, *no*, baby." He pulls back and his eyes are full of hurt. "He was inside you? You let him *inside* you?"

I'm crying too hard to admit it. I'm crying too hard to deny it.

His entire face pulls into a grimace, as if he thinks this is the absolute worst thing that could possibly be happening right now. *He just shot a guy upstairs, and he's more upset that I might have cheated on him?*

I turn my head to the side and squeeze my eyes shut.
This is it.
This is how I'm going to die.

Asa buries his head in the crevice of my neck and shoulder and mutters, "I can't remember if I locked the door."

When he crawls off me, I try to process what he just said, but it was so random and my pulse is racing too fast to process thoughts,

I don't even know what to think. As he's walking toward the door, I turn my head to find Luke. His hands are cuffed behind his back around the desk chair. But he quickly stands, slipping his arms up and over the back of the chair, and then he sits down again, this time with his arms directly behind his back without the barrier of the chair. It all happens so fast, it takes me a second to realize that he's not even cuffed to the chair.

Asa must not realize this or he'd never turn his back to him.

My eyes flick to the door and Asa is locking it. My eyes flick back to Luke's and he's shaking his head, warning me to stay calm. He can't bring his thumb to his lip, but he's biting it, running his teeth across it.

I tug at a strand of my hair, just as Asa rests his back against the bedroom door. He places his gun flat against his cheek and looks straight at Luke. "I already told you about the first time *I* fucked her," he says. "It's your turn."

FORTY-ONE

Asa – Several Years Earlier

My Dad is standing at the window, watching for the men. He watches for them all the time. He tells me if they find out where we live, they'll shoot him. Then they'll shoot my mom and then they'll shoot me. He says after they shoot us, the men probably won't even tell the police. They'll leave us all here and our bodies will rot inside this house and the mice and roaches will eat them.

"Asa!" he yells from the window, pointing at the front door. "Check the door again!"

I already checked it for him two times, but he never believes me that it's locked. He says, "Check the door again," every time he looks out the window.

I don't know why some days he thinks the men are coming for him and some days he doesn't care. I slide off the couch and crawl to the door. My legs work, so I could walk to the door just fine, but sometimes I'm scared if the men show up, they'll shoot me, so I crawl when I pass the big window.

I check the door. "It's locked."

My Daddy looks at me and smiles. "Thank you, son."

I hate it when he calls me *son*. The only time he calls me son is when he's scared of the men who are going to shoot him and then my mom and then me. When he's scared, he's really nice to me and makes me help him do things, like push the couch against the door and unplug all the things that have electricity. I've been helping him a lot today and he keeps calling me son. I like it better when he doesn't call me anything and he just sits in his chair all day.

I crawl back to the couch, but before I make it there, I feel my dad squeeze my arm. "They're here, Asa!" he whispers. He pulls me to my feet and says, "You have to go hide!"

My heart beats real fast inside my chest and I nod.

My dad is scared of the men a lot, but they've never actually shown up before. I look out the big window while he pulls me across the living room, but I don't see anyone. I don't see the men.

My dad pulls me out the back door and down the steps. He kneels and grabs my shoulders. "Asa, hide under the house and stay there until I come get you."

I shake my head. "I don't want to." It's dark under there and once I saw a scorpion.

"You don't have a choice!" he whispers real loud. "Don't come out until I come for you or they'll kill all of us!"

He pushes me toward the opening that leads under the house. I fall to my knees and my hands sink into the mud. I don't look behind me. I crawl as far as I can so the men don't see me.

I pull my knees up to my chest and I try to be quiet when I cry so the men don't hear me.

I got really cold and hungry and cried until the sun came back up. But my daddy said not to move, so I didn't. I still haven't moved. I hope he doesn't get mad, but I peed on myself while I was sleeping. I haven't peed on myself while I was asleep since before my last birthday. If the men haven't killed him yet, he's going to be so mad at me for what happened.

I can hear them walking around inside the house. I don't know if they killed my dad. My mom was in the bedroom where she stays most of the time, so they might have even killed her, too, if they found her.

But they didn't kill me, because I did exactly what my dad said. I stayed here and I'm not moving until he comes for me.

Or until the men are gone.

I got really cold and hungry and cried until the sun went down again. But I still didn't move. My daddy said not to, so I didn't. But my legs don't feel like they're a part of my body anymore. My eyes keep closing. I'm not so thirsty anymore because there was a little water coming out of a pipe next to me and I put my mouth on it and drank some of it.

I think the men killed my mom and dad, because it's real quiet in my house now. I haven't heard the men walk around since the sun came up, so maybe they left.

I know my dad said not to move, but if my dad were still alive, he would have been back to get me.

But he never came back.

I crawl out from under the house. It's real dark out now, so that means I've been under the house for more than an entire day now. I don't think the men would kill my mom and dad and then stay at our house for more than a whole day, so I think that means they're probably gone now and it's safe for me to go inside.

When I try to stand up, I fall back down. My legs are tingly and my fingers hurt. I crawl up the back stairs and that's when I realize my clothes have mud all over them. I'm scared to get the floor dirty. I try to wipe some of it on the rug, but I just keep spreading it around on my clothes.

I grab the door handle and pull myself up. I still can't feel my legs very well, but they're working now. When I open the door and walk into the house, I can see my father's dead body. It's in the recliner in the living room.

I hold my breath. I've never seen a dead body before and I really don't want to see one now, but I know I have to make sure it's my dad and not the men. I tiptoe into the living room and I'm so scared, it feels like my heart is beating in my neck.

When I reach his chair, I take a deep breath and then step around it to look at him. I'm a little surprised to see that dead people don't really look all that different from the people who are still alive.

I thought he'd have blood all over him, or be a different color—like a ghost. But he still looks the same.

I lift my finger to touch his cheek. I heard dead people are colder than people who are alive, so I press the tip of my finger into his cheek to see what his skin feels like.

His hand goes around my wrist and he squeezes it. His eyes pop open and it scares me so bad, I scream.

My dad's eyes are real mean when he looks down at my clothes. "Where the hell have you been, boy? You're filthy!"

I thought he was dead.

He's not dead.

"Under the house where you told me to go yesterday. You said you'd come get me."

He squeezes my wrist real tight and he leans forward and says, "Don't ever fucking wake me up from a nap again, you little bastard! Now go get in the shower, you smell like a goddamn sewer!"

He pushes me away from him. I step back, still confused how he's alive.

I thought the men came. I thought they killed him.

He squeezes the back of my neck and shoves me until I stumble out of the living room. He said he would come get me, but I don't think he even remembered I was under the house.

I can feel my eyes start to get warm, so I run out of the living room. I can't cry in front of my dad or he'll get really mad.

I walk down the hallway toward the bathroom, but really all I want to do is eat something. My stomach has never been this hungry before. When I pass the bedroom where my mom stays most of the day, her door is open. She's asleep in her bed, so I walk inside her bedroom to ask her if I can have something to eat. I shake her and try to wake her up, but she just groans and rolls over. "Let me sleep, Asa," she says.

I don't like how much she sleeps. She says she can't sleep very well on her own, so she takes lots of pills that help her sleep better. She says the white ones are for the nighttime, but she takes them when the sun is up sometimes. I've seen her do it.

She has some yellow ones, but she says those are her *special* pills. She says she saves those for the days when she wants to go somewhere else in her mind.

I look at her bottle of pills and I wonder if she would notice if I stole one of the yellow ones. Because I want to go somewhere else in my mind. I don't want my mind to be inside this house anymore.

I pick up her bottle of yellow pills and I try and try, but I can't get them open. I'm not very good at reading because I'm only in the first grade, but I finally figure out that the lid says I have to push down and then twist it open.

When I do that, it opens this time. I look at my mom, but she's still facing the other way. I hurry up and take one of her yellow pills and I put it in my mouth and chew it. My face crinkles up because it's the grossest thing I've ever eaten. It's real bitter and makes my mouth dry. I take a drink of my mom's water so I can wash it down.

I hope she's right. I hope this pill takes me somewhere else in my mind, because I'm getting really tired of being in this family.

I put the lid back on the bottle and I sneak out of my mom's room. By the time I get to the bathroom to take a shower, my legs already feel like they aren't mine again.

So do my arms. My arms feel like they're floating in the air.

I look in the mirror after I turn the water in the shower on, because it feels like my hair is growing. It doesn't look longer, though. It looks the same. *But I can feel it growing.*

My toes start to tingle just like my legs. I feel like I'm about to fall down, so I hurry up and sit down in the bathtub. I forget to take my clothes off, but that's okay because my clothes are really dirty. I think my clothes need the water, too.

I wonder how long I was under the house for. I probably missed a day of school. I don't really like school that much, but I really wanted to go today so I could see what Brady's mom packed him for lunch.

Brady sits next to me at the lunch table and he brings a lunchbox every day. One time his mom packed him a piece of coconut cake. He doesn't like coconut cake, so he told me I could have it. It was so good. I went home and told my mom how good it was, but she still hasn't bought me coconut cake.

Sometimes Brady's mom writes notes and puts them inside of his lunchbox. He reads them all to us and he laughs because he thinks they're dumb. I never laugh, though. I don't think the notes are dumb.

One time I saw one of the notes he threw in the trash and I picked it up. It said, "Dear Brady. I love you! Have a great day at school!"

I tore the top of the note off that had Brady's name on it and I kept it. I pretended my mother wrote it for me and sometimes I would read it. But that was a long time ago and I lost the note recently. That's why I wanted to go to school today because if Brady had another note from his mom, I wanted to steal it and pretend it was for me again.

I wonder how it would feel to have someone say those words to me.

I love you!

No one has ever said that to me.

I feel dizzy. It feels like my head is floating on the ceiling and my eyes are looking down at my body, sitting in the bathtub. I wonder if this is why my mom likes the yellow pills. Because it makes her feel like the important parts of her are floating high in the air where no one can reach her?

I close my eyes and whisper, "*I love you,*" to no one while I float in the air. Someday I'll find someone and I'll make them like me enough to want to say those words to me. I want it to be a girl. A *pretty* girl. One my dad doesn't think is a whore.

That would be nice. Maybe she'll love me enough to make me coconut cake. I really like coconut cake.

If I ever find a girl who says those words to me and makes me coconut cake, I'll keep her. I won't throw her away like Brady throws away the notes from his mom.

I'll keep her forever and I'll never let her leave me. I'll make her tell me she loves me every single day.

"I love you, Asa," she'll promise me. "I'll never leave you."

FORTY-TWO

Asa

’ve never killed anyone before. Not until just a few minutes ago when I shot the guy upstairs for trying to take what wasn't his.

I'm still not sure how I feel.

I should probably be worried, because murder comes with repercussions. I should also be pissed, because as soon as I shot the guy and pulled Sloan into this room, the rest of those fuckers I hired scrambled like eggs.

I guess they're scared I'll shoot them, too.

I suppose I am a little worried about the repercussions and all that shit. Normally when a gun is fired, someone calls the cops. Which means they're probably on their way here right now, thanks to a nosey goddamn neighbor.

And I'm referring to the *real* cops. Not this poor excuse sitting in front of me right now.

I'm disappointed this isn't going down how I had planned. I shoot *one* guy out of self-defense and the rest of them just give up on their fucking duties and scram? That means Jon, Kevin, and Dalton are no longer being detained by them. Which means at least one of them is about to come beating on this door, wondering why the fuck I set them all up like I did.

Which means...*I'm kind of in a bind right now*. I'm running out of options. I think the only option I really have left is to shoot Luke in his goddamn smug face and get Sloan out of here while I still can. Sure, she's going to be a little traumatized. But we could go to therapy or something whenever we get settled again. She's going to need it after being brainwashed like she was.

It's kind of sad that I'm only left with one option and I only have a minute or so to follow through with it, because I really wanted to hear Luke tell me what it was like when he fucked Sloan.

Not because I would have been turned on by it. *I'm not fucking morbid.*

I wanted to hear it, because I need the vision. I need to know what he said to her to make her fall for it. I need to know if he had to talk her into it like I did. I need to know if she made the same noises that she sometimes makes when she's with me. I want to know what position he fucked her in. Was he on top? Was she? Was he behind her?

I just need to know so I can make sure I don't do or say any of the things he said to her when I make love to her in the future. I need to make sure I never fuck her in the same positions *he* fucked her in.

But now I'm out of goddamn time, because someone is beating on the door and Luke still hasn't opened his mouth.

"Asa!"

It's Dalton.

I'm still not sure what to think about Dalton. I really like him. He's coke, everybody likes coke. But everyone knows cocaine is one of the most widely impersonated drugs there is. A whole hell of a lot of imposters. Dealers selling crushed up aspirin on street corners to half-dead crack addicts who can't even tell the difference.

Dalton may not even *be* cocaine. He's probably a bottle of fucking *Advil*, crushed up and poured into a baggie.

"Asa, open the door!" Dalton yells.

I reach behind me and make sure the door is locked. "Where did everyone go?" I yell to Dalton. "It's quiet out there!"

"Open the door so we can talk." He's right on the other side of the door now.

I laugh and repeat myself. "Where *is* everyone, Dalton? Where are Jon and Kevin?"

"They left. They got paranoid and left."

Of course they did. Fucking best friends for life. *Assholes.*

I look over at Sloan. She's sitting at the head of the bed, her knees pulled up to her chest. She's watching me, wide-eyed.

Luke is watching me, too. It doesn't matter where I'm standing or what I'm doing, his eyes are always fucking on me. Have been since the day I met him. The day *Dalton* introduced me to him.

I tilt my head until my mouth is close to the crack in the door. "Why are you still here, Dalton? Waiting on your backup to arrive?"

Dalton isn't so quick to respond this time. After a pause, he says, "I'm here because my friend is in there. If you let him go, we'll leave."

I can't believe I fucking fell for this. Months of practically living with these fuckers and all they were here to do is destroy me.

Kind of feels like my childhood all over again.

At least Sloan loves me.

At least.

I drag my eyes across the room until they land on her. "Remember when I was in the shower earlier and you asked me if I wanted anything from the grocery store?"

She nods, but barely.

"I told you I wanted a dessert for the celebration. Did you get one?"

She nods again. "Your favorite," she whispers. "Coconut cake."

See? She fucking loves me.

"Dalton," I say, demanding his attention. Not that it ever left me.

I should probably move over. He's right on the other side of this door. Wouldn't put it past the fucker to shoot me through it.

I step against the wall and reach down to make sure the door is locked. "Do me a favor, will you? Bring us the coconut cake."

Again, Dalton pauses for a moment before responding. "You want *cake*?" he says, confused. "You fucking want *cake*?"

Why does that sound so ridiculous?

"Yes, I want cake! Bring us the fucking coconut cake, asshole!"

I hear Dalton's footsteps fade as he walks into the kitchen. Luke is staring at me like I've lost my mind.

"You got a problem?"

He shakes his head and opens his mouth to speak. *Finally.*

"There's medication that can help you, Asa."

Medication?

"What the fuck are you talking about?"

Luke glances at Sloan and then back at me. I hate it when he looks at her. It makes me want to rip his fucking eyes out and swallow them like my mother's yellow pills.

"You've checked the lock on the door fifteen times in the last five minutes," he says. "That isn't normal behavior. But it can be controlled. Just like your father's behavior could have been controlled."

This is where I cut the fucker off. "Talk about my father again, Luke. I *dare* you."

His eyes meet the gun that's pointed straight at him now, but for some reason, he still doesn't shut the fuck up.

"Did you know he was diagnosed with paranoid schizophrenia when he was only twenty-seven? I read it in his file. He never took his meds, Asa, not even once. The things going on inside your head—they can stop. It can all stop. You don't have to be like him."

I stride across the room and press the fucking gun to his head. "I'm *not* like him! I'm *nothing* like him!"

Before I pull the trigger, Dalton beats on the door.

"How am I supposed to give you the cake?" Dalton yells.

Fuck. Good question.

I start to walk to the door, but the anticipation of coconut cake is ripped from me when I hear sirens. The sound is far off—maybe four or five streets over.

I still have time. If there was a fucking window in this bedroom, I could grab Sloan, shoot Luke, and be out the window and to the car before they get here.

But mother-fucking Dalton is standing in my way.

If he's standing at the door holding a cake, that means he's probably right...about...*there.*

I aim my gun and as soon as I fire it, something hard meets my back. I fall forward, my knees hit the floor, and the gun flies out of my hands. I look behind me and Luke is standing over me, pulling his leg back to kick me in the face. I roll to the side and swipe my leg across the floor, knocking him off balance. He lands on his back.

He immediately starts trying to pull his legs through his arms so his hands will be cuffed in front of him rather than behind him. I sit up and reach for my gun, but Sloan jumps off the bed and lunges across the floor. Our hands reach the gun at the same time, but mine are more experienced and know where to grab it to get the better grip. Her hands fumble around mine until she's aware that the gun is firmly planted back in my hand. I shove her away from me, back in the goddamn corner.

She hits the wall and scoots as far away from me as she can. By the time I get the gun pointed at Luke, the fucker somehow got his hands around to his front. He's pulling himself to his feet, so I stay a step ahead and pull the fucking trigger. I watch as the flesh of his thigh explodes into tiny pieces.

Fuck, that looks like it hurt.

He's on his knees.

His back slams against the wall. He's wincing, pressing his hands against his wound. Dalton is beating on the door now. "Asa, open the fucking door or I'm shooting it open! Three...two..."

"If you open that door, they're both dead!" I yell.

Dalton never makes it to one.

I look at Sloan and she's huddled against the wall, hands over her ears, tears pouring out of her eyes. She's staring at Luke, looking like she's about to flip the fuck out. I need to get her out of here before she does. But the sirens are closer now. More than likely on this street.

Fuck.

Think, Asa. Think.

I smack my gun against my forehead three times. I can't lose her. I can't. If I'm arrested, I won't be able to protect her. I won't be able to touch her. She'll fall for someone else's lies. Maybe even *Luke's* again.

She's the only person who has ever loved me. I can't lose her. I can't.

I crawl over to her and try to grab her hands, but she keeps pulling away from me. I have to point the damn gun at her head just to get her to be still. I press my forehead to the side of her head. "Tell me you love me, Sloan." She's shaking so hard, she can't even speak. "*Please*, baby. I need to hear you say it."

She tries three times to get her voice to work, but she keeps stuttering. Her lips are trembling harder than I've ever seen. She finally gets out one sentence. "Let Luke go and I'll say it."

I squeeze my hand around the gun. I wrap my other hand in her hair and squeeze. She's trying to fucking *negotiate* for him?

I blow out a steady breath through my nostrils. My jaw is wound up too tight to let any air through my mouth. When I calm myself enough to speak, I grit my teeth and whisper, "You love me, right? You don't love him. You love *me*."

I pull back and meet her petrified eyes. She lifts her chin and says, "I'll answer that after you let him go. He needs a doctor, Asa."

A doctor? He doesn't need a *doctor*. He needs a mother-fucking miracle.

"I don't need you to answer that," I say to her. "I have a feeling if I kill him, I'll be able to tell if you love him based on your reaction."

Her eyes widen and she immediately begins shaking her head. "I don't," she blurts out. "Please don't kill him, it'll make things worse for you. I love *you*, Asa. Please don't kill anyone else."

I'm staring right at her, looking back and forth between her eyes. It's hard to see any truth there, because all I see is the concern she has for Luke written across her face. "Don't worry, Sloan. He's probably wearing a bullet-proof vest."

I turn my head and lift my gun, aiming it straight at Luke's chest. I fire the shot. Luke's whole body jerks against the wall. His hands go to his chest just as the blood begins pouring through his fingers. He immediately falls limp onto his side.

"Oh. My bad. I was wrong."

Sloan is screaming. Screaming his fucking *name*, screaming *no*, screaming *what have you done*, screaming his *name* again, *screaming, screaming, screaming.*

She's fucking *screaming.*

She has fucking *tears.*

For *him.*

I grab her by the goddamn arms and pick her up, dropping her back down on the bed. I straddle her while she covers her head and screams even louder, the tears flooding down her face.

"Why are you fucking *screaming*, Sloan? *WHY!*"

I can hear my father's voice repeating *whore, whore, whore.* I smack my forehead to get it to stop.

Stop, stop, stop.

She doesn't love him. She loves *me.* Forever.

"You don't love him, Sloan," I say, my face twisting in pain. "You *don't*, he brainwashed you." I grab her cheeks and press my lips to hers. She's trying to pull away from me, trying to fight me.

"Yes I do!" she screams. "I love him, I hate you, I love him, I fucking *hate* you!"

She's going to regret this. She's going to regret this more than she's ever regretted anything in her whole fucking worthless life. If she thinks she's sad now watching that bastard die, wait until she sees *me* die.

She barely knew the guy. She's loved me for *two fucking years!* My death would fucking *devastate* her. She'll be crying so hard, she won't have enough air to say she hates anyone.

Whore, whore, whore.

I smack my hand against my forehead again and then I press my forehead to hers. She's no longer screaming now. She's just sobbing uncontrollably.

"You're going to regret this, Sloan. You think you're crying hard now? When I die, it'll fucking *kill* you. *It. Will. Fucking. Kill. You.*"

She shakes her head back and forth, sobbing through her words. "It's *too late* to kill me, Asa. You killed me a long fucking time ago."

She's delusional.

She's goddamn delusional.

I laugh, knowing how much this is going to upset her. I laugh, knowing how much she's going to regret everything she just said to me. I wish I could be here to see it when she finally realizes how much I mean to her. How much I've done for her. What her life will be like without me.

I press my mouth against her trembling lips.

I press the gun to the side of my head and I pull the fucking—

FORTY-THREE

You know what they say dying feels like?

No. You *don't* know what they say, because no one *says* it. The people who die aren't around to tell us what it felt like when it happened. The people who lived never died to begin with, so they're unable to describe it.

But I'm in it. So let me tell you about it while I still can.

There's a moment—a split second right before you close your eyes for the very last time—when you can actually feel yourself embracing death.

You can feel your heart as it begins to slow down, preparing to come to a halt.

You can feel your brain shutting off, the circuits slamming shut like doors.

You can feel your eyes closing—no matter how fucking hard you try to keep them open. And you realize that whatever you're looking at in the moment you close your eyes—that's the last thing you're ever going to see.

I see Sloan. She's all I see.

I see her screaming.

I see Asa pick her up and throw her on the bed.

I see her trying to fight him off.

I see her giving up.

That's why I refuse to close my eyes.

I look down at the blood pouring from my chest—the life seeping out of me and onto the floor. I've made enough mistakes that caused Sloan to be in the position she's in right now. I refuse to die without correcting a few of them.

It takes everything in me—but I stretch my arms out until I'm able to reach the gun at my ankle. There's blood all over my hands, so I struggle getting a grip on it, but finally manage. I may not be the best at my profession in a lot of areas, but I have one hell of an aim.

Right when I lift my gun, Asa points his gun at himself.

No fucking way is he getting off that easy.

I refuse to close my eyes as I wrap my finger around the trigger and squeeze, watching as the bullet penetrates his wrist, sending his gun several feet across the room.

I refuse to close my eyes when the sounds of three more shots penetrate my ears, this time coming from the direction of the bedroom door.

I refuse to close my eyes as I watch Ryan kick open the door and rush in, followed by several other men.

I refuse to close my eyes until Asa is on the floor—several feet away from Sloan—being handcuffed.

I refuse to close my eyes until they meet Sloan's.

She's off the bed, across the room, on her knees, pressing her hands to my chest, doing everything she can to keep the rest of the life from seeping out of me.

I don't even have enough energy left to tell her it's too late.

I close my eyes for the last time.

But it's okay, because she's all I see.

She's the last thing I'll ever see.

FORTY-FOUR

Sloan

This feeling is nothing new to me. I've experienced living through the death of someone I've loved before. Horrendous, heart-wrenching, soul-crushing death.

It was one month before I turned thirteen.

I had twin brothers, Stephen and Drew. From early on I basically became their caretaker. Both my brothers had a lot of medical issues, but my mother used to leave all hours of the night, regardless of their needs. She would go through spurts where she could be the mother she needed to be. She'd get them to their doctor's visits for the medications they needed in order to convince the state she was a decent mother. But then she'd leave the majority of their everyday care up to me while she went out and partied or did whatever it was she did until the early hours of the morning.

The night Drew died, my brothers were in my care. I can't remember all the details because I try not to think about that night too much, but I remember hearing him fall in his bedroom. He had seizures frequently, and I knew he had more than likely just had a seizure, so I ran to his room to check on him.

When I opened the door, he was on the floor, his whole body jerking from the seizure. I dropped to my knees and held him as still as I could, but since he had turned ten, it became increasingly difficult for me to help him due to the fact that he and Stephen were already bigger than me. I did my best, holding his head until it was over.

It wasn't until the seizure had stopped completely that I noticed the blood. It was all over my hands and on my clothes. I started to panic when I saw the gash on the side of his head. Blood was everywhere.

When he had fallen from the seizure, he hit his head on the door hinge going down. We didn't have a phone, so I was forced to leave him alone in the room while I ran to a neighbor's house and called 9-1-1.

By the time I returned, he was no longer breathing. I'm not sure he ever took another breath after the moment I left him. I wasn't aware at the time that he had died from the blow to his head, but I realize now that he had probably died before I even dialed 9-1-1.

I changed after that night. Before that moment, I still held on to a little hope for my life. I knew that no one could be cursed as a child with such awful parents, only to then go on to have an equally awful adolescence and adulthood. Until that point, I thought maybe everyone's life had an equal balance of good and bad and the only difference was that the good and bad luck was dispersed to each person differently at different points in their lives. I had hope that all my bad luck had been dispersed early on in my life and that things would only get easier.

But that night changed my way of thinking.

Drew could have fallen anywhere in that bedroom other than where he did. In fact, the doctor said the location of his injury was so unfortunate, he could have fallen a mere six centimeters to the left or right and he would have been fine.

Six centimeters. That's all that separated Drew from life.

The impact to his temple killed him almost instantly.

I obsessed over that six centimeters for months. Long after my mother had stopped pretending to grieve his death.

I obsessed over it, because I knew that if he had fallen six centimeters to the left or right, his survival would have been referred to as a "miracle."

But what happened to Drew was the opposite of a miracle. It was a tragic accident.

A tragic accident that made me lose my belief in miracles altogether. By the time I was thirteen, anything labeled a "miracle" pissed me the hell off.

That's one of the main reasons why I never partook much in social media. The amount of "miracles" seen in my Facebook newsfeed would make my eyes practically roll out of my head. So many people "cured" of cancer, thanks to the prayers of all their Facebook friends. *"It's benign! Hallelujah! God is so good to me!"*

There were so many times I wanted to reach through my laptop screen and grab those people by the shoulders and scream, "Hey! Guess what! *You aren't special!"*

Lots of people die from cancer. Where was *their* miracle? Did their Facebook friends not pray enough? Why did their chemotherapy not work? Because they didn't post enough public prayer requests on social media? Why didn't they get their miracle? Does God think less of their lives than those whose lives he spares?

No.

Sometimes cancer is cured...sometimes it isn't. Sometimes people hit their heads and die, most of the time they hit their heads and survive. And anytime you hear of a person beating the odds... that's all they're doing. *Beating the odds.*

Because people never really think about how, in order to beat the odds, a lot of unfortunate deaths have to occur for that particular survival to be considered "out of the norm."

Maybe Drew's death hardened me to the idea of miracles, but in my mind, you either survive or you don't. The journey from first breath to death has nothing to do with miracles, how much you pray, coincidences, or divine intervention.

Sometimes a person's journey from first breath to death isn't always part of a master plan. Sometimes the only thing that separates your final breath from your death is a mere six centimeters.

That's why—when the doctor walked into the waiting room to update me on Luke's condition—I had to sit down when he said, "*If the bullet had made impact just six centimeters to the left or right of where it did, Luke would have died instantly. Now all we can do is pray for a miracle.*"

I failed to tell the doctor that I don't believe in miracles.

Luke is either going to survive...*or he's not.*

<hr>

"You should go grab some coffee," Ryan says. "Stretch your legs."

Luke came out of surgery over eight hours ago. He lost a lot of blood and had to have a transfusion, and I've refused to leave his side since.

I shake my head. "I'm not leaving until he wakes up."

Ryan sighs, but he knows there's no talking me out of my decision. He walks to the door, "I'll bring you a coffee, then."

I watch as he exits the room. He's been at this hospital the entire time I have, even though I know there are probably job-related things he should be doing right now. Giving statements about what happened last night. *Taking* statements. Dealing with a murder, an arrest, an attempted murder.

I never saw them take Asa out of the bedroom last night because I was too worried about Luke to care what happened to him. But I could hear him. The whole time I was pressing my hands against Luke's chest, waiting on the paramedics to arrive, Asa was behind me yelling, "Let him *die*, Sloan! He doesn't love you! I love you! *I* do!"

I never turned around to acknowledge him or his words. I continued to try to help Luke while they pulled Asa out of the bedroom. The last thing I heard him say was, "It's *my* fucking *cake*! Let me take my fucking coconut *cake!*"

I don't know what's going to happen next with Asa. I'm certain there will be some sort of trial, but I honestly don't want to testify. I'm afraid if I testify, he'll get off easier than he should. Because I would have to be honest. I'd have to tell them about all the things I've witnessed in his behavior, specifically the drastic changes in recent weeks. It's obvious to everyone who knows him that he's more than likely developing symptoms of schizophrenia—the same hereditary illness his father had. But if that's the case, he'll more than likely be sentenced to a high-security mental health facility than a prison.

And even though I do want him to get help for whatever is going on with him, I also want him to pay. I want him to pay for every single thing he's ever done and I want him to pay forever. *In a prison.* Where he'll rot with men who are probably twice as evil as he could ever dream of being.

Some might call that bitter. I just call it karma.

I grip the arms of my chair and whisper to no one. "I'm done thinking about you, Asa Jackson."

And I am. He's taken up way too much of my life already and now I just want to focus on the future. On Stephen. *On Luke.*

There are tubes and wires and IVs hooked up to him, but I'm somehow still able to find an area on his bed where I can fit if I curl up just right. I crawl onto the bed with him and I wrap my arm over him, lay my head on his shoulder, and close my eyes.

Several minutes later, Ryan's voice pulls me out of my slumber. "Coffee."

I open my eyes and he's sitting on the chair by the bed, holding a coffee out to me. It's probably the fifth cup I've had since Luke came out of surgery, but I'm pretty sure I'm good for about a million more if it takes that long.

Ryan sits back in his chair and takes a sip of his coffee, then grips it with both hands and leans forward.

"Did he ever tell you how we met?" Ryan asks.

I shake my head.

I can see a nostalgic smile begin to play on Ryan's lips. "We were assigned a job together a while back. He broke cover the second night we were there," Ryan says, shaking his head. "I was so angry at him, but I knew why he did it. I can't go into all the details, but if he hadn't outed himself when he did, a kid would have lost his life. Luke couldn't have lived with himself if that had happened. I knew in that moment that he had the worst kind of heart for this job. But as pissed as I was at him, I respected the hell out of him for what he did. He cared more about the life of a kid he didn't even know than he did about his own career. And that's not a flaw, Sloan. That's a character trait. Pretty sure they call it compassion," he says with a wink.

Ryan's story makes me smile for the first time in forever. "That's the sexiest thing about him," I whisper. "His compassion."

He shrugs. "I don't know...he's got a great ass."

I laugh. I wouldn't really know—Luke was sitting down when I had my only chance to see it.

I put my coffee on the bedside table and then lean in and give Luke a peck on the mouth. I've made sure to kiss him every chance I get, just in case I don't get many more chances.

When I pull my lips from his and start to rest my head on his pillow, I hear a quiet noise come from his throat. Ryan leaps out of his chair at the same moment I lift my head back up.

"Did he just make a noise?" Ryan asks, his voice full of disbelief.

"I think so," I whisper.

Ryan waves his arm toward Luke. "Kiss him again! I think it woke him up!"

I do. I kiss him lightly on the lips again and there's no mistaking the noise Luke makes this time. He's definitely waking up.

We both stare at him for a moment while his eyelids flutter open and then shut, several times. "Luke? Can you hear me?" Ryan asks.

Luke finally forces his eyes open, but he doesn't look directly at Ryan. Instead, his eyes move painfully around the room until he's looking down at me, curled up at his side. He stares for a moment, and then with a weak voice he whispers, "Kaleidoscope belt buckles see leprechauns when the fog drops it like it's hot."

Tears immediately form in my eyes and I have to choke back my cry.

"Oh, God," Ryan says. "He's not making any sense. This isn't good. I'll go get the doctor." He runs out of the room before I can tell him that Luke is perfectly fine.

I lift my hand to Luke's face and touch his lips. I whisper, "Depressed baguettes linger on the playground eating bowls of cereal until the slugs wilt." My voice cracks with my relief—with my happiness—with my gratefulness. My lips meet his, and even though I know this isn't good for him and he's probably in a lot of pain, I hug him wherever I can and kiss him in all the places I can reach on his face and neck. I wrap myself around him, careful to keep my arms and hands away from his injuries. I lie quietly with him while the tears roll down my cheeks.

"Sloan," he says, his voice gravelly. "I can't remember what happened after I fucked everything up. Did you end up saving me?"

I laugh and lift up on my elbow. "Not really," I say quietly. "You shot Asa's gun out of his hand and then I ran over to you and put pressure on your wound until the paramedics got there. I'd say it was a mutual save."

He tries to force a smile. "I told you I wasn't very good at my job," he says.

I smile in whole-hearted agreement. "It's not too late to quit, you know. You could go back to school and become a Spanish teacher."

He winces with his laugh. "That's not a bad idea, Sloan."

He struggles to lean forward in order to kiss me, but it takes everything in him. He's only six centimeters away.

A mere six centimeters between breath and life.

When I close that six-centimeter gap and kiss him, I know I'm closing a chapter. A really dark chapter that I've been waiting more than two years to end.

And this kiss is just the beginning of a whole new book. A book where maybe miracles aren't that far-fetched.

FORTY-FOUR

Asa

I sit up straight and open my eyes.Not that I was sleeping. No one could sleep in this goddamn place. I breathe in through my nose and out my mouth, wondering why it's just now hitting me.She didn't say *harder*. She fucking said *Carter*! "Fucking whore!"

THE END

EPILOGUE

Sloan

I tap lightly on the door to his hospital room, but no one responds. When I push it open and peek inside, Luke is asleep. The volume to the TV is low, but audible. I glance over to the couch and Ryan is lying on his side, a ball cap covering his eyes. He's asleep, too.

I hold the door while it closes, not wanting to wake either of them, but Ryan hears me and sits up on the couch. He stretches his arms over his head and yawns, then stands up.

"Hey," he says. "You gonna be here a while?"

I nod. "I'll probably stay here tonight," I whisper. "You go get some rest."

He glances over at Luke again and says, "The doctor came by earlier. Says he'll get to go home tomorrow, but he'll need someone to stay with him for a while. He's on strict bed rest. I would offer, but I'm sure he'd rather you do it."

I set my purse down on the couch. "It's fine. I can stay with him if he's okay with it."

"I'm perfectly okay with that," Luke says from his bed. I glance in his direction and he's smiling at me lazily.

Ryan laughs and says, "I'll stop by in the morning after my meeting with Young."

Luke nods and then motions for me. "Come here."

I walk toward him as Ryan leaves the room. Just like every other time I visit him, he scoots over and makes room for me to lie with him.

I wrap my leg over his and my arm over his chest, resting my head on his shoulder.

"How's your brother?" he asks.

"Good," I say. "Really good. You'll have to go with me soon if you're up for it. He kept looking up at the door like you were going to show up, so I know he was disappointed that you weren't with me."

I feel the light laughter in Luke's chest. "I tried to sneak out and go with you today, but someone is being overprotective."

I shake my head. "You got shot in the chest, Luke. You almost died. I'm not taking any chances." I lift my head from his shoulder and rest my head on my hand. "Speaking of taking chances, what exactly did the doctor say about your release tomorrow? Bed rest? No strenuous activity?"

He runs a hand through my hair and smiles at me. "What if I told you he said plenty of bed rest *and* strenuous activity?"

"I'd call you a liar."

He makes a face. "Four to six weeks," he says. "Doctor says my heart needs to take it easy. Do you know how difficult that's gonna be with you taking care of me?"

I run my fingers over his chest, feeling the bandages beneath his hospital gown. "Four to six weeks is nothing when we have forever."

He laughs a little. "Easy for you to say. Guys think about sex every seven seconds."

"That's a myth," I tell him. "I learned in biological science that it's actually only thirty-four times a day."

Luke stares at me for a few quiet seconds and then says, "That's still almost a thousand times in the next four weeks I'll have to refrain."

I shake my head with a smile. "I'll try to make it easy on you, then. I won't shower or brush my hair or put on makeup for the next month."

"That won't help," he says. "Might even make it worse."

I lower my head and press my lips to his neck. "If it's too hard on you, we can hire a male nurse to take care of you instead of me," I tease.

Luke tightens his arm around me and yawns. "No one is taking care of me but you," he whispers.

I can hear the pain meds kicking in by the sound of his voice, so I don't respond to him. We lie there for a while, until I'm almost certain he's asleep. But then he says, "Sloan? Where are you staying?"

I was waiting for this question. He's been here in the hospital for two weeks now and every time he starts to bring up my living situation, I tell him we'll talk about it later.

I have a feeling he's not going to let me redirect the conversation this time.

"In a hotel."

He instantly stiffens, reaching to my chin to lift my face to his. "Are you kidding me?"

I shrug. "It's fine, Luke. I'll find an apartment soon."

"Which hotel?"

"The one on Stratton."

His jaw hardens. "You're checking out today. You shouldn't be there alone, it's not a safe neighborhood." He tries to adjust himself to where he's sitting up, lifting the head of the bed several inches. "Why have you not told me this?"

I flick my hand at him. "You almost died, Luke. The last thing you need right now is to stress over my situation more than you already have."

He drops his head back to his pillow, raking his hands over his face. He locks eyes with me. "You'll stay with me. I need the help, anyway. There's no point in you paying for a hotel."

"I'm not moving in with you. I'll come take care of you for however long you need me to, but we barely know each other. That's too much, too soon."

He lowers his chin and stares at me, hard. "You're staying with me, Sloan. I'm not asking you to make it permanent. But until I'm recovered and you have your own apartment, you aren't going back to that hotel."

It really is a scary hotel, but it's all I could afford. After Asa was arrested, I grabbed my hidden stash and a few items of clothing and haven't stepped foot back inside that house.

I nod. "Two weeks, tops. Then I'll have my own place."

He sighs, relieved that I'm not arguing. But I honestly have no idea how I'll be able to afford an apartment in two weeks. I'll have to find a job and a car. I had to borrow Luke's car to visit Stephen today, but I can't keep doing that.

I feel Luke's hand slide through my hair and wrap around the nape of my neck. When our eyes meet, there's a softness in his that wasn't there a few seconds ago. "Stop overthinking it," he says quietly. "You aren't in this alone anymore, Sloan. Okay?"

I release a sigh. "Okay," I whisper.

It's the first time in my life I feel like my burdens aren't all mine. I've never met anyone who brings more relief to my life than they do stress. Until Luke.

Love shouldn't feel like added weight. It should make you feel as light as air.

Asa made everything in my life heavy.

Luke makes me feel like I'm floating.

I guess that's the difference between being loved the right way and the wrong way. You either feel tethered to an anchor...or you feel like you're flying.

———

"You need anything else?" I ask him.

It's the first time I've ever been to Luke's house, and I was shocked to see that it's very normal. A home in a neighborhood about an hour or so from where I lived with Asa. It's even closer to my brother's facility.

Luke says he rents the house, he doesn't own it. He never knows what his jobs are going to be, so he hasn't been ready to commit to a mortgage yet.

"I'm fine," he says. "Stop worrying. I'll let you know if I need anything, okay?"

I nod. I glance around his bedroom, not really knowing what I should do with myself. He probably wants some sleep. It just feels weird with this not being my house.

"You want to crawl in bed with me and watch a movie?" he asks, lifting the blanket.

"That sounds like heaven."

I crawl into bed and snuggle up to him just like I did at the hospital every day. He turns on the TV and begins flipping through the channels. After a minute or so, he says, "Thank you, Sloan."

I glance up at him. "For what?"

His eyes scroll over my face, slowly. "For everything," he whispers. "For taking care of me. For being as strong as you are, despite everything you've been through."

I know the doctor said no strenuous activity, but I doubt the doctor knew Luke could say such appealing things. I press my lips to his, because it feels hella good being thanked. And complimented. Heck, just having someone be nice to me is so new, it makes me melt every time he opens his mouth.

His hand comes around to the back of my head and he kisses me harder.

This isn't good. Luke is right. Four weeks of this and we're expected to refrain? Jesus Christ. We're screwed.

But then we're spared by a loud knock on the door.

"I'll get it," he says, pulling back the covers. I yank the covers back over him.

"No you won't. You'll rest. I'll get the door."

He grabs my hand as I'm sliding off the bed. "Check the peephole first," he says. "If it's Ryan, he'll scratch his neck to let you know it's safe to open the door. If he doesn't scratch his neck, do not open that door."

I pause, wondering why their silent codes are even necessary. I don't ask, though. This undercover shit is going to take some getting used to. I hope Luke was serious when he said he was switching professions.

When I reach the front door and check the peephole, sure enough, Ryan is scratching at his neck. But there's someone else with him. A girl.

"There's a girl with him!" I whisper loudly as I run back into Luke's bedroom.

"Long blonde hair?" he asks.

I nod.

"That's fine, it's just Tillie."

Tillie. Great.

I go back to the living room and enter the passcode to the alarm, then open the door.

"Hey," Ryan says, making his way inside, followed by Tillie. She smiles at me, but I'm already intimidated by her. She's a few inches taller than me, decked out in sleek black pants and a tucked in white collared shirt. She has the top two buttons open, revealing a shiny silver braided necklace. I've never seen simple look this good.

"Tillie, this is Sloan. Sloan, Tillie."

She reaches out to shake my hand and it almost hurts, she has such a good grip. I can't help but think about the fact that she's made out with Luke. Even if it was just for work, it still makes my stomach feel weird knowing this fact about them. I don't let it bother me too much though. I get it.

As if she can read my mind, she says, "I'm sorry about making out with Luke in your house. It was necessary, but will never happen again. Believe me. It's almost as bad as when I had to kiss this one for show," she says, pointing at Ryan.

Ryan rolls his eyes. "Tillie, Tillie, Tillie," he says. "That was over a year ago and you still can't stop thinking about my tongue in your mouth."

She nods. "Nightmares are hard to overcome."

I laugh. I instantly like her. I close the door behind me and point to the bedroom. "He's in his room," I tell them both.

Ryan glances toward the room and then back at me. There's something in his expression that concerns me, but he's trying to hide it with a forced smile. "You mind if we talk to Luke alone?" he asks.

I cross one arm over my stomach and grab the other. I look back and forth between him and Tillie. "Does it have to do with Asa?"

I can see Tillie look briefly in Ryan's direction, her eyes revealing that Asa is exactly what they intend to talk to Luke about.

"I want to know," I say to them. "If you don't let me hear what you're going to tell him, I'll eavesdrop at the door."

Ryan doesn't laugh. His lips tighten together and he just nods. "Fair enough," he says.

They both turn to walk into Luke's bedroom and I'm forced to inhale a calming breath.

This doesn't look good.

LUKE

I can see Tillie and Ryan making their way into my bedroom, but my eyes are on Sloan. She's standing in the living room with her eyes closed, looking like she's about to be sick.

"What'd you say to her?" I ask Ryan.

Right when I ask him that question, she blows out a rush of air, opens her eyes, stands up straight, and walks toward my bedroom.

Ryan shakes his head. "Nothing. She's insisting on being in here for what I'm about to tell you."

Sloan is in the bedroom now, leaning against the door, watching as Ryan and Tillie make their way around the room to the couch. The last thing I want is for Sloan to be involved. If I could have my way, she'd never have to hear Asa's name again. But I know we've got a long road ahead of us and a lot of court hearings. Possibly even testimonies on the stand. So until Asa is convicted and put away for good, I know I'm not going to be able to protect her from all of it. Instead, I pat the spot beside me on the bed and encourage her to come sit with me.

She does. Once she's settled next to me and we're both propped against the headboard, I look at Ryan. "What is it you don't want to tell me?"

He shakes his head and leans forward, clasping his hands in front of him. "I don't even know where to start," he says, his eyes meeting mine. "I met with Young today."

"And?"

"It wasn't good," Ryan says. "I don't even know how to sugar coat this, so I'm just going to explain it in a way you'll both understand."

Sloan's hand wraps around mine and I can already feel her shaking. I squeeze her hand for reassurance. Ryan tends to overdramatize situations; I just wish Sloan knew that so she wouldn't be this worried.

"Asa is claiming he shot the guy in his bedroom out of self-defense."

Sloan scoffs. "It wasn't self-defense!" she says. "I was there!"

Ryan nods softly. "Not in defense of *himself*," Ryan says. "He claims he was defending *you*. That he heard you screaming for help, and when he walked into his room, the guy was attacking you and he was holding a gun. He claims he had no other choice but to stop him before he killed you."

Sloan is shaking her head. "It wasn't..." She looks at me. "Luke, he didn't have to kill him."

I knew Asa was going to pull this shit. I wrap my arm around Sloan and refocus my attention on Ryan. "What does this mean exactly?" I ask. "When it goes to trial, his defense won't stand up to Sloan's testimony?"

Ryan blows out a quick breath. "That's what we're hoping," he says. "If it goes to trial."

"*If?*" Sloan says, voicing my exact thought.

Tillie speaks up this time. "The thing is..." she says. "It's a solid case of self-defense. The guy was holding an unauthorized weapon. Sloan was screaming for help. He was attacking her. Even with her testimony, Asa's defense holds up. And the gun he used was a legal firearm, registered in his name. Unlike the victim. Also, Asa is claiming to have no knowledge of who the men were who broke into the home. And the police haven't located any of the men who fled. Only the victim, who, so far, has no ties to Asa that we can prove."

I rake my hands down my face. I can hear Sloan's breaths speed up as she begins to realize what Ryan and Tillie are telling us.

"But what about the three of us?" I ask Ryan. "It's our word against his. We know he orchestrated that entire thing. He admitted to it out loud."

Ryan nods. "He admitted it to you, Luke," he says. "I never heard him say it, so I won't be able to testify against him. I wasn't in the room with the two of you. And..." Ryan pauses.

Tillie leans forward and says, "He's claiming the two of you set *him* up."

I sit up straight. "Are you fucking kidding me? What jury is going to believe that shit?"

This is ridiculous. They're in here saying absurd shit and upsetting Sloan. I shouldn't have let Ryan talk to me about this in front of her.

"I know this sounds crazy," Ryan says. "We all know how guilty he is. But to a jury...how do you think it's going to look that Asa's fiancée was knowingly sleeping with the undercover cop who was trying to have him arrested? How do you think it's going to look to a jury when it's Asa's fiancée and that undercover cop's word against his?"

Sloan's hand slips from mine and she covers her face. My chest is starting to ache with all of this.

"You knew I was pursuing her, Ryan. If I knew it would jeopardize the case..." I was about to say I wouldn't have done it, but I shut my mouth. Because I *would* have done it. I *did* do it. I pursued her, no matter the consequences, and now it's putting us in a huge fucking bind.

"Depending on the judge," Tillie says, "he might throw the case out before it even goes to trial. Most cases of self-defense are ruled justified homicide if there's a witness to corroborate the defendant's story."

"There's no one to corroborate his story, though," I say.

Both Ryan and Tillie look at Sloan. Ryan nudges his head at her. "Sloan's story will most likely corroborate his claim of self-defense."

"How?" Sloan says, flabbergasted.

Ryan stands up and walks around the bed, leaning against the wall nearest Sloan.

"Was the victim attacking you?" he asks.

Sloan nods.

"Was he holding a gun?"

Sloan nods again.

"Was he impersonating an officer?"

Another nod.

"Did you scream for help?"

She doesn't nod this time. A tear just pours down her cheek. "Twice," she whispers.

"And how did you feel when Asa walked into the room?" Ryan asks. "A jury is going to ask you these questions under oath."

A sob breaks from her chest. "Relieved," she whispers through tears. "Terrified. And relieved."

Ryan nods. "That's enough to back up his claims, Sloan. He rescued you from an attacker. That's hardly murder in the eyes of a jury, no matter how evil we all know he is. His whole character isn't what will be on trial. Only that one action."

"But..." Sloan wipes tears from her eyes. "He didn't have to shoot him. He could have stopped him without killing him."

Ryan nods in agreement. "I know he could have. We all do. But the jury won't know Asa like we do. And they'll put you up on the stand and tear you apart, Sloan. They'll make Asa look like the victim, because you're his fiancée. Yet you were knowingly having an affair with the undercover cop who was developing a case against him. That will lend sympathy to Asa's case and your testimony against Asa will lose any and all credibility in the eyes of the jury."

"But," she stands up, wiping at her eyes. "What about *your* case against Asa? Won't that back up my claims? Won't that have any bearing on the potential murder charge?"

Ryan's eyes meet mine. He releases a rush of air and then walks back to the couch. "That's another reason why we're here," he says. "Young doesn't want to move forward with any charges in our investigation. None of our reports were complete because our investigation was still ongoing. Young is afraid if we press charges and this goes to trial, the department will be ripped to shreds in the press. It doesn't look good that one of our cops was involved in an affair with our main subject's fiancée. The fact that we broke cover to fake agents. They're afraid the chances of Asa actually being charged with anything are far less than the chances of us ruining the department's reputation. Young is requesting the case be closed and no charges be filed. He says it's not worth the risk."

"Oh my God," Sloan says, taking a seat on the bed. She drops her elbows to her knees and holds her head in her hands. "This is all my fault," she whispers.

I reach over and pull her hand to mine. "Sloan, it's not your fault. It's my fault. I was the one on duty." I look up at Ryan. "What about the fact that he tried to kill me? He shot me in the chest and that wasn't self-defense. He'll be charged with that, right?"

I can see the roll of Ryan's throat as he swallows.

"You have to be fucking kidding me," I whisper, dropping my head against the headboard.

"He's claiming self-defense in that case, too," Ryan says. "You both shot each other. Sloan was the only witness in the room. I can only testify to what I heard from outside the door."

"He almost killed me, Ryan!"

Ryan and Tillie both glance at each other. Tillie clears her throat and then says, "The thing is, Luke...with the shit storm of that whole day, if the DA charges him with anything, chances are, you'll be charged, too. And you'll both go to trial."

"I'll be charged? What the fuck will I be charged with?"

"It depends on the judge. Felony assault...attempted murder. And without the department taking the case to court...it will look like you and Asa just had a standoff in a bedroom. The result of a love triangle gone wrong."

I can hear Sloan crying now.

I can't even force another question; my mind is going in all fucking directions now. "So you're telling me that not only does this sick fucker have a chance at getting away with everything he did...I'm looking at facing charges?"

Ryan nods, slowly. "Unless...we work out some sort of a plea deal. His lawyers are pushing for it. They want us to agree to drop the charges in exchange for information on Jon and Kevin and a few other people in the investigation. Like I said, Luke, it all depends on the judge. And the District Attorney, of course. That's a good thing, because the DA likes you. I don't see him pushing for anything when it comes to charges against you, but if we push for charges to be brought against Asa, his lawyers are going to push back. So you need to think about that long and hard."

I can't even believe what I'm hearing right now.

"What about everything else he's done?" Sloan asks. "All the times he forced himself on me? Can I not press charges against him for that?"

Tillie nods. "You can, but what exactly are you claiming? Rape? Did he rape you?"

Sloan glances at me, then back at Tillie. She shrugs. "I don't even know," she says quietly. "There were several times I...I was terrified he would hurt me so...I just let him."

Tillie stands up and walks over to the bed, sitting next to Sloan. "Did you ever tell him no? Did you ever ask him to stop and he refused?"

Sloan pauses in thought, and then shakes her head. "No, I was too scared to say no. I pretended I was okay with it every time."

Tillie tilts her head in sympathy and squeezes Sloan's hand. "I'm afraid that won't hold up in court," she says. "All he has to do is claim he wasn't aware that you didn't want to have sex with him. If the accused is never told no and assumes you're willing based on your actions..."

Sloan's head falls back into her hands. Then she just leans toward me and collapses against my chest. I wrap my arms around her and press my lips to her head.

"I'm sorry," Tillie says. "There were several things that could have been handled differently to prepare for a solid case against him. Several things that prevent us from pursuing Asa like we wish we could."

"You mean several things I messed up," I interject.

Ryan stands. "Don't be so hard on yourself, Luke. I encouraged several of those mistakes. Sometimes cases are cut and dry. Sometimes we get everything we need before the end of an investigation. Unfortunately, this isn't one of those. This one was messy from beginning to end, and there isn't much we can work with at this point. They found nothing in his house after Jon and Kevin cleared out with whatever would enable us to file charges. All they found was some unexplained cash and a stash of prescription pills. It's not enough to go after him—not with the way Asa and his lawyers are going to fire back at us. Sometimes it's just not worth the fight."

I feel Sloan tense against me. She lifts up and glares at Ryan. "Not worth the fight?" she says. "He murdered someone! And he would have killed Luke if it weren't for six fucking centimeters! Now you're saying he'll likely walk free? He's going to be able to find me? To find Luke? Because he's not giving up, Ryan! He won't give up until Luke is dead and you *know* that!"

"Sloan," I say, pulling her back to me. "Stop. We don't know that he won't be convicted of anything yet. Try to calm down."

She cries against my chest and I hold her while Ryan stares down at her, the regret and sympathy evident in his expression. He just nods slightly and says, "I'm sorry, Sloan. I really am." He looks at me and his eyes are saying the same thing to me. I nod, letting him know I understand. This isn't Ryan's fault. This isn't anyone's fault but my own.

Ryan and Tillie both walk toward the door. I pull Sloan against me and hold her, trying to ease her fears. But her whole body is wrecked with tremors. I never knew just how scared she was of Asa until this moment.

I press a kiss to the side of her head and I whisper, "It'll be okay, Sloan. You aren't alone this time. I'm here and I won't let him hurt you. I swear."

I hold her until she falls asleep in my arms from pure exhaustion.

ASA

"Do you have any questions?" my lawyer asks.

His name is Paul. Same as my father. I almost refused him when I found that out, but he's got the best reputation in the state. I won't hold it against him that he shares a name with the person I hate the second most in this world.

Luke is the first.

"No," I say. "We walk into the courtroom, I plead self-defense, and the judge decides whether or not it goes to trial."

Paul nods. "That's right."

I stand up, the cuffs digging in to my wrists. I hate that Sloan is going to see me with these on. It's a little emasculating and I hate for her to see me in any other light than she always has. At least they let me wear a suit today and I don't have to walk in with that ridiculous standard-issue orange jumpsuit on. Orange is not my color and I know for a fact that this suit is Sloan's favorite.

"Let's do this," I say to Paul. "Piece of fucking cake."

Paul nods quickly and stands. I can tell he doesn't like my confidence. He hasn't liked it since the moment we met. I'm also not sure that he likes *me*, but I couldn't give two fucks what he thinks of me. As long as he clears me of these charges, he'll be my favorite person in the world.

Well...*second* favorite. So far, Sloan is still in the top spot.

Sure, she's done a lot of fucking shit to piss me off, but I know it was all thanks to Luke and the lies he told her. I'm sure she's spent enough time with him now and enough time apart from me to be coming to her senses.

I follow Paul out of the room, quickly flanked by four guards. Two in front and two behind me. A fifth guard opens the door to the courtroom, and as soon as we file through the door, I scan the crowd for her.

I see him first. The cocky fucking bastard, sitting second row, next to his little bitch-friend Dalton. Or Ryan. Whatever the fuck his name is.

Sloan isn't sitting next to him, though. She's sitting in the far corner on the back row by herself. I smile at her, but she glances away as soon as her eyes land on mine.

There's one of two reasons why she isn't sitting with Luke. She either figured out his bullshit by now and wants nothing to do with him. Or they were advised not to sit together in the courtroom, thanks to their little indiscretion behind my fucking back.

I'll go with the former.

I take my seat, but I keep my eyes on Sloan. Doing so means I'm turned sideways in my chair, not facing where the judge will sit. But that's fine. I'm not looking away from her until she makes eye contact with me again.

"All rise for the honorable Judge Isaac," a guard says.

I rise, but I don't stop staring at Sloan. I can hear doors open and steps being taken, but I'm not going to fucking look at that man until she makes eye contact with me. She's wearing a new dress. A black one. It looks like she's going to a fucking funeral. Her hair is pulled back and up in a twist. She looks sophisticated. Fucking sexy as hell. My dick twitches in my pants and I wish I could ask for a bathroom break and take her to a hallway and pull her dress up around her waist and press my fucking face between her legs.

I miss the way she smells. I miss how soft her thighs are against my cheeks. I miss the way her whole body tightens up when I shove my dick inside her.

"You may be seated."

I sit.

Fucking hell, it's hot in here.

I hear the judge start talking at the same time Paul slides me a piece of paper. I glance down at it long enough to read it.

"You need to face forward out of respect for the judge."

I laugh under my breath and grab the pen.

"Fuck the judge and fuck you, Paul," I write. I slide the note back to him and return my eyes to Sloan.

She's looking at me now. Her eyes are locked with mine and her lips are pressed together real tight like she's nervous. I like that. I love it, actually. She's feeling something while she looks at me and I can tell she isn't thinking about Luke at all right now.

"I love you," I mouth.

Sloan's eyes drop to my mouth and I smile at her. Then that stupid fuck—*that ridiculous fuckface motherfucking stupid fuck*—stands up and walks to the back of the courtroom, right to where she's seated. He makes his way down the aisle until he plants himself right next to her. He wraps his arm around my fucking fiancée and she squeezes her eyes shut and buries her face against his shoulder, like she's relieved he moved to be next to her. My eyes meet his—*the fucking motherfucking fuckface brainwashing fuck*—and he leans forward, blocking my view of her. He stares at me, hard, like he's threatening me to turn around.

I want to kill him. For a few seconds, I try to think of ways I can do that.

Grab the security guard's gun and shoot him.

Run to the back of the courtroom and break his fucking neck.

Grab the pen that I just wrote Paul the note with and shove it right in his carotid artery.

But I don't. I refrain, because I'm pretty sure this case is going to go in my favor and I'll be out on bail until the next hearing.

His murder can wait.

It needs to be planned out with more precision and preferably without the eyes of a judge on me.

I decide to turn around. Not because Luke threatens me to do so with that fucking look in his eyes—but because I need to convince this judge that he's making the right decision when he throws this case out due to self-defense.

I try to follow along as both lawyers stand up and speak. I try to follow along as the judge responds to each of them. I smile when the judge looks at me. But inside, my blood is boiling. Knowing Luke is back there, sitting next to her, holding her. That means she's probably been with him at night while I'm forced to fuck my own hand, alone in my jail cell. It also means he's probably been inside her. His fingers, his dick, his fucking tongue. Tasting and taking what's mine. What was supposed to be *only* mine.

My pulse is raging when the judge's gavel comes down. "This court session is adjourned."

I breathe in slowly through my nose. I release it when I look at Paul. "What the fuck just happened?"

He makes a face like I'm supposed to keep my voice low. My eyes flick to the back of the room when I hear Sloan's cry. Luke is helping her stand, but her arms are around him and she's crying. Sobbing.

She's upset. That can't be good news for me. She's upset for me.

"Is this going to trial?" I ask Paul. "You said this wasn't going to fucking trial!"

Paul shakes his skinny little head. "The judge decided not to take it to trail," Paul says. "Which means your claims of self-defense were upheld. You'll have to go back to your cell, but only until I can bail you out on the other charges pending against you. It may be four or five hours, but I'll come get you once your bail is posted."

I glance back at Sloan, watching as Luke helps her out of the courtroom. *Why is she crying, then? If the charges against me were dismissed, why is she crying?*

"How long do you think it takes someone to recover from being completely fucking brainwashed?"

Paul looks at me. "What are you talking about, Asa?"

"Like how much therapy do you think a person will need in order to get over being brainwashed? A few weeks? Months? More than a year?"

Paul stares at me a moment and then shakes his head. "I'll see you in a few hours, Asa."

He stands, so I stand. The same four guards escort me out of the courtroom.

I should probably be fucking ecstatic that this case just got thrown out. The next one should be even easier, because Paul says Luke's department isn't pressing charges. So as long as I cut a plea deal, undergo some psychiatric treatment, and give them the information they want on Jon and Kevin, I more than likely won't be charged with shooting Luke in the fucking chest.

That says a lot about our court system. I fucking come within six centimeters of killing a guy in cold blood, and I walk free because I tattle and claim a mental illness?

I fucking love the USA.

It almost feels like all my efforts have gone to waste, though. Since the moment I started growing suspicious that someone was brainwashing Sloan, I've been concocting this elaborate scheme and I'm not even really getting credit for it. I had to deny having anything to do with the fake raid, which was really hard for my ego. I'm fucking proud of that and I want to brag to the world that I pulled it off flawlessly.

Not to mention the fucking schizophrenia shit. *Shower with your clothes on, check the lock on a door a few times, and people think you're losing your fucking mind.* I had to do it, though. I know myself and I knew if I found out my suspicions were true and Sloan was fucking someone else, that I would more than likely lose my shit and murder the guy. I can't very well murder someone and run the risk of being tried as a mentally competent adult. I had to have a back-up plan so I wouldn't rot in fucking prison like my father did most of his life.

Maybe it wasn't a complete waste. I at least have the "schizophrenia" to fall back on if I ever need it. Which I probably will eventually, because Luke is still breathing.

When I make it back to my cell, I fall down onto the bed as the bars clank shut behind me. I can't help but smile.

This whole thing is turning out so beautiful. Sloan will take some time to come around again, but I know she will. Especially once Luke is out of the picture for good. I'll have to somehow look past the fact that Luke has been inside her. I can fuck him out of her, though. I'll just have to fuck her a whole goddamn bunch and in every position until I no longer think about him when I look at her.

"What are you so fucking happy about?" a voice says.

I turn my head and look at my cellmate. I can't remember his name. He's asked me about a million questions since I was thrown in this cell with him, but this is the first time I actually answer him.

"I'm about to be a free man," I tell him, staring up at the ceiling with a huge goddamn fucking smile on my face. "Which means I finally get to marry my fiancée. In a real wedding. With a three-tier coconut cake."

I can't help but laugh, just thinking about it.

I'm coming for you, Sloan. Whether you think you want me to or not.

You promised to love me.

Forever.

And you fucking will.

SLOAN

I bring the cup of coffee to my mouth. My hands are shaking so bad, it makes tiny little black waves of coffee crash against the sides of my cup.

I glance over at the clock on the far wall. *Three in the morning.*

It's been two days since Asa's case was thrown out. He was bailed out that afternoon. Luke and I were sent to this apartment in the city for protection until the next hearing.

It's a nice apartment, but when I'm too scared to step outside or even look out the window, it feels more like a prison. Luke has assured me over and over that there's no way Asa will find us here. But what Luke probably doesn't understand is that even if Asa is locked up in prison the rest of his life, I'll still constantly be looking over my shoulder. If it isn't Asa himself who could hurt me or Luke, I wouldn't put it past him to hire someone else to do it.

I turn my head when I hear the bedroom door open. Luke walks out, rubbing the sleep out of his eyes. He's wearing black jogging pants that hang off his hips and no shirt. The bandages from his wound cover part of his chest. He's barefoot, shuffling across the hardwood floor toward me.

He reaches the back of the couch and I lean my head back and look up at him. He leans forward and kisses my forehead upside down. "You okay?"

I shrug. "I can't sleep. Again."

His eyes are sympathetic and he lifts a hand, brushing my hair off my forehead. "Sloan," he says quietly. "You don't have to worry here. He can't find us. We're safe until his next trial, I promise."

I nod again, but his words do little to comfort me. I'll never trust Asa, no matter how safe I should feel.

He walks around the couch and sits down, pulling me onto his lap until I'm straddling him. He wraps his hands around my lower back and says, "What can I do to help you sleep?"

I smile. I like his distraction methods. "It's only been two weeks since you were released. You have two more to go."

His hands cup my ass beneath his oversized T-shirt I'm wearing. He slides his fingers beneath the edges of my panties, sending chills over me and forcing Asa out of my head for a few seconds. "I wasn't thinking about sex with you," he says. "I was thinking more along the lines of what I could do *for* you."

One of his hands slides around to my stomach and then up to my breast. His thumb brushes my nipple at the same time his tongue slides across my lips. He kisses me, deep, then pulls back just as I start to grow dizzy.

"I'll be careful," he says. "My hands and mouth will do all the work, but I'll make sure the rest of me takes it easy. Okay?"

I know I should encourage his recovery, but every time he touches me, it calms me down. Makes me less nervous.

I need that right now.

"Okay," I whisper.

He smiles as he pulls off my shirt. Then he pushes me until my back is against the couch and he's hovering over me. His lips drag across my mouth, my neck, my breasts. His breath warms up every part of me while his hand works its way inside my panties. I open my eyes, just as his fingers slip inside me. I moan, struggling to keep my eyes open, but he likes the eye contact.

I like it, too. It's new for me.

In the past, with Asa, I've always kept my eyes shut tight because I never wanted to look at him.

With Luke, I'm scared I'll miss something. I don't want to miss the way he looks at me, the way he responds to my noises. I *love* the eye contact.

We only have to keep eye contact for two minutes, because that's all it takes for his touch to completely send me over the edge. As soon as I start shaking beneath him, he claims my mouth with his, swallowing his name as it flows from my lips. He kisses me until it's over and then lowers himself until he's pressed against me. I can feel him bulging through his sweatpants and it creates another need in me.

"I think I'm better," he says, moving his hips against me. "I'm pretty sure it's safe to be inside you now."

His voice is gravelly—needy—and it would be so easy just to push down his sweatpants and let him fill me. But I would feel terrible if something bad happened because we were too impatient to wait the recommended time. His heart may not be strong enough for that yet.

"How about we compromise? One more week and then we'll take it really slow."

Luke groans against my neck, but pulls back. "One more week," he agrees. "But then be prepared for multiple times a day. I have a lot of catching up to do." I laugh as he sidles up to my side, pulling me against him. I'm facing him, my hands on his chest. I trace my fingers around his bandage.

"I wonder what your scar will look like," I whisper.

His hand meets my hair and he runs his fingers through it, down my back, over my arm. "I don't know. I just hope you kiss it a lot."

I laugh. "Don't worry, once we're in the clear, you're gonna have a hard time keeping my mouth off you. I like your body too much." I look up at him. "Is that shallow? That I like looking at you with your shirt off?"

He shakes his head with a grin. "Nah. The first thing that attracted me to you was your ass."

"I thought it was the drool on my chin when you woke me up in class that first day."

He nods. "Yeah. You're right. It was definitely the slobber."

I laugh. I love that he's able to make me laugh at a time like this. Our lips meet and we kiss for a solid five minutes. Until he starts to press into me again. I feel terrible that he's being tortured so much, but there's no way I'm allowing him to go against doctor's orders. I need him to be as healthy as he can as *soon* as he can. I push him away and try to change the subject to something that will help him recover.

"Do you think you'll get to see your mother soon?"

He talks about his mother a lot. I hate that we're in hiding right now, because that means he can't see her until the next hearing is over and Asa is hopefully behind bars again. Of course, there's a chance he'll walk free again. But we don't talk about that possibility.

"We'll see her when this is all over. She's going to love you for me."

I smile, wondering what that's like to have a mother who loves you. I start to think about my only family—Stephen—and then my smile fades.

Luke notices, because he runs the backs of his fingers over my cheek. "What's wrong?"

I try to shake away his concern. "Just thinking about Stephen. Hoping he's safe during all this. I hate not being able to visit him."

Luke's hand finds mine and he slides his fingers through it. "He's safe, Sloan. He has twenty-four-hour security. You don't have to worry about him, I made sure of it."

I hate that Asa has put us in this situation. A situation where I can't even see my brother. Luke can't even see his mother. We can't leave this apartment. And we have to have security for anyone we love.

It isn't right.

I hate Asa Jackson. I hate that I ever met him.

"I want him to pay for everything he's ever done, Luke." I can't look him in the eyes when I'm full of this much hatred. "I want him to suffer in the worst possible way. And that makes me feel like such a terrible person."

His lips meet my forehead, soft and gentle. "He deserves to go to prison for the rest of his life, Sloan. You shouldn't feel guilty for wanting that."

I pull back and make eye contact with him. "No, not that kind of revenge. Prison wouldn't affect him like it would most people. I want him to *really* hurt. To know that I don't return his psychotic, obsessive feelings in any way whatsoever. I want him to see how much I love you just so he'll hurt as much as he's made everyone else in his life hurt. I want him to be forced to realize that I love you and would pick you over him. It would cut him to his core."

Contemplation flashes in Luke's eyes as he stares down at me. "If that makes you a bad person, then we're both evil. Because I would give anything for him to have to suffer like that."

It's twisted, but his words make me smile. I guess when you're pushed far enough, revenge becomes the only thing that could help you move on. That's not healthy. I know that and I'm sure Luke knows that. But knowing the difference between right and wrong doesn't change the way you feel. It just makes you feel guiltier that you feel that way.

I tuck myself into him and press my head against his chest. "Sometimes," I whisper. "I have these terrible thoughts..."

I stop speaking, because I'm not sure I should even say it out loud. Luke's lips meet the top of my head. "Tell me."

"You'll think bad of me."

"I could never."

I close my eyes, not knowing what Luke will think of my confession. But it feels good just getting it out—letting someone else know how much hatred I'm harboring. "Sometimes...I wish that just once...Asa would have to watch you fuck me. It's the only thing that would kill what's left of his soul. I sometimes wish he could somehow be forced to watch you take what he thinks belongs to him."

Luke doesn't respond for a long time. I start to grow embarrassed that I admitted that out loud. I don't want him to think I have this fantasy that involves Asa watching us for pleasure. It's far from that. With everything Asa has put me through, I know that this would hurt him more than anything. That's all that fantasy is—a way for me to get the ultimate revenge on him.

"Sloan," Luke finally says. "He did a lot to you that you didn't deserve. So much more than anyone should ever have to endure. It's perfectly normal for you to want him to suffer. Don't ever feel guilty about that. Ever."

I sigh with relief at his words. "What would be your ultimate revenge?"

Luke laughs a little. "My only revenge would be watching you get *your* ultimate revenge. I just want to see you vindicated. Justified. So I want whatever it is that would get you that."

I love him. I really do. So damn much. I pull my face away from his chest and say, "I love you, Luke."

He cups my face and says, "I love you too, baby." Then we kiss.

But then we stop.

Banging.

Loud banging on the center of the apartment door. I immediately feel the terror, the chills all over my skin, the shaking return to my hands.

Luke is standing now. I don't even know when he jumped off the couch. He throws me my T-shirt. He moves across the living room and grabs his gun off the counter.

More banging on the door.

He motions for me to get up and come stand by him. I do.

"Who knows we're here?" I ask him.

"Just Ryan," he says, walking to the front door. I follow him. He leans forward and looks through the peephole. He pulls back and presses his back to the wall by the door. "It's Ryan."

"Thank God," I whisper.

Luke doesn't move. His gun is still drawn and his eyes are boring into mine.

"What's wrong?"

Luke inhales a quick breath, then releases it. "He's not scratching his neck."

LUKE

Sloan's whole face drops. She knows mine and Ryan's non-verbal signal for when everything is safe. And she realizes now that everything is not safe.

I glance out the peephole again, hoping I just missed the signal. But he's still not scratching his neck. And it's four o'clock in the morning. Why would he be here?

"Open the door, Luke," Ryan says. "I know you're in there."

Ryan is looking straight into the peephole. But I know him well enough to know that he's hoping I don't open the door.

If Asa is behind this, why would Ryan lead him here?

I look out the peephole again and I can see Ryan looking to his left, like he's listening to someone give him orders. Ryan inhales, then stares at the door again. "He took Tillie. If you don't open the door, he'll let them kill her. He's the only one who knows where she is."

"Fuck," I whisper, dropping my head against the wall. "Fuck."

I can't believe Ryan would put Sloan in this situation. I can't believe he would bring him here. There has to be something else to this. Ryan would put his own life in danger before he would risk anyone else's. I glance over at Sloan and tears are pouring down her cheeks. Her eyes are wide with fear. I look out the door again, just as Asa walks into the frame, pointing a gun against Ryan's head. "Don't forget to tell him who else I have," Asa says, loud enough for me to hear him through the door.

Ryan closes his eyes regretfully. "Luke," he says. "He has someone parked outside my little sister's house. I'm sorry, Luke. I'm so sorry."

I close my eyes. Ryan's little sister is the one thing he would protect more than anyone in this world. It makes sense now. And the fact that Asa was smart enough to pull that off makes me scared for Sloan's life. I reach for my phone to dial 9-1-1.

"If you call the police and have me arrested, they're both dead," Asa says. "Tillie. Ryan's sister. And Ryan. My guys have strict orders. I'm giving you three seconds to open this door."

Sloan is crying hard now, shaking her head, begging me not to open the door. I take two steps until I'm standing right in front of her. I brush my thumb across my bottom lip and whisper, "I'm so sorry, Sloan." Then I grab her arm and pull her to me, press the gun against the side of her head, and open the door.

Asa looks at Sloan first. Then his eyes meet the gun I'm holding to her head. "Son of a bitch," he says.

I back us both into the living room as Asa makes his way inside, holding the gun to Ryan's head. "Looks like we have a predicament."

I shrug. "Not really. What you have of mine is disposable. What I have of yours is not."

Sloan is shaking so hard against me, and it fucking kills me that I'm doing this to her. But she knows she's the only bargaining tool we have to work with. He would never want her dead, so I hope she realizes that this may be our only way out of this.

It's a risk, but we're out of options.

Asa's eyes are hard on mine. "Let her go, Luke. I'll release Ryan, Sloan and I will leave, and things can go back to how they're supposed to be."

I'll never push her into Asa's arms. Even if he has to kill me first.

"Asa," I say, backing her away from him. "Do you remember the last time we were locked up in a room together? You were very curious about the details of my first time with Sloan."

He swallows hard.

"You still interested in hearing about it?"

Asa cocks his gun in a threatening gesture, pushing it beneath Ryan's chin, forcing his head up.

I do the same to Sloan. It makes her cry even harder.

"The first time I kissed her was in your bedroom," I say. "Right next to your bed."

"Shut your fucking filthy mouth, Luke," Asa yells. "I'll blow his fucking brains out all over this apartment."

I nod. "If you do that, you'll see exactly what Sloan looks like on the inside."

He winces. I'm getting to him.

"You think I care if she dies?" I say. "There are a million more girls just like her, Asa. She doesn't mean shit to me. She got me closer to you and that's all I ever cared about. She's a white-trash cunt who used you for your money. Do you really think I would take a girl like that home to my mother?"

Asa lowers his head until his eyes are narrowed in my direction. "You think I believe that? Nice try, Luke. I know you want to keep her all to yourself or you wouldn't fucking be here with her. Now tell me what it'll take for you to give her to me. Alive."

"I can't do that yet, Asa. You're right, I don't want to give her up. I've only been able to fuck her once. She owes me a good fuck or two."

Asa pops his neck. I can see his focus changing more to me and less on Ryan. I push him a little further.

"You want to know what it was like the first time I fucked her or not? Last chance."

Asa shakes his head. "Not particularly. What I'd like is to not have to fucking kill you or your partner. What I'd like is for you to hand me Sloan so we can move on with our lives."

"You were passed out in your bed upstairs." I press my cheek against Sloan's, rubbing my face against her. I can feel her tears and my fucking heart is regretting every second of putting her through this, but I have no other choice. "Sloan had just gotten out of the pool. Her bra and panties were soaking wet. Nipples were hard as fucking rocks. You know what she did, Asa?"

He doesn't respond, so I continue.

"She walked right up to me, pressed those hard nipples against my chest, and then she called me out on my bullshit. Said she knew I was undercover. She threatened to tell you. So I did what any guy would do in that situation. I pulled her to the side of the house, shoved her against the wall, and kissed her to shut her up." I force a smile. "She loved it, Asa. Moaned so loud I was afraid she might wake you up. Then she wrapped her legs around me, letting me know how much she wanted it. I carried her to my car and she straddled my lap. She fucked me in the backseat of my car while you slept upstairs. She fucked *me*, Asa. She didn't fuck Carter. She fucked *Luke*. The cop. She fucked me, knowing I was there to bring you down."

I push Sloan forward a step, getting just a little bit closer to Asa, digging that knife in a little bit deeper. "How does that make you feel? Knowing it turned her on more to know that I was an undercover cop building a case against you than it did when she thought I was just another dealer like you?"

Asa's nostrils are flaring. He's staring at Sloan, hatred in his eyes. "Is that true, baby?" he says. *Sloan is right. She's the only thing that can break him.* "Did you know he was a cop when you fucked him?"

Sloan is staring at Asa, her fear forcing her chest to heave up and down. She nods. "It's true, Asa," she whispers. "And it was the best fucking orgasm of my *life*."

There's a split second when I can actually see her words breaking his heart. Cracking his entire soul right down the middle. His eyebrows draw apart and he blows out a quick breath, refusing to believe the words she just spoke to him.

That split second is all it takes to aim my gun in his direction. I pull the trigger, hitting him in the arm that's holding the gun. The second the bullet makes contact, Ryan breaks free and grabs Asa's gun, shooting him once in each leg to ensure he's immobile.

Sloan is wrapped around me, one of my arms holding her tight while the other is aimed straight at Asa's head. My finger is around the trigger and it's taking everything in me not to shoot him. To end his fucking worthless life for good.

Ryan can see it on my face. "Don't do it, Luke," he says.

Asa falls to the floor and Ryan is on top of him, cuffing his arms behind his back. "Where's Tillie?" Ryan demands.

Asa makes eye contact with him. He has three bullet wounds in his body—none of them necessarily life threatening—but he has a solemn look on his face, like he can't even feel the physical pain.

"Fuck if I know."

Ryan reaches back and smashes the barrel of his gun across Asa's face. Blood splatters on the wall. He grabs Asa's phone out of his pocket and says, "You're going to call them off! Right now! You're going to free Tillie and my sister, you piece of fucking shit!"

Asa is staring up at him, laughing. "Your sister was a lucky guess," he says. "Found her online. Looked up her address. I don't even have people at her house, you gullible piece of shit. That picture I showed you was taken last night."

Ryan stares at him long and hard. He pulls his phone out and dials a number.

"Are you okay?"

He pauses then says, "Tillie, are you fucking okay? This isn't a joke! Where are you?"

Ryan closes his eyes, and then in a split second, his gun smashes against Asa's head again. "You pathetic fuck!"

He hangs up the phone and calls his sister. "Hey," he says. "I'm sending police to your house. Don't freak out, I just need to make sure you're okay."

When he hangs up the phone, he looks at me. He shakes his head. "I'm sorry, Luke. There was no way I knew if he was lying or not. I couldn't take any chances."

"I would have done the same thing."

Ryan makes sure Asa's cuffs are secured to the mantel and then walks toward the door. "I'll call the station and have this sorry fucker picked up. I'll show them up. Keep your gun on him until they come get him."

As soon as the door is shut, I pull Sloan to me, squeezing her. "I'm sorry. I'm sorry I did that. I'm sorry I put a gun to your head and said those things."

She lifts up on her toes and kisses me. "You saved my life, Luke. Don't apologize, I knew what you were doing."

"Get the fuck off her," Asa grumbles.

We both glance over at him. He's handcuffed to the mantel, his jeans covered in the blood that's coming from his legs. But he still doesn't seem to care that he's been shot three times. He's staring at Sloan, rage in his eyes. All I can think about is Sloan and how relieved I am that this fucker is definitely going to prison now.

She'll feel safer, at least.

But she still won't feel vindicated.

ASA

Stupid cock-fuck. His hands are on her, his lips in her hair. My stomach feels like someone went after it from the inside with a fucking machete. Every time he touches her, I can taste vomit.

"Get your hands off her," I demand.

Sloan's eyes meet mine. She casually walks to the door and locks it, then walks back to Luke and presses her back to his chest. She pulls his arms around her waist. "I don't want his hands off me," she says. "He makes me feel things, Asa. Things you never could."

She lifts her shirt and slips one of his hands inside it.

What the fuck is she doing?

My breathing is getting real fucking hard to control right now. I've never hated something this much. If it took me going to church just so I could believe in a hell Luke would rot in, I'd never miss a fucking service.

Luke's eyes are locked with mine as he lowers his mouth to her neck. I can see his hand moving inside her shirt, straight up to her breast. He squeezes her breast and I fucking gag.

"Sloan," I say, my voice desperate. "Baby, *stop*. Stop letting him touch you like that, you don't like it." I'm yanking my wrists so hard, attempting to break this fucking mantel, they start to bleed from the cuffs cutting into my skin.

She leans her head back until it's resting on Luke's shoulder, but she's still staring down at me. "Remember the first time we had sex, Asa? The night you took my virginity?"

I shake my head, wanting her to shut up. That was special. Luke doesn't need to hear about that from her, it's mine. *That night is mine to share. Good girls don't talk like she's talking right now. Only whores talk like this.*

His other hand presses flat against her stomach and begins slowly sliding down. She moans right in front of me.

Fucking sick fuck.

"I told you I wasn't ready," she says to me. "But when I woke up, you were on top of me."

I shake my head. "Stop, Sloan. Don't talk like this to me, baby. You don't mean it."

"Every time I think about that night, I throw up bile. It fucking burns my throat every time I think about how you took something so special from me and treated it like it was yours to do with as you pleased."

My eyes watch Luke's hand as it disappears inside Sloan's panties.

I feel stuff on my face. Wet shit. Tears. I'm gonna fucking kill him so slowly until he begs me to take his life.

She begins to stiffen beneath Luke's hand.

Her arm goes up behind her and she snakes it around his neck. "I hate you, Asa. I hate you so fucking much. When you would have sex with me, I would cry. When you would come to bed at night, I would pray that you didn't put your hands on me. When you kissed me, I wondered if death tasted better than you."

She spins around and leans against the couch, pulling Luke to her. She lets him kiss her while his hand is still inside of her.

I can't fucking watch.

I turn my head.

"Open your eyes, Asa," Luke says.

"Fuck you!"

I hear him march across the floor and then I feel him grab my hair. He bashes my head into the mantel behind me and holds it there until I look up at him.

"You'll fucking watch or I'll staple your goddamn eyes open!"

He walks back over to Sloan and pulls her panties down to her ankles. She kicks them off.

I would turn away, but I still don't believe she'll do it. There's no fucking way she would do this to me. She doesn't have it in her.

Oh, God.

She won't do it.

She won't let him inside her.

She would never do that to me.

Sloan grabs his hair with both hands and says, "Fuck me, Luke. Fuck what's yours now."

I can't breathe.

She reaches in his pants.

Puts him inside of her.

God. No.

"Luke," she breathes.

No.

Baby, no.

My chest hurts.

Fuck.

Fuck.

No.

No, no, no!

I'm dragging in breaths, trying to find enough air to beg her to stop, but I can't fucking speak.

I bash my head against the mantel behind me.

Once.

Make her stop.

Twice.

Make him stop.

"Luke!" she says. "I didn't know it could feel this good."

Three times.

Four times.

The physical pain doesn't even come close to what she's doing to me. She wraps her arms around his neck. "I love you," she lies to him.

Her teeth meet his shoulder when he says, "I love you too, baby."

I bash my head again for the fifth time.

Sixth time.

She says, "I'll love you forever, Luke. *Only* you."

And then she fucking rips my heart out of my chest. She throws her head back and moans.

I want to die.

I hear him groaning. Groaning against her neck, buried inside her, not even using a fucking condom. He's tainting her. *Ruining her.*

I want to fucking die.

I close my eyes so I don't have to see the aftermath. "Kill me," I whisper. "Just fucking kill me."

I hear sirens.

Fucking goddammit! The last thing I want to do is live with these visions in a fucking prison.

I open my eyes just as Sloan is pulling her panties back on. "Fucking whore," I mutter. Then I scream. "You fucking whore! Just kill me!"

Sloan presses her lips to Luke one more time, and then she stands up straight and walks toward me. She bends down in front of me. I would reach out and strangle her, but I'm fairly certain I've lost too much blood to even lift my arms now.

"No one is going to kill you, Asa. For the rest of your life, every time you close your eyes in that prison cell, I want you to see me. With Luke. Making love to Luke. Marrying Luke. Having Luke's babies."

She leans in closer until I can smell the sex on her. She's whispering when she looks me dead in the eyes and says, "And every year on April twentieth, my beautiful family will be celebrating your birthday with a big, huge, delicious coconut cake, you sorry fucking bastard."

Luke unlocks the door, seconds before it's shoved open.

Guns are drawn.

Pointed at me.

But all I see is Sloan.

The whore is fucking smiling, and it's all I see.

PROLOGUE

Sloan
Two Years and Some Months Earlier...

I t's been two weeks since Stephen began receiving funding for his group home. It couldn't have come at a better time—right when my first semester of college started.

I'd be lying if I said I wasn't worried about him living apart from me, but it's way more of a relief knowing he's there than at home with my mother. My ultimate goal, of course, is to move him in with me eventually, but it's hard to do that when I don't even have an official place to stay.

My whole life, I've been Stephen's caretaker. So, growing up, I didn't even think college was going to be an option for me. It wasn't until a month before I graduated high school that I found out from the school counselor about financial aid and that I could get financial assistance from the government for Stephen. Apparently it was always available for my mother to apply for, but why would she need to when that required effort on her part? Besides, she had me to take care of him.

I just assumed since my mother was his legal guardian and he was only sixteen that he'd be stuck living with her until he was old enough for some sort of assistance as an adult.

But now, here we are. I discovered financial aid and am now an official college freshman. My only issue was that I didn't get enough aid to cover the cost of living in the dorms, so I'm still at home for the time being.

Sort of.

I stay with friends (okay, more like acquaintances) sometimes because my house is an hour away from campus. I usually take the bus to school, but that's only when I have the money to do so. But on the days I have two class days back to back, I just try to find somewhere to crash. That's been happening more and more often, because every time I'm in the same room with my mother, it turns into a fight. I've been avoiding her as much as I can, and now that Stephen no longer lives there, it's so hard being there.

It's kind of stressful when I think about my life too much. The fact that I'm not living in the dorms, I don't have enough aid left to rent an apartment, I'm crashing on people's couches in hopes I can rotate those places enough that they don't realize I'm living out of my backpack just to avoid going home to my mother.

But I feel like karma has to lean on my side eventually. And maybe it's starting to. I don't have to worry about Stephen as much as I used to, now that he's in the group home. Which means...I might actually have time for a life now. Every day has been the same routine growing up. Wake up, get dressed, get Stephen dressed, take the bus and drop him off at his school, go to my school, pick him back up at his school, ride the bus home, start dinner, help him eat dinner, give him his meds, bathe him, get him ready for bed, do my homework, sleep, repeat.

But now...I feel somewhat free. Not that Stephen ever felt like a burden to me. I love him and would do anything for him, but it's nice to finally have some time for myself. I just wish I knew what to do with it. I feel lost after class and spend most of my time in the library. I've applied for student-work positions on campus and am on a waiting list for two of them. I also applied to work at the McDonald's down the street from the college, but apparently every other poor college kid wants to work there, too.

In the meantime, until I can get one of those jobs and start saving up for a place for Stephen and me, I'll just continue trying to get by. And continue to hope that Stephen's new care facility is something he grows to love. The ultimate dream would be that the funding he receives never gets cut, and that he grows to love it there and they take good care of him. Because there's no way I could provide him with what he needs if he lived with me while I was trying to go to college and find a job.

All in all, my life isn't ideal right now, but it's getting better. Slowly but surely.

And sitting near this guy who occasionally shows up to history class is one of the few pleasures I get out of life right now.

I'm always really self-conscious when he does show up for class, hoping he never looks in my direction. I've never really had the money to buy nice clothes or get my hair or nails done. I'm nothing like the girls who flirt with him in class. My hair is dark and straight and since I can never afford to get it cut and styled, I just let it grow as long as I can until it's easy for me to trim the edges myself.

I sometimes feel like I stick out at this college, and not in a good way. I'd much rather just blend in. Disappear into the crowd.

I want to be the exact opposite of this guy. *Asa*, I think is his name. He's probably one of the best-looking guys I've ever seen in real life. And it's not even entirely because of his looks—it's because of his confidence. I've never seen anything like it. He walks in the classroom with such confidence, holding his massive shoulders back, his head lifted up, his eyes scanning the room like he's daring someone to say anything about how he rarely shows up once a week. Even the teacher fails to reprimand him and seems sort of nervous to do so.

When every other student walks into the classroom, their heads are down, eyes to the floor, scurrying to their desks so they don't notice everyone staring at them. But Asa almost seems like he wants everyone to stare at him. Like he'd be upset if he didn't have the attention of every person in the classroom.

As far as I can tell, he has nothing to worry about. He gets that attention and then some.

I'm staring at him while the teacher drones on and on about the Civil War. Asa has really great hair. I can't help but imagine what it looks like wet. What it would look like with my hands in it. What it would look like if he were facing me—staring at me like he wanted to touch *my* hair, too.

I'm not sure he's ever even laid eyes on me, but I like to imagine he does sometimes. I imagine what it'd be like to be *anyone's* focus, really. I've never had time for guys due to taking care of Stephen. I mean, it's like a babysitting job that never ends—not even on weekends or holidays. Guys would ask me out in high school a lot, but I was never able to find a way to get Stephen covered. I wanted to date, though. I wanted all the things normal high school girls wanted. A boyfriend, their first kiss, and everything that comes with that.

Once, I was so desperate to hopefully get that first kiss, that when the guy I had a crush on finally asked me out, I suggested we go to my place instead. That way I could get to know the guy and keep an eye on Stephen at the same time. My mother wasn't home that night, so before the guy showed up, I put a lot into getting ready for him. But right before he rang the doorbell, Stephen started having a meltdown at the dinner table. It took all I had to finally restrain him, but by the time I had, we were both a mess. Food all over us, my hair covered in sweet potatoes, my shirt ripped at the sleeve.

I opened the door like that—panting from exhaustion. The guy took one look at me and one look at Stephen and the mess he'd made in the kitchen and he backed right out of the house. "Maybe another time," he suggested.

But he never asked me out again. And I'm pretty sure he told every guy in school what had happened, because no one ever asked me out again after that.

Guys can be real fuckers sometimes.

I look away from Asa and glance toward the board, catching up on all the lecture I just missed while I was lost in thought. I'm scribbling away at my notebook when my pen runs out of ink.

I shake it and try to write again, but it doesn't work.

I didn't bring my purse to class, so I don't have an extra. I continue to try to make it work, only noticing that I'm making noise with the pen scratching at the paper when I feel Asa's stare.

I don't even have to look up. I can feel his eyes on me as he takes in my shitty clothes, my shitty nails, my shitty hair, my lack of makeup. I want to crawl under the desk and hide from his scrutiny, but it's too late.

"Here."

Shit.

I don't want to look at him, but he's reaching out with a pen in his hand, trying to give it to me. I immediately feel warmth spreading over me—from the surface of my skin, deep down to the pit of my stomach.

When I look up at him and meet his eyes for the first time, I gasp. His face is perfection. A strong jaw, two plump lips that are wet and inviting. When he smiles at me, dimples form just at the corners of his mouth, giving the harshness of his strong features just the right touch of boyish charm.

I could go on and on about the perfection of his physical appearance, but I'm not that type of person. I'm not that shallow.

Right?

It doesn't matter to me that his hair looks thick enough to grab fistfuls of. It doesn't matter to me that his defined arms look like they could lift me up without a struggle. It doesn't matter to me that the heather-blue T-shirt he's wearing fits him in all the right places, and I don't even have to slide my hand inside his shirt to know where every contour of his six-pack is.

None of that matters. I'm not that kind of person.

So why am I finding it so hard to breathe?

He's still reaching out, trying to hand me the pen. He chuckles at my lack of response and then he lifts out of his chair far enough to lay the pen on my desk. He winks at me and then faces forward again.

I look down at the pen. I look back at him and he's no longer taking notes.

He gave me his only pen?

I pick it up and force myself to finish taking notes, even though I'm consumed with the fact that I'm going to have to give this pen back to him and thank him. Which means I'll have to actually speak to him.

By the time the professor ends his lecture, my hands are shaking. I'm completely ridiculous. I pack my backpack, and before he's even standing, I walk past him and mutter a "thanks" as I lay the pen on his desk and rush away.

I exit the classroom on two flimsy excuses for legs. When I make it about ten feet from the door, I feel a hand on my elbow.

"Hey."

I close my eyes because that voice sounds even sexier when it's being tossed in my direction from this close. When I turn around and look at him, he's staring down at me, his dimples sinking in with his smirk. His eyes scroll over my features, one by one, and I'd give anything to be able to know what he's thinking as he checks me out. He leans against the locker beside me and says, "What's your name?"

Oh, God.

He's going to ask me out.

The guy I never thought would notice I existed has noticed. And for some reason, he wants to ask me out. I thought I'd want to say yes, but I don't. Not after seeing him up close. Not after feeling what his voice alone does to my insides. I'm no match to his experience. I can tell by the look in his eye that he would eat me alive.

I need to ease my way up to someone like him. I can't dive into the dating world with him as my first attempt, never even having *kissed* a guy.

I immediately turn around and walk in the other direction. A few steps later, I feel a hand on my elbow again. "*Hey*," he says, laughing this time.

I stop again and face him. "I already thanked you for the pen."
Why am I being such a bitch?

That stupid, adorable smile is still affixed to his face. Even his teeth are sexy. *Who the fuck has sexy teeth?*

"I realize that," he says. "And you're welcome. But now I'm kind of in need of a return favor."

I may not know anything about dating, but I know what it means when guys like him ask for favors. "You let me borrow a pen. That's hardly a favor worth repaying."

He lifts an eyebrow. "I let you borrow my only pen. Now I need a copy of your notes."

Oh. Maybe he doesn't want to ask me out. "You show up to one out of every four classes and now you're worried about missing ten minutes of notes?" I say. "Seriously?"

His eyes squint in the corners a little. "Actually," he says, leaning forward. "I'm trying to flirt with you, but you're making that a little difficult."

Oh.

I chew on the corner of my lip for a moment, trying to hide whatever reaction that comment just elicited. But he's probably used to that reaction because I'm sure I'm the only girl left in the whole school he hasn't flirted with yet. "I'm Sloan. And I'm not interested in being flirted with."

"Sloan," he repeats with a smile. "Very nice."

Seriously? How do those three words cause chills to run down my arms?

He takes a step closer. He smells like peppermint. "Sloan...you should go to dinner with me tonight. I promise to be a gentleman for as long as you need me to be."

His comment repulses me and turns me on at the same time. I have no idea how. I feel like my body and my conscience are at war. Especially now that I'm staring at his mouth, wondering if he's going to be the first guy I ever kiss. I imagine kissing a guy is sort of like how it feels when you eat a pineapple. Kind of satisfying and sticky, but you can feel it on your tongue hours after you eat it.

He lets me borrow a pencil and now I'm daydreaming about kissing him? My thoughts are not safe around this guy.

I shake my head and turn around to walk away.

I have no idea why I just turned him down. It's not like I have anything better to do tonight. But something about him tells me I'll be getting in way too deep. He's not safe. He's not shallow water where people normally tiptoe in, ankle deep. He's the shark-infested deep end of the sea and if I agree to go out with him, I'll be walking the plank, right off the boat and into his dark depth.

How am I supposed to do that when I don't even know if I can swim?

He's in front of me now, causing me to come to a sudden stop. He takes a step forward and I take a step back.

"We don't have to call it a date," he says. "I'm just really fucking attracted to you and I'd like to eat a meal and be able to stare at you while I do it. Will you let me pick you up tonight so I can stare at you while I eat food?"

A playful smile breaks out on his face and I can't help but laugh at him. And damn. He has a potty mouth. *Why do I find that such a turn-on?*

He mouths the word, "Please," while looking at me desperately. I don't know why I love that he mouthed that word and didn't voice it.

I take a moment to think about all the things I was just telling myself in class earlier. I'm young. It's my first time to experience life now that Stephen is in full-time care. If I don't start to experience things soon, I'm going to be too far behind to ever catch up.

I blow out a breath and nod. "Fine. I'll let you watch me while you eat. Weirdo. Pick me up in front of the student union at seven."

He shakes his head. "I'll pick you up at eight thirty. I'm free then."

"That's a really late date."

He smiles and says, "So it is a date." He leans forward, his lips coming close to my ear. "Wear the dress you wore to class last Tuesday, please. The one with the yellow flowers on it."

He brushes past me and walks away, and I don't even get to see his expression after those words. I feel like those words sent a charge of electricity coursing through me.

He noticed what I was wearing last week?

I cover my smile with my hand and walk to my next class.

———

I got ready at the laundromat.

How sad is that?

The dress Asa asked me to wear was dirty and I don't have access to a washer or dryer at my house or at the girl's house I've been staying at the last few days. So I grabbed my dirty clothes and went to the laundromat and did my hair and makeup in the laundromat bathroom while my clothes washed.

I wonder if he'd still be attracted to me if he knew that.

I've noticed the name brand clothes he wears. The new pair of shoes he always has on when he decides to show up to class. Even the pen he let me borrow looked more expensive than this dress.

I still can't figure out why he wants to take me out. Don't get me wrong, I don't have huge issues with self-esteem. I just wonder why, out of all the girls I see flirting with him, he asked *me* out on a date. I'm not loud, I don't seek out attention, I don't dress to impress. If anything, I do what I can to avoid guys like him for this very reason. Because I hate the unknown.

When you go your whole life without interacting with guys in a flirtatious or sexual way, you just get to a point where you feel so far behind, there's no way you'll ever catch up to the people your age.

I feel like I'm in a completely different race than they are. I stare at all the people passing me as they go in and out of the student union. Some stare at me, some don't. Two guys have asked if I need help.

I don't know if they were hitting on me or if it's because I've been standing here for half an hour now. One of my least favorite things about a person is tardiness. I've already deducted a point and we haven't even started the date yet. I'll give him ten more minutes and if he isn't here, I'm leaving.

One minute passes.

Three.

Seven.

Eight.

Nine.

Time's up, asshole.

I wrap my purse around my shoulder and turn to head back toward the bus stop. Just as I'm rounding the corner, I hear a car screech into the parking lot and come to a stop. I hear a door slam, but I don't turn around. I keep walking.

"Sloan!"

I can hear him running toward me. I'm relieved he's here. It means he didn't stand me up. But he's still almost forty-five minutes late.

I come to a stop when he appears in front of me.

"Hey," he says, his eyes scrolling down my body with a grin. "You ready?"

I laugh incredulously. *Is he serious? He's not even going to apologize for being late?*

"I waited forty minutes for you," I say, irritated. "I got so hungry I'm past the point of hungry and now I'm just ready for bed. Goodnight, Asa."

His eyes immediately grow apologetic and he grips my shoulders. "No. No, don't say that. I'm sorry, I got held up. I would have called, but I don't have your number."

"I don't have a phone," I say.

He raises an eyebrow. "Why not? Who doesn't have a cell phone these days?"

"*Poor* people, Asa. People who can't afford modern luxuries. People who spend their last three dollars at the laundromat, washing the dress they were asked to wear by the guy who showed up late. People who don't have time to be stood up this late at night, because their only means of transportation is the bus, and the last one leaves in ten minutes. So if you'll excuse me, I need to get to the bus stop."

I try to push past him, but he slides his hands to my face. "Please don't leave. I've been looking forward to this date all day. I did everything I could to get here on time and I know I'm late, but I'm here. So can we please start over? Can we pretend I said the date started at ten past nine and I'm perfectly on time and you're really excited to see where I'm taking you?"

He's looking back and forth between my eyes desperately. He's really kind of endearing on top of all that cockiness. What a deadly combination.

Shit.

I force a smile. "Where are you taking me?"

He grins. "*Thank* you," he says, his whole face breaking out into a smile. "It's a surprise. And we're walking there, is that okay?"

I nod and try to move past the fact that he's so late. Lots of things could have happened to make him half an hour late and he's right. He's here, so it obviously wasn't intentional. I probably shouldn't be so hard on him.

He reaches down and laces his fingers through mine. To him, it's probably a very casual move that he does with every girl he takes out. But to me, it's way more than casual. It's monumental. It's the second time I've ever held hands with a guy. The first was when I was twelve, so I don't even know if that counts.

"You look amazing," he says, switching hands so he can walk backward a few steps and admire my dress. His eyes rake down my body, pause at the hem against my thighs, and then drag back up again until he's looking at my eyes. He smiles and then switches hands again, falling back into step with me.

"When I saw you in that dress for the first time, I couldn't sit still in class. I tried to catch up with you when class was over, but I lost you in the hallway."

I smile. "I didn't notice."

He laughs a little bit. "You don't notice a lot of things, Sloan. Trust me."

"Like what?"

He gives me a sidelong glance. "Oh, just the fact that every goddamn male in history class can't keep their fucking eyes off you. Me included."

I definitely would have noticed if he ever stared at me. "You're delusional."

He shrugs his shoulders. "I'd rather be delusional and on a date with you than sane and with any other girl in the world."

That shuts me up. I don't know whether to be flattered by the things he's saying or insulted. He's so smooth; I'm positive he's used every line in his book on more than one girl, more than once. I'm not special to him.

So why are the things he's saying having such an effect on me?

My stomach is in knots and it's getting really hot, despite the fact that it's kind of chilly out and I'm in a sleeveless dress.

But seriously. Attraction is what gets girls in trouble with guys like him, obviously. I know his lines are as genuine as a dollar bill with Kanye West on the front of it, but I'd be lying if I said I didn't like the compliments a little. Even if this goes nowhere, it's still fun hearing them for a few hours.

I should try to just enjoy it. I've gone so long without doing the things other girls my age do, I should just enjoy this tonight, even though in the back of my mind I know it's all just attraction. He doesn't know me at all—he just knows he likes the way this dress looks on me.

He finally says, "It's at the end of this street."

I've gone to this college for most of the semester and I've never been on this road before. It's cute. Christmas lights in the trees, even though it's nowhere near Christmas. There's music playing, coming from speakers attached to the light posts. I can see the restaurant at the end of the street and I'm a little disappointed we're almost finished walking. It's been a while since I've taken the time to enjoy some fresh air.

I wonder what we're going to talk about while we eat? And if that's all we're doing is eating and then parting ways? I've never been on a date, so I don't know all the steps.

"What's your favorite part of dates?" I ask him, trying to get some information from him while not appearing as clueless as I am.

He glances at me and smiles. "The kiss, Sloan. Definitely the kiss."

So that's happening tonight?

I suddenly don't have an appetite because I lose it to nerves. He's going to be so disappointed when my tongue has no idea what to do inside his mouth.

I clear my throat. "Does that always happen at the very end of a date?"

"That all depends on the couple. Sometimes it happens during. Sometimes it doesn't happen at all. Sometimes it happens at the beginning."

Wouldn't that be nice? Getting it over with?

"When do you predict ours will happen?" I smile and wonder if it's obvious that I'm flirting with him. He pulls on my hand, making a sharp left between two buildings. We're still about thirty feet from the restaurant, so I'm taken aback that we're taking a detour.

We're in an alley now. A very narrow, empty one. He turns to face me and I gasp when I see the look in his eyes. His hands meet my hips and then my back meets the wall of the building.

"I think now is a good time," he says, right before his mouth connects with mine. My hands clench his shirt in two tight, nervous fists. His tongue slides against my tight lips and it practically causes me to melt against him. My lips part and I sigh, just as his tongue touches mine.

I don't even feel nervous anymore. An instinct kicks in that I didn't even know existed, and I just follow where his kiss takes me. Stroke for stroke, breath for breath, I do everything he does. I'm pretty sure I have the hang of it after about thirty seconds, but as soon as I'm positive, his mouth leaves mine.

He presses his hands into the wall behind me, and the side of his head meets mine. I can feel his quick breaths crash against my ear. I'm glad he's not looking at me, because I'm smiling.

That was nice. It wasn't nearly as intimidating as I thought it would be. I'm feeling so confident, I have no idea why I blurt out, "That was my first kiss," because I instantly feel him tense against me and I regret saying it.

He pulls back, his dark eyes even more intense after our kiss. "You're kidding, right?"

I should laugh and say of course. Instead, I shake my head.

"You've never been with a guy?"

I shake my head again. "No."

He tilts his head while he stares down at me. "Is it some weird religious thing?"

I laugh. "No. Not at all. I'm not a prude or saving myself for marriage for any particular reason. I've just been...busy. My whole life I've been busy from morning to night. I've never had a free second to date."

He stares at me disbelievingly then says, "So... you've never been touched by a guy? Or kissed? *Any* guy?"

Again, I shake my head. "Never. This was the first. You...kissing me. That's the most experience I've had. So don't judge me too harshly if I sucked at it."

He releases a very slow, deliberate breath. "Holy fuck." Then his mouth is immediately back on mine, much harder this time. It catches me off guard for a moment, but it doesn't take long to catch up with him.

He's devouring me now, kissing me desperately, pressing himself against me. I throw my arms around his neck because the intensity of this kiss is making me feel less stable. My body is growing so weak; I can't even rely on it anymore to hold me up.

I can't keep up with him. I'm gasping for breath as he kisses down my chin, down my neck, back up to my mouth again. His hands are in my hair and then mine are in his. He groans as he releases my hair and bends down, grabbing my legs and lifting me, sliding me up the wall a few inches.

It's amazing how different our second kiss is from the first.

I wonder what the third one will be like.

He wraps my legs around him and he slides his hands up my thighs until he's gripping me beneath my dress, making sure I'm stable against the wall. When his lips meet my neck again, I let my head fall back against the building. "Asa," I whisper. "We probably need to eat at some point."

I feel him laugh against my neck. "I know," he mutters. "I can't help it. Knowing you're...that you...*fuck*, Sloan. I can't stop kissing you. I'm trying." His mouth is against my neck again and then my focus is no longer on the food or the kiss. It's on the way my legs are wrapped around him, the way our bodies are fused together, the way I just started moving against him to feel things I've never felt before.

"Jesus Christ," I whisper, wrapping myself around him even tighter.

"I thought it wasn't a religious thing."

His comment makes me laugh against his kiss. My laugh makes him groan and then he's lifting me off the wall, placing me on my feet. He kisses me on the forehead and then pulls back and presses his forehead to mine, staring down at me. He laces his hand through mine, and without saying anything else, he pulls me out of the alley and toward the restaurant.

I don't know if it's because it's so late at night or if the restaurant isn't very good, but when we walk through the door, we're the only ones here. The host comes out of a back room and grabs two menus. He's older than us, about mid-thirties. "Thought you'd never make it," he says to Asa.

Asa shrugs. "We got held up."

The guy nods and points to a room leading off the main dining area. "Right this way."

We're led into another empty room, all the way to the left. There's a circular booth tucked privately in the corner, complete with a bottle of wine already on ice and two wine glasses. I want to point out that I'm not old enough to drink, but I get the feeling that it wouldn't make a difference.

Asa lets me slide in first and then he's right next to me, his hand on my knee. The guy sets our menus in front of us and then proceeds to open the bottle of wine and pours us both a glass.

I hardly ever drink, but tonight seems like a good enough occasion. Especially if no one is going to card me. Asa picks up his glass like he wants to toast me, so I pick up mine when he says, "To first kisses. First dates. And first...whatever the hell else you allow me to have."

I laugh. "Dessert, at least." We clink our glasses together and then I taste the wine. It's not sweet like I expected it to be, but I like it. When I set my glass down, Asa leans in and kisses me on the corner of the mouth.

"Maybe I should have waited until the end of the date to kiss you."

"Why?"

"Because it's all I can think about now. But there's so much I don't know about you and I should be a good date and ask you a million questions."

I feel like there's not much about my life worth talking about. At all.

"I'm eighteen," I say. "My birthday is next month. I have a mom that should have been required to pass a test before birthing children. I have a brother I love dearly. Now you already know more about me than any other guy in existence. How's that?"

He watches me a moment, his gaze locked on mine. "I like you." And then we're back to kissing.

Slow kissing this time as his fingers explore my outer thigh. Through all the kissing, we've somehow completely turned toward each other in the booth. The only thing that tears us apart is the presence of the waiter clearing his throat.

"Do you know what you'd like to eat?" he asks.

Asa laughs before pulling away from me. "Fuck yes," he says. "In the meantime we'll both take the special."

The waiter nods and walks away.

I take a few more sips of my wine while Asa does the same. "You just ordered for me? What if I don't like the special?"

He smiles. "Then I'll order you something else." His mouth returns to mine and we start kissing again. This time, his hands get braver. Or maybe the wine makes me less resistant.

We kiss for so long, I don't even notice his hand moved to the inside of my thigh. His fingers are slowly stroking up and down, in circles, getting more and more daring. I think he's doing it because I gasp every time he gets to the top of my thigh, near my panties.

"Asa," I whisper.

He shakes his head. "I know. I know what you're about to say. I'll slow down."

And he does for a while, but that may only be because our food comes.

It's Indian. Lucky for him, Indian is my favorite. We try to eat without interruption, but he leans in every now and then to brush his lips against my jaw or my ear. Every time he does it, I have to drink more wine.

I'm on my third glass when we're finished eating and he orders a dessert. He requests it not to come for at least fifteen minutes, though. I could be on my fourth glass of wine now. I'm not sure.

All I know is that kissing feels good. Great. So much more than I imagined it would feel, especially being my first experience with it.

I freeze with that thought. What if I'm letting him do too much? I don't know. I have no idea what eighteen-year-olds do at this age in restaurants with guys who seem to know exactly the right words and the right way to move their mouth against yours.

"What's wrong?" he asks, pulling back. I try to focus on his eyes, but my focus is on his hand that's on my thigh again, still inching up.

"I..." I blow out a quick breath. "I don't know. I think maybe we should slow down."

His fingers trail a slow circle over my thigh and I feel so much, I have no idea how I can possibly be asking him to slow down right now. But I should. I shouldn't be allowing him to touch me like this yet.

Should I?

"Sloan," he says, brushing his thumb over my cheek with his other hand. "Do you not like the way you feel right now? Does this not feel good to you?"

I nod. "Yes, but...we just kissed for the first time an hour ago. I feel like I'm letting it get too far."

His nose brushes mine and then he pulls back again. "Funny, because I feel like I'm not taking it far enough."

"But..." I close my eyes. "I feel stupid for having to ask this." I open them again. "Is this normal? Like...am I being too...slutty?"

I can feel the laughter in his chest. He presses his mouth to mine and then pulls back. His eyes are playful and the look on his face is endearing. "You're a grown woman, Sloan. If it feels good to you, that's all that matters. This date is our date, not anyone else's." He kisses my jaw. "Do you want me to stop kissing you?"

I shake my head. "Not really. No."

His mouth reaches my ear. "Good. I don't want to stop. And that doesn't make you slutty, Sloan. It's kind of hard to be a whore when you've only ever kissed one guy, right?"

His logic makes sense. Kind of. I think. I feel woozy.

His fingers begin moving on my thigh again. He pulls back and he's biting his bottom lip. My eyes focus on his mouth. His teeth release the pressure against his lip and he smiles at me.

"The only thing you need to worry about is if the way I touch you feels good. Okay?"

I exhale and nod, just as his fingers begin to crawl the rest of the way up my thigh. "Do you feel good right now?" he whispers.

I let my head fall back against the booth. "Yes," I whisper, my breaths heavy. My whole body jerks when his fingers meet my panties. He's not kissing me. He's watching me, his eyes focused on my mouth as he drags a finger up my center, outside my panties. It causes me to shudder.

"How about that?" he whispers. "Does that make you feel good?"

I try to say yes, but I can only whimper instead.

I think about the fact that we're in public. I think about the fact that our waiter is bringing us dessert in a few minutes. I think about the fact that I shouldn't be acting like this, right here, right now.

But then I think *why not?*

His lips barely touch mine when he says, "I need you to reaffirm this for me. No guy has ever touched you like this?" His fingers meet the edge of my panties and he hooks his fingers inside and pulls at the fabric. I gasp when he says, "No one knows what you feel like?"

My heart is beating in every part of me, but my pulse is throbbing between my legs, wanting him to be the first to touch me, but fighting my conscience as it tells me that shouldn't happen here. But I'm so relieved that he's not turned off by my inexperience. If anything, he might even be turned on by it. That's not something I expected.

"No one, Asa," I whisper. "No one has ever touched me like this. You're the only one."

He exhales heavily, and I realize I'm right. He likes that he's the first. He might even love it.

His tongue dives into my mouth the same moment I feel the pressure between my legs. His finger slides into me unexpectedly, but I do nothing to stop it. His mouth swallows my moans and gasps as I try to relax against his hand. I try to become familiar with it—the way it moves against me.

"That's it," he says, whispering against my lips. "Relax. Let me make you feel good."

His thumb presses into me and the sensation makes my legs tense so hard, I slide away from him. It doesn't deter him. He just moves closer. Presses his mouth even harder to mine.

I'm shocked at the instinctual way my body begins to move against his hand. When I first do it, he groans, so I continue doing it.

I can feel the pressure of two of his fingers inside me as he presses them as far into me as he can reach. "Fuck," he groans. "You're so fucking tight, Sloan."

His voice does things to me when it's this deep and full of desire.

"I can't fucking wait to be inside you." His lips drag down my neck. "It's killing me that I can't fuck you right here. Right now."

Jesus. I think I might like dirty talk. That surprises me, but hearing him talk about wanting me is making me want to give it to him. Just not yet. Definitely not tonight. We're already going too fast, but he makes it seem perfectly okay.

"I want to taste you," he whispers. "I want to climb under this fucking table and devour you."

"Asa," I whisper.

It's all I can say, because I'm scared if I try to say any more than that, I'll ruin the mood. I don't think I can talk like him. The way he's talking...

"Do you like this?" he asks.

"Yes."

My words must be exactly what he wanted to hear, because the next thirty seconds go by in a blur. His tongue is devouring mine, his hand is touching me in just the right spot that I start to shake. To shudder. Tremors take over and I'm trying to scoot away from him because the sensation is too much, but he's coming at me with even more force, drinking my moans up like the wine.

His fingers stay inside me, but his hand is still now as he pulls back to watch me recover from what he just did to me. His chest is heaving against mine and he's somehow pressed against my thigh so hard, I can feel how hard he is through his jeans.

I wait until I've caught all my breaths before I'm able to find my voice. And then, for whatever reason, I choose to say, "What happens now?"

I say this mostly because I don't know if I'm supposed to do something for him. Tit for tat. Return the favor. I feel like an idiot. Like a rejuvenated idiot.

He grins. "Now...we eat some fucking dessert."

As soon as the words are out of his mouth, his hand leaves me and the waiter rounds the corner. I sit up straight, attempting to hide the fact that my hair is a mess and I'm still panting.

The waiter pretends not to notice anything is amiss. I appreciate him for that. He places a plate of one huge slice of coconut cake in front of us, then sets two forks on the plate. "Enjoy your dessert," he says.

Asa dips his finger...the one that was just inside me...into the coconut cake. I watch as he slides it into his mouth and sucks it. He slowly pulls his finger out of his mouth. "This is my new favorite flavor," he says, smiling. "Coconut cake mixed with you."

I blush.

He picks up his fork and then I pick up mine. I take a bite and smile.

I like him. He makes me feel...I don't know. Good and dangerous. It may not be a good combination, but it's nice right now. Here. Tonight. What's the worst that could happen? I'm eighteen. It's not like I'm going to spend my future with him.

"Spend the night with me," he says, after swallowing a bite.

I don't answer him.

I think about his request. I don't really have a place to crash tonight. It's already too late to catch a bus home and I'd feel bad showing up at any of my friend's places so late.

"On one condition."

He nods. "I promise I won't ask you to do anything you don't want to."

I don't even have to name the condition. He just laid it out for me. "Okay," I say.

He puts his fork down and yells, "Check, please!"

We were kissing as we entered his house. I didn't get a good look at it, but I glanced around enough to know that I'm not at all shocked by it. Based on the way he dresses and the car he drives, this house isn't so out of line with his wallet. The only thing that seems odd is the fact that he owns it. He told me so on our way here.

He lifts me and carries me up the stairs, kissing me all the way to his bedroom. I told him on the ride over that I don't think I'm ready to have sex yet. That I've already experienced more tonight than I can wrap my head around.

He assured me that wouldn't happen—that we'd just kiss until we fell asleep. But I get the feeling he's going to need something more than just simple making out.

I don't know what. I've never given a guy a blow job before, so I feel like that's even moving so much faster than I planned to in the next year. But I feel guilty. I've taken more than I've given tonight.

We're in his bedroom now. His door slams shut and then I'm against it, him pressed against me. His hands are on my dress, lifting it over my head.

Holy shit.

Wasn't expecting to be half-naked this quick.

Naturally, I go to cover myself, wrapping my arms in front of my bra. As soon as I do it, I feel stupid. But I just wasn't expecting that.

He grabs my wrists and pulls them away. "I want to see you, Sloan," he says, his voice gentle. He takes a step back and stares at me. Luckily, I washed a set of matching bra and panties before the date.

"Fuck," he whispers, his eyes trailing slowly down my legs. "Are you positive you don't want me inside you tonight?" He takes a step closer until his hands are on my panties, pushing them over my hips, down my legs.

It's too fast.

"Asa," I whisper. "Stop."

My mind is still hazy from the wine, but even drunk, I know that the panties should stay on a little longer. Until I'm absolutely ready for them to come off.

Which may not even be tonight.

He slides up my body, stopping to kiss me in several different places. When he reaches my mouth, he whispers, "What's wrong?"

I exhale and my breath comes out shaky. Nervous.

"It's too much," I tell him, pushing around him. "The whole night...I wasn't prepared for all of this. I feel like..." I hold in my words until I can sort through and find the exact right ones. Asa is still facing the door as he blows out a slow, seemingly frustrated breath. "I feel like you think I'm a different type of girl than I am," I say. "But I'm not used to doing these things, Asa. I'm not experienced; I'm not comfortable like you are right now. You make me nervous. And it's not your fault; I think you just assumed I was different than I am. Maybe...maybe you should just take me home."

He's facing me again, so I see it when he winces, like maybe I didn't choose the right words. Hell, maybe I didn't. I don't know what I'm doing—what I'm saying. This whole night has been a huge reminder of just how different I am from him. How much more experience he has at life than me. And just because I let him get too far already doesn't mean that's his pass to go all the way.

I need to put the brakes on, no matter if that upsets him or not. That's selfish of me in a way, I guess. But I can't help that I suddenly feel uncomfortable. Being in a guy's house I barely know. Staying the night with him.

I suspect there's more of a chance of him reaching for his keys and rushing me home than there is of him engaging in a mature conversation about how getting my first kiss and losing my virginity on the same night may be too much, too soon.

He rakes a hand through his hair and then grips the back of his neck while he stares at me from across the room. Then, in a display of sheer determination, he walks swiftly toward me, grabbing my face and forcing me to look up at him.

"You think I don't know what kind of girl you are?" His voice is quiet but firm as his gaze scrolls over my face. "I've been watching you in class for weeks, Sloan. I know *exactly* what kind of girl you are. I've studied you. I've admired you. And I've thought about you way too much. And lately—I've developed this idea that you're exactly what's missing from my life. You're the type of girl I've dreamt about. You're the type of girl I failed to believe existed for the majority of my life. But you're real and...you're so fucking special to me already. In my life...special things are difficult to come by. *Real* fucking difficult. You just might be the first special thing I've ever been this close to having all to myself. So if I'm coming on too strong or too fast, that's why. It has nothing to do with my expectations of tonight. It has nothing to do with your inexperience. I can't keep my hands off you because I'm scared to death that if I move too slow...if I don't take things too fast...I'll be too late."

I don't allow air to move in or out of my lungs.

I wait until I have time to absorb every word he just said to me.

Before I'm finished soaking everything in, he continues talking. "Stay the night with me. Please. You can put your panties back on, your dress back on. Hell, you can take your bra off and sleep completely naked. I don't care. I just want you in my bed, that's all. I swear, Sloan. I just need to fall asleep next to you."

His expression is sincere. His words even more so. That's why I'm nodding...because for whatever reason, I trust him right now. And I've never trusted people easily.

"Okay," I say.

Rather than find my dress, I reach behind me and unfasten my bra. I let it fall to the floor. His eyes are all over me as I stand in front of him, completely bare.

"Let's go to sleep," he whispers, his voice gruff.

I walk to his bed and climb under the covers. When I look back at him, his shirt is off and he's sliding off his jeans. He keeps his boxers on as he climbs into bed with me. He moves to my side. "Roll over so I can spoon you."

I laugh and roll over. I never expected this night to end with spooning, but I love that it is.

He wraps his arms around me tight and presses a kiss against my head. "Sweet dreams," he whispers.

"You, too."

I can't tell if I like the feeling of being drunk. It's the first time I've ever had more than one glass of wine in a single night. Heck, I think I had five glasses at dinner alone. I think I drank so much because it calmed my nerves—made me feel more comfortable with myself. Too comfortable, maybe. Because now I'm straddling that line from being in a dead slumber to being too buzzed to actually sleep.

Everything feels heavier when you're drunk. Your head weighs more, your body grows too heavy to control, your emotions somehow even feel heavier. And now air feels heavier—like the whole world is balancing on top of me while I struggle to open my eyes.

But being drunk also has its advantages. Somehow—in the midst of feeling all the weight—there's a lightness on the inside. It's reminiscent of a feather, tickling the inside of my stomach. Tickling my lips. It makes me crave pressure...touch. It felt good tonight when Asa would touch me. The alcohol made me enjoy it, even when my conscience was fighting to warn me I shouldn't.

Even now...in the throes of sleep...I feel it. The warmth of him, the strength of his hands, the sound of his voice.

I'm suspended somewhere between reality and dreams and I can't figure out which one I'm in yet. And I really don't want to wake up, but it feels so real. His hands on my breasts—his mouth between my legs. It feels so real; I wince from the stubble of his jaw cutting into the soft flesh of my thighs.

I gasp.

My heart is thrashing around in my chest. My hands are gripping the sheets at my side.

I'm not dreaming.

This feels too real.

Too soon.

Too fast.

"Asa," I whisper.

I'm confused as to where he is exactly. I feel his hands on me... they move from my breasts to my waist.

He's...*Oh God.*

"Asa," I whisper again, my entire body tensing. How did this happen? When did we get to this point?

Despite the way his tongue is making me feel, the fact that I'm waking up to this seems wrong. Right and so wrong. Did I ask him for this? While I slept?

Or did he just take it?

I try to force my legs shut—force his mouth away from me. But he just grips my waist tighter and slides his tongue up the entire center of me—slowly.

I moan.

I want to cry, but I fucking moan instead. My voice is a traitor.

"Please," I whisper, the word being released between heavy breaths.

I feel his tongue leave me. His lips press softly against my inner thigh. I'm highly aware of his every movement now, because I can't understand how I can want so badly to push him away while at the same time, want his mouth back on me.

"Relax," he whispers, his breath hot against my inner thigh. "You deserve this. You deserve all the good things, Sloan."

The room is spinning. His hands are running over my stomach, caressing me, making me feel like thinking this is wrong is somehow wrong.

His palms slide down my hips, over my thighs and to my knees. He puts pressure against the inside of my legs, opening them wider. "Just close your eyes and relax. Please let me do this for you."

Before I can agree or disagree, his mouth returns to me, his tongue dipping into me, stroking up, all the way up, back down. My back arches off the bed and I'm still gripping the sheets for dear life.

His tongue begins to make smaller journeys until he's circling just my clit.

I've never felt anything like it.

I squeeze my eyes shut and feel myself starting to accept it. I let the weight and the lightness of the alcohol take me in all the right places, and seconds later, I allow my voice to betray me even louder.

"Asa." I'm moaning.

I'm gasping.

My hand leaves the sheets to find his hair and I grip it, pull it, need him closer.

"Don't stop," my voice says, even though my conscience is screaming STOP!

Don't stop.

Stop.

Don't.

Yes.

No.

"Yes." My head falls back against Asa's pillow.

My body gives in to him completely while my conscience is slow to catch up. I begin to tense in a different way this time. Both of my hands are in his hair now as my body begins to respond in all new ways. He's right. This is good. It feels so good. So good, I don't allow myself to think of what this will cost me when it's over.

I don't get good things in my life. I need this. I need to feel something good.

I'm shaking now. My whole body. His tongue and his lips are moving against me with eagerness, like his only desire in the world right now is to please me. The feeling begins to intensify...my breathing grows more erratic, my moans more desperate.

And then it happens.

I feel it so deep, I question if I'm actually awake. I have to be dreaming. Nothing in life can feel like this. It's so intense; I freeze as the feeling moves through me. I stop moaning, I stop shaking, I stop breathing. Seconds pass as the feeling holds me tight. More seconds pass as it releases me, freeing me, sending me plummeting.

I'm shaking again, panting. His mouth leaves me and he crawls up my body until his mouth is on mine. I taste myself on him...his tongue in my mouth, his wet lips against mine.

"Fuck," he mutters into my mouth. "I was wrong. *This* is my new favorite flavor."

His tongue dives deeper into my mouth and I swallow his groan as he settles himself on top of me.

I'm fighting for air. I lost all mine right before he kissed me, and now I can't catch a breath because he's kissing me so fiercely I can't breathe. My head is heavy but my thoughts are light, and I want to tell him to slow down. I want to tell him to give me a second to breathe. I want to say so many things, but the room is spinning and I'm drowning in guilt for allowing what just happened to transpire when I'm not sure I even wanted it to.

He finally tears his mouth from mine and I gasp for air as he presses our cheeks together.

"Hold your breath, Sloan. This might hurt."

I feel his palm press against my stomach and I have no idea what he's doing or what's about to hurt. "What might hurt?"

I hear my answer in my own scream.

Pain rips through me as he forces inside me with one quick, uninvited thrust.

And then another.

"Asa!" I scream.

His mouth finds mine again, just as the tears make their way out of my eyes.

"Sloan," he murmurs, closing his lips over mine, thrusting against me a third time. A fourth. I try to squeeze my legs shut, I try to force him out of me and I use my hands to push against his shoulders. His hands find mine, one at a time, and he brings them above my head, pressing them into the mattress.

This doesn't feel good. Having him inside me feels so much different than when his mouth was on me.

"You feel fucking incredible, Sloan," he whispers. "Thank you. Thank you so much for giving me this."

Giving me this?

Did I give him this? I don't even remember him asking if I was ready. If I *wanted* this. He just took it.

I think.

Who would do that? Everything he said earlier made me believe he was willing to wait.

I squeeze my eyes shut and try to think. All I can feel is the pressure inside me. My thighs are burning from being forced apart while I try to squeeze them back together.

I woke up to this. To him touching me...kissing me. And I didn't stop him.

I said *yes.*

I spoke that word out loud.

I said *don't stop.*

He misunderstood me—what I was asking of him. What I was willing to do.

I was careless with my words, and that's not his fault. That's *my* fault.

I'm no longer a virgin, and I have no one to blame for that but myself.

His lips glide across my cheek and I feel his tongue as it follows the trail of my tears. "You won't feel the pain next time," he whispers, moving his mouth to the other side of my face. "I promise."

If he thought for a second that he just took my virginity without my permission, he's not acting like it. He's thanking me for giving it to him. He's fully aware of what's happening between us and I still feel half-asleep and confused, not sure if this was consensual or not. *It had to be.*

He wouldn't be doing this if it weren't. If I didn't want this to happen, what was I doing sleeping next to him? Naked? I barely know him.

I should have been more prepared.

Prepared.

I gasp. *We aren't prepared.*

He's not even wearing protection. I try to move my hands from his grasp above my head, but he doesn't budge. "Asa," I plead. "Condom."

He groans against my neck. "It's on, baby. Don't worry." He squeezes my hands and pulls back, staring down at me. "You are so tight," he says. "This is a fucking dream."

Or a nightmare.

He releases my hands. The whole time he's been having sex with me, I haven't once told him no.

Not once.

And I'm not even sure I want to now. What's done is done. I'm not a virgin anymore, and I would feel bad making him stop now. Not when he thinks I wanted this. It would make me feel even more immature and inexperienced compared to him. To take selfishly from him...twice tonight...and stop him when it's his turn?

One of his hands is behind my knee now, lifting my leg, wrapping it over his waist.

I wince, because the new position makes him dive into me even deeper.

"Does it hurt?" he whispers.

I nod. "Yes."

He smiles a little, and I feel that smile rip at me. *Why did he smile?*

"It'll hurt worse if I stop," he says. "It won't feel like this next time. I promise. Just breathe through it, okay?"

It'll hurt worse if he stops? Oh, God. I didn't know first times were like this. Why did I ever feel pathetic for waiting so long? I could have happily waited a lifetime if I knew first times were so painful.

"Put your other leg around me," he says. "It'll feel better if you stop resisting."

I do what he says and I try to relax. Anything to make it not hurt so much.

His lips come down against mine, and then his teeth tug gently at my bottom lip. I close my eyes and do whatever I can to stop my body from resisting. How could I want him so much before this started and then suddenly feel the complete opposite? That's not really fair to him. To selfishly take what feels good to me and then want to deny what feels good to him.

"You are so sweet, Sloan. So fucking sweet." His thrusts grow faster. Harder. I hope that means it's almost over.

One of his hands meets the headboard and he holds himself up. His weight being pressed against the headboard causes it to crash into the wall every time he pushes against me. It's almost as if he's turned on by the sound—by the fact that marks are likely being left on the wall—because he pushes harder with every thrust.

"Fucking hell," he groans.

I can't close my eyes. Watching him above me—seeing the way he's engrossed in the way it feels to be inside me—it almost makes the pain fade.

Almost.

I try to find enjoyment in it. I think part of me does. The way he's watching me—grunting—touching me with his free hand. He palms my breast and says, "Do you like it yet?"

I whimper, because I do. A small part of me is starting to like the way he's looking at me. His thumb brushes over my nipple and then his other hand leaves the headboard. He lowers himself until his lips are on my breast, sucking gently. He's no longer fucking me.

He's gentle now. Barely moving inside me.

This is better.

This doesn't hurt as much.

His mouth moves to my other breast and he lifts his eyes to meet mine while his tongue circles my nipple in slow strokes. "Do you like this, Sloan?"

I finally nod. He smiles, still teasing me with his mouth. He closes his mouth over my nipple and sucks once, hard, biting gently with his teeth. Then he releases my breast and his lips feather mine.

"Thank you," he says with a slow thrust inside me. "Thank you for trusting me. Thank you for giving me what you've never wanted to give to any other man." His tongue slides softly against my bottom lip. His hand slides up my chest and wraps around my throat.

Despite the leap it causes my heart to take when I feel him squeeze my neck, it's a gentle squeeze.

He must see the fear enter my eyes, because he whispers, "I need to touch your throat. I won't hurt you, but I want my hand here. Is that okay?"

I have no idea what's normal and what isn't during sex. I've only had ten minutes of experience with it.

I swallow and then nod softly.

He closes his eyes and presses his forehead to mine. His lips barely touch mine, but he doesn't kiss me. He just begins to move slowly, all the way in, part of the way out, all the way back in. Every movement against me comes a little faster. A little more deliberate. He's breathing hard against my mouth, his hand still against my throat. Gentle, though. And even though this feels nothing like his mouth felt between my legs, it's a different kind of feeling. A feeling of desire to want him to like this. To like how I feel to him.

I keep my eyes open the entire time, fascinated by the intensity of him. He keeps his head pressed against mine, his lips still don't fully take mine, his hands begin to grip me tighter.

"Fuck," he whispers against my mouth. "*Fuck*," he says again. He begins to shake as he releases, and my breaths have matched his in desperation. I'm gasping with him as the tremors take over and he shoves into me again. He holds himself still, his lips resting between mine, his breaths colliding with mine.

He collapses against me and buries his face against my neck for a full minute before his mouth meets my skin. "Thank you," he whispers.

I don't say you're welcome.

I stare up at the ceiling, wondering why I feel so conflicted. I liked that I made him feel good. I liked when he made me feel good.

But I didn't like the rest of it.

I guess that's why I've read that sex in real life is different from sex in books and on TV. In real life, it's uncomfortable. Awkward. It even feels wrong and unwanted at times. Hopefully it won't feel like that every time. Hopefully it only gets better.

His hand meets the side of my head as he presses his mouth to my ear. "You're gonna have a hard time getting rid of me now."

I smile. At least he has me convinced that this actually meant something to him. That he didn't just see me as a one-time thing. That has to be a positive thing. I still find it hard to tell with him. Sometimes the positive things seem negative and the negative things seem positive. He's a haze of confusion to me. But I have nothing else to compare this to. No one else to compare *him* to.

"I'll be right back," he says, pushing himself off the bed. He stands up and it's the first time I've seen him naked. Every single muscle is cut and defined. He reaches down and carefully pulls off the condom and tosses it into the trashcan.

I don't even remember him putting it on. That must have happened when I told him I'd have sex with him. That's what happens, right? You discuss sex and then get the condom. I must have been half asleep.

I hate that there were moments when I doubted him tonight. He's been nothing but nice to me. Honest with me. I'm punishing him for my unspoken feelings of indecisiveness. How could he stop when I didn't even find my voice to say no?

Asa leaves his bedroom, but comes back in less than a minute. He closes the door behind him and walks to the bed, lowering himself beside me. He's holding something. He leans over me and puts a hand on my knee, spreading my legs open. Then he presses something warm against me. Something wet.

"I want to help with the pain," he says, his eyes full of concern. "Let me hold this here for a minute or two."

I nod and relax my legs while he holds the warm washcloth against me. We don't speak. The whole thing is kind of strange and surreal, and I don't want to make it even more so with words. I have no idea what to even say right now.

He kisses the top of my knee and then uses the rag to clean me up. "You bled a little," he says. "It's okay, it stopped."

He tosses the rag into the hamper and then moves to lie next to me. He pulls the covers over us and we're facing each other.

"Did you enjoy it?" he says, brushing a strand of hair from my face.

I don't want to hurt his feelings, so I lie. "Yes," I whisper. "It hurt. But I liked it."

He kisses my cheek. "Well, I *loved* it." He wraps his arm over me, his hand cupping my ass. He pulls me against him. "I'll take you home tomorrow," he says, wrapping himself around me. "But I hope you stay long enough for me to make you love it. I promise you will. The first time is always the hardest."

For the next several minutes, his lips meet every part of my neck and shoulder. Never his tongue, though. Just his lips—soft and gentle against my skin. I've never felt so delicate. Every time I think he's asleep and I'm on the verge of it, his lips meet my skin again. It's like he's scared to go to sleep for fear that he'll wake up and this will all have been a dream.

I'm almost asleep again when his mouth presses against my neck, jerking me awake.

"Asa," I whisper. "Go to sleep. I'm not leaving."

I feel him move suddenly, so my eyes flick open. He's propped up on his elbow now, staring down at me fiercely. I don't know what I just said, but it upset him. Or maybe it had the complete opposite effect. I'm not sure.

"You swear?" he says, his eyes boring into mine. "You won't leave?"

I nod, because it looks like he needs the affirmation. "I swear."

He exhales, his forehead dropping to mine again. And then he's kissing me. "I don't want you to leave," he says between kisses. "Don't leave me, Sloan."

I don't like the sound of his voice. The fear in his plea. I have no idea why he's saying this and if he's just talking about right now—tonight—or forever.

Surely not forever.

Whatever it is, it makes me wonder what kind of things must have happened to him to make him so intense. He was either loved deeply or hated deeply. Hopefully it was the former.

"Promise," he says, kissing me again. "Say you won't leave."

I take his face in my hands and whisper, "I won't, Asa. I promise. I'll be here when you wake up."

He pulls me to him and holds me tightly for so long, the only time he releases his grip is when he finally falls asleep.

I stare at him for a moment. He looks less like a man when he's asleep and more like a vulnerable young boy. His features are softer; his mouth isn't set so tight. He's relaxed in his sleep. Relaxed with me in his arms.

I adjust myself slowly until I'm on my stomach. His arm is still around me, but I turn the other direction and face the wall, allowing my arm to dangle off the side of the bed. I close my eyes and think about today.

I was kissed for the first time.

I went on my first date.

I had sex for the first time.

And even though it was nothing like I thought my first time would have or should have been, Asa already treats me better than anyone has ever treated me in my whole life. I've known him for one day and I already feel more important to him than I ever felt to my own mother.

I find myself relishing in the way he's holding me. It feels good to be wanted. It feels even better to be needed. I'm almost asleep when I feel him move next to me. His lips meet the center of my back and he presses a gentle kiss there.

"You sleep on your stomach?" he whispers. "I don't know why, but I fucking love that so much."

His head comes to rest against my back, his cheek pressed against my skin.

And that's how we fall asleep.

Me on my stomach.

Him half on top of me, ensuring I don't leave, even in his sleep.

EPILOGUE TO THE EPILOGUE

Asa

There was a case on the news recently about some dude who raped a girl. He got a few months in jail because he was white, or because he won some medals, or some shit combination like that.

The whole fucking nation went nuts over it. Everywhere anyone looked, his lenient sentence was all anyone saw. It flooded the news for weeks. I don't know all the details of it, but it's not like the guy was a serial rapist. Pretty sure it was just his first or second offense, but everyone acted like he was motherfucking Hitler.

Not that the stupid fuck didn't deserve whatever jail time he got, or an even longer sentence. I'm not defending the cocksucker. I'm just a little irritated that my case hasn't received one single goddamn second of national news coverage. I fucking *murdered* a guy and didn't even get charged. I ran the biggest campus drug ring since college was fucking *invented* and didn't get charged. Even after holding a gun on Ryan, the judge releases me on fucking house arrest until my trial.

House arrest. Six whole glorious months of it.

It's a joke. This entire nation and the racist fucking hypocrites who run it are a joke, and guys like me are the ones who benefit from it. I would be ashamed of this country if I didn't love it so much for its lack of repercussions.

And while we're on the subject of white dudes having non-consensual sex with chicks without repercussions...I'm pretty sure I don't even have enough fingers on both hands to count how many times I've been inside a girl without permission. Hell, I can't even count the times I was inside Jess without her actually wanting me there. In all honesty, that's one of the only reasons I even bothered with her. I liked how much she hated me.

I just don't understand why I can get away with all that shit and no one makes a big fuss about it. I'm better looking than most of the dudes who get national media coverage. I'm also not a pussy... which most of them seem to be. What is it with pussy-ass, ugly white dudes getting all the fucking screen time?

Is it because I don't come from wealth?

That's probably it. I grew up an orphan with two piece-of-shit parents. The media knows people don't eat stories like mine up, simply because I don't have two privileged white parents by my side supporting me.

Figures. My one chance at notoriety and my parents are still fucking things up for me.

Paul, my bitch-ass lawyer, tells me it's a good thing that the media hasn't picked up this story. He says when the media grabs hold of shit, they spin it a certain way, and the judge feels more compelled to hand down a stronger sentence. *To make an example.* Makes sense, I guess, but I'm not sure Paul realizes what an effect I have on people. I'm fucking charismatic. The media would love me. And then Sloan would be forced to follow the story because it would be on every news channel every time she turned on the TV.

Fuck, I did it again. I let thoughts of her enter my head. I've been trying to listen to my psychiatrist...trying not to think about her. Every time I think about her it feels like I'm an overweight old dude with sky-high cholesterol, dropping dead from a heart attack. Hand clenches my heart, knees want to meet the ground.

I choke on my own nerves, just thinking about what she did to me.

My Sloan.

It's my own fault. I should have known not to love something as much as I loved her. But I couldn't help it. It was like she was made for me. It was as if she was put on this earth to make up for all the shit I endured growing up. For a while, I thought she was God's apology to me. Like he pushed her straight down from the heavens, saying, "Here, Asa. I've created this ray of light to make up for all the darkness cast upon you by your parents. She is my gift to you, child. With her, your pain will vanish."

And it did. For more than two years I had my own little piece of heaven whenever I wanted it. Sloan was like Eve before the fucking serpent corrupted her. She was sweet and innocent. Untouched. My own little angel in human form.

Until Luke.

Luke is the Satan to my Eve. The serpent. Tempting her with his apple, introducing her to sin. Corrupting her.

When I think of Sloan—which is every fucking second of every goddamn day—I think of the pre-Luke Sloan. The Sloan I loved. The Sloan who lit up like a fucking Christmas tree any time I'd pay her even the smallest amount of attention. The Sloan who made me coconut cake and spaghetti and meatballs just because she knew it would make me smile. The Sloan who would sleep in my bed every night, waiting for me to come wake her up by making love to her. The Sloan who would express her love for me by caring for my house like the good women do. The women who aren't whores. I fucking loved watching her clean. She never complained about all the pigs who didn't respect my house. She would just clean up after them, because she knew how much I loved a presentable house.

I miss her. I miss how much she loved to love me. I miss when she was innocent...my angel...my very own apology from God.

But now...after falling for that fucking serpent...I want her dead. I want them both dead. If she's dead, I don't have to think about how she isn't the same person I fell in love with. If she's dead, I don't have to think about the sounds she makes when she's being fucked by Luke. If she's dead, I can move past the hatred I have for this *post-Luke* version of Sloan that took over all the parts of her that I once loved.

I've wondered if I kill Luke—if he's out of the picture—can she change back to the Sloan I know is still there? Sometimes I think about giving her one last chance. Maybe if I were to kill Luke first and give her time to readjust to life with me again, I could learn to love her the way I used to love her.

It's wishful thinking. He's been inside her. Not only her body, but her head. He's made her think that he's better than me, that he can offer her more than I can. I'm not sure I want to forgive her for being that fucking stupid.

Her shine has worn off. She's a dull toy now. Too many kids have played with her.

Damn shame.

It won't be long, though. I've figured out where to get to them. It's just a matter of how.

I lie back on the couch and close my eyes. I slip my hands in my boxers, wondering when I'll stop having to think about Sloan just to get off. Even hating her as much as I fucking hate her, she's the only thought that can get my dick hard.

I think about pre-Luke Sloan. I think about the first night I kissed her in that alley. I think about the fact that my lips were the first to ever touch hers. I think about how fresh and innocent she was. How fascinated with me she was. How she looked at me like she couldn't get enough. Like I was God Himself.

I miss the Sloan I fell in love with.

Just when I'm getting nice and hard, someone knocks on my door.

"Fuck." I groan and pull my hands out of my pants. This dude has the shittiest timing. I stand up, wondering if the weight of the ankle bracelet will ever stop feeling foreign to me. Three months of this and I'm about to go fucking crazy. No way I can make it three more. I might as well invest in NyQuil stock and sleep my way through the next three months.

I look through the peephole and then unlock the door to let Anthony in. He already knows not to say too much out loud. I'm not stupid, I know those fuckers probably have my house bugged.

"Hey, man," I say, grabbing the backpack from him.

"Hey," he says, glancing around like a paranoid twit. "Found that coconut cake you were looking for."

Coconut cake is code for computer. Bakery is code for Sloan.

I refuse to use either of the two computers still left in my house. When the District Attorney is trying to build a case against someone, they don't just leave their computers in their house. They confiscate them. The fact that both of my computers are still here proves they want me to search stuff because they're watching me.

Just to piss them off, I've spent a good hour every day using the computers to search things like, *"How to find redemption through Jesus Christ."*

I even click on church podcasts and let them play so they'll think I'm actually changing for the better. Hell, last night I took it so far that I created a Pinterest account. That's right. *Asa Jackson has a Pinterest account.* I pinned recipes and inspirational quotes for three hours straight just to confuse them.

What a ridiculous fucking world this is.

I take a seat at the dining room table and open the backpack. It took me a month to finally find a guy I knew wouldn't rat me out. I have too much information on him. He'd go to prison for life if he ratted me out. Besides, Anthony is desperate enough for easy money, he'd probably agree to kill Sloan and Luke for less than I paid him to get this laptop. The only downfall with Anthony is that it has taken him for fucking ever to finally pin down Sloan or Luke. He somehow found a guy who was able to locate an address for them. I didn't ask too many questions because the less I know about his methods, the better, in case they come back to bite me in the ass. But I'm almost positive there's a crooked fucker in Luke's department that spilled the beans for even less than Anthony demands from me.

That's the thing about humans. We'll *all* do despicable things for money.

"Did you find the bakery?" I ask him. He nods.

Fucking hell.

He found the fucking bakery.

"I went and checked it out myself." He smirks. "You were right. That's a nice fucking bakery."

I ignore the fact that it feels like my guts are lodged in my throat because he's telling me he saw Sloan, and I focus on the fact that I'm pretty sure he just said Sloan was hot. *Who does this fucker think he is?*

"What's so special about this bakery, anyway?" he asks, kicking back in his chair. He's wanting to know why I forked over a clean ten grand for a computer and her address. Another five grand was promised if he was able to get some actual surveillance footage, proving that she actually lives at the address.

"That bakery is one of a kind, Anthony," I say as I pull the laptop out of the bag. Anthony wrote all the instructions down for how to access the surveillance footage he'll be uploading for me. Also in the bag is a Wi-Fi box set up in his name so it's not traceable to me in any way.

"Did you get any cupcakes at the bakery?" I ask him. *Cupcakes* is code for surveillance footage. We sound like two tools with all this baked goods talk, which is why I switch it up every time he comes over. Last week it was TV shows.

He smirks again. "Yeah, they're in the bag," he says, pulling out more sheets of paper from the backpack. He unfolds one and points to an email address and a password, letting me know that's where I can find all the footage.

My pulse is raging inside me and I'm trying to calm it down, but it feels like my heart is in the middle of a fucking mosh pit.

I want Anthony to leave so I can pull up the footage. I need to see her. It's been three months since I've been able to lay eyes on her. I need to fucking see her.

I stand up and walk down the hallway to retrieve the money I owe him. I toss it on the table and point at the door, letting him know he's no longer needed today. He slides the envelope in his back pocket. "Anything else you need? I can stop back by tomorrow."

I shake my head. "Nope. I'll let you know when I run out of cake."

He grins and heads for the front door.

I set up the Wi-Fi and log in to the account. There's a message along with the email that links to the Dropbox. The message is from Anthony.

Recorded about eight hours of footage yesterday and cut it down to actual visual of the couple. Got a couple of minutes of some dude leaving and returning. Halfway through the footage, you'll see the girl take out the trash. End of footage shows both of them. I'll record more this week. If you want, we can set it up on a live feed that you can access from this computer. Takes two seconds. Just let me know.

I email him back before I even download the footage.

Of course I fucking want live feed. Why the fuck are you just now telling me this?

I hit send and then download. It takes almost five fucking minutes to download the video in the Dropbox. Once it's complete, I get up and lock the front door. I don't want any interruptions.

I also make myself something to drink because my mouth is fucking dry. I feel like puking, just thinking about seeing her for the first time in three months.

I sit back down at the table and hit play. The video is thirteen minutes long. Three minutes is of Anthony just focusing his camera on the front door of their apartment. The angle is high, like he's filming from the second floor of the apartment complex.

I knew wherever Luke and Sloan were staying, Luke would be extra paranoid. He's probably personally hired someone to make sure no one is watching the apartment while he's not there. I had Anthony rent out an empty apartment in the complex with a view of their front door, just so he could get good footage without being obvious by sitting in a parked car.

At three minutes and thirty-one seconds into the video, the front door to their apartment opens. Luke walks out, glancing left, then right. I like that he's paranoid. I like that every time he opens the door to his apartment, he's thinking of me. Wondering if I'm there, ready to get my revenge.

The film cuts out and then back in.

That's when I see it. The front door begins to open.

I see her arm as she swings a trash bag out and onto the ground next to the front door. I barely get a glimpse of her hair as she slams the door shut again. It looked like she was trying to hide. Like she fears she's being watched. She's scared to be there alone.

Fucking *Luke* just leaves her there, all alone, probably for several hours a day. I don't care if he needs to work to pay their bills. If that were me and I was with Sloan, I'd fucking find a way to protect her. If I knew there was a guy out there who posed a danger to her, she'd never leave my fucking sight.

That's my first clue that he doesn't love her like I do.

Like I *did*.

I don't love her anymore.

Do I?

Fuck.

I rewind the clip no less than twenty times, watching that arm as she swings the trash outside. Watching her hair sway over her shoulder as she slams the door. My heart speeds up every time I watch it and slams to a stop every time the door closes.

Fucking hell. I do. *I still love her.*

I fucking love her and it's killing me that she's alone in that apartment, too scared to even open the door all the way. That stupid fucking bastard just leaves my Sloan all alone and scared while I'm locked in this stupid fucking house and can't get to her, thanks to him.

"I see you, baby," I whisper to the computer screen. "Don't be scared."

After a few more replays, I finally let the video continue. It skips forward to a few hours later. Luke's car pulls up in front of the complex. He gets out and opens the trunk. He begins to pull groceries out of the trunk.

How cute. The motherfucker went grocery shopping for his fake little family.

He walks them to the door and uses his key to unlock it. He tries to push it open, but it's still locked from the inside.

Smart girl. Never trust a single lock.

Sloan opens the door to let him in. Luke disappears inside the door as Sloan walks—*no, she practically fucking skips*—to the car. She's smiling. She reaches into the trunk to grab some groceries when Luke walks back outside, holding up his hands. It looks like he's telling her to stop, that he'll get the groceries. He points at her, toward her stomach, and says something to make her laugh. She presses her hands against her stomach and that's when I see it.

That's when I fucking *see* it.

I pause the screen.

I stare at her hands, pressed against her stomach. I look at the smile on her face as she stares down at her hands, holding her belly. It's barely noticeable under her shirt. Barely.

"Motherfucker."

I'm frozen. Counting days, months, trying to make sense of this.

"Motherfucker."

I don't know a lot about the circle of life. The only time I ever knocked up a girl, I forced her to get an abortion because she wasn't

Sloan. But one thing I know for a fact...it takes at least a few month for someone of Sloan's size to start showing.

A few months ago...it was *me* who was inside her. It was *me* who was making love to her at night.

Luke had her *once* during that time.

I had her daily.

"Motherfucker," I say again, smiling. I can't help it. My whole face breaks out into a huge fucking grin. I stand up, needing to take a moment to breathe. To regain my bearings. For the first time in my life, I feel like I might pass out.

"Holy shit," I say, staring down at the laptop, paused on my Sloan. "I'm gonna be a dad."

I sit down again and rake my hands through my hair. I stare at the screen for so long, it starts to get blurry.

Am I fucking crying?

I wipe my eyes and sure enough, there are tears on my hands.

I can't stop fucking smiling. I zoom in on her stomach and then lift my hand to the screen. I place my hand right over both of hers, on top of her stomach. "Daddy loves you," I whisper to our baby. "Daddy's coming for you."

TWO MONTHS EARLIER

Luke

I unlock the door to our apartment and wait for Sloan to unlatch the deadbolts.

All five of them.

I hate that we have to be paranoid. I hate that I call her every hour just to check on her, even though I know she has 24/7 surveillance parked right across the street. I hate that we're the ones who are forced to hide, even though Asa is monitored and on house arrest until his trial, which will, without doubt, put him behind bars for a while.

I don't know how the last couple of months have affected Sloan. I tried to talk her into seeing a therapist, but she insists she's fine. Or she says she *will* be, once Asa is behind bars.

There's no possible way for anyone to remove an ankle monitor without it notifying the police, so that's one small reassurance we have. If Asa does something stupid and decides to leave his house, we'll know within ninety seconds. But it isn't Asa I'm worried about—it's all the people he has on his side who will do his work for him.

The judicial system in this country is fucked, to put it lightly. It feels like Sloan is the one being punished, simply because people like Asa are considered innocent until proven guilty in a court of law. I keep telling myself that we're lucky he got house arrest. The judge could have allowed him to post bail and walk around free until he faces trial.

We have that much on our side, at least.

It hasn't been so bad until a few days ago, because he was recovering from his gunshot wounds in the hospital. But now that we know he's healed and at home, with visitors free to come and go as they please, we don't feel as safe as we've been feeling. I attached the extra four deadbolts to the door yesterday for added protection.

We're two hours away from him now and no one outside the department knows where we're staying. It takes me over an hour just to drive home every day because I take so many side roads, just to ensure I'm not being followed. It's exhausting. But I'll do whatever it takes to keep her safe, short of walking through Asa's front door and putting a bullet in his forehead.

I hear the deadbolts unlatch and as soon as she begins to pull the door open, I slip inside and shut it. Sloan smiles and stands on her tiptoes to kiss me. I wrap an arm around her waist and kiss her back as I spin her to where I can reach the deadbolts and lock them. I try not to make it noticeable, because the more I worry, the more *she* worries.

She pulls back as I'm latching the last deadbolt. I can see the concern flash in her eyes, so I redirect her.

"Smells good," I say, glancing into the kitchen. "What are you cooking?" Sloan is an incredible cook. Better than my own mother, but I'm not telling my mother that.

She grins and grabs my hand, pulling me toward the kitchen. "I'm not sure, to be honest," she says. "Soup, but I just threw in what sounded good." She opens the pot and dips a spoon in, bringing it up to my mouth. "Taste it."

I sip from the spoon. "Holy shit. That's delicious."

She grins and puts the lid back on the soup. "I want it to simmer for a while, so you can't have any yet."

I pull my keys and cell phone out of my pocket and toss them on the counter. Then I reach down to Sloan and grab her, lifting her up into my arms. "I can wait to eat," I say as I carry her to the bedroom. I toss her gently onto the bed and crawl up her body. "Did you have a good day?" I ask, planting a kiss to her neck.

She nods. "I got an idea today. It might be dumb, though. I don't know."

I roll onto my side and stare down at her. "What is it?" I place my hand on her stomach and inch her shirt up so I can touch skin. I can't get enough of her. I don't remember a time in my life that I've been with a girl I couldn't stop touching. Even when we're just lying here having a simple conversation, I'm either tracing patterns over her stomach or up and down her arms, or touching her lips with my fingers. She seems to like it because she's the same way and I *definitely* don't mind.

"You know how I can cook pretty much anything?"

I nod. She really can.

"I thought about compiling some of my best recipes and making a cookbook."

"Sloan, that's a great idea."

She shakes her head. "I wasn't finished." She lifts onto her elbow. "There are too many cookbooks flooding the market, so I want something to stand out. I want it to be different than the rest of them. So I thought about playing up the fact that I learned to cook so well when I was practically forced to cook every night by Asa. So I thought the title could be something funny, like, *'Recipes I learned to cook while living with my asshole, controlling ex-boyfriend.'* And then I could donate half the proceeds to victims of domestic violence."

I give her a moment, to make sure she's done sharing her idea.

I'm honestly not sure what to think. Part of me wants to laugh, because she's right, a title like that would be catchy in a strange way. But part of me cringes that Asa is the reason she cooks so well.

Because he was controlling and she had no choice. It reminds me of the first time I took her out to lunch and she acted like she'd never been to a restaurant before.

"You think it's stupid," she says, falling back onto her pillow.

I shake my head. "Sloan, no. I don't." I cup her cheek with my hand so she'll look at me. "It's a catchy title. It would make people look twice, that's for sure. I just hate that it's so...*accurate*. It would be funny to me if it was a joke, but it isn't. That's really why you cook so well, and I fucking hate that son of a bitch."

She forces a smile. "Thanks to you, that's not my life anymore."

I constantly have to remind her that I didn't save her. "Thanks to *you*, that isn't your life anymore."

She smiles again, but since the moment I walked through the front door, her smile has seemed forced. Something bigger is bothering her and I don't know what it is. It could just be the stress of being locked in an apartment all day. "Are you okay, Sloan?"

She waits a second too long to nod, which lets me know she's not okay.

"What is it?"

She sits up on the bed and begins scooting off of it. "I'm fine, Luke. I need to stir the soup."

I grab her arm to stop her. She stays at the foot of the bed, but doesn't turn back to look at me. "Sloan."

She sighs with her whole body. I release her arm and then join her at the foot of the bed. "Sloan, he can't leave his house, if that's what's bothering you. We'll know if he does. Not to mention the surveillance outside. You're safe."

She shakes her head, letting me know that's not why she's upset. She isn't crying, but I can tell by the small quiver in her lip that she's about to.

"Is it your brother? We'll go see him this weekend. We'll go with an escort to make sure we're safe, and he's still got security outside his room." I tuck a strand of hair behind her ear, wanting her to know that I'm here. She's safe. Her brother is safe.

She lowers her head even more and somehow folds in on herself, gripping her arms with her hands.

"I think I might be pregnant."

———

She didn't want to be in the bathroom while we waited the two minutes for the results. I stand here, staring down at the stick. Waiting.

As soon as she told me she might be pregnant, it felt like I had failed her. Like all that I've done to protect her was for nothing. She sat there with tears streaming down her cheeks, her head lowered and her voice barely above a whisper, and there wasn't anything I could say to take her fear away. I couldn't tell her not to worry, because this is definitely something to worry about. We can do the math. She's been with both Asa and me in the last couple of months. The odds of it being mine are even slimmer than the odds of it being his, so if I were to tell her not to worry, I'd be lying.

The last thing she needs right now is the stress of carrying part of that man inside her. Something that would tie her to him for the rest of her life. The last thing she needs right now is the stress of caring for a baby, no matter *whose* it is. The next few months are crucial to her safety. She's going to be locked up inside this apartment, waiting for the trial. Not to mention once the trial begins—if she's pregnant—she'll have to testify on stand near the time she would be due to give birth.

I inhale slowly as I stare down at the test. It's the kind that doesn't show a line. It actually displays the words, "not pregnant" or "pregnant." I went to the store as soon as she told me. The last thing I want her to do is wonder. The sooner she knows, the quicker she can decide what she wants to do.

I wait, my hands raking through my hair, my feet pacing the small bathroom. I'm facing the other direction when the timer on my phone chimes, indicating the wait time is up.

I blow out a calming breath, and when I turn around and see the word pregnant, I make a fist, prepared to punch the wall. The door. Anything. Instead, I punch the air and cuss under my breath, because I know I'm going to have to walk out of this bathroom and break that girl's heart.

I don't know if I can do it.

I debate staying in here for another few minutes, just until I can shake off the anger. But I know she's out there, scared and probably even more nervous than I was. I open the door, but she isn't in the bedroom. I walk into the living room and she's in the kitchen, stirring the soup again. It's been simmering for over an hour now, so I know she's just wasting time. She hears me, but she doesn't turn around to look at me. I walk into the kitchen, but she doesn't look up at me. She just continues stirring the soup, waiting for me to break the news to her.

I can't. I open my mouth three times, but I can't fucking find the words to tell her. I grip the back of my neck and watch her for a moment, waiting for her to look at me. When she refuses to look up and I can't find the words to speak, I close the distance between us. I wrap my arms around her from behind and pull her back to my chest. She stops stirring and she grips my arms that are wrapped around her. I can feel her whole body begin to shake with her quiet sob. My silence is all the confirmation she needed. All I can do is hold her tighter and press a kiss into her hair.

"I love you, Sloan," I whisper.

She turns around and presses her face against my chest while she cries. I close my eyes and hold her.

This isn't how it should be. This is *not* how a girl should feel when she finds out she's a mother. And I feel partly responsible for her sadness.

I know we'll have time to talk about it later. We'll have time to discuss all of the options, but right now I just focus on her because I have no idea how incredibly difficult this must be for her.

"I'm so sorry, Luke," she says against my chest.

I squeeze her tighter, confused as to why she's apologizing. "Why are you saying that? You have nothing to apologize for."

She lifts her head, shaking it, looking up at me. "You don't need this stress. You're doing everything you can to keep us safe and now I've gone and made it even worse." She pulls away from me and picks up the damn spoon and starts stirring again. "I'm not going to put you through this," she says. "I'm not going to make you watch me carry a baby that you don't even know is yours or not. It isn't fair to you." She sets the spoon down and grabs a napkin, dabbing it beneath her eyes. She turns and looks at me, her face full of shame. "I'm sorry. I can..." She swallows like the next words are too hard for her to get out. "I can call tomorrow and see what I need to do to get it...to get an abortion."

I just stare at her, letting all of that soak in.

She's apologizing to *me*?

She thinks *I'm* the one who will be stressed by this?

I take a step forward and slide my hands through her hair, lifting her gaze to mine. Another tear begins to roll down her cheek, so I wipe it away with my thumb. "If there was a way we could find out this baby was mine, would you want to keep it?"

She winces, and then shrugs. And then she nods. "Of course I would, Luke. The timing is shit, but that's not the baby's fault."

As much as I want to wrap my arms around her in this second, I continue to hold her face in my hands. "And if you knew right now for a fact that this baby is Asa's, would you want to keep it?"

She doesn't respond for a moment. But then she shakes her head. "I wouldn't do that to you, Luke. It wouldn't be fair to you."

"I'm not asking about *me*," I say, my voice firm. "I'm asking *you*. If you knew this was Asa's baby, would you want to keep it?"

Another tear falls and I let it roll down her cheek. "It's a baby, Luke," she says quietly. "It's an innocent baby. But like I said, I wouldn't do that to you."

I pull her to me and I kiss the side of her head and hold her there a moment. When I find the words I want to say to her, I pull back and force her to look at me again. "I'm in love with you,

Sloan. *Madly* in love with you. And this baby growing inside of you is *half you*. Do you know how lucky I would feel if you allowed me to love something that was a part of you?" I lower my palm to her stomach and rest it there. "This baby is mine, Sloan. It's yours. It's ours. And if your decision is to raise this baby, then I'm going to be the best damn father that ever walked the earth. I promise."

She immediately brings her hands to her face and begins crying. She cries harder than I've ever seen her cry. I pick her up and I take her to our bedroom where I lay her on the bed again. I pull her to me and I wait for her tears to subside. After several minutes, the room is quiet again.

She's now lying with her head against my chest, her arm wrapped around me. "Luke?" She lifts her head and looks at me. "You're the best kind of human there is. And I love you so, *so* much."

I kiss her. Twice. And then I lower my face to her stomach and I lift her shirt and I kiss her skin. And I smile, because she's giving me something I never even knew I wanted. And as much as I can hope this baby is mine and not Asa's for Sloan's sake, it truly doesn't matter. It won't matter because this baby is part of the one person I love more than anything else. How lucky am I?

I sidle up to her side again and kiss her cheek. She's not crying anymore. I brush the hair back from her forehead. "Sloan? Did you know that concrete pillars dissolve into donuts every time a clock falls off a turtle's head?"

She laughs, hard, and her smile is huge. "Well, a victory isn't a victory if the empty room fills with dirty socks when the Christmas fruitcake is stale."

Our baby is going to have the strangest two parents in the whole world.

PRESENT DAY

Asa

I'm not sure if I inherited my intelligence from my mother or my father, because if you ask me, they're both a couple of ignorant fucks who somehow managed to only get one thing right during their combined years on this earth: My conception.

I didn't know my grandparents, but sometimes I like to imagine my paternal grandfather, *rest his soul*, was a lot like me. They say things skip generations, so I probably looked a lot like him. I probably act a lot like he did. And like me, he's probably disappointed as fuck that his son—*my father*—turned out to be such a fucking twat.

He's more than likely proud of me, though, and he's probably one of the few humans, dead or alive, who appreciate what a goddamn fucking *genius* I am.

Let me explain.

Ankle monitors. They're impossible to beat. You cut them, you get caught immediately. The fiber optic sensors inside of them will send an immediate signal as soon as they're tampered with and the police will show up at your door within seconds.

You can't just let the battery die, or the police will be notified. You can't possibly slip them off your foot because feet don't bend the way wrists do, and God didn't take ankle monitors into consideration when he designed the human skeleton, *the fucking selfish bastard.* You can't leave the perimeter of where you're confined to or the police will be notified. Hell, you can't even get drunk. Most ankle monitors come with sensors that periodically test alcohol levels in your skin. Not that I'm upset by that. I was never one to need alcohol. I just enjoy it, but I can do without.

Unless you're a tech geek with more knowledge than the tech geeks who invented the motherfucking ankle monitor, there's absolutely, without a doubt, no way to get around them without the police immediately being on your tail.

Which sucks, because knowing Luke, he's set it up so that he'll be notified as soon as my monitor indicates I've left my house or that the monitor has been tampered with in any way. There's no way I could make it from here to their place without them being given plenty of advance warning. And yes, I could send someone to their apartment to do my work for me, but where's the fun in that? Where's the fun in watching a bullet stop Luke's heart when I'm not standing in front of him, smelling the gunpowder? Where's the fun in making Sloan realize what a pathetic life choice she's made when I'm not the one tasting her tears when she cries for mercy?

It's a good thing I'm a big planner. I plan everything. I look at all possible scenarios and I develop ways around them before the events even occur. Because I'm a motherfucking genius. *Just like good ol' grandpa.*

I remember when I was a kid, there was a moment I thought I was going to die. I had slipped into my mother's bedroom and had stolen some pills from her. Fuck, I was so little I couldn't even read yet. I had no idea what I was taking, I just knew I wanted to feel whatever she felt. I wanted to chase whatever feeling it was that she loved more than her own child.

I woke up a few hours after I had taken them and my ankles looked like fucking baseballs. Both my legs were swollen. Back then

I thought it was because I was dying and all my blood was pooling in my feet. But now I know it was because of the medication. Antidepressants, pain pills, calcium channel blockers. They all cause severe edema, which was what I was experiencing as a kid. I just didn't realize it then.

A few months ago, Pansy Paul told me there was a chance I might get house arrest while we waited for the trial. Most defendants in my situation would be offered some sort of bail so they could walk around free, but with my record, he was almost certain I'd be confined to my house until a verdict was reached at trial. That's one of the few things I'm grateful to Pansy Paul for. The forewarning. It gave me a good solid week to obtain and consume as many fucking pills I could to guarantee a good couple of inches on each ankle. Wasn't hard to do since I was already in a hospital, thanks to those two fuckers who thought it'd be a good idea to actually fucking *shoot* me. Pricks.

Since the ankle monitor was attached, I've had to keep up with the medications just so the follow-up visits from the probation officer wouldn't raise any red flags. Stupid fucker has never even thought twice about the fact that my ankles and calves are the size of tree trunks. His name is Stewart. *Who in real life is really named Stewart*? Stewart thinks I'm just "big boned." I rejoice in his stupidity with every visit. I also kind of like the guy, because he feels bad for me. He thinks I'm a good guy because I laugh at his lame jokes and I talk to him about Jesus. Stewart fucking *loves* Jesus. I even had Anthony bring me a crucifix. Before Stewart's visit this morning, I hung it on my living room wall above the flat-screen TV where I watch hours upon hours of porn. Ironic, huh? When Stewart saw the Jesus-on-a-stick, he commented on it. I told him it was my grandpa's. I told him he was a Baptist preacher and it helps to look at that crucifix and know that grandpa is looking down on me.

It's a lie, of course. I doubt my grandpa ever even stepped foot inside a church. And if he really did own a crucifix, he probably used it to beat people with.

Stewart liked it, though. Said he has one almost identical to it, but it's not quite as big. He also checked my ankle monitor and told me everything looked great and that he'd see me in a week. I gave him a slice of coconut cake before he left.

Now I'm standing here, staring down at the bottle of hydrochlorothiazide in my hands. I have to be smart with it, because taking too much could drop my blood pressure like a motherfucker. But I need to take enough to get rid of the edema. Enough to create a large enough gap between me and my ankle monitor so that I can slip it off and onto Anthony's wrist.

That's where the genius comes in. If a person could actually slip an ankle monitor off without tampering with the fiber optics, the chances of it picking that up are slim to none. Ankle monitors are monitored periodically throughout the day. Set up on timers and shit. So the switch from my foot to Anthony's wrist will go completely unnoticed, so long as the actual piece of equipment isn't tampered with. They thought ankle monitors were foolproof because they don't slip off the ankles of people of average intelligence.

It's the geniuses like me they should have been more concerned with. Now I just have to be able to trust Anthony enough not to leave my fucking house or drink any alcohol until I tell him it's done. Then I'll put the ankle monitor back on my ankle and it'll look like I never left my house.

In the meantime, I still have more planning to do. I open the bottle and pop four of the pills. I open my laptop and begin searching obstetricians while I place phone calls for two hours straight. By the time I finally figure out which obstetrician Sloan is seeing, I've already pissed four times. The ankle monitor is already starting to feel loose. I was thinking this would take a few days, but I think this can actually happen as soon as tomorrow morning.

The person who answers the phone puts me on hold while she searches the file for what I'm assuming is a confidentiality agreement. HIPPA compliance and all that shit.

"Sir?" she asks to see if I'm still on the line.

"Here," I tell her.

"What did you say your name was?"

"Luke," I tell her. "I'm the father."

Ha! I laugh internally at all the Star Wars jokes that poor fucker must have endured in his lifetime.

"Can you confirm your address and date of birth?" she asks.

I confirm both of them. Because I know both of them. Because I'm a *genius*. Once my "identity" is confirmed, she says, "And what is it you were wanting to know?"

"The due date. I'm having a video made for our family to announce the pregnancy and I don't want to ask Sloan, because she'll get mad that I forgot the exact due date. So I'm hoping you can just share that information with me to keep me out of the doghouse."

The woman laughs. *She likes that I'm such a loving and caring man, excited about the birth of my child.* "Looks like the conception occurred in March. Due date is...Christmas Day! Not sure how you could forget that, Dad," she says with a laugh.

I laugh, too. "That's right. Christmas Day. Our very own little miracle. Thanks for checking."

"No problem!"

I hang up the phone and look at a calendar. Sloan was still living with me in March.

Luke was around in March. *A whole fucking lot.*

I'm not sure when the brainwashing started, or when she gave herself to him. My whole body stiffens at the thought. I can't believe he fucked her. *My Sloan.*

I can't believe she *let* him. I have no idea if they even used a condom. I know for a fact the fucker didn't use one when he decided to take her right in front...

Not going there.

I will not allow those visions to repeat in my head. The worst fucking moment of my life. I keep telling myself it was a nightmare, that everything I saw—the words that came out of her mouth, the noises they made—it was a nightmare. I had been shot four fucking times, I lost a lot of blood. It could *not* have been real. There's no way that bitch stood in front of me and allowed another man to stick his...

Not. Going. There.

I stand up, filled with renewed rage. I pick the chair up I was just sitting in and I throw it across the room, watching it smash against the door. I sprint across the living room and pull the fucking crucifix off the wall. I bash it against the TV, cracking the screen.

That feels good. Sloan was with me when I bought that TV. It feels good to fucking smash it. I look for something else to smash. A mirror. I run toward it and slam the crucifix against it three times until all the glass is shattered on the floor.

Fucking bitch. I can't believe she had the nerve to do that right in front of me.

I take my crucifix down the hallway to the bathroom. I stare at myself in the mirror, wondering if that baby inside her is mine. Just knowing there's a chance it could come out looking like Luke makes me fucking hate it. Knowing it was inside her when he fucked her right in front of me makes me fucking *hate* it.

I swing the crucifix at the mirror and smash it over and over.

Fucking bitch.

I walk upstairs and do the same to that mirror.

I don't even want this fucking baby. It's been inside her since March, and there's no telling how many times Luke has been inside her since then. Even if it *is* my baby, he's already tainted it. Pretty sure fetuses have ears, and every time Luke speaks out loud in the vicinity of Sloan, that baby probably thinks Luke's fucking disgusting voice is its father.

When Sloan grows my baby inside her, Luke won't fucking be around to corrupt my child.

I walk through every room, finding more things my tiny Jesus-on-a-stick can destroy. Lamps? Done. Vases? Smashed. Jesus-on-a-stick is on a rampage.

Fucking bitch.

Fucking baby.

Fucking *Luke.*

Every fucking nice thing I've ever had in my life has been destroyed by that man. My empire. The love of my life. My potential child. Everything that's ever meant anything to me now means absolutely nothing to me because of him.

When I make it back to the kitchen, I open the bottle and swallow another pill. The sooner I'm able to get this ankle monitor off, the sooner I can destroy what he's slowly corrupting.

I'll be a dad when I'm goddamn ready to be a dad, and it'll be to a child who isn't a single goddamn part of that pathetic piece of shit.

This thing growing inside Sloan right now wasn't made from love. Even if it's mine, it wasn't created innocently. She was allowing another man to corrupt her while I was making love to her at night. If I'd have known that, my dick would have never been inside her. I would have ended her before she went and made all the stupid decisions she's made. She wouldn't have had a fucking viable womb capable of creating life if I'd known what she was doing behind my back.

Now I just need to put a stop to it. I look at the screensaver on my laptop. It's a screenshot of the moment she put her hands on her belly and smiled down at that fucking abomination. I pull a new chair around and I sit down and change my screensaver. I find a picture of Sloan from back when she was sweet. I make it my screensaver and I stare at it, wondering how she let this happen. How does she still have the audacity to smile when the whore doesn't even know whose baby is inside her?

"Fucking whore." I look down at the crucifix in my hand. "Jesus-on-a-stick, do you want to go on a little road trip with me tomorrow? I know a girl who has some serious repenting to do."

S L O A N

In the last two weeks, I've cooked and photographed twenty-seven meals. Maybe it's because I'm trying to keep my mind off the fact that I can't leave my apartment, but this cookbook idea has completely taken over my thoughts.

When I'm not thinking about the pregnancy, of course. Which is every other moment.

I don't know what I'd do without Luke. Part of me thinks he's too good to be true. That men like him don't really exist and that this is all some sort of wishful thinking on my part. I live in constant fear that he was only brought into my life so I would have to endure the pain of him being taken out of it. I hate those thoughts and I try not to think them, but I do. Constantly. I fear losing him more than I fear death.

But every afternoon when Luke comes home and wraps me in his arms and asks how "we're" doing, it completely reinforces his claim that this baby is his. No matter who is biologically responsible for the conception, Luke loves it, simply because it's inside me. That's enough for him. And somehow, he makes me think it's enough for me. When I'm actually in Luke's presence, I feel a sense of self-worth. I feel all the things that Asa stripped from me.

I don't know if I'm as good at forgiveness as Luke seems to be. He didn't even make me feel ashamed, not even for a second. And he continues to remind me of how lucky he is, even though I know it's the other way around. He always redirects my thoughts when I start to worry about Asa finding out about the pregnancy, or when I worry about the upcoming trial. But when he's not here, like right now, the only thing that can redirect my thoughts is this cookbook.

I'm making lasagna tonight. I'm not sticking to a certain type of food, like specifically Italian or Asian. I'm including all of my favorite foods. I'm even including some of Asa's favorites, like his damn coconut cake. I like that his favorite recipes are going in a cookbook that goes against everything he is as a person. It feels a little like revenge. For every two dollars this cookbook makes, it's a dollar that helps women who have suffered at the hands of men like Asa.

So yes, I'm including his stupid fucking coconut cake and his stupid spaghetti and meatballs and even his stupid protein shake that he used to wake me up at the butt-crack of dawn to make for him. As much as I hate all the times he demanded I cook for him, at least some good will come of it. This whole cookbook is like a huge middle finger to Asa Jackson.

That's a good idea, actually. I think I'll incorporate a tiny little hand flipping the bird on all the pages, somehow. A cute little middle-finger emoji.

When I finish layering the noodles and sauce, I set the pan up to take another picture. I snap a few and then place the pan in the oven.

"What smells so good?"

I grip the counter at the sound of his voice.

Right behind me.

No. *No, no, no, no, no, no, no.*

It isn't possible. The door is still dead bolted. All the windows are locked from the inside. *I'm dreaming, I'm dreaming, I'm dreaming.*

I can feel myself slowly sinking to the kitchen floor as my body starts to fail me. I'm going into shock. I can feel it, I can feel it, *no, no, no.*

I'm on the floor. I slide my hands through my hair and against my ears, my palms shaking. I try to cover up the sound of his voice. If I don't hear it, it's not there. He's not there. *He's not.*

"Jesus, Sloan." He's closer now. "I thought you'd be a little more excited to see me."

I squeeze my eyes shut, but I can hear him as he hoists himself up onto the counter next to me. I open my eyes and see his feet swinging close to the floor as his legs dangle at my side. There's no ankle monitor. He wants me to see that. I know how his fucked up mind works.

How is this happening?

Where is my phone?

I feel sick. I force myself to breathe so I don't pass out from fear.

"Lasagna, huh?" He tosses something onto the counter. "Never liked your lasagna much. You always used too much tomato sauce."

I'm crying now. I scoot away from him, unable to find the strength to stand up. I keep scooting, knowing I won't get anywhere, but hoping I somehow do.

"Where you going, baby?" he asks.

I try to pick myself up off the floor, but as soon as I come to a half-stand, he jumps off the counter and has his arms around me from behind. "Let's go have a little chat," he says, lifting me effortlessly off the floor.

I cry out in fear and a hand immediately clamps over my mouth. "I'm going to need you to be quiet while we chat," he says, carrying me through the living room and into my bedroom. I still haven't laid eyes on him yet.

I won't.

I refuse to look at him.

Luke. Please, Luke. Come home, come home, come home.

Asa tosses me onto the bed and I immediately begin to crawl to the other side, but he grips my ankle and yanks me back. I'm on my stomach. I try to kick his hand off. I grab at a blanket, a pillow, anything my hands can touch, but my strength does little to defend me against him. In what feels like slow motion, he flips me onto my back and pins my hands down with his knees as he straddles me. He's sitting on top of me, putting pressure against my stomach, and it's then that I know he knows. It's not something I can hide at this point.

That's why he's here.

I feel his fingers press against my eyelids and he forces them open. When I see his face, he's smiling. "Hey, beautiful," he says. "It's rude not to make eye contact with someone when they're trying to have a serious conversation with you."

He's fucking insane. And there's nothing I can do to protect myself. Nothing I can do to protect my baby.

I cough up bile with my tears. Despite the fact that he has me pinned to the bed, completely at his mercy, I somehow still have lucid thoughts that flash through my head. Right now, in this second, I'm wondering how my life can mean so much to me. How the thought of dying fills me with so much fear, when just a few months ago, I honestly wouldn't have cared. I used to pray Asa would just kill me and put me out of my misery. That was back when I had nothing to live for.

Now I have everything to live for.

Everything.

The tears fall from my eyes and into my hair. He looks at the tears sliding down my face and then he leans forward, bringing his face to mine. He moves his mouth to my temple and I feel his tongue as it draws up some of the tears. When he pulls back, his smile is gone.

"I thought they would taste different," he whispers.

I start sobbing. My pulse has gotten so fast, it's one constant beat now. Or maybe it stopped altogether. I close my eyes again. "Just get it over with, Asa," I whisper. "Please."

Some of the pressure on my stomach decreases, as if he's readjusting himself on top of me. Then I feel him lift my shirt and press a hand to my stomach. "Congratulations," he says. "Is it mine?"

I keep my eyes closed and refuse to respond to him. He rubs his hand over my stomach for several seconds. I feel him move closer again and his mouth is at my ear. "Are you wondering how the *fuck* I got inside your apartment?"

I was, but now I'm wondering how the fuck I can get him out.

"Do you remember this morning when your good friend, Luke, let the maintenance man in to change the filter on the air conditioning?"

The maintenance guy? What? No, that isn't possible. Luke asked for his identification. Verified his identity with the manager. We know everyone who works on this property, and that man has worked here for over two years.

"He did me a small favor and unlocked the window while Luke had his back turned. You know how much he did it for? Two grand. No questions asked. He knew you were here, he knew you were pregnant, and he knew I had something terrible planned because why else would I pay him two grand to pretend he was doing routine filter changes? He didn't *care*, Sloan. Two grand is all he needed and then he walked away, no questions asked."

I'm sick.

Sick.

Humans are sick.

If that man knew what Asa was capable of, he never would have done that. He never would have unlocked the window. He probably thought Asa was breaking in to steal a TV.

I might be crying even harder now, disappointed that humanity fails to live up to even the minimum morals.

"Your little surveillance buddy out front never even saw me, because sadly, Luke doesn't think you're worth the money to hire surveillance for every point of entry into this apartment. Does he really think I'm stupid enough to go through the front fucking door?"

The more he talks, the less I hear. Somehow, my fear is numbing me. I can't feel my body anymore. I can't feel Asa on top of me.

I slowly stop feeling anything.

But my conscience isn't doing me any favors. I'm still aware.

I'm aware of the fact that he's removing my clothes. Piece by piece.

I'm aware of the fact that his tongue is in my mouth.

I'm aware of the fact that he's doing these things to me, on the bed I share with Luke, in an apartment I naively thought was safe.

I'm aware of the fact that he's inside me now.

I can't feel him.

I can't see him.

But I know.

I am aware.

I am aware that this is what my death is. This is how my shitty, despicable joke of a life is going to end. This is how my baby's life will end, because I couldn't do enough to protect us.

I don't deserve Luke. If I did, this wouldn't be happening. Luke was put in my life so that when I experienced this, it would hurt infinitely more to know that I'm losing him.

I'm not sure what I did to God to deserve this. But for Asa to be here, right now, doing these things to me, I must have done something terrible in this life. Or in a past life.

I deserve this. I'm sure I do.

I choke on my tears; I choke on his tongue.

I am aware, and it's the last thing I want to be right now. *I'd much rather be dead.*

ASA

"That felt different."

I'm still panting, recovering from that unplanned moment between us. I pull out of her and collapse on top of her.

She never even tried to stop me. She just let me fuck her and she never even said no.

Fucking whore.

It was better back when I knew I was the only one who had ever been inside her. But just then, every time I pushed into her I felt like I was sharing her. Knowing Luke knows what it feels like to be a part of her made me want to put my hands around her throat and squeeze both lives out of her. I probably would have if she'd have put up a fight, but she didn't.

She misses me. Any other woman in the world would have done whatever she could have to fight me off of her, but not Sloan. She knows that's where she belongs. Beneath me. Surrounding me.

I lie next to her and prop myself up on my elbow. She still has her eyes closed and she's trembling. I don't know if it's because she's scared or because I brought her close to orgasm. Probably both.

I hate that she's still just as fucking beautiful as she was when she was innocent. That same shiny dark hair, long enough to cover her breasts. Those same sweet, soft lips that used to belong only to me and my body. I drag my finger down her stomach, over the tiny bump, and then I cup my hand between her legs. I sigh as I look down at her. I fucking miss her. I fucking hate her so fucking much, but I miss her.

"Look at me, Sloan."

She whimpers and tries to choke back another sob.

"Sloan, *look* at me."

She does, slowly. She opens her tear-filled eyes and tilts her head just enough to make eye contact with me.

"I miss you, baby." I rub my hand between her legs while I talk to her, reminding her of how I used to make her feel. Maybe if she remembers how good we were together, we can somehow get back to that. "I miss wrapping myself around you at night while I slept. Do you know how fucking lonely it is in our house, Sloan? It's fucking lonely without you there. I *hate* it."

She closes her eyes again. I smile, because I know how hard it is for her to keep them open when I make her feel things with my hands like this. I loved watching her build until her eyes squeezed shut and she'd scream out my name. I slide a finger inside her and just like I hoped, she squeezes her eyes even tighter.

I press a soft kiss against her lips. "I thought I was over you," I say, thinking back to yesterday. To the rage-filled rampage I went on with Jesus-on-a-stick. "I hated you, Sloan. I don't like hating you, baby."

She sucks in a long rush of air, and my mouth is so close to hers, she steals some of my breath. I give her more. I press my mouth to hers and I kiss her, filling her mouth with my tongue. Just like when I was inside her a moment ago, she refuses to kiss me back.

"Sloan," I whisper, dragging my lips across hers. "Baby, I need you to kiss me back. I need to know if I still mean anything to you."

I remain patient, still touching her, watching her. She finally opens her eyes. A huge tear, bigger than the rest, rolls down her face.

And then she remembers. She lifts her head, parting her lips for me.

She remembers how much I've fucking done for her. She remembers how much I fucking loved her. How *hard* I loved her. When her tongue slides against mine, I want to fucking cry. My chest fills with fire and if I'm not inside her again, I'm scared I'll combust.

"Baby, I've missed you so much," I say to her. But then I shut up, because she's kissing me like she used to kiss me, before she was corrupted. She's kissing me the way she kissed me that first night in the alley when my mouth was the first one to introduce her to a kiss.

She's moving now, lifting her arms, rubbing her hands up my neck. Her fingers slide through my hair and I needed this so much. It was worth the risk of removing the ankle monitor. *So* worth it. I know I came here with different intentions, but that's because I was angry. Luke makes me feel so much hatred, it caused me to confuse what I feel for him with what I feel for Sloan. It made me think she was evil, but she's not.

She's a victim.

She's simply Luke's victim and she just needed me to remind her of how different it feels to be held by me. She needed to feel me inside her to remind her that she's being brainwashed to forget me. But she didn't forget me.

She remembers.

"Asa," she whispers, saying my name with desire. "Asa, I'm sorry."

I pull back, shocked that I can even force words out when I need her so fucking much I can't even breathe. "Baby, don't," I say, brushing the hair back from her face. "It's okay. We'll get past this. He made you hate me, and for a moment he made me hate you. But that's not us, Sloan. You don't hate me, Sloan."

She shakes her head. "I don't, Asa. I don't hate you."

I can see the apology all over her face. I can feel the regret in her words and in the tears that are still falling.

"I love you," she says, completely fucking murdering me with those three words. "I'm sorry for everything. I miss you so much." I kiss her again, and then I slide on top of her because those three words have already made my dick so fucking hard, I can't think straight. I push into her and she gasps for more air. I go slow this time. I don't fuck her like I did a few minutes ago, because that was when I thought I hated her.

I kiss her, and I'm gentle with her, because she's been through so much. I make love to her and I watch her face the whole time because I love her. She's the only good thing that's ever happened to me and I somehow almost forgot that. "I was wrong, baby," I say to her. "It doesn't feel different. It feels exactly like it used to feel. You feel perfect."

She forces a smile, but it's hard for her because this is so fucking intense. Being reunited with her like this, feeling her hands on me and the way her legs wrap around me, wanting me deeper inside her. It's the most intense feeling I've ever had. It almost makes the entire last few months all worth it.

This is heaven. *This* is God's apology.

"I forgive you," I whisper, and I'm not sure if I'm forgiving Sloan or if I'm forgiving God. Maybe I'm forgiving both of them, because this is worth all the forgiveness in the world. She feels so fucking good right now, I might even consider forgiving Luke.

Okay, that's not true. I'll never forgive that piece of shit. But I'll worry about him later. Right now I'm preoccupied with the love of my life, remembering every curve of her body, every curve *inside* her body.

I try to make it last, to make love to her like she deserves, but I've missed being inside her so much, I can't even hold back the second time around. I press my face against her neck and wait for her moans. She always moans when I release inside her.

As soon as that precious sound glides up her throat, I fucking lose it.

362

"Fuck," I say, thrusting hard into her once. Twice. "I fucking love you, Sloan. I fucking *love* you, baby, fucking *hell*."

It's the best thirty seconds of my life.

She's still holding on to me when I'm finished. She's shaking. I love that I make her whole body tremble with mine. I love it. I love *her*.

"Don't leave me again, Sloan," I say quietly. I roll onto my side and I pull her against me. I can't even describe this. I thought I loved her before, but it doesn't compare to this moment, to the intensity rushing through my veins. My heart beats for her. She's why my heart still beats at all, and I'm not sure I realized it to the extent I realize it now. "Don't ever fucking leave me again. If you break your promise again I don't know if I can be as forgiving."

Maybe this feels so different because I love more than just Sloan now. I love what's growing inside her. The feeling I got while I was inside of her was more than I knew I was capable of feeling, and I don't think I realized until this moment that it's because there's more of her to love. There's her and then there's the tiny little piece of heaven that we created together, growing inside her body. And *fuck* Luke. Luke wouldn't be capable of creating life that's due on Christmas fucking *Day*.

I know I created this baby with her because I wouldn't feel this way if it were Luke's baby. This feeling is God, letting me know that a part of me is inside of Sloan, and that I need to do what I can to protect both of them from Luke.

I press my cheek to Sloan's stomach. I lay my palm flat against her skin and I squeeze my eyes shut, but the tears still come. I can't believe I'm fucking crying right now. *What the fuck?* Does realizing you're a dad instantly turn men into pussies?

I squeeze her tight and I kiss my baby. I kiss her over and over. Her stomach is so beautiful, and I know the life we created together will be beautiful, just like Sloan. She runs her hand through my hair, and the next words she whispers to me will never leave my soul. Ever.

"You're gonna be a Daddy, Asa."

I laugh and I keep fucking crying, and then I'm on top of her again, kissing her. I can't get enough of her. "You're so beautiful, baby. You're so beautiful. If I knew how fucking beautiful being pregnant would make you, I would have tampered with your birth control way sooner than I did."

I feel her freeze for a second and it makes me laugh. I pull back and look down on her, but she gives me a half-hearted smile. "What?" she says. Her voice cracks a little. It's so fucking cute.

I laugh and kiss her again. "You can't be mad at me, Sloan." I put a hand on her stomach again and look down on her. "I did it for us. So you wouldn't leave me." For some reason, she's still crying. But so am I. I laugh again, wiping away some of her tears. "And now look at us. We've been through fucking hell, but look at us. We're having a baby." I lower myself on top of her again. I kiss her. Slow, deep, promising. When I pull back, I leave my lips pressed lightly against hers. "You won't leave me again, Sloan. Not with my baby inside of you. Right?"

She immediately shakes her head. "I won't, Asa. I promise. I love you. I'll never leave you."

I have no idea how it happens for a third time, but hearing those words makes me hard again. I'm already on top of her and I barely have to move to slip inside her. I squeeze my eyes shut. I kiss the tears off her cheeks. And I move inside her, slowly, over and over, needing to make up for all the nights we've been apart. I can feel the sweat sliding down my forehead. I can feel my heart as it increases its pounding against the walls of my chest. My whole body is exhausted because our third time together goes on for so long, I start to grow weak. But I could make love to her like this forever. And I *will*.

For fucking ever.

S L O A N

There was a moment.

It was a split second, almost too quick to notice. It was right when Asa pulled back and looked down on me, begging me to kiss him back. It was a moment of desperation. *And I took advantage of it.*

I know if I fight him right now, I can't win. Fighting back is what every part of my soul is screaming for me to do. It's been screaming for me to fight, to defend myself, for the entire time Asa has been inside this apartment. I'm not even sure if he's been here for a whole hour yet, but it feels like an eternity. I can feel my soul, clawing at my insides, begging to be set free from this pathetic shell of a body it's been stuck in since the day I was born.

But this is the moment my soul and I need to finally become one. This is the moment my body needs to align with the rest of me, to calm the nerves, to protect the baby growing inside of it, to preserve our lives for as long as it possibly can. And the only way that can happen is if I give this body to Asa.

That's all I'm doing. It's just a body. My soul is still strong. It's fighting the only way it knows how. But my body needs to give in... just long enough to save me.

I tell him what he needs to hear. I touch him like he needs to be touched. I make the noises I've trained myself to make for him. I speak the lies to him that I've trained myself to speak.

I've been pretending to love him for two years. *What's one more day?*

Finally, after he finishes...*again*...I feel it. A sense of peace. A quiet calm, letting me know that my soul and my body and my mind and my perseverance have all come together in understanding. We are going to fight Asa with the only weapon stronger than he is. *We're going to fight him with love.*

He falls to my side again and pulls me so that I'm facing him. I smile and cup his cheek with my hand. "What now?" I ask him, gently stroking his face with fingers I've somehow convinced to stop trembling. "How do we get out of this mess, Asa? I can't lose you again."

He grabs my hand and kisses it. "We get dressed and walk out the front door, Sloan. Simple as that. And then we go somewhere... anywhere. We get far away from here."

I nod, taking in all that he just said.

Asa is dumb as shit, but somehow, he's also one of the smartest people I've ever met. I've always had to try to stay a step ahead of him. This is no different. Every move he makes from here on out is a test. I dissect his words and flip them over in my head.

He knows we can't go out the front door. He knows about the surveillance. That's why he came through the window.

I shake my head. "Asa, you can't walk out the front door," I say, forcing myself to sound worried for him. "Luke has me under surveillance. If whoever is out there sees me with you, they'll call Luke."

Asa grins.

It was a test.

He leans forward and kisses me on the forehead. "We'll go out the window, then."

"I need to pack first." I start to get up, but he pulls me back down.

"I'll pack for you," he says. "Don't get off the fucking bed."

He stands up and looks around the room. I can see the veins in his neck bulging as he notices all of Luke's things. I try to distract him from his own anger.

"There's a bag in the top of the closet." I point toward the closet and I see his eyes as they scan the distance from the bed to the living room. He walks toward the closet and slams the bedroom door shut as he passes. His way of letting me know that I better not even try to run.

I take in my physical posture on the bed and realize that it looks like I'm poised to jump at any second. I'm not being convincing enough.

I lie back on my pillow and try to look relaxed. He walks out of the closet and scans me, smirking. He likes that I didn't try to run. He's letting down his own guard.

"So fucking beautiful, love," he says, tossing the bag onto the bed. "What do you want me to pack?" He looks around the room. His eyes fall to the dresser—at the picture of me and Luke. I printed it out a week ago and framed it. I can see the roll in Asa's throat. "Excuse me for a second," he says, walking toward the bedroom door.

"Where are you going?" I ask, sitting up on the bed. He opens the door and walks into the living room.

"I left *Jesus-on-a-stick* near the window. I need Him."

What the fuck?

He's back before I can process what he said, and he's holding something in his hand.

"Is that a crucifix?"

What in the hell?

He smiles with his nod, and then he brings the crucifix up over his head with both hands, and then straight down again, right on top of the framed picture on the dresser. I flinch with the first blow, but he bashes the cross against the frame, over and over, until it's in a dozen tiny pieces.

I'm *absolutely* terrified. But I force myself to laugh. I don't know how. Every part of me wants to scream out in terror right now, but I know that's the last thing I need to do. I'm playing a part, and that character needs to laugh for Asa, because he needs to know that I have no feelings for that picture frame.

He glances at me and enjoys the smile on my face. He grins from ear to ear, so I point at the nightstand. "There's one over there, too."

His gaze falls on the other picture frame, and he glides across the room. He swings the crucifix like it's a bat, knocking the picture off the nightstand and straight into the wall. Even knowing it was coming, I still flinch. I cringe at the amount of hatred he has for Luke.

This entire time, I've been silently praying that Luke will miraculously come home early. But now I'm praying he doesn't, because I'm not sure any man can withstand the person Asa is right now. He's completely irrational. He's void of compassion, of empathy. He's delusional. He's dangerous. And I'd rather get Asa out of this apartment and be forced to accompany him, than to have him here when Luke returns home.

Asa looks around the room. When he doesn't see anything else that makes him vengeful, he tosses the crucifix on the bed. "When does Luke get home?"

He knows when Luke gets home.

I could lie and say he'll be home any minute, but if Asa somehow knew our address, then he more than likely already knows our every move. He knows Luke gets home at six every night.

"Six," I say to him.

He nods. He pulls his phone out of his pocket and checks the time. "It's gonna be a long wait," he says. "What do you want to do for the next few hours?"

Wait...what?

"We're *waiting* for him?"

He drops down onto the bed next to me. "Of course we are, Sloan. I didn't come all this way to take back my girl and not get revenge on the bastard who stole her from me."

He somehow says all this with a smile on his face.

Once again, I swallow my fear. "We could eat lasagna. If I don't take it out of the oven in the next two minutes, it'll be inedible."

Asa leans over me and presses a kiss to my mouth, making a loud pop when he pulls back. "Fucking genius, babe." He scoots off the bed and pulls me up. "I'm starving. You can put your clothes back on if you want."

He lets go of my hands and walks into the bathroom. He leaves the door open and he watches me the whole time he stands over the toilet. I put my clothes back on, trying to stop my hands from shaking too noticeably. He flushes the toilet and walks back into the bedroom, toward the living room. "I was just kidding earlier," he says. "I don't hate your lasagna. I feel really bad for saying that, I was just really upset with you."

I walk past him and stand on my tiptoes to kiss him on the cheek. "I know, baby. We all say things we don't mean when we're angry."

I walk into the kitchen. The lasagna has been in the oven way longer than I intended for it to be, but I don't think it's burnt yet. It just won't make for very good pictures for the cookbook.

I laugh as soon as I have that thought.

Seriously? My life is in fucking danger and I'm thinking about a stupid cookbook?

I walk into the kitchen, but Asa isn't far behind me. I'm sure he's on my heels because he's not convinced I won't go for a knife. He's smart, because if he wasn't a step behind me, I'd absolutely go for one. I grab the empty boxes of ingredients strewn across the counter and toss them toward the trash, but as soon as I do, I see there's no trash bag lining the can.

That's because I took the trash out of the can.

I look at the trash bag, tied at the top, sitting next to the empty trashcan.

I look at the empty trashcan.

My pulse begins to race and I do everything I can to hide it.

I forgot the fucking trash!

Calm down, calm down, calm down. I grab an oven mitt and I pull the oven door open. I set the pan of lasagna down on top of the stove. Asa reaches over my shoulder and opens a cabinet to grab a couple of plates. He kisses the top of my head in the process. He grabs a spatula and cuts into the lasagna, refusing to bring a knife into the equation. The whole time he cuts at the lasagna, I'm staring at the empty trashcan.

I didn't take out the trash.

LUKE

look at my phone again.

"You aren't listening," Ryan says, bringing my attention back to him.

"I'm listening." I set my phone on the table, face up. I stare at it and pretend to be listening to Ryan, but he's right. I'm not.

"What the hell, Luke?" He snaps his fingers. "What the fuck is wrong with you?"

I shake my head. "Nothing, it's just..." I don't even want to say it out loud, because I'll sound like an idiot. The measures Sloan and I have gone to just to feel safe are ridiculous, even by my standards. "It's five after."

Ryan leans back in his seat and takes a sip of his drink. We're at some pizza joint just a few miles from my apartment, discussing what we always discuss when we meet: Asa's case. He goes to trial in a few short months and I'll be damned if we don't do everything we can to make this as cut and dry as possible. The longer he's sentenced and the more he's convicted of, the better off Sloan will be.

"It's five after what?" Ryan asks.

371

"Twelve o'clock. *Six* after, now." I look at my phone. It's 12:06 and Sloan hasn't taken out the trash yet.

Ryan leans forward. "Please elaborate, because you're really starting to piss me off with how *not present* you've been in our conversation."

"That guy who does daytime surveillance...Thomas...he always texts me right at noon to let me know Sloan took the trash out. She puts it outside the door every day at noon so I'll know everything is okay."

I pick up the phone and begin texting Thomas.

"Why don't you just call and check up on her?" Ryan asks, as if that's the most obvious answer.

"This is extra protection. If something happens and someone is with her, they could force her to answer the phone and pretend everything is okay. We do other things aside from phone calls for added reassurance."

Ryan stares at me a moment after I hit send on the text. I know he thinks I'm being overly paranoid right now, but surely he can't blame me. Asa is fucking psychotic and unpredictable. I'm not sure anyone could ever be too safe when it comes to him.

"That's actually pretty genius," Ryan says.

"I know," I say, getting ready to dial Sloan's number. "It was her idea. And so far, she's never missed a single day. She sets the trash out like clockwork." I bring the phone to my ear and wait while it rings. She's never not answered her phone.

I wait.

She doesn't answer her phone. Right when it goes to voicemail, I get a text from the surveillance guy.

Still waiting. Trash hasn't been taken out yet.

My fucking heart falls straight to the floor. Ryan sees it. He stands up at the same time I do. "I'll call for backup," he says, tossing money onto the table. I'm out the door before I can respond. I'm in my car. I'm cussing traffic and honking my horn and doing everything I can to get there.

Four minutes.

Four fucking excruciating minutes.

That's how long it's going to take me to get there.

I dial a number and hit send on my phone.

"Yeah?" he says.

"Is it out yet? Did she put the fucking trash out yet?" I'm trying to remain calm, but I can't.

"Not yet, man."

I beat my fist on the steering wheel. "Did anyone go through the front door today?" I'm yelling my words, no matter how hard I try to remain calm.

"No. Not since you left this morning."

"Go around back!" I yell. "Check the windows!"

He doesn't say anything.

"Now! Check the windows while I'm on the phone with you!"

He clears his throat. "You hired me for surveillance. I don't even have a gun, man. No way I'm going back there if it's got you this worried."

I grip the phone tighter in my hand and scream at him. "Are you *FUCKING KIDDING ME?*"

The line goes dead.

"Fucking son of a bitch!"

I slam on the gas and power through a red light. I'm two blocks away now. I'm almost through the intersection when it happens.

My whole body jerks with the impact. I saw the eighteen-wheeler out of the corner of my eye, and then I didn't. My airbag deploys. My car begins spinning. I know it's all happening faster than anyone witnessing it can possibly even comprehend, but the crash goes in slow motion for me.

It drags. On and on and fucking on.

By the time my car comes to a stop, the blood is already rushing into my eye. I hear horns and people yelling. I reach down for my seatbelt, but I can't move my right arm. It's broken.

I get my seatbelt unbuckled with my left arm. I press my shoulder into the driver's side door and push it open.

I wipe the blood off my forehead.

"Sir!" a man yells from behind me. "Sir, you need to stay in the car!"

Someone grabs my shoulder and tries to stop me. "Get off me!" I yell. I try to regain my bearings long enough to see which direction I'm facing. I catch sight of the convenience store on my right. I turn left and I push through the crowd beginning to form around my car. People are yelling at me to stop running, but I can't run fast enough.

Two blocks.

I can do that in less than a minute.

The entire time I'm sprinting toward my apartment, I make excuses for why she's not answering the phone. I pray I'm wrong, that I'm overreacting. But I know Sloan. Something is wrong. She wouldn't not answer her phone.

She wouldn't not take the trash out right at twelve.

Something is wrong.

When I finally reach the complex, I'm not in a vehicle, so the sensor on the fucking gate doesn't open for me. I look around for a door to walk through, but it's locked. I back up several feet and then sprint for the gate, somehow pulling myself over with my good arm. I don't land on my feet. I land on my right fucking shoulder and the pain shoots through me like a bolt of lightning. It knocks the breath out of me. I'm forced to take a second until I can take in air again. Then I'm back on my feet.

I see Thomas, the surveillance guy. He's standing outside of his car. When he sees me, his eyes widen at the sight of me, and then he throws his hands up. "I'm sorry, man, I was about to go check on her." He backs up and I can't help myself. I punch him right in the throat with my good hand. I keep walking as he falls against his car door.

"Stupid fuck!" I yell over my shoulder. I sprint toward the apartment and go straight past the front door, around the side of the building, to the wall our living room and bedroom windows line. I run up to the living room window and it takes all I have not to scream out her name when I see the lock on the inside of the window.

It's unlatched.

I know instantly how it happened. The maintenance guy. It's my own fucking fault. I should have been a step ahead of Asa. I don't give myself time to think over it. I press my back against the wall next to the window and I try to listen.

I reach down to my side and I pull out my gun. I close my eyes and inhale.

I hear voices.

I hear Sloan's voice. I want to cry a river knowing I'm not too late, but I'll do that later. Right now, I inch over toward the window and try to peek inside. I can barely see anything because of the curtains.

Fuck.

My pulse is pounding. I can hear sirens in the distance and I have no idea if they're coming here because Ryan called them or if they're going to the wreck I just caused at the intersection. Either way, if I don't do something in the next five seconds, whoever is inside this apartment will hear them.

And they'll be forced to take action.

I drop to my knees and hold the gun in my left hand while I inch the window open with my right. I peek inside and I can see Sloan. I can also see someone else. His back is to the window. He laughs.

He fucking laughs, and I know instantly that it's him. He's in there with Sloan. He hasn't hurt her yet. She's standing in the kitchen.

If he hears the sirens, he *will* hurt her. He'll panic and he'll do something stupid. I don't know how she has him this calm, but it doesn't surprise me. My Sloan is smart as fuck.

I raise the window another inch. For half a second, Sloan makes eye contact with me.

Half a second.

A glance.

She drops her fork and I know she does it on purpose. The second she does it, she says, "Shit!" She bends over to pick it up. I raise the window a little higher as Asa is scooting back in the barstool. He's walking around the bar for whatever reason. To make sure she's not trying something? I lift my gun, barely able to grip the trigger with my right hand.

He takes the fork from her and tosses it in the sink and then hands her a new one. Right after she grabs it, she falls to the floor and screams, "Now!"

Before Asa can even comprehend what's happening, I pull the trigger. I don't even wait to see where it hit him. I push the window up and climb inside, running across our living room until I get to her. She's crawling around the bar, toward me.

"Again!" she yells in desperation. "*Please*, Luke! Shoot him again!"

Asa is lying on the floor with his hand against his neck. Blood is rushing through his fingers, spilling down his arm. His chest is heaving up and down as he struggles to drag in breath. I aim the gun at him.

His eyes are wide and he glances around, looking for Sloan.

She's standing behind me now, gripping the back of my shirt in fear. His eyes land on her. "Fucking whore," he manages to mutter. "I lied. I hate your fucking lasagna."

I pull the trigger.

Sloan screams and buries her face against my back.

I turn around and pull her against me. She's crying, holding on to me with all the strength she has.

I can't stand up anymore.

I grip the bar and lower us both to the floor. I pull her onto my lap and she curls up against me. I try to ignore the pain in my arm as I hold her. I press my face into her hair and I breathe her in. "Are you okay?"

She's sobbing, but she manages to nod.

"Are you hurt?" I'm trying to inspect her, but she looks okay. I put my hand on her stomach and I close my eyes and exhale. "I'm so sorry, Sloan. I'm so sorry." I feel like I failed her. I did everything I could to protect her and he somehow still got to her.

She wraps her arms tightly around my neck and I can feel her shaking her head. "Thank you." She's holding me as tight as she possibly can. "Thank you, thank you, thank you, Luke."

The sirens are directly outside now.

Someone is beating on the door.

Ryan climbs through the window and assesses the situation, then walks to the front door and unlocks it. Several uniformed officers file in, yelling orders at each other. One of them tries to address Sloan and me, but Ryan pushes him aside. "Give them a minute. Goddamn."

They do. They give us several. I hold her until the medics come inside. I hold her while they check Asa's pulse. I'm still holding her when one of them announces his time of death.

I'm still holding her when Ryan slides to the floor next to us.

"I saw your car," he says, referring to the wreck. "You okay?"

I nod. "Did anyone get hurt?"

He shakes his head. "Just you, it looks like."

Sloan pulls back and looks at me. "Oh my God, Luke." She presses her palm against my head. "He's hurt! Someone help him!"

She crawls off my lap and a medic rushes over. He looks at my head for a brief second. "We need to get you to the hospital."

Ryan helps the medic lift me up off the floor. I grab Sloan's hand as I'm passing her and she holds it with both of hers. She's in front of me now, walking backward as she looks at me, frantic. "Are you okay? What happened?"

I wink at her. "Just a little fender bender. You can't drown in Fred water if the cruise ship is full of salmon tacos."

Sloan smiles and squeezes my hand.

Ryan groans and looks at one of the medics. "You need to check him for a concussion. He did this last time he was injured. Just started saying random stuff that didn't make any sense."

They put me in the back of the ambulance, but I'm still holding Sloan's hand. She sits next to me and leans over and presses her lips against mine. She pulls back and smiles down at me, her eyes still full of worry. "Is it over, Luke? Is this nightmare finally over?"

I nod and bring my hand up to her cheek. "It's over, Sloan. For real this time."

LUKE

spent three days in the hospital due to my wreck. Sloan stayed with me because I didn't want her to be in the apartment alone after everything that had happened.

She still doesn't talk about what happened before I showed up that day. As much as I hope she can open up and tell me about it one day, I don't push her. I know what Asa was capable of and I don't even like to think about what she might have had to endure. She's been going to therapy, and it really does seem to help, so that's all I can ask of her. I just want her to continue to do what she can to help herself move past the situation, at whatever pace she needs to do it.

The day I was released from the hospital, there was a funeral planned for Asa. Sloan and I were at the apartment that morning packing a few belongings when Ryan called to let me know about it. I relayed the information to her, but knew that she wouldn't want to attend his funeral after all he'd put her through.

Later that morning, on the drive to my parents', Sloan told me she wanted to go to the funeral. She asked me to turn the car around. Naturally, I tried to talk her out of it. I was even a little upset that she would want to subject herself to that, but I had to remind myself that she knew him better than anyone. Even though she was terrified of him, she was one of the few people who meant something to him. As fucked up as he was in showing it.

When we arrived, we were the only two who showed up.

I tried to imagine what that must have been like for him. To have no family at all, and the friends you *did* have weren't even real friends. He didn't even have anyone to set up funeral arrangements, so it was a minimal burial. There was no one else there. Just a preacher from the funeral home, me, Sloan, and another employee from the funeral home. I'm not even sure a prayer would have been said had we not attended.

I don't want to say that helped me to understand him better, because he was the reason no one showed up to his funeral. But I did feel sorry for him more in that moment than I ever had. But he harmed everyone in his path throughout his life and you can't really blame anyone but Asa for that.

Sloan didn't cry during the funeral. It was just a graveside burial that lasted about ten minutes. The preacher relayed a quick sermon and said a prayer, then asked if either of us wanted to say anything. I shook my head, because I was honestly only there for Sloan's benefit. But Sloan nodded. She stood next to me, her hand in mine, and she looked down at the casket. She exhaled a careful breath before speaking.

"Asa..." she said. "You had a lot of potential. But you spent every day of your life expecting the world to repay you for a few really shitty years you were dealt as a child. That's where you went wrong. The world doesn't owe us a thing. We take what we're given and we make the most of it. But you took what you were given and you shit on it and then expected more."

She stepped forward and released my hand. There were no flowers, so she bent down and picked up a dandelion, placing it on top of his casket. And then in a quiet whisper, she said, "Every child deserves love, Asa. I'm sorry you were never given that. For that, I forgive you. We both do."

She stayed quiet for several minutes. I'm not sure if she was saying a prayer for him or if she was silently saying goodbye, but I waited for her. She stepped back eventually and grabbed my hand, then turned and walked away with me at her side. In that moment, I was happy we decided to attend. I think she needed to be there more than I knew.

Since that day over seven months ago, I've thought about that moment a lot. I thought I understood what she was saying in that moment at Asa's funeral. But right now, standing over my son's crib and looking down on him as he sleeps peacefully, I think it just hit me what she was saying when she said "...*I forgive you. We both do.*"

At the time, I thought she was referring to the two of *us*. Her and me. That both of us forgave Asa for all he had put us through. But I'm not so sure she was referring to me now that I look back on it. She was referring to our son. When she said *we*, she meant herself and our son.

She was telling Asa that they forgive him, because even though she was only a few months pregnant at that point, I think she's known all along that Asa is most likely our son's biological father. I believe that's the reason she needed to go to the funeral. She didn't need closure for herself. She needed closure for the child that Asa would never know.

We've only spoken once about the fact that our son, Dalton, may not biologically be mine. It was two weeks after he was born. Sloan had purchased a paternity test because she feared that it was bothering me not knowing if Dalton was mine or Asa's. Sloan was afraid that not knowing for certain if I was the father was going to eat at me, and she didn't want to be what stood between me and the truth.

That paternity test has been sitting in our bathroom cabinet since that day. I haven't opened it yet. She hasn't asked about it. And right now, staring down at my little boy while he sleeps, I feel like I already know the answer.

It doesn't matter who fathered this baby, because Sloan is this baby's mother.

There was a moment once, the first time Asa introduced me to Sloan. She was standing in her kitchen, swaying back and forth, washing dishes. She was absolutely mesmerizing. And there was this peacefulness on her face that I'd soon come to know was very rare.

I see that same peacefulness in Dalton when he sleeps. He has her dark hair, her eyes. And her spirit. And that's all that matters to me. I wish she believed that. I wish she knew that whether or not those test results would prove that this baby is biologically a part of me or a part of Asa, it changes nothing. I don't love this child like I do because I have a biological responsibility to love him. I love this child because I'm human and I can't help it. I love him because I'm his dad.

I reach into the crib and I run my hand over the top of his head.

"What are you doing?"

I turn around and Sloan is leaning against the doorway to the nursery. Her head is resting against the frame of the door and she's smiling at me.

I pull Dalton's blanket up a little higher and then I turn around and walk toward Sloan. I grab her hand and pull the door to the nursery halfway shut. Sloan intertwines her fingers in mine and follows me as I make my way through our bedroom and into the bathroom.

She's still behind me, gripping my hand, when I open the cabinet and take out the paternity test. When I face her, I can see a quiet fear in her eyes. I kiss her to wipe her fear away, and then I keep my hand wrapped with hers as I make my way toward the kitchen. I open the door to the small room off our kitchen that contains our trashcan, and I take the lid off of it. I take the paternity test—still in its packaging—and I throw it away. I replace the lid, close the door, and turn to face Sloan.

There are tears in her eyes, and as hard as she's trying to hide it, there's a smile tugging at the corner of her mouth. I wrap my arms around her and for several seconds, we just silently stare at each other. She's looking up at me and I'm staring down at her and in this moment, we both know everything we need to know.

It doesn't matter how the members of my family came to be. What matters is that this is my family. We're a family. Me and her and our son.

THE END

You can find more works from the author
of this book by visiting www.colleenhoover.com

If you want to stay up to date, follow Colleen Hoover at:

www.instagram.com/colleenhoover

www.facebook.com/authorcolleenhoover

www.twitter.com/collcenhoover

Send an email to Colleen at colleenhooverbooks@gmail.com

Made in the USA
San Bernardino, CA
01 December 2016